Praise

'Great fun!' – CAROL DRINKWATER

'Chapman delivers on every level in this intriguing murder mystery' – *Lancashire Evening Post*

'A delightful Dales tale to warm the cockles!' – *Peterborough Telegraph*

'A rollicking read' – *Craven Herald*

'For, above all else, there is warmth and heart to her novels' – *Yorkshire Times*

'Bags of Yorkshire charm and wit' – *Northern Echo*

'A delightful read' – *Dalesman*

'A classic whodunit set in the spectacular landscape of the Yorkshire Dales, written with affection for the area and its people' – CATH STAINCLIFFE

'Charming . . . full of dry wit and clever plotting . . . will delight and entertain the reader' – *Countryside*

'Nicely told and rather charming, so it should give traditionalists hours of innocent delight' – *Literary Review*

'An engaging twist on the lonely-hearts killer motif . . . should leave readers eager for the sequel' – *Publishers Weekly*

'An engaging cast of characters and a cleverly clued puzzle move Chapman's debut to the top of the English village murder list' – *Kirkus*

Date with Destiny

Julia Chapman is the pseudonym of Julia Stagg, who has had five novels, the Fogas Chronicles set in the French Pyrenees, published by Hodder. *Date with Destiny* is the final book in the Dales Detective series, following on from *Date with Justice*.

By Julia Chapman

Date with Death
Date with Malice
Date with Mystery
Date with Poison
Date with Danger
Date with Deceit
Date with Betrayal
Date with Evil
Date with Justice
Date with Destiny

Julia Chapman

DATE WITH DESTINY

PAN BOOKS

First published 2025 by Pan Books
an imprint of Pan Macmillan
The Smithson, 6 Briset Street, London EC1M 5NR
EU representative: Macmillan Publishers Ireland Ltd, 1st Floor,
The Liffey Trust Centre, 117–126 Sheriff Street Upper,
Dublin 1, D01 YC43
Associated companies throughout the world
www.panmacmillan.com

ISBN 978-1-0350-4480-1

1 3 5 7 9 8 6 4 2

A CIP catalogue record for this book is available from the British Library.

Map artwork by Hemesh Alles

Typeset by Palimpsest Book Production Limited, Falkirk, Stirlingshire
Printed and bound by CPI Group (UK) Ltd, Croydon, CR0 4YY

Visit **www.panmacmillan.com** to read more about all our books
and to buy them. You will also find features, author interviews and
news of any author events, and you can sign up for e-newsletters
so that you're always first to hear about our new releases.

For Bruncliffe fans

Thanks for taking this town
and its inhabitants to your hearts

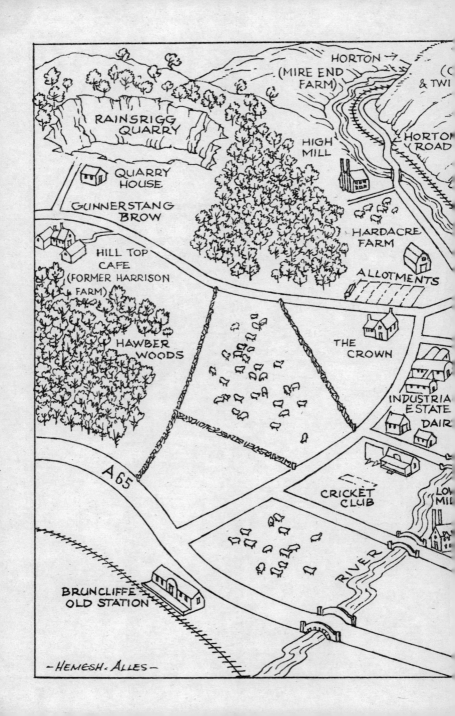

HORTON →
(MIRE END FARM)

(C
& TWI

HORTON
ROAD

RAINSRIGG QUARRY

HIGH MILL

QUARRY HOUSE

GUNNERSTANG BROW

HARDACRE FARM

HILL TOP CAFE
(FORMER HARRISON FARM)

ALLOTMENTS

HAWBER WOODS

THE CROWN

INDUSTRIAL ESTATE

DAIR

A65

CRICKET CLUB

LOW MILL

BRUNCLIFFE OLD STATION

RIVER

- HEMESH · ALLES -

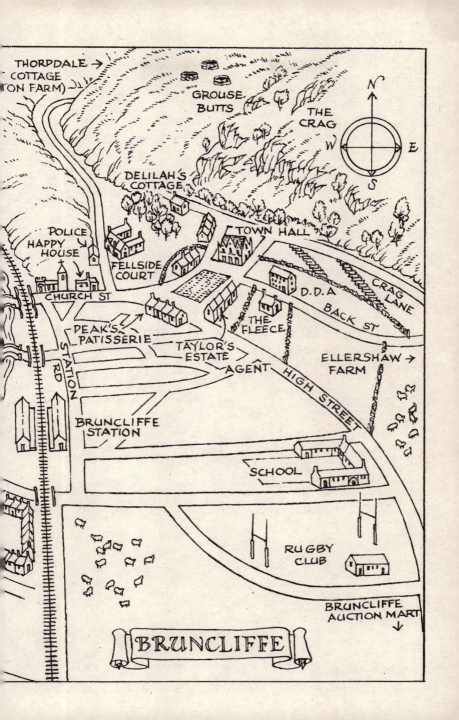

1

'They're death threats.'

Samson O'Brien looked at the screenshot displayed on the mobile being held out across the desk and found himself shrugging.

'Could be,' he said. 'Or they could be just the usual social media trolling which has no substance.'

Laconic eyebrows raised over chiselled cheekbones, even the act of surprise looking nothing short of perfection on the face opposite. 'I wish I shared your nonchalance. But then, you're used to danger. The most reckless my life gets is when someone hands me a pair of scissors the wrong way round.'

The statement was accompanied by a self-deprecating smile, brown eyes twinkling, auburn curls framing the features of an angel.

And Samson found himself wondering why he felt such antipathy towards the man sitting across the desk from him on the ground floor of the Dales Detective Agency. Granted, the visitor was dressed in a lurid outfit – a tracksuit bottoms and puffer-jacket combo, the entirety made of corduroy in a gaudy floral pattern bright enough to induce a migraine. Not to mention the acid-green trainers which completed the get-up. But Samson knew nothing about haute couture and was the last person to judge another by their sense of fashion. Particularly when the person in question made his living cutting cloth to fit the rich and famous and had become a celebrated reality TV host because of it.

Tyke. A man of such renown he bore only a single name, like a Brazilian footballer. Darling of the society pages. A constant on red carpets of all descriptions, various beauties dangling off his arm. And host of *The Nines*, one of the most popular programmes on British TV. He'd come a long way from the gawky lad who'd spent his summers visiting relatives in Bruncliffe and answered to the name of Jake Ramsbottom.

The moment Samson had arrived at the building on Back Street and Ida told him, in an awed whisper, that he had a very important client waiting, he'd sensed something was up. It took a lot to impress Ida Capstick and, given that the four occupants of the downstairs office were currently drinking tea from the daintiest of cups, replete with matching saucers and slices of fruit cake on bone-china plates, Ida was impressed with this TV icon. Normally mismatched mugs sufficed, a couple of biscuits if they were lucky.

But Ida's veneration wasn't enough to sway Samson. He shook his head.

'I'm sorry, Mr Ramsbottom—'

'Tyke, just Tyke,' the man intervened with a grin, turning his focus to the preternaturally still figure sitting next to Samson. 'That's all anyone calls me.'

There was a slight intake of breath in response from Samson's colleague. Nothing more. Delilah Metcalfe might as well have been turned to salt, like a modern-day Lot's wife. Perched on the edge of her chair, she was unable to tear her gaze from Tyke's face, not a single interjection leaving her lips. In fact, since she'd entered the room alongside Samson and been introduced to their guest, she hadn't uttered a word.

Which, for anyone who knew Delilah, was a miracle of major proportions.

She was star-struck. As was her Weimaraner, Tolpuddle. Normally the dog didn't dispense his friendship so easily where newcomers were concerned but the second he'd seen the man sitting in one of the clients' chairs, Tolpuddle had made a beeline for him. His large grey head was currently resting on Tyke's lap, his ears were being ruffled and his face was bearing an expression of canine ecstasy.

Samson knew, in a searing moment of honesty, he was jealous. Of the ease with which Delilah's and Tolpuddle's affections had been stolen. Affections normally bestowed only on him. He also knew that was why he was so reluctant to offer up the agencies of the Dales Detectives to this man-god.

His frank self-assessment didn't change his mind.

'I'm sorry, but we're just flat out at the moment. I don't see how we can take anyone else on,' he persisted.

'Please.' Tyke leaned forward, hands on the desk, fingers splayed out, attention back on Samson, as though aware that the other partner in the business was beyond coherent conversation. 'I'm begging you. I need your help. I'm a nervous wreck since these threats started coming in. Please.'

'I'm sorry, but we can't—'

Samson's reply was halted by a kick to his shins from Delilah and their prospective client simultaneously jumping to his feet.

'If it's money,' Tyke protested, arms outstretched, giving Samson a full view of the extraordinary creation he was

3

wearing, 'I'll pay whatever you ask. Eloise, have you got the cash?'

He addressed the latter to the woman sitting next to him. Tall, with a gamine look emphasised by her elfin haircut, she'd been introduced as Tyke's assistant at the outset, but had remained as mute as Delilah throughout the meeting. It wasn't just in that respect she was the more understated of the two visitors. Her jeans, black Converse All Stars, military-style vintage khaki jacket and black T-shirt were a study in restraint compared to her flamboyant companion.

She reached into the satchel on her lap, pulled out a thick wedge of banknotes and put them on the table. The top note was a fifty.

Delilah's gulp was audible.

'Whatever it costs,' continued Tyke, genuine consternation on his features now. 'I've got a launch for my latest collection to organise and I don't want to be watching over my shoulder all the time, afraid someone is going to try to harm me.'

If anything, the ostentatious display of wealth made Samson even more obstinate. He shook his head.

'This doesn't change a thing,' he said, gesturing at the cash. 'We're not equipped to provide security in a genuine case concerning death threats.' He stressed the word 'genuine'. 'I suggest you contact one of the many companies which do offer such services. Or the police.'

He pushed the money back across the desk towards the still silent Eloise and got to his feet, noting with satisfaction the surprised look on Tyke's face. Clearly not a man accustomed to being turned down.

But Samson was walking towards the door. He pulled it open and waited pointedly as Tyke tugged his baseball cap on, gave Delilah a rueful smile and left the room, Eloise scooping the banknotes back into her bag before following him into the hall. Only when the front door had closed behind them did Samson turn to confront his partner.

Delilah Metcalfe was standing by the desk looking like thunder. And Ida Capstick was descending the stairs, looking just as furious.

Caught in the crosshairs of their annoyance, Samson found himself wondering if he'd been wise to allow his emotions to overcome good business sense.

Samson wasn't the only one in thrall to errant emotions. Across town, Arty Robinson was feeling murderous. It was a feeling which didn't sit well in the chest of the retired bookie, a man far more given to magnanimity, a man who revelled in the company of others.

Not today. With the early summer sunshine streaming through the high windows of the communal lounge and filling the residents of Fellside Court retirement complex with communal joy, Arty knew his dark thoughts were at odds with those of his friends and neighbours. And it was all because of that bast—

'Penny for them?' Joseph O'Brien was leaning over the arm of his chair to murmur in his friend's ear.

'Sorry,' Arty shook his head, managing a smile. 'Miles away.'

'You mean you weren't hanging on to his every word?' Joseph cast a look towards the far side of the lounge where a man was holding court, sitting on a high stool brought in for the occasion. Every sofa and armchair in the large room was occupied. Every head was turned his way, faces rapt with attention, his droll tales of life in a glamorous world the residents could only dream about eliciting lots of laughter. 'You've got to give him credit. He's a natural entertainer.'

'Natural something,' muttered Arty, letting his feelings show.

Joseph nodded slowly. Understanding. 'You know you've nothing to worry about,' he whispered, glancing at the woman sitting a few seats away, her sharp features focused on the speaker, an amused smile on her lips. 'That gobshite doesn't mean anything to Edith.'

Arty smiled. Tried to make it convincing. Tried to conceal the agonies of insecurity that had settled on him since Vinny King, Bruncliffe's answer to royalty, had arrived at Fellside Court three months before. After a lifetime in showbusiness, Vinny had announced in an interview in *Hello!* magazine that he'd decided to retire back home to the Yorkshire Dales, to live among folk who knew him.

Problem was, some of the folk knew him better than others. As Arty watched Edith, mesmerised like everyone else by the stories Vinny was spinning, he had to accept that his concerns were warranted.

For it wasn't every day that the former fiancé of the woman you loved, the woman you'd been looking forward to a wonderful future with, came to live at the same retirement complex and threw all your plans into the air. It was no surprise, then, that Arty was wishing Vinny King dead. No matter the man's pedigree.

There were few places better to while away a couple of hours than Bruncliffe's market square on a Thursday morning in late May. Especially when the sun was shining overhead, the sky was the kind of blue that made the heart swell, and there was a sense of gaiety as the locals congregated to sample the wares of the stalls set up around the cobbles, the high fells arching green above the town in the background.

Basking in the warmth of what was shaping up to be a gorgeous day, Clive Knowles was leaning against the wall outside the bank and taking in the scene with an air of contentment.

Truth be told, he wasn't one for markets. Not unless they were of the ovine sort. But his lass liked this weekly event, took pleasure from haggling with the stallholders for tomatoes or carrots, and declared that the fish van was exceptional. Which, for a native of coastal Bridlington who'd been raised on the bounty of the sea, was high praise indeed. So Clive was happy to make the trip into town from Mire End Farm every Thursday, because bringing pleasure to the life of the woman who'd recently become Mrs Knowles meant the world to him.

Not that you'd know she was pleased as she leaned in over the vegetables, pinching at potatoes with a frown and casting a critical eye over the cabbages. But Carol Knowles wasn't a woman to waste her smiles, a fact which endeared her even more to her newly-wedded husband, making those rare moments when her lips curved something he'd learned to treasure.

She glanced over at him, as though sensing his regard. Nodded briskly, and then turned back to her business, unaware that her curt acknowledgement of Clive's presence had been enough to catapult his heart around his ribcage. He was like a teenager, bowled over by this amazing woman who'd turned up unexpectedly in his life.

Sending a general note of thanks up to the gods, the Fates, Cupid, or whatever agency had been behind this change in his existence at an age when he'd been resigned to bachelordom, he pushed himself off the wall and started to walk across the cobbles. He'd go and get the bag of shopping Carol had already amassed and leave her free to peruse the rest of the market without any encumbrances.

She saw him coming. Turned towards him. And as she did so, he saw her jerk back in surprise, eyes widening, jaw dropping. Her expression was sufficient to make Clive spin round to see what had caught her attention. He dismissed Lucy Metcalfe standing on the steps of her cafe, taking in the sunshine. Likewise Mrs Pettiford, who was just leaving the bank on her break, the sight of neither woman being enough to cause such alarm. So it had to be the man walking down the pavement towards him.

Clive had time enough to notice the outlandish attire. The garish colours. The ridiculous lime-green trainers and the baseball cap pulled low. Then it all happened too fast for him to remember much else.

The man started to cross the road as though heading for Peaks Patisserie, and out of nowhere, a motorbike came roaring along High Street. A blur of speed. The man in the middle of the road. The bike not slowing down.

Clive was moving before he knew it. Long legs carrying him towards the pedestrian with an agility he hadn't shown since his days on the right wing for Bruncliffe rugby club. Aware of the bike, the proximity, the danger, he lunged.

A face full of fabric, the crash of contact as two bodies collided heavily and he was falling to the ground, the man beneath him. Then a shout of pain or surprise, the blast of a horn, the wheels of the motorbike screeching ever closer. Close enough that Clive squeezed his eyes shut, expecting the worst.

2

It missed them by mere inches.

Ears filled with the roar of the engine, Clive felt a peppering of gravel on his head, the scorch of the exhaust, his heart going way too fast for a man of his age. Then the bike was gone.

As it roared away down Church Street, the marketplace – which had been frozen into a tableau of open mouths and shocked expressions – came back to life. People shouting at the fleeing motorcyclist as he disappeared off into the distance. Others rushing over to check on the two men. It was Carol who reached them first.

'Are you okay?' she asked just as Clive rolled off the man he'd flung to the ground, her voice steady despite the pallor to her face.

'Aye, lass,' muttered Clive, heart still ricocheting wildly in his chest.

Relief washed over her. But then he glanced down and saw the rip in the sleeve of his jumper, the one she'd knitted which had been the catalyst for their romance. The soft blue wool was torn where he'd made contact with the road.

'Damn it,' he muttered.

'Easier darn a sweater than a body,' she murmured. 'And you?' She turned to the man, who was sitting up, gingerly rubbing the side of his face, his bulky jacket ripped and stained, baseball cap lying on the tarmac. 'Mr Tyke? Are you all right?'

'Tyke, just Tyke,' he mumbled. He nodded. Looked dazed.

Realisation came to Clive in a flash. The bloke off the TV show Carol loved – *Nine Lives* or whatever it was called. One of those blasted reality programmes, set around the theme of making clothes. Not his cup of tea but he was happy to sit and watch them with his wife, getting joy from her acerbic comments about the various creations the contenders produced each week.

'I think you saved my life. How can I ever thank you?' The man was looking at Clive now. Those auburn curls framing a face so well known but looking so different as shock set in. The perfect skin was drawn tight across the sharp cheekbones and marred by a scarlet slash of blood, and the famous grin had morphed into a grimace as he held his side.

There was a fair crowd around them now, people murmuring as they made the connection between the unfortunate pedestrian and the TV star.

'No thanks needed,' said Clive, getting to his feet and extending a hand to the man, helping him stand. He gestured at the tattered clothing. The gash on the man's face which was bleeding profusely. 'Sorry about that. I reacted without thinking.'

Tyke shook his head. 'Don't apologise. I'm just grateful you acted as fast as you did. That motorbike . . .' He hesitated, gazing down Church Street.

'It came out of nowhere,' said Carol. She looked at Clive, eyes narrowed, and then at Tyke. 'And if I'm not mistaken, it were aimed straight at you.'

Tyke, already the colour of a newborn lamb, turned an even starker shade of white.

'You must have lost your bloody marbles! They were offering enough to see us through to the back end of summer. What the hell did you turn it down for?!'

Samson tried to appear more resolute than he felt. After several minutes of being harangued by his colleagues, he was finding it hard to defend his decision. Especially as Delilah was right – it *had* been a lot of money. 'Like I said,' he muttered, falling back on the sole justification that carried merit, 'it's beyond our capabilities.'

Delilah glowered at him. In the wake of Tyke and Eloise's departure she had recovered her voice – and her strident opinions – and had used both to good effect as she paced up and down between the desk and the large window which overlooked the street. There were no signs of her tiring. Not when she was being backed up from the other side of the room, where Ida Capstick was standing inside the office door, arms folded, having made no attempt to hide her disbelief as she took in the news of what had transpired in her absence.

'Tha's gone daft, lad,' she muttered. 'Think of the exposure. The agency would have been flooded with clients if tha'd had the gumption to take him on.'

'I genuinely didn't think he needed our services,' protested Samson.

'Seriously?' Delilah was standing over the desk now, leaning on it in a way that made Samson want to reach up and kiss her. He valued his life too much to even risk it. 'Did you *read* those tweets he received? "I'm coming for you!" followed by a knife emoji? Or "You'd best sleep with one eye open!" with a gun and skull motif thrown in for good measure? You really think that's just trolling?'

Samson shrugged. The threats had seemed intense all right. Certainly enough to warrant concern and a request for help. It was just that Samson didn't want to be involved in providing that assistance. Or rather, he didn't want Delilah involved.

'And as for that lame excuse you gave him . . . Flat out? We're struggling to keep our heads above water financially and you're willing to walk away from what could be a lucrative contract?'

Another half-hearted shrug was all Samson could manage. Because yet again, she was spot on. Since he'd given up his position as an undercover operative with the National Crime Agency and resigned from the Metropolitan Police at the end of the previous year, the Dales Detective Agency was now having to support him full-time. Along with Gareth Towler, the former gamekeeper showing no signs of wanting to secure other employment. There was also Ida to consider, her original position as cleaner having merged into a combined role of receptionist and detective, plus teenager Nina Hussain, both only part-time but key members of the team. Things were tight and if it wasn't for Delilah's success in her other ventures, they would be looking at laying someone off. Thankfully her expertise in IT was in high demand and the Dales Dating Agency was also going from strength to strength, bringing in much needed revenue, paying the overheads of their shared office space.

That revenue didn't stretch far though, and with a wedding looming, not to mention the expenses incurred in trying to get Twistleton Farm to a state they could move into permanently, Samson and Delilah were feeling the pinch.

It wasn't what Samson had envisaged back in September when all his dreams seemed to be answered on that glorious day out at his childhood home. An auction of which he was the unexpected beneficiary, bringing the family farm into his ownership. And an impulsive proposal to a woman he worshipped.

When Delilah had said yes, Samson had seen nothing but bliss ahead of them. Not bills. Not stress. And certainly not her seeming reluctance to actually commit to getting married.

He stifled a sigh. Ran a hand through his hair and tried to get a grip on his rampant paranoia. Because that's all it was. Delilah was simply being laid-back. That's why she wasn't fussing about the minutiae when it came to their big day. She'd assured him that the date was booked. The venue too. As for the rest of it, it would happen in due course. It didn't matter that she kept putting off sending out invitations. It didn't matter that she had yet to find a dress with only three weeks left until the big day – he was content to exchange vows with her in running kit if that's what she wanted.

But no matter how much he told himself that there was nothing to worry about, what had started out as a niggle of unease in the New Year was now, five months on, growing into fully fledged anxiety.

What if that impulsive proposal was the problem? What if Delilah was regretting her equally impulsive acceptance – an acceptance which had been forced from her in a very public setting? And now she didn't want to humiliate him by backing out but was reluctant to proceed at the same time?

With everything on their plates on the work front, not to mention the possibility that Delilah would soon be testifying in a major court case, Samson didn't feel he could add more stress to the situation by trying to talk to her about it. Nor did he want her family and friends weighing in on the topic – which is exactly what would happen if they knew there was the slightest doubt in her mind, this being Bruncliffe, where opinions were abundant and widely shared. Samson would rather not get married at all than have her agree to go through with it simply because of peer pressure.

So when Tyke, with his puppy-dog eyes and easy charm, had turned up asking for help and beguiling Delilah in the process, jealousy had breached Samson's already weakened defences, causing him to reject a valuable client and, more importantly, judging by the tweets, someone whose life might genuinely be in danger.

Feeling beleaguered, Samson glanced towards the corner of the office, but if he'd been hoping for some canine support, he was out of luck. Tolpuddle was curled up in his bed, head on his paws, large eyes mournful as though the sunshine which had been warming his heart had been extinguished by a sudden cloud.

What was it with the lot of them?

The front door crashed open, taking attention off Samson momentarily.

'Is he still here?!' Nina Hussain bundled into the hallway, Delilah's nephew Nathan on her heels, both in school uniform, a babble of excited language issuing from them. 'We came as soon as the lunchtime bell went.'

'It's the talk of the school!' declared Nathan. 'Everyone's going around saying "Clothing gets you noticed!" and "A stitch in time doesn't always save nine!".'

Seeing Samson's puzzlement, Nina rolled her eyes. 'They're the catchphrases from his show, *The Nines*. Don't tell me you don't watch it?' Then she grinned. 'So are we going to be working for him?'

'Wait till everyone hears!' Nathan's grin was as wide as hers.

Ida turned to Samson. Arms folded even higher on her thin chest, chin at an angle that brooked no argument. 'Reckon tha can break the bad news, seeing as it's tha doing.'

'Bad news?' Nina looked around the office, took in the atmosphere and wheeled round to face Samson. 'You didn't take the case? We're not working with Tyke?'

Samson took a deep breath. 'It's not that simple' – a snort from Delilah cut across him – 'he wanted services we don't provide.'

'Like what?' asked Nathan.

'Personal protection.'

Nathan blinked. Looked at Delilah. Who shrugged in mutual incomprehension.

'Why don't we do that?' asked Nina.

Samson ran a hand over his face. 'Because it's outside our remit. And besides, I really don't think there's a credible threat to life in this instance.'

'Remember last time you said that,' muttered Delilah.

He could tell from the blush which followed the words that she wished them back as soon as they were said, but it was too late. They'd found their target, bringing silence to the room.

Alice Shepherd. Samson remembered her all too well, the resident of Fellside Court who'd sat on the other side of this very desk eighteen months ago and told him her life was in danger. He'd dismissed her claims as the ramblings of an elderly person losing their grasp on reality. He'd been wrong and the guilt still haunted him.

'This is different,' he said tersely. 'Tyke is not a vulnerable pensioner, for starters. And secondly—'

He was spared from having to think up a spurious second reason as the front door swung open again and Clive Knowles came into view, Carol following, and none other than Tyke supported between them.

Tyke, who had a gash on his grey face pouring blood down his right cheek and whose high-end clothes were all dirty and torn.

'I don't know what reason you gave for turning this lad down when he asked for your help,' boomed Clive with a glare. 'But I can tell you now, Samson O'Brien, someone damn near just tried to kill him!'

3

The Dales Detective Agency sprang into action. Nina ran upstairs to grab the first-aid kit, Nathan going with her to get more chairs and Ida hustling after them to get a brew on. While Delilah helped Clive lead a dazed-looking Tyke to a seat across the desk from Samson.

Samson, who was sitting there shocked. Awash with remorse. Cursing himself for his arrogance and petty jealousy.

'I'm so sorry—' he began.

Tyke went to brush the apology aside, but the motion triggered a low groan, sending his hand to his ribs instead. 'Not a word of it,' he said. 'I get your reticence – high-profile clients can be a nightmare.' He managed a lopsided grin, which just made Samson feel worse.

'What happened?' Delilah had sat down next to Samson and was flipping open a notepad, pen in hand, already making notes. While her partner was wallowing in shame, she was all business.

'Bloody motorbike came out of nowhere,' said Clive, as Nathan entered the office carrying several folding chairs. The farmer took two, opened one out for his wife and sank onto the other, wiping his forehead, shock etched on his craggy face. 'Out of nowhere.'

'Where were you?'

'In the marketplace,' said Carol. 'Clive was just coming to get my shopping when we noticed Mr Ramsb— I mean, Mr Tyke, walking towards Church Street. He'd reached the edge of the pavement and had begun crossing it when the motorbike came roaring up High Street.'

'I was on my way to visit my uncle,' explained Tyke. 'And yeah, I admit that I was deep in thought, worrying about those blasted messages I've been getting. But I swear I didn't see the bike when I stepped off the kerb.'

'Happen that's cos it weren't there to be seen,' grunted Clive. 'Isn't that right, lass?'

Carol nodded, her focus now on cleaning up the cut on Tyke's face, courtesy of the first-aid kit Nina was holding out with a look of rapture.

'Was Eloise with you?' Samson asked Tyke, thinking another witness would be helpful.

Tyke shook his head. 'She went back to the house we've rented to catch up on some admin.'

'And what about the bike? Could you describe it?'

'Not a chance.'

'Likewise,' said Clive. 'I was too busy praying it wouldn't hit us to get a proper look.'

'It were a trail bike,' said Carol, taping gauze to Tyke's cheek. 'A Triumph. Black. Off-road tyres. The number-plate was too mucky to read.' She flipped the lid of the first-aid box closed and sat back to scrutinise her efforts, before becoming aware of the impressed gazes around the room, Clive looking at her with unabashed admiration. She shrugged it off with a frown. 'I recognised the name as it flashed by, that's all. Happen one of our neighbours had a Triumph back when we were nippers. Always razzing around on it like he thought he were Steve McQueen or summat.'

Ida, entering the room with a tray laden with teapot and a multitude of mugs just as Carol was concluding her story, sniffed. 'Aye. I remember that. Daft ha'p'orth. Wasn't much of a Great Escape when he failed to clear the garden fence and ended up in hospital.'

Carol made a sound somewhere between a laugh and a snort.

'So a classic bike, then?' asked Delilah.

'No. It were modern.' The brief flash of humour evaporated, leaving the residue of Carol's severe expression behind. 'Sorry, I didn't catch the model. And I can't say much about the rider either, other than he were dressed all in black. I was so caught up watching these two escaping death, I didn't notice owt else.'

Tyke blinked. Ran a hand over his face. 'Jesus,' he muttered, as though realising just how close he'd been to meeting his maker. 'I thought it was just an accident.'

'No accident that.'

'How can you be so sure?' Samson's question brought Carol's fierce gaze onto him.

'Because, lad, it happened right in front of me.'

'But you've said Tyke was in the road. If he stepped out in front of a motorbike, what was the motorcyclist supposed to do?'

'The bike wasn't there when I stepped off the pavement—' Tyke began. His protest was cut short by Carol's sharp tone.

'I can see how this could look like an accident,' she said. 'Mr Tyke not paying attention. A motorbike having to swerve to avoid him. Thing is though, that's not what happened.'

'You mean Tyke is right in saying the road was clear?' asked Samson.

'I mean,' said Carol, leaning across the desk now, voice firm, 'the motorbike didn't swerve to avoid him. It changed direction to try to hit him!'

There was a shocked moment of silence then a long low whistle came from the doorway. Gareth Towler was standing there, his large figure almost filling the space, eyebrows raised up towards his thatch of russet hair, a hand rubbing his thick beard in disbelief.

'Not much of a welcome home, Tyke!' he said, ruefully.

'Gareth!' exclaimed Tyke in pleased surprise. He tried to jump up, winced in pain, and managed a grin instead, the former gamekeeper crossing the room to embrace him.

'Wasn't expecting to bump into you here,' Tyke murmured, then yelped as he was enveloped in the bigger man's arms. 'Watch the ribs, mind!'

'You always were a bit delicate,' laughed Gareth, standing back to appraise the fashion designer. And his clothes. 'What the heck's this lot?' he asked, tugging at the ripped puffer-jacket. 'Bit overdressed for these parts.'

'"Clothing gets you noticed!" remember,' said Tyke, taking the jibe with the humour it was intended to provoke, as he flashed the inside of the jacket to reveal an even brighter pattern in different hues.

Gareth grinned. 'They're certainly doing that!'

'I've called them Retro Reversibles – a choice of styles in one garment. It's my new line. The one I was hoping to launch here . . .' He tailed off. Apprehension clouding his features.

'Tha's holding the launch in Bruncliffe?' asked Ida, the surprise and excitement in her voice mirrored on several faces around the room.

'That's the plan . . . It was a spur-of-the-moment decision last week. I just thought it would be a lovely way to acknowledge my heritage now that my uncle's moved back here.' Tyke grimaced. 'But it's not worth risking my life for.'

'I heard right, then?' said Gareth, looking to Samson and Delilah. 'Someone tried to kill this lad?'

'That's what we're trying to establish—'

'Yes!' said Delilah, interrupting her partner. 'It seems that way. He's been getting death threats, too.'

'And we're investigating, I presume?' Gareth's question brought all eyes onto Samson and a heavy silence filled the room. 'What? Is there a problem?' the gamekeeper asked, looking around the agency team.

'Mr Tyke has asked us to provide personal protection, but Samson thinks we're too stretched,' muttered Ida.

'It's not . . . I didn't . . .' Samson sighed. Ran a hand through his hair. 'We *are* stretched,' he said. 'But it's not just that. If that bike really did take aim for you, Tyke, then this is a matter for the police.'

'We already suggested that,' said Clive Knowles. 'Lad's dead set against it.'

Tyke splayed out his hands. 'Sorry. No can do. I don't want the police involved.'

'Why not?' asked Gareth. 'Surely they should be notified about what's going on? Death threats shouldn't be taken lightly.'

'My thoughts exactly,' muttered Samson.

But Tyke was shaking his head. 'It would jeopardise the launch of my collection and I simply can't have that happen. There's too much riding on it.' He grimaced. 'I don't need the media attention notifying the police would bring, either. Because I guarantee you, no matter how much I ask for an official investigation to be kept under wraps, someone would leak it on social media.' He turned to Samson. 'That's why I came to you. My uncle's friends said you were the best.'

'Your uncle?' Samson asked at this further mention of the man.

'Vinny King,' said several voices in unison, Ida adding a tut of reproval at his ignorance of Bruncliffe connections.

'Vinny's your uncle?' Samson was staring at Tyke now, seeing the similarity between the young man and the TV talk-show host who'd recently become a resident at Fellside Court. And the penny dropped. He groaned. 'Those recommendations you mentioned . . . they weren't from my father and his mates?'

Tyke nodded. 'I happened to say I might need the services of a private detective while I was visiting Uncle Vinny earlier this week and I was told to try here.' He smiled. 'They were very effusive in their praise. And offers of help. One woman – Clarissa, I think she's called – even said they could organise a stakeout if I needed it.'

Samson groaned again. The thought of Clarissa Ralph leading an investigation in the wake of his refusal to do so was one that was not only credible, but also too scary to contemplate. He was between a rock and a hard place – if he didn't take this case on, the pensioners at Fellside Court quite possibly would.

'Perhaps we could work something out,' he muttered.

'Thank goodness!' Tyke's head dropped in relief, shoulders sagging.

'We can do shifts,' said Delilah, with a sudden animation which sent Samson's paranoia rocketing. 'Gareth, Samson and myself. And work all our other caseloads around your needs.'

'I'm in,' said Gareth, grinning as he ruffled Tyke's hair. 'Always looked after this little runt when he was up here on holidays with his folks. Shouldn't be any different now.'

Tyke laughed. But then shook his head. 'Sorry if this sounds pompous but when it comes to my security, I want Samson on it full-time.' He gave an apologetic shrug. 'He's got the experience and I'd feel a lot happier knowing he was the one watching my back. Plus I need it to be as discreet as possible.'

Delilah was opening her mouth as though about to object, but Samson got in first.

'I agree,' he said. 'No disrespect to my colleagues, but given the gravity of what occurred this morning, that aspect of the case is best left to me. So I'll provide the protection needed and Delilah can lead the investigation into the attempted hit-and-run and the online threats.'

'I'm not going to argue with that,' said Gareth. He gestured at his immense frame with a laugh. 'Not as though I'm suited to being discreet anyhow!'

His comment triggered laughter.

Samson turned to Delilah, whose jaw was set in a solid line he recognised. 'You okay with that? I mean, those messages Tyke's been getting – with your IT expertise, you're the best placed out of all of us to get a lead on who's behind them. And in a situation like this, prevention is better than cure.'

She gave a slight nod of the head.

'That's great,' said Tyke. 'I've just got one final request – I can't stress how important it is that the press don't get wind of what's going on, so I have to ask that not a word of this leaves this room.'

He looked around at the gathering, getting nods of acquiescence from everyone.

'Thanks,' he said with a smile of appreciation. 'You've no idea how much of a load you've taken off me.' Then he turned to Clive. 'And you, I literally owe you my life.'

Clive went to brush off the gratitude but Tyke continued.

'I know this won't repay my debt in any way but . . . how would you like to star in my launch-night fashion show? I was hoping to use some local models and you fit the bill perfectly.'

'He'd love it!' replied Carol before Clive could even find his voice.

'Excellent!' Tyke smiled at her, a hint of red coming to her cheeks. 'And thanks for this.' He reached up to touch the bandage on his face. 'Not just a sharp-eyed witness but a competent nurse, too.'

'Happen us Capsticks are observant,' commented Ida, with a sharp humph and an even sharper glance at her dumb-struck cousin.

'You're related?' Tyke looked from one to the other.

'Cousins,' they both muttered.

Tyke nodded, well acquainted with Bruncliffe's inter-locking lineage. His smile switched to Delilah. 'Like us,' he said.

Samson turned so quickly to look at her, he felt a snap of pain in his neck. 'I didn't know you two were cousins.'

She shrugged in that nonchalant way she had when it came to her family. As though the connections were so cemented in centuries of existence, they were simply a way of life, beyond the need for explanation. Something Samson, as an only child a long way from his father's Irish relatives and ostracised from his mother's, couldn't comprehend.

'Through the Giffords, I think,' she said. A memory of young Megan Gifford who worked out at the auction mart flitted through Samson's mind. 'Although,' continued Delilah, 'I think it's more a connection through marriage.'

'Kissing cousins, then?' quipped Gareth with a wide smile.

Delilah blushed while Tyke grinned. 'Sounds good to me,' he said.

The pain in Samson's neck was surpassed by an even sharper one in his heart. As Tyke shook hands with him to seal the deal, Samson's only consolation was that he'd denied Delilah the opportunity to spend hours in the fashion designer's handsome company.

Or at least, he hoped he had.

4

News never took long to circulate around Bruncliffe. Those interconnections which baffled the likes of Samson, the threads of family winding unseen through the town which he could never untangle, were utilised in times of drama, becoming effective communication lines the moment anything of note happened. And as many of those familial threads were woven into the brilliant tapestry which represented the occupants of Fellside Court, news often reached the retirement complex way before the rest of the population.

Today was no exception. A potential road accident taking place in the market square, averted at the last minute by an heroic act which saved a life, was definitely something of note. Even more so when the life saved was that of a celebrity fashion designer, who also happened to be the nephew of a national treasure and current Fellside Court resident.

Having finished his talk to rapturous applause – which Arty Robinson had participated in with only half a heart – Vinny King was taking his time walking through the lounge, accepting praise with a humble smile, pausing to have a quick word here, a shake of hands there. When he reached the group of friends sitting over by the windows, he sank down into the only available chair with a dramatic sigh.

'Thank goodness that's over!' he exclaimed, giving an exaggerated mop of his brow.

'Likewise,' said Arty under his breath, garnering a snort from Eric Bradley next to him.

'So what did you think?' Vinny's question was aimed at the group but his gaze came to rest on Edith, the former headmistress at her most sphinx-like as she simply nodded her head.

'Oh it was wonderful!' enthused Clarissa Ralph, beaming, her effervescent nature the polar opposite of her sister's more measured take on life. 'How exciting to have rubbed shoulders with all those greats of the screen and stage!'

Vinny gave a shrug, smiling. 'They're just people. Most of them not a patch on folk around here.'

'Too bloody right,' retorted Arty. Louder this time. Edith flicking him a glance.

But Vinny was oblivious to the hostility, his warm smile turning to the woman Arty loved. 'Edith? What about you? I know I can rely on you to tell me the truth – did I just make a complete idiot of myself?'

Edith smiled back, an easy familiarity between them. 'Well, I thought—'

'Oh!' The sharp cry came from a woman in the centre of the lounge who was looking at her mobile. She stood, eyes focused on them. Hand over her mouth, she approached, reaching out to grasp Vinny's forearm as her perfectly shaped eyebrows arched in shock beneath her immaculate platinum-blonde bob. 'Oh my goodness!'

'Blasted drama queen,' muttered Edith at a volume only loud enough to be heard by Arty. She was airing an opinion shared by many in the room, for everyone knew Geraldine Mortimer liked a bit of melodrama, particularly if it was at someone else's expense or could place her centre stage.

Right now, however, Arty could have kissed her, as she'd broken whatever that moment had been between Vinny and Edith.

But as she stood there making the most of her time in the spotlight, there was something in Geraldine's expression which made Arty hold back on agreeing with Edith's normally astute assessment. Something which suggested there really was a drama in the offing. It was sufficient to bring Vinny to his feet.

'What is it?' he demanded.

'It's your nephew!' exclaimed Geraldine. 'There's been an accident!'

Vinny King paled, staggered backwards, Edith's hand going out to steady him as a collective gasp echoed around the room. 'Tyke? What do you mean? Is he okay?'

'What's going on?' Ana Stoyanovic, recently reappointed as manager of Fellside Court by the new owner and – in Arty's opinion – the best thing to have happened to the retirement community in the past twelve months, was walking towards them, a frown creasing her angelic face.

'It seems Vinny's nephew has been involved in some sort of accident,' said Edith, guiding Vinny back down into his armchair. 'But we're a little short on the salient details so Vinny's understandably upset.' She glared at Geraldine.

'I'm sorry,' snapped Geraldine. 'I thought it imperative to pass on the news immediately—'

'Tyke's fine!' said Clarissa, looking up from her mobile before pausing, a wheezing cough momentarily taking her breath.

Edith regarded her sister with concern. 'Did you call the doctor like I told you to?'

'How about a suck of oxygen?' Eric was holding out the mask attached to the cylinder by his side. 'Would that help?'

Clarissa ended the coughing fit on a laugh. 'Thanks, Eric – I'll be fine. And Dr Naylor's coming this afternoon, Edith, so stop fussing. But going back to Tyke, I put a shout out on the WhatsApp group and Lucy saw Clive Knowles leading him away from the marketplace. Apparently he's got a few cuts and bruises but nothing major.'

Vinny let out a loud sigh, shoulders slumping, and Edith put her arm around him.

'Thank goodness,' she murmured.

Arty tried to quell the surge of jealousy threatening to engulf him. A man's life had been in danger and he was behaving like a teenager.

'Do you know what happened?' he asked Clarissa.

She was scanning her phone, the Bruncliffe WhatsApp group set up by Delilah back when Samson's life was in danger having proved its worth many times over in the last twelve months. When Clarissa looked up, her eyes were wide with shock.

'Lucy saw it all – she says a motorbike came out of nowhere as Tyke was crossing the road in front of her cafe and almost ran him over. If it hadn't been for Clive's intervention . . .'

'Crikey!' said Eric. 'Sounds like he had a lucky escape.'

Murmurs of agreement echoed around the group.

'But that's not all,' continued Clarissa, excitement making her breathless, the rasp in her chest more pronounced. 'Mrs Pettiford was on the other side of High Street by the bank and she told Lucy that it didn't look like an accident from her angle.'

'What do you mean?' asked Ana.

'She said it looked like the motorbike was trying to hit Tyke on purpose!'

Her words triggered a gasp from Vinny, whose skin was now a worrying shade of grey.

'Clarissa!' Edith's tone was sharp with remonstration as she stared at her sister. 'You should know better than to be repeating the view of the town's gossip before we have any corroboration from a more reliable source.'

'I think we might have that corroboration,' came the reasoned lilt of Joseph O'Brien. He gestured at his phone. 'Barry saw Clive and Carol going next door to his with Tyke.'

'Barry?' Vinny looked around, puzzled, a newcomer to town. 'Who's Barry?'

His question fell into silence, everyone else making the connections and looking worried, Eric even reaching for his oxygen as his breath started to come in short pants.

'Barry Dawson,' he muttered, between inhalations. 'He owns Plastic Fantastic on Back Street.'

'And? How is that relevant?' Vinny was getting exasperated. 'Edith? What's going on?'

She shook her head, placed her hand over his and squeezed. 'Plastic Fantastic is next door to both the Dales Dating Agency and the Dales Detective Agency. I'm guessing that it wasn't the former they were visiting.'

Vinny still looked puzzled. 'Tyke's gone to see a private detective?'

'So it would appear. But don't worry. He mentioned the other day that he was thinking about engaging someone to protect his new clothing range from corporate spies. It's probably just that.'

'Or he might have decided his own backside needs protecting,' muttered Eric, undermining Edith's attempt to play down the situation.

Vinny slumped in his seat, getting it now. 'Do you think . . . could that lady be right? Someone tried to kill Tyke . . . ?' He was shaking his head, struggling to take it in.

'Whatever it is,' said Clarissa as Vinny gripped Edith's hand and leaned against her shoulder, 'Tyke's done the right thing. If anyone can establish whether this was a murder attempt or not, it's Samson and Delilah. They're the best in the business.'

There was a strong rumble of agreement around the group. Vinny was taking little consolation from it, however, looking like a husk of the man who'd been holding the room enthralled only moments before. While Arty's insecurity was reaching new levels as Edith murmured in Vinny's ear, her hand clasped in his, the pair of them looking every bit the betrothed couple they used to be.

Arty turned away, remonstrating with himself for being so immature, and saw Geraldine Mortimer, her focus also on the two former sweethearts. And for a brief second before her face assumed an expression of perfect concern, he saw his own feelings reflected in her gaze.

Seemed like he wasn't the only one being tormented by pangs of envy.

'So,' said Samson, forcing himself to be businesslike and overcome his personal reservations now that the agency's services were committed, 'how are we going to reallocate the rest of the cases if I'm on bodyguard duties?'

With their new client having departed along with Clive and Carol, and Nina and Nathan having been reluctantly shooed back to school, the rest of the DDA team were gathered around Samson's desk, Ida studying the agency's schedule on her laptop, lips pursed in contemplation.

'Bodyguard?' came a loud voice from the hall as Delilah's oldest brother, Will, appeared in the office doorway. 'What's this all about?'

'We've had a request from someone for personal protection.

You'll never guess who,' said Delilah, face alight with excitement.

'Clive Knowles? Those sheep of his are finally after his blood for being dyed pink?'

Ida snorted and Gareth let out a loud laugh, Clive's candy-floss Texels the subject of local legend.

'Tyke!' announced Delilah, unable to hold it in any longer.

'*The* Tyke?' Will asked.

Samson waited for an expression of awe to descend on the features of the farmer as it had done with everyone else so far. But none materialised, a simple puzzled frown remaining on Will's face.

'The very same,' Delilah confirmed. 'He's in the area to launch his summer collection and has received death threats. He wants us to provide surveillance while he's here.'

'*Me*,' clarified Samson. 'He wants *me* to provide surveillance.'

Delilah waved a hand as though it was a trivial point, but it wasn't for Samson. He'd been relieved beyond measure when Tyke had expressly stated that he wanted only Samson on the case.

'Who'd have thought it,' murmured Ida, shaking her head. 'That scrawny boy who used to come up every summer, turning into someone so famous.'

'So famous he's adopted a ridiculous name,' muttered Samson, feeling like a curmudgeon but unable to enter into the excitement his colleagues were experiencing.

'Jake Ramsbottom hardly has the same ring to it,' Gareth laughed. 'Besides, it was Will who gave him that nickname. Remember, Will? We'd be hanging out in Hawber Woods and he was always trailing after us. The lad was so cheeky, never took no for an answer. So Will just started calling him "Tyke". And now he uses it for his clothing range and everything.'

Will gave a dry laugh. 'Aye, that's true enough. Happen I should be on commission or something for coming up with his branding.' Then he turned serious. 'But is it true? Did he really get death threats?'

'Not just death threats. Some bugger tried to run him over this morning in the marketplace,' said Ida.

'We don't know that for sure—' began Samson.

Delilah shot him a look. 'Sounds very much like we do. Carol Knowles isn't one to make things up and according to the WhatsApp group, Mrs Pettiford attested to the same. The motorbike appeared to change direction and head straight towards Tyke. But for Clive's quick thinking, we'd be looking at a murder investigation.'

'Bloody hell!' muttered Will, his frown deepening as he glanced towards Delilah.

'Don't!' she growled.

He raised both hands in appeasement. 'I didn't say a word.'

'You didn't need to! I'm thirty, and yet you still think you have to worry about me.'

'Given you've been involved in several near-death encounters in the last eighteen months, I can hardly be blamed for looking out for my little sister,' he said gruffly, reaching over to ruffle her hair. He flicked a look at Samson above her head, a silent entreaty.

It was an entreaty Samson couldn't promise to fulfil. Not when Delilah Metcalfe had a penchant for seeking out trouble and a stubborn refusal to stay out of it once she found it.

'So what does this personal protection involve?' asked Will, with an air of resignation.

'Mostly surveillance,' said Samson. 'And whatever Delilah and the rest of the team can dig up in the background.

Hopefully we'll be able to find the perpetrator before they make good on their threats.'

Will nodded. 'Well, Tyke couldn't have chosen anyone finer to ask for help. While I'm no fan of his taste in fashion, he's certainly shown sense in placing his life in your hands, Samson.'

The rare praise from the oldest Metcalfe sibling brought raised eyebrows around the room. And a sense of guilt to Samson's heart. Because he wasn't sure his new client would have been so keen to secure his services if he could have seen the resentment being harboured by his bodyguard.

Not that Samson held anything against the man personally. He remembered seeing him around in the summers when they were kids, Jake – as he was then – visiting grandparents at the Ramsbottom place, a ramshackle cottage on Crag Lane, tucked under the crag and permanently damp. He'd been a slip of a lad, a couple of years younger than Samson and Ryan Metcalfe, and without the robust physique that the local kids had from living on farms and spending most of their time outdoors. But that had never held him back, the boy refusing to heed the older lads' pointed comments when he tagged along. Refusing to be cowed when they deliberately chose activities which would test the city-dwelling youngster.

Samson had always had a grudging respect for him. Although, once Samson's mother died and his time became tied up with keeping the family farm going and keeping his father out of the pub as much as possible, he saw very little of Jake Ramsbottom. Until now. When he'd entrusted Samson with his safekeeping.

'Does he still run?' Will was asking his sister.

'Don't know – it didn't crop up. But he looks fit, so maybe. Although I can't see him getting much hill training down in London.'

'He's a fell runner?' asked Samson.

'Used to be a good one,' said Will. 'Beat Delilah in the Bruncliffe Hills race back in the day.'

'I don't remember that.' Samson turned to Delilah, surprised. For she'd been the queen of the fells in her teens, winning every race which came before her and leaving even the likes of Samson, five years her senior, in her wake. 'In fact, I don't remember you ever losing the Bruncliffe Hills in your age category.'

'It was a few years after you left town,' murmured Delilah. 'My first race as a senior. Tyke was up visiting family and decided to enter. Although in my defence, it wasn't exactly a fair contest.'

Will laughed. 'Over a decade ago and you're still smarting, sis? Never say a Metcalfe can't hold a grudge.'

'What happened?' asked Gareth.

'Tyke cheated.' Delilah gave a small smile. 'He didn't go to the final checkpoint. He swears he did and the rain smeared the ink but I was ahead of him and then suddenly he was ahead of me on the track as we hit the descent. The only way it could have happened was if he cut a corner.'

'And so Delilah, being Delilah, threw herself down the fellside trying to catch him. Left the track and went down the steep bit.' Will was shaking his head at the memory.

'Down the bit by the Crag?' Samson asked, thinking of the sheer drop that marked the side of the limestone outcrop which hung over the town. Thinking of the dizzying steepness of it. One false foot and it would be certain death.

'Yep.' Will looked at Delilah. 'Complete madness. So insane that it got named Delilah's Descent there and then, but no one has been foolhardy enough to try it since.'

'Tha's got to give the lass credit,' said Ida. 'Not one to give up easily.'

Delilah grinned. And Samson felt his heart twist with pain. Because Ida was right, as she so often was. The woman who'd agreed to marry Samson was a fighter. Not someone to walk away from a problem. Yet why was it Samson had the distinct impression that she was currently walking away from their relationship?

'So, this schedule,' said Ida, bluntly bringing the conversation back on track. 'I'm thinking Gareth could pick up the suspected pilfering case out at the dairy which Samson was working on.' She glanced over at the former gamekeeper. 'Tha can run that alongside the insurance claim verifications tha was already doing.'

Gareth nodded.

'And I'll take over the running of the Dales Dating Agency,' continued Ida. 'That should give Delilah a bit more time to investigate the death threats and the motorbike incident. With the rest of us helping out where and when needed, including Nina at weekends, Samson should be freed up completely for his undercover work.'

'It's asking a lot of all of you,' said Samson, hoping one of them would baulk and provide the excuse he wanted to jettison the case.

But the three of them were shaking their heads.

'Fine by me,' said Gareth. 'Possible theft sounds a lot more interesting than insurance claims.'

'Just as well,' muttered Ida, 'as there's no other option if we're to take on Tyke.'

'Which we *are* doing,' said Delilah, giving Samson a pointed look. Seeing right through his attempted subterfuge.

'Right.' Samson nodded with resignation. 'Let's get started, then.'

He made to get up but Will cleared his throat, looking uncharacteristically hesitant at the end of the desk.

'Sorry, Will, was there something else?'

'Yeah . . . it's just I wanted to ask . . . well, Harry asked me to ask. And Ash, too, in fact . . .'

'Good lord, lad,' snapped Ida. 'Cut to the chase! We've got work to be getting on with.'

The farmer's ruddy cheeks turned a deeper shade of pink. 'How's the wedding planning going?' he blurted out.

The unexpected question caught Samson unawares. 'Oh . . . great . . . good, all fine,' he said, trying not to look at Delilah, whose mobile had suddenly captured her complete attention. 'Nice of you to ask.'

Will nodded. Coughed again. 'So you've made all the big decisions?'

Samson risked a glance at his fiancée. She was busy scrolling through a website, lips tight, face pale. 'We're getting there,' he said. Trying not to think about all the things which had yet to be arranged and which the bride-to-be seemed reluctant to discuss.

'Right. Okay.' Still Will lingered, an awkwardness to him that didn't fit the confident farmer.

'Was there something in particular you wanted to know?' Samson asked, puzzled by Will's interest in the fripperies of the impending wedding when normally anything outside the sphere of livestock, agriculture and rugby failed to hold his attention.

'Erm . . . like I said . . . Harry and Ash wanted to know—'

'Who's going to be Samson's best man?' interjected Gareth

Julia Chapman

with a loud laugh. 'Don't tell me – there's a book opened at the Fleece and you three are the front runners?'

A shameless grin lit up Will's face. 'Something like that. Just thought I'd throw my hat in the ring seeing as the odds are set against me.'

'You're betting on the wedding?' Samson asked, turning to see if Delilah was as stunned as he was. But she was still studiously looking at her mobile.

'Just who'll be best man. It's only a bit of a laugh,' shrugged Will.

'What are the odds on thee?' asked Ida with sudden interest.

'Ten to one. Ash is currently at five to one and Harry's odds-on favourite. And if you want to really gamble, Troy's got himself down as an outsider at a hundred to one.'

Gareth burst out laughing, while Ida was looking contemplative.

'Troy?' managed Samson, looking across the road to the Fleece where Troy Murgatroyd was the landlord. Given the man's surly demeanour and miserly nature, he was hardly best-man material. 'People really think I'd choose him?'

'You might get free beer!' said Gareth.

Ida snorted. 'Happen there's more chance of thee getting charged for his services!'

'So,' persisted Will, 'you're not going to give me a heads up as to who it is?'

Samson shook his head. 'Sorry, but it's a secret,' he lied, not having given the matter any consideration. He was too worried about whether he'd have a bride next to him at the altar to be concerned about a best man.

Will laughed. Slapped him on the back. 'Don't blame you. But I meant what I said. I'm happy to throw my hat in the

38

ring if you're stuck, bet or no bet. I'd be honoured to be by your side when you marry my sister.'

The comment finally dragged Delilah's gaze from her mobile, her shocked features reflecting Samson's own reaction. For it wasn't long ago that her brother's sole interactions with him had featured the farmer's broad fists or, at the very least, verbal abuse.

Touched by this unexpected vote of approval, Samson held out his hand. 'Thanks, Will. I can't think of anyone better to have as a brother.'

'Right,' said Delilah, springing to her feet. 'Time I was off. I'll walk you out, Will?'

Will nodded and started making for the door, Ida and Gareth gathering up their things to follow.

'Have you got a second, Delilah?' Samson asked.

It was as though she could read his mind. Could see the anxious questions waiting to be asked.

'Sorry,' she said, smile wide, tone breezy. 'I promised Barry I'd drop by and help sort out some teething problems he's having with the bookshop software. It'll probably take all afternoon.'

'No worries,' said Samson. Equally breezy. Both of them putting on a display for the others. 'I'll see you at home.'

She nodded. Not a verbal commitment. Not a hint either that she hadn't been home with him for days, choosing to stay at her cottage at the back of town rather than join him out at Twistleton Farm, the poor broadband connection in the more remote Thorpdale having been cited as the reason.

'So it's true, then?' asked Gareth. 'Barry Dawson is opening a bookshop in the old Taylor's premises?'

Delilah switched her attention to Gareth, her shoulders dropping, the tension around her eyes relaxing. She was happier talking about their neighbour's expanding commercial operations than she was about their imminent marriage.

'Yep. He should be opening on Monday, if I can get the technical glitches sorted.'

'It'll be nice to see something there rather than a burned-out husk,' muttered Ida, referring to the double-fronted retail space on the market square which had once housed Taylor's Estate Agents, but more recently had been a charred reminder of the bad times which had struck the town.

'Books and brooms,' said Will with a laugh, gesturing to the window beyond which the colourful display of buckets and mops spilling out from Plastic Fantastic next door could be seen. 'Barry's taking over Bruncliffe one shop at a time!'

'Aye, well, better him than someone like Rick Procter,' muttered Ida.

The name threw a shadow over the room. A year on from his arrest, the disgraced property developer was finally about to undergo trial for his role in the human trafficking and drugs racket he'd been running from his property empire. He was also facing charges of murder and attempted murder. While the former was going to be hard to prove, the evidence that he'd killed Pete Ferris thin on the ground, the prosecution was banking on a star witness to testify for the latter: Delilah herself.

Her reluctance to discuss her upcoming ordeal – because Samson had no doubt that's what her time in court would be as she was forced to relive those dreadful hours when she'd been left for dead – made him wonder if the trauma the case had resurrected was the cause of her current behaviour.

He could hardly blame her if that was so. Being trapped in a burning building would be enough to trigger nightmares for life. But if she wouldn't talk to him about it, he was at a loss as to how he could help.

'Any idea when you'll be called up?' asked Gareth.

'Any day now,' muttered Delilah, the tension back in her face. Then she shook her head, looked at her brother and said, 'Come on. I need to get to Barry's.'

The Metcalfe siblings left the building, Tolpuddle in tow, and with Ida and Gareth not far behind. All alone in his office, Samson slumped back down behind his desk and stared out of the window.

The Fleece stared back, its stone facade almost as sullen as the man who ran it.

Samson gave a wry laugh, thinking about the betting shenanigans taking place inside the pub. He wondered what odds Troy would be offering on the wedding even happening if he knew how things stood between the engaged couple.

5

'Shock, nothing more.' Dr Naylor made his diagnosis as he straightened up, his tone on the harder edge of brusque.

From her position on the other side of the armchair which contained Vinny King, Ana Stoyanovic tried not to let her surprise show. In all her dealings with the doctor during her previous spell as manager of Fellside Court, she'd never seen him quite so abrupt with a resident. Normally he had time for everyone. But today, as the afternoon sun lit up the fells beyond the corner windows of Vinny's lounge and cast a golden glow into the room, the doctor seemed far from sunny in disposition and in no mood to dwell with his patient.

It had been Edith's idea to bring Vinny back to his apartment and ask Dr Naylor to stop by, the talk-show host not showing signs of recovering his usual ebullience after Geraldine Mortimer broke the dreadful news about the near miss at the marketplace. Even the arrival of his nephew in the communal lounge hadn't eased Vinny's anxiety. In fact, the sight of Tyke's bruised and battered features seemed to have set him back even further. Given how pale he looked, Ana had concurred with Edith and, accompanied by Tyke and Arty, they'd escorted him to the two-bedroomed flat on the first floor, what used to be a guest suite before the new owner took over the complex and reallocated the flat for residential use.

Date with Destiny

One of many changes which had been made since Fellside Court was auctioned off in the wake of Rick Procter's fall from grace. All changes for the better, as far as Ana was concerned, her own reappointment included. When she'd had to go back to her native Serbia eighteen months ago due to visa issues, she'd been devastated to leave the place and its lovely residents. But last October she'd been asked if she would be interested in taking up the reins again at her former place of work. She'd accepted immediately – getting to return to Fellside Court was a dream come true.

The increased salary had also been a bonus, enabling her to rent a small house in Bruncliffe, the extra space needed as she now not only had her young son, Luka, living with her, but Grigore Vlaicu, too, the Romanian who'd stolen her heart. They'd both agreed to give it a six-month trial, Grigore working for an engineering company in Shipley, who'd seen the news about his brave actions in helping to break up Rick Procter's human-trafficking ring and had offered to sponsor his visa. Ana was quietly – and happily – confident the trial would become permanent.

But while Ana's own circumstances had influenced her decision to take the position at the retirement complex, she'd also been swayed because she'd known who the new owner was. Despite efforts to keep the identity of the person who'd bought the place a secret, in a town like Bruncliffe it hadn't taken long for rumours to flourish, and Nancy Taylor's name had featured in every single whisper. Her reasons for keeping her role in the purchase under wraps were well understood, afraid that her deceased husband's part in the dreadful events which had almost brought the town to its knees would make the residents fearful of having a Taylor at the helm. So far, however, Nancy had brought nothing but joy to Fellside Court.

The outdoor gym which had been set up on the grass beyond the courtyard was proving very popular, especially the tandem air-walker which allowed two people to exercise while chatting away. Equally the new residents' committee, which met once a month with the management, had been a hit and had already organised regular day trips as well as visits from a mobile cinema during the winter months. All in all, Fellside Court was a happy place.

At least it had been. Until the arrival of Vinny King. Since the national celebrity had moved in three months ago, Ana had detected an undercurrent of tension within the community she worked for. While the majority of the residents were overjoyed to have someone so famous decide to make Fellside Court his home, there were definitely a few who seemed a bit ruffled by his presence. Arty Robinson was one of them.

From what she'd seen of him recently, the former bookie was a bit out of sorts, which was surprising given that he'd moved in with Edith and all should have been rosy in his world. He was currently standing to the side of Vinny's lounge, looking at what could only be described as a vanity wall.

Spanning the entire width of the room were photos of the rich and famous. People Ana knew from watching television. Some she even recognised from the movies. And one or two politicians. In every image Vinny was featured front and centre, the smile that had endeared him to households across the country beaming out.

Ana wondered what Arty was making of this vulgar display of fame. Although, now that she looked again, she could see that his interest wasn't being held by the photos, nor was it focused on the sideboard beneath, on which were displayed an astonishing number of trophies, presumably all accolades in recognition of Vinny's talent. Instead, Arty was staring at the only item which didn't pay tribute to the apartment's occupant. He was leaning forward, studying a large painting of an outdoor swimming pool, a white diving board cutting across turquoise water, the texture of the piece refracting the light and making it look like the water was rippling in a breeze. It was simple. But breathtaking.

'Don't get too close. That's my pension,' said Vinny, casting an eye at Arty as Dr Naylor snapped the clasp on his bag closed. 'A Hockney. Original. I take it you've heard of him, Arty?'

Ana, who didn't have a clue who Hockney was, had enough awareness to know a put-down when she heard one. Seemingly the lack of enthusiasm Arty was feeling for Vinny King cut both ways. Arty merely stepped away from the wall with a small smile, while Edith's eyebrows shot up.

'It's definitely an original?' she asked, moving across the room to peer at the painting.

Vinny nodded. 'Treated myself one year when my career was on a high.'

'Who is Hockney?' asked Ana into the ensuing silence.

'David Hockney – one of the most influential British artists of the twentieth century,' intoned Vinny. 'And a Yorkshire lad to boot. As I keep telling Tyke here, invest in art while the going is good. It'll look after you in the hard times. Last valuation put that piece at over two million.'

Ana gasped, swivelling to stare at the pool and diving board. 'Two million pounds?' she squeaked.

'At least.'

Edith let out a little noise, eyes wide, while Dr Naylor grunted, his mouth fixed in a stern line, his focus not on the artwork but on his patient.

45

'If we're quite done with the art-history lesson,' he said sharply, 'I'll be on my way.'

'That's it?' asked Tyke, concerned. 'My uncle has no need for any medication or anything?'

'As I said, it's just shock, no doubt resulting from hearing about your accident—'

'It wasn't an accident,' Vinny muttered, interrupting the doctor, his hands grasping the arms of his chair as his gaze switched to Tyke. 'I heard that someone tried to kill you.'

Tyke smiled and patted his uncle on the shoulder. 'Just rumours, that's all. Nothing to them. Honestly, it was a simple accident.'

'But you were seen going into a detective agency. What was that all about if everything's okay?'

There was no hiding the surprise which flitted across the young man's face at his uncle's knowledge of his movements, Edith letting out a droll laugh.

'Welcome to Bruncliffe,' she said. 'We don't have a bush telegraph so much as a farmers' fax – news usually arrives outdated, illegible and often at the wrong number. But more often than not there's a grain of truth in it somewhere.'

Tyke grinned, Ana recognising the easy charm which was so apparent on the TV screen. 'Remind me not to try to keep secrets around here!' he laughed.

'So why do you need a detective?' persisted Vinny.

'It's nothing serious. When I was last in to see you I happened to mention to your friends that I was thinking of hiring someone to provide security for my clothing collection ahead of the official launch – they were kind enough to recommend the DDA.' Arty and Edith were nodding, corroborating his story. Tyke shrugged. 'This morning seemed as good a time as any to stop by and set it up. So you can rest easy, Uncle Vinny – there's nothing to worry about. I just need to look more carefully when I cross the road.'

He ended on another smile, doing his best to reassure his uncle. But still Vinny didn't seem at ease, shifting in his chair, his hands shaking, a frown marking deep creases in his forehead.

'Well, looking on the brighter side of things, Vinny,' said Ana, 'I've just had confirmation from Bruncliffe Taxis. Our minibus is all booked for Tuesday evening.'

'Oh, that's great news!' Edith said, while Vinny's frown finally shifted, a look of eager anticipation taking its place.

'Going somewhere nice?' asked Dr Naylor.

'Bruncliffe Community Hall is live-streaming the Royal Shakespeare Company's *Romeo and Juliet*,' explained Edith. 'Vinny suggested we have a group outing to see it.'

'You can't beat a good production of the Bard,' said Vinny, an animation to him which had been missing earlier. 'Did I ever tell you about the time I had Judi Dench on my show? One of the best Shakespearean actors this country has ever known . . .'

As Vinny continued to regale his audience with his anecdote, Dr Naylor simply nodded at the assembled group and turned towards the hallway. Ana followed him.

'Are you sure he's okay, Doctor?' she murmured once they were out of earshot of the others. As a fully qualified nurse, she had enough experience to be worried about the waxy sheen to Vinny's face, which remained despite his new-found energy.

'Quite sure,' came the terse response. 'What he'd benefit from most is a bit of rest rather than waffling on about his past glory. Now if you'll excuse me, I've got a full round this afternoon and need to get on.'

Ana stepped back in surprise. Not just at the tone but at the strange look on the usually affable features of Dr Naylor. Almost at retiring age himself, he was customarily seen with a wide smile beneath his grey hair. Today he was struggling to hold back a frown.

Noticing her reaction, he ran a hand over his face.

'Sorry,' he muttered, looking weary. 'Got a lot on. Normally I can balance it all out but . . . Liz hasn't been having the best of days of late.'

Immediately Ana felt contrition at having pushed the man so far. His wife had been diagnosed with terminal cancer in February, a diagnosis which had shocked the town, especially Ana. A quiet woman who never indulged in gossip, Liz Naylor had been one of the first to make her feel welcome when she'd arrived in Bruncliffe and they'd bonded over a preference for weak tea, a view considered heresy in the Dales town. Ana's contrition was amplified at the realisation that it was over a month since she'd last visited Liz. Between moving house, sorting a school place for Luka and settling down in a new job, not to mention living with Grigore, Ana just hadn't found the time.

'I've been meaning to get round to see her one of these days. How is she doing?'

'She'd love that. Just . . . just don't leave it too long before you do . . .' His words tailed off into a sad silence.

'Oh! I didn't realise . . . that's so quick . . .'

'For the best, perhaps.' The doctor sighed, then gave a brisk nod, opened Vinny's front door and let himself out into the corridor beyond. He turned, gesturing back in towards the lounge behind Ana. 'You did the right thing sending for me. Mr King has certainly had a shock but rest assured, he'll be fine. His heart rate and blood pressure are already down.'

'Thanks,' Ana said.

'To be honest, I'm more concerned about my next appointment.' He indicated the flat next door, now home to Clarissa Ralph following her exchange of properties with Arty. The poor woman's excitement about having her own place after years of living with her sister had been cut short by a nasty chest infection she just couldn't seem to shake. 'I thought Clarissa would have been over the worst by now, but that cough is still plaguing her.'

'And it's not like she's taking it easy either,' said Ana with a smile. 'She wouldn't listen when I told her to give the armchair aerobics session a miss the other day. And she won't stay off the air-walker outside. She said she'd have plenty of time for taking it easy when she's six feet under in a box.'

Dr Naylor laughed. 'Perhaps she's right. The world needs more folk like Clarissa.'

Ana closed the door and re-entered the lounge where Tyke was now entertaining his uncle with some story about an episode of his TV programme, *The Nines*, which had gone wrong, while Arty was back at the vanity wall, staring at the painting of the swimming pool. Edith crossed over to Ana's side.

'Is he okay?' Ana asked Edith quietly, nodding towards Arty. 'I mean, is there a problem between him and Vinny?'

A rare flush tinted Edith's cheeks. 'He's fine,' she said, a look of affection resting on the former bookie. 'Just so happens he's more discerning than most.' She turned her gaze onto Vinny King, her features becoming inscrutable. 'Not everyone falls for a veneer of bonhomie.'

With that, she called over to Arty and, making the excuse that Vinny needed some rest as the doctor had ordered, the pair took their leave. Ana was puzzling over Edith's cryptic parting comment when she heard voices at the front door, one of them raised in indignation.

'Is something the matter?' she asked, arriving in the doorway to see Edith and Arty in the corridor with an affronted-looking Geraldine Mortimer, who was holding a freshly made apple pie, the tantalising smell of warm pastry wafting up from it.

'I called by to see how Vinny is,' Geraldine said, pouting in annoyance, 'and Edith said I shouldn't disturb him.'

Ana nodded. 'Well, Dr Naylor has just said that he needs some rest, so perhaps—'

'It's only me, Vinny,' Geraldine called through the open door. 'I've brought you a treat.'

There was the distinct sound of a resigned sigh from the lounge. Then Tyke appeared in the hallway.

'Geraldine – it is Geraldine, isn't it?' he asked with a smile that could melt a polar ice cap. 'I'm afraid Uncle Vinny is really tired after all the stress I unwittingly put him through today. Do you think you could call back later? Maybe tomorrow even?'

Geraldine nodded, smiling back at the young man, eyes fixed on his handsome face. 'Of course!' she murmured. 'Totally understandable. But here, take this. It might be just the tonic he needs.'

She offered out the apple pie, Tyke taking it from her and leaning down to smell it, giving a groan of appreciation.

'Really, Geraldine, you shouldn't have gone to the trouble.' He looked up at her and winked. 'But I'm glad you did.'

Geraldine giggled, while Tyke gave one last powerful smile and turned back towards the lounge, the divine scent of the pie lingering in his wake. Ana stepped out into the corridor and closed the door to Vinny King's apartment behind her.

'There. See.' Geraldine had turned to Edith, her voice rich with triumph. With a flounce of her perfect platinum bob, she walked away.

'Some folk are gluttons for punishment,' Edith muttered before linking her arm through Arty's and heading off towards their apartment at the far side of the building.

Ana was left standing in the corridor thinking that as far as enigmatic comments went, Edith Hird was proving herself unparalleled. She also had a strong sense that if the harmony of Fellside Court was to be maintained, she might need to brush up a bit on her local history. Because whatever was causing the ripples in this normally tranquil pond, Ana was betting – as with much that went on in Bruncliffe – its roots lay back in the past.

6

Delilah hadn't been lying when she said she needed to call in and see Barry in his new premises. But as she closed the fire-engine-red doors of Barry's Books behind her and slipped back out into the sunshine bathing the cobbled square, she felt a twinge of guilt.

She'd known it would only take an hour to get things sorted. Not the entire afternoon as she'd implied to Samson. And considering that Barry had done everything she'd asked and been more than ready when she called in, she'd been able to sort out the glitch faster than she'd anticipated. There'd even been time for him to show her around, proudly displaying the renovations – carried out by her own brother, Ash – which had turned the former estate agents into a vibrant bookshop.

Shelving in bright yellow, armchairs in bold colours, and flooring which looked like Jackson Pollock had been let loose with an entire spectrum of paint, gave a trendy and yet cosy feel to the place. As her brother had wryly commented when he'd finished the refit, it was as though Barry had taken his inspiration from the pavement display outside Plastic Fantastic.

The upbeat vibe of the bookshop was a far cry from Delilah's present frame of mind. She stood in front of the doors, wondering what to do next. Not in the mood for returning to Back Street and the DDA building.

Another twinge of guilt. With the agency suddenly inundated with work, here was she moping around, doing her best to avoid being at the office.

To avoid being with Samson.

'You understand, don't you boy?' she murmured, as a heavy weight came to rest against her right leg, Tolpuddle leaning into her. Knowing the hound, she knew better than to convince herself this was his way of agreeing with her. It was affection-seeking and nothing else. She ruffled his ears, letting the sunshine warm them both, trying to relax.

She needed advice. Someone she could talk to without feeling like she was being a traitor.

She glanced to her left, Peaks Patisserie on the other side of the road, the tables inside busy. Lucy would be flat out with the afternoon-tea brigade and while Delilah knew her sister-in-law would drop everything in order to help her out, it felt like an unfair demand. Besides, Delilah already knew what the advice would be.

Snap out of it.

After all, that's what she'd been telling herself for the past five months. Not that it had done any good.

So who else could she turn to? Her mother? It would seem like such a betrayal. Ida?

Delilah let out a laugh. The thought of it. Of Ida's face if Delilah laid out her worries in front of her. The things which were keeping her awake at night.

It had been weeks since she'd slept properly, the effects showing in the dark circles under her eyes. At this rate, she'd be walking up the aisle looking like a panda. If she walked up the aisle at all . . .

'What do you reckon?' she enquired of her Weimaraner.

He gazed up at her, eyes half-closed in the sun's warmth.

Yawned. And shook himself. What would he say, she wondered, if he knew what she was contemplating?

He'd never forgive her, because he loved Samson every bit as much as he loved Delilah.

With a heavy heart, she started walking. Aimlessly. Away from Back Street and towards Church Street. She didn't make a conscious decision, but when she found herself starting up the steep incline past the library, she knew she'd made the right choice. If she could find help anywhere, it would be here.

Market day in Bruncliffe usually brought brisk business to the Fleece. Usually. But while the mercenary in Troy Murgatroyd – which even he would admit formed the largest part of his character – should have been bemoaning the brilliant sunshine beyond the deep-set windows for causing the scattering of empty chairs in the dark interior of his pub, he was in good humour. Partly because he happened to be a man whose moods were closely tied to meteorological conditions, his naturally sullen disposition distilled by the sun's warmth – which, given this was the Yorkshire Dales, wasn't that often. But also because whatever losses he'd sustained due to the clement weather, he'd more than made up for on the side hustle he was operating.

The race to see who would be Samson O'Brien's best man was on and the wagers had been coming in thick and fast, with money landing heavily on some key names – livestock auctioneer Harry Furness being the hottest of favourites. And now Troy was about to make the easiest money of all.

'Are you sure?' he asked the prospective punter standing across the bar from him. Not something he would normally do, figuring that fools and money deserved to be parted. But this particular person was no fool and Troy had no desire to get on their wrong side by accepting what seemed to him a ludicrous bet without giving them a chance to reconsider.

'Aye. A tenner.' Chin jutting out in stubborn determination, Ida Capstick waggled a ten-pound note at him and tapped the piece of paper she'd placed on the counter.

Troy looked again at the name written there. Raised his glance to Ida. She stared defiantly back at him.

'And good odds, too, mind. Tha'll not have to pay out more than this one.'

Impressed and amused by her misplaced confidence, Troy shrugged. Wrote down a couple of numbers on the paper. Ida nodded.

He signed the slip, pocketed the tenner and turned to make a note of the transaction in the small blue notebook by the till. When he looked up, she was shoving her receipt into the pocket of her combats, a rare glint in her eye. Troy would spend the rest of the day wondering if he was the one who should have been heeding his own warning.

For someone who'd been reluctant to take on the role of Tyke's personal protection officer, Samson was already on the job. He'd fixed an appointment to visit the fashion guru late afternoon at the house he was renting in the exclusive Low Mill development on the edge of town, at which Samson would draw up a risk analysis to determine the protection schedule to be set in place. But for now, he was using the intervening time to brush up old skills.

It was seven months since he'd carried out surveillance. More if you counted the fact that he'd been placed on desk duty once he'd handed in his notice with the NCA. To say he was feeling rusty was putting it mildly. Especially given the unique circumstances of his operational sphere.

While London offered someone in his line of work ample opportunity to blend in and go unseen as he tailed drugs barons or spied on money-laundering networks, this was Bruncliffe . . . a small town in the Yorkshire Dales where everyone knew everyone and the slightest hint of 'outsider' or behaviour beyond the normal was duly noted. And commented on. What chance would he have trying to sneak around unnoticed while watching Tyke's back?

Which was why he was currently crouched down in a clump of bushes at the rear of Fellside Court. Tyke had mentioned he was heading straight from the DDA offices to the retirement complex to complete the visit to his uncle which the purported attempt to run him over had interrupted. Samson figured that if he could maintain watch of the premises for the length of time his client was in there without some well-meaning pensioner spotting him and raising the alarm, he would be ready for the task he'd signed up for. Because out of everywhere in town, Fellside Court was the toughest place to carry out covert operations. A fact which could be attributed to a large group of people having nothing much to do all day but look out of the window, or could be explained by the razor-sharp intellect and excellent powers of observation possessed by a section of the population others were all too keen to dismiss as useless.

Given his experience with the current residents, Samson was inclined to opt for the latter.

He watched two women come into the courtyard, the large wall of glass which spanned both floors of the middle section of the U-shaped building towering over them, offering yet more vantage points for people to see out. The women crossed the paving stones and walked up onto the grass to where the new outdoor gym had been installed beneath some trees. Without a break in their conversation, they stepped up on one of the contraptions, side by side, and proceeded to exercise, their legs moving in synchronicity while their voices floated over to him.

'Shock, they said . . .'

'Not a surprise given the news. Ooh, look who it isn't – coming back from Vinny's no doubt. She didn't waste any time offering succour!'

The two women laughed, their gazes on the glass wall and the figure clearly visible striding purposefully along the corridor up on the first floor. Samson recognised the blonde bob of Geraldine Mortimer. She disappeared out of sight and the chatter resumed beneath the trees.

Knees beginning to ache, Samson was about to leave, satisfied that he'd managed to remain concealed long enough to prove to himself he was capable of carrying out his duties, but at that moment two familiar figures came around the corner of the building.

Delilah and Tolpuddle.

While Delilah had her head down, clearly miles away, Tolpuddle was alert, nose up, sniffing. He looked over towards where Samson had remained concealed, barked once and tugged at his lead. Samson braced himself, convinced he was about to be unmasked and greeted by a canine embrace, but Delilah merely glanced at the Weimaraner, made a soothing noise and apologised to the ladies, thinking the dog was barking at them.

Samson grinned, seeing the confusion on Tolpuddle's face. He'd done it. Mission accomplished.

He went to stand up, intending to reveal himself and head over for a hug from both of them. And that's when it hit him. What was Delilah doing at Fellside Court? She'd said she'd be at Barry's all afternoon.

It was probably nothing. An innocent explanation. But from his position in the bushes, he had a brilliant view of Vinny King's lounge window and as he glanced up, he saw Tyke looking out. Saw the fashion designer spot Delilah from above, Delilah looking up at the same time, the two of them waving at each other before Tyke moved out of sight.

Samson remained crouched down, eyes on the woman and dog as they entered the building. They crossed the foyer and there, coming down the stairs at pace, was Tyke. Laughter, the silence of it from this distance making it seem illicit.

He watched them chatting. Then he pulled out his phone and typed in a message, asking Delilah where she was, saying that he needed to talk.

Through the glass, he saw her turn to her mobile, frown, then her fingers were tapping . . . Seconds later the reply appeared on his screen.

> *Still at Barry's. Going to take a while.*
> *Catch you tomorrow? xx*

Samson looked up, heart hurting, just as Tyke slipped his arm through Delilah's, the pair of them walking off towards the cafe.

Pain. Anger. Confusion. It sent Samson shooting upright with a barely muffled exclamation. And nearly gave the two elderly women heart attacks, one of them almost falling off the exercise equipment.

With a curt apology thrown their way, he stormed off around the side of the building and down to the library, where he'd parked his motorbike, all the while conscious that, if someone made an attempt on his client's life, at that precise moment he wouldn't give a damn about trying to prevent it.

7

'Two million?!' Eric gasped. For once his restricted breathing was caused by shock rather than the emphysema which had plagued him for the last few decades.

'That's what he reckons,' said Edith. She lifted the teapot on the table in front of her and poured dark brown tea into five cups.

With the late afternoon bursting with sunshine and the glorious May warmth beckoning, Eric, Edith, Arty, Joseph and Clarissa had decided to take a walk into town. The five friends had ambled slowly towards the marketplace, their pace kept leisurely as much to enjoy the delightful weather as to accommodate Clarissa's frequent outbursts of coughing, and after a peer through the window of Barry's Books, which was yet to open for business, they'd crossed the cobbles to sample the delights of Peaks Patisserie. Seated inside the window with a fine view of the town hall, they were now discussing Vinny King's extravagant taste in art over a brew and some of Lucy Metcalfe's divine strawberry cheesecake.

Joseph shook his head. 'That's crazy. Spending that amount of money on a painting. It would have to be something special.'

'Is this special enough?' Edith held out her mobile and the others leaned in over the screen.

'It's just a swimming pool!' exclaimed Eric. 'Not even the full view of it.'

'Oh, but that shade of green,' sighed Clarissa. 'And the water actually seems to shimmer. It's exquisite.'

'Two million pounds' worth of exquisite?' asked Edith dryly. Eric grunted. 'Some folk have more money than sense.'

'What do you think, Arty?' Ever sensitive to those around her, Clarissa had noticed Arty's unusual restraint when it came to voicing an opinion. In fact, she'd noticed that he hadn't really been himself of late, almost as though the euphoria of moving in with Edith was starting to wane. While she hoped this wasn't the case for her sister's sake, Clarissa was also worried on a purely selfish level. Relishing living on her own after most of her adult life had been spent living with others, Clarissa was hoping she wouldn't have to swap back apartments. 'Has Vinny wasted his money or made a wise investment?'

Arty finished his last piece of cheesecake and sat back in his chair, the air of contentment which normally accompanied such an act conspicuously absent. He shrugged. 'Not my place to say. But I can tell you now that Vinny's spot on with his estimate. Hockney originals sell for a fortune – as much as ninety million dollars in one instance.'

'I didn't know you were such an art expert,' said Edith, surprised.

'Bookies are allowed to know stuff,' muttered Arty. Then he gave another shrug. 'Truth is I know bugger all about art, just about David Hockney. Happens he was at school with our Joe in Bradford so I've always had an interest in him.'

'You've never mentioned that!'

Arty gave Edith a look. 'Aye, well we all have things in our past we don't always talk about.'

Clarissa started coughing, not just because she felt the need, this blasted chest infection really having a hold on her, but also because she wanted to break up the tension which was developing between two of her favourite people.

'Talking of bookies,' said Eric once Clarissa had fallen silent, 'have you heard about the book Troy's running at the pub?'

'On what?' Arty was all interest.

'The wedding.' There was no need to identify the participants, the upcoming nuptials between Samson O'Brien and Delilah Metcalfe having been wildly anticipated by the town since last September when the O'Brien lad had proposed in front of everyone. 'Who'll be best man to be more precise.'

'Oooh!' Clarissa clapped her hands. 'We should all have a flutter. See who gets it right.' She glanced at her sister, expecting a reprimand for suggesting something some might think was crass. But Edith was smiling, a roguish glint in her eyes.

'My money's on Harry!' she declared.

Arty laughed, slapping her on the back, a flicker of his usual vigour for life returning. 'Great shout, lass!'

'I reckon Ash is worth a punt,' said Eric. 'You'd get good odds on him.'

'I'm going for Will,' said Clarissa.

The others stared at her. 'Are you mad?' asked Edith. 'He's spent the last twelve months threatening to kill Samson at various intervals. Why on earth would Samson choose him for such an important role?'

Clarissa shrugged. 'Dark horses are always a good bet.'

'What about you, Arty?' Edith turned to him, placing a hand over his. 'What are all your years of gambling expertise telling you?'

He tapped the side of his head. 'Firstly, consider the course and not just the horse. And secondly, back what you know.'

'Which means what exactly?' demanded Eric.

Arty nodded towards Joseph, who, mobile in hand, was busy replying to a text.

'Our lad, here. Father of the groom, he'll win it hands down. In fact,' he said, gesturing at Joseph's phone, 'I'd even take a bet on that being a message from Samson right now discussing it all.'

Joseph looked up, protesting, something furtive about him. 'No . . . it's not . . . I don't know what you're talking about.'

'Huh!' said Eric. 'That's what you would say. Samson and Delilah have probably heard about what's going on, and you've been told to keep it under wraps!'

'I'd say it's definitely worth a wager,' said Edith, smiling impishly at Joseph.

He shrugged. 'Go ahead and waste your money but don't say I didn't warn you when you realise I was telling the truth.'

'So,' said Clarissa, leaning over the table conspiratorially, 'when do we place our bets?'

'No time like the present,' said Arty. 'Let's wander over to the Fleece and get our money down while the odds are still in our favour.'

They rose from the table en masse, just as Lucy Metcalfe approached, apron around her waist and a warm smile on her face.

'Off home?' she said, as she began stacking up their plates.

Arty grinned and shook his head. 'We're off to see a man about a horse.'

A loud burst of laughter broke from the other four and Lucy watched them leave the cafe, Arty's arm through

Edith's, Joseph, Clarissa and Eric still laughing as they crossed the cobbles. She found herself smiling until they disappeared down Back Street. Whatever they were up to, it was doing them good.

Samson wasn't a betting man, but having carried out an inspection of the property Tyke was renting in the Low Mill development, he would have put money on his client making a good living out of the fashion business. Situated at the end of a cul-de-sac on the opposite side to the now infamous – and empty – home of Rick Procter, the house sat behind high stone walls, a gravel driveway leading up to an ornate portico, a red Porsche Cayenne parked in front of it. Inside had revealed five spacious bedrooms, two en suite, an impressive kitchen-dining room with views through bifold doors up onto the Crag and the fells behind, and a hot tub in the back garden. It was worlds apart from the tiny cottage the Ramsbottoms had owned on Crag Lane with its moss-covered slates and the white render turning green.

'Not a bad little spot to spend time in,' said Tyke, as he joined Samson at the open bifold doors, a warm breeze drifting in from the garden. Behind them, Eloise was making coffee.

When Samson had arrived at the appointed time, Tyke hadn't been back from his clandestine meeting with Delilah – a fact Samson had been grateful for, not sure he was in the mood to deal with the man while his own personal life was in such a mess. Instead, it had been Eloise who'd shown him around. She hadn't spoken much during the inspection, just watching with that wary gaze she had, as though expecting life to deal her a blow at any second. While Samson had tested window locks and made notes on possible security updates, she'd followed like a silent shadow. But when they'd entered the rear bedroom, where an easel had been set up to face the view and a makeshift bench was cluttered with jars of brushes and tubes of paint, she'd come alive.

'Is this your work?' Samson had asked, crossing to a homemade drying rack which had been ingeniously fashioned out of a cot turned on its end, sheets of plywood slatted between the cot sides to make shelves.

'The drying rack or the paintings?' she'd asked, with a soft laugh. Then she gave a shy shrug. 'Both are mine, as it happens.'

Samson reached towards one of the paintings. 'May I?'

She scrunched up her face. 'Sure. But they're not very good.'

He pulled the top piece towards him. It was a painting of the Crag as seen from the window, the patchwork of fields and stone walls, the ever-present sheep. But it was the colours Eloise had used which caught the eye – joyous purples and greens and crimsons, depicting the scene in a way Samson had never thought possible.

'That's beautiful!' he said.

'You think so?'

He looked up, to see if she was being coy. But the earnest expression on her face demonstrated her lack of faith in her own talent.

'Honestly, yes I do,' he said. He placed the painting back and took out the next one, a grin forming as he recognised a familiar face. Broad charcoal sweeps had rendered Tolpuddle perfectly, sitting in his basket in the corner, eyes looking up mournfully in the martyred countenance he was apt to adopt whenever treats were in the vicinity. There was a vibrancy to the drawing which defied the simplicity of the style.

'Let me guess,' said Samson, 'this was when the cake was brought into the meeting.'

Eloise nodded. Smiling now.

He held on to the drawing, glancing down at the rack of art, taking in the fact that each shelf held different types of work. Small tiles covered in colourful abstract swirls, more traditional paintings of the marketplace, but with that trademark use of colour which made Bruncliffe shine.

'They're all so different,' he said.

She grimaced. 'That's my problem. I'm a jack of all trades.'

'And these?' Samson pointed towards a pile of pencil drawings fanned across a small table to the side, androgynous figures swathed in baggy bomber jackets and baggier trousers, the psychedelic patterns jumping from the page. Bright pink orchids, zigzags in orange, dazzling geometric shapes. They all seemed to pulse with life. 'These are your bread and butter?'

'Yes.' Her lips twisted on the word, Samson guessing this wasn't what she really wanted to be doing, producing the templates for Tyke's creations.

'Aren't you tempted to go out on your own? Try your hand at selling your work?'

'I'd love to, but I owe Tyke a lot.' She must have sensed Samson's curiosity because she continued, a small smile forming as she spoke. 'We bumped into each other on the street one day and he totally turned my life around. I'm lucky to be working for him. And besides,' she gestured at the drying rack, 'I've been told I don't really have a unique style. It's why I'll never make it as an artist.'

'I beg to differ,' said Samson. He held out the charcoal drawing of Tolpuddle. 'How much?'

She blinked. 'You want to buy it?'

'Yes. I know someone who'll love it just as much as I do.'

The door slammed downstairs, Tyke's voice calling up to them. Eloise took the painting from Samson's hands and slipped it back into the rack, before hurrying him out of the room.

Now she was tipping beans into the coffee machine, while Tyke chatted on.

'So what do you think? Do you need to make any changes or am I safe inside the house?'

'As long as you're cautious, I don't see any need for major changes. But until we get a better idea of where the threat is coming from, keep windows and doors locked at all times. And perhaps consider getting one of those video doorbells installed, too.'

Tyke nodded. 'I'll have a word with Delilah. She seems to have a good grasp on the tech side of things.'

Samson turned back to the view, kicking himself for providing a valid opportunity for the man to exercise his charm on Delilah once more. Because there was no denying he was charming. Which made it even harder for Samson to feel animosity towards him.

'Anything else?'

Samson shook his head. 'Not in terms of the property. As for the rest, I'll do a surveillance run for a couple of days, in the grounds and just around the area, including overnight. See if anyone is watching the place. And then we'll take it from there.'

A look of relief passed over Tyke's face. 'I was hoping you'd suggest that. To be honest, I'm a bit shook up after what happened earlier. I wasn't taking the threats seriously but now . . . so I was going to ask if you could keep watch, especially during the night. At least until you get some concrete leads into who is behind all this. I think we'd both sleep better knowing you were out there.' He looked at Eloise and she nodded.

'Sure,' said Samson, sounding more convinced than he felt.

Given the only viable threat so far had taken place in the daytime and in a public place, Tyke's request for overnight surveillance at the house seemed excessive. But Samson wasn't in a position to push back. Not just because he was dealing with a client, but because he'd already made the mistake of not believing in the danger that client was in. It wouldn't hurt to comply on this – apart from the additional strain it would place on the detective agency's already stretched resources. And his own sleep.

'Brilliant! Only thing is,' added Tyke, 'I have to ask if we could keep it covert. It's just I don't need some neighbour getting irate because someone is hanging around outside in the dark. The headlines would write themselves – *Fashion designer's bodyguard spied through my window.*'

He grinned as he said it but Samson got a glimpse of the pressure living with such a level of fame brought. Where every move had to be calculated for any potential bad publicity.

'You won't even know I'm there,' he promised. 'And in the meantime, I strongly suggest that if you've developed any routines since you've been here, you change them.'

'Like what?' asked Eloise.

Samson shrugged. 'Shopping, going for walks, going to the pub . . . Anything you do on a regular basis which could be monitored and used as the starting point for a possible attack.'

Tyke winced and Samson regretted his blunt choice of words.

Regretted not having Delilah with him as she was much better at dealing with folk when it came to this side of things.

'And, as I gather you're into fell running,' he resumed, trying to be more diplomatic, 'consider setting up a tracking app before you hit the hills. Or even better, go with someone.'

'Great advice.' Tyke nodded. 'Seeing as I'm here, I was planning on entering the Bruncliffe Hills race, for old times' sake. I was already thinking about asking Delilah to take me up onto the tops for a route recce – seeing as she's part of your team, that would kill two birds with one stone.'

'Good idea,' said Samson from between gritted teeth. All the while wondering what was with him today. He seemed determined to throw Delilah into Tyke's company. 'In terms of the virtual world,' he continued, 'you also need to exercise caution on social media. No posts to suggest your location and no advance notice of your schedule—'

'No can do, I'm afraid.' Tyke was shaking his head. 'I've got a major collection about to be launched – there's no way I'm going dark on socials. It would be commercial suicide. We have to advertise the fashion show and that means disclosing its location as well. The world needs to know I'm in Bruncliffe.'

'Perhaps commercial suicide is preferable to real-life murder?' muttered Samson, diplomacy failing him in the face of his client's stubbornness.

Tyke went to speak but Eloise interrupted.

'Samson's right,' she murmured. 'It's not worth the risk. Maybe we could just scale back a bit, at least for the next couple of days until we have a better idea of where these threats are coming from.'

'Okay!' Tyke raised both hands in submission. 'But a couple of days, no more. Social content is half the battle in brand recognition. Without it, we could be looking at my new line being brought to the world with no audience—'

'Audience?' asked Samson.

'Of course. In twelve days' time the elite of the fashion world will be descending on Bruncliffe. Not to mention journalists, models, stylists . . .' Tyke saw Samson's expression and wagged a finger at him. 'Don't even consider asking me to cancel. Death genuinely would be better than that.'

Twelve days! The Dales Detective Agency had less than two weeks to discover what was going on before the place became a carnival and Tyke's potential killer had even more opportunities to finish off what he'd tried to do that morning.

'Besides,' continued Tyke, 'I've been thinking about it since that . . . incident with the bike . . .' He paused, gave himself a slight shake. 'So yeah, I've got a gut feeling the person who wants me dead doesn't come from the haute-couture industry.'

'What makes you say that?' asked Samson.

Tyke shrugged. 'It's a cut-throat business. Everyone gets screwed by someone at some point in their careers – it goes with the territory. It's happened to me and, if I'm honest, I've probably been guilty of dishing it out a bit too over the last decade. But I've never heard of anyone taking things to this extreme. We're all used to it.'

'Remind me never to work in fashion!'

Tyke laughed, his eyes raking over Samson's jeans and T-shirt. 'I don't think I need to feel threatened in that department.'

Samson found himself grinning back at the man, resplendent in his vibrant clothing. 'So where do you think it's coming from if not from your work?'

'Oh, I think it could be from my work all right. From my TV work.'

'*The Nines*?'

Tyke nodded. 'Have you watched it?'

'Sorry, I have to admit I haven't.'

'No apology needed. Between you and me, it's the usual reality fodder – I'm not even sure I'd watch it if I wasn't in it.' That grin flashed again. 'But basically I take nine hopeful designers each series and over eight episodes, I whittle them down to the best of the bunch. Which means, of course, that some people's hopes and dreams get crushed along the way.'

'So you think it could be a disgruntled contestant?'

'Yeah. Someone who got booted off the show and holds a grudge because I ruined their career.' Tyke glanced towards Eloise. 'There's been a few of them, haven't there?'

She nodded. 'I can think of one or two straight away who didn't take their dismissal from the show lightly.'

'Could you put a list together and email it to me?' Samson held out a business card to her. 'It'll give Delilah and the others something to be going on with. And if you think of anyone else who might be behind all this . . .' He turned back to Tyke.

'Believe me, you'll be the first to know,' said Tyke.

'Great,' Samson said, trying to sound more reassuring than he felt. Because given the multiple angles to this case and the high-profile nature of his client, identifying the mysterious threat to Tyke's life wasn't going to be straightforward in the least. All of which left Samson seriously concerned that preventing another attack might be beyond the abilities of the Dales Detectives team.

With a mind beset with troubles, Samson returned to the office, riding his Royal Enfield down the ginnel which ran at the rear of the terraced houses until he reached the small yard at the back of the building. He eased the motorbike through the gate and parked on the concrete slab in the corner, sitting astride the bike for a few moments, contemplating the logistics of the surveillance he was about to embark on.

The Enfield wasn't the best vehicle for undercover work. Chrome and scarlet, the vintage machine caught the eye. It also meant that any overnight work would have to be carried out in the open, rather than in the comfort of a car interior. But the alternative?

He thought of the bright orange Mini currently parked outside the front of the building, the pink intertwined hearts and the DDA logo on the side. Not exactly inconspicuous either. Shaking his head in dry mirth at his Hobson's choice and not relishing a night spent bivouacking in downtown Bruncliffe, he took off his helmet and as he did, noticed a shadow flit across the first-floor window overlooking the yard.

Delilah was still here.

He went from elation to angst in a matter of seconds. Should he confront her about why she'd lied when he'd asked where she was earlier? Or was it better to let things be? To give her space to tell him in her own time what was bothering her? Because something was.

Ideally, he'd love to persuade her to get a takeaway from Rice N Spice, to sit in her cosy cottage up the hill and talk through whatever this was which had come between them. Lately, with the renovations at the farm in Thorpdale taking all of their spare time and living conditions there far from comfortable, they never seemed to find the opportunity to simply relax. At first they'd found romance in the farmhouse's basic conditions, the rustic living an adventure as they worked to make their future home. But now Delilah was finding more and more excuses to stay in town in her cottage of an evening, Samson unsure whether the appeal lay in the running hot water or in the distance from him.

Perhaps that was the problem? Maybe Twistleton was draining both of them? Demanding so much attention that Delilah didn't have the energy for pushing forward with the wedding? Add in the training she was doing for the Bruncliffe Hills race, which was just over a week away, and the stress of the Rick Procter trial looming over her like the sword of Damocles, was it any wonder she wasn't herself.

If only that takeaway was a feasible option, he'd be able to find out if he was right. But he didn't have the time, having promised Tyke he'd be on surveillance within the hour.

Weighed down with frustration and foreboding, Samson got off the bike and headed for the back porch. As he came through the utility into the hallway, he saw Delilah and Tolpuddle coming down the stairs.

'Thought I'd stay at the cottage,' Delilah was saying, focus on Tolpuddle's lead. 'Seeing as you'll be out at Tyke's.'

Samson nodded. 'Sensible option.' He bit back the questions. Tried not to stare at her pale face, the dark shadows under her eyes. Whatever comforts her cottage was offering, sleep didn't seem to be one of them.

'Catch you tomorrow?' she said, placing a quick kiss on his cheek as she went past.

He gave Tolpuddle a head rub, resisted the urge to pull Delilah back into his arms, and simply watched instead as the rear door closed behind them.

At least, he thought ruefully as he headed for the stairs and the kitchen to get supplies to tide him over, there was no chance of him dozing off on the job tonight. Not with the way his head was spinning with so many worries.

Delilah always walked faster when she was perturbed. As she made her way up the steep steps which ran from the ginnel to Crag Lane, legs pumping, heart thudding, she was almost running, the muddle in her head driving her on. It was only as she reached the top and Tolpuddle let out a whine of protest, having not long been disturbed from a delightful dream involving Dog-gestives and beer and therefore not fully awake, that she realised just how wrought-up she was.

She stood by the stone wall overlooking the town, letting the Weimaraner shake himself, letting her heart rate slow, trying to let her worries go even if just for a moment. The looming court case, the fast-approaching wedding, between the two she was a nervous wreck, the nights being passed in the scourge of insomnia and the days finding her irritable and fatigued. As she looked out on the familiar jumble of slate roofs and the impressive gables of the town hall, for the first time in her life she found herself wishing she was anywhere but Bruncliffe.

A soft breath of wind caught her, carried across from the fells opposite. It was early evening, the sun still a long way from setting, the sky a benevolent blue and a lingering warmth to the air. A perfect evening for a stroll through the streets or even a run up onto the fells. Followed by a.takeaway. A bottle of wine maybe. The things couples did. The things she'd done with Samson until recently. Until he'd proposed . . .

That life seemed a long way away now. And Delilah wasn't sure how to get back to it. Not when she was carrying such trouble in her heart. How could she spend time with Samson when she wasn't sure about their future? Or when she wasn't sure about the words she'd said back in September . . . ?

She took a deep breath to quell the rising panic. At least today she'd taken the first step towards getting help. Something which might enable her to see things from a different perspective and allow her to consider her options. Even though it felt wrong to be going behind the back of the man she loved.

Because she did love Samson. Of that she was sure.

She just didn't know if she loved him enough to spend the rest of her life with him.

At the sound of voices, she turned. A couple were coming her way, the young woman laughing, the man's arm resting around her shoulders. They nodded, walked on by, wrapped up in their own world.

Delilah gathered Tolpuddle's lead and headed for her cottage. One way or another, she needed to sort this out. It wasn't fair to keep Samson dangling.

Hours later, as night moved closer to dawn and the majority of Bruncliffe's inhabitants were immersed in blissful sleep, Delilah was still wide awake, lying in bed, staring out of her curtainless windows at the stars strung across the sky. As her thoughts tumbled through her tormented mind, the only consolation, had she known it, was that across town, crouched under a hedge and keeping watch on the dark windows of Tyke's impressive house, Samson was equally wide awake and thinking of her.

8

Friday passed in a blur for all connected with the Dales Detective Agency. With Samson out on surveillance, Delilah rarely emerging from her office and Gareth kept busy at the dairy on the other side of town on the suspected pilfering case, Ida had made use of the peace and quiet to catch up on overdue admin duties. She felt like she'd spent the day chasing her tail. Inputting the latest batch of new customers into the dating website, drawing up invoices across the two businesses and sending out firm reminders for outstanding payments took way more time than she'd anticipated and saw her literally running down Back Street with her cleaning bucket at the end of the afternoon, late for work at Dales Homes, where she cleaned twice a week.

Early Saturday morning found her riding into town on her bicycle from Thorpdale and hoping for an easier time of it. Stopping first at the office building, she fired up her frying pan to make bacon butties for the troops. Then Nina and Nathan were set to work on paperwork, Gareth was dispatched back to the dairy to gather more evidence, while Delilah ensconced herself in her office with the door shut, trying to trace the origins of the threatening messages sent to Tyke and working through a list of former contestants on *The Nines* which Eloise had provided as potential suspects. Ida just about had time to give the office building a quick lick before setting off to her next job.

She stepped out onto Back Street and was glad of her jacket pulled tight over her thin frame. The balmy weather of the last week had changed dramatically overnight, the temperature plunging into single figures and a soft mist now draped on the tops which had been bathed in sunshine only the day before. For those living in the Yorkshire Dales, this capriciousness of the climate was nothing new. A fact easily observed when Ida began crossing the marketplace, negotiating her way through the usual Saturday bustle of locals, all dressed appropriately for the colder weather. By contrast, there was a significant number of tourists easily identifiable by their optimistic shorts and T-shirts and their air of indignant surprise at being so caught out by the conditions.

'Ne'er cast a clout till May is out,' Ida found herself muttering smugly as she hurried past the under-attired visitors.

A few minutes later, she reached the U-shaped building which formed Fellside Court and made her way round the back, cutting across the car park towards the beautiful courtyard with its glorious cherry trees. As always, the sheer expanse of glass that reared up above the patio area, impressively linking the two wings of the building, caught her eye and she entered the foyer thinking about the effort involved in just keeping that amount of window clean.

Out of respect for its residents, the temperatures inside the building were kept on the toasty side so she slipped her jacket off before crossing the reception area, heading for the stairs to the right. At the top, she pushed the door open into the corridor, the light pouring in from the wall of glass, and turned towards the store cupboard to the side where the spare guest linen and her cleaning equipment were kept. Stepping into the spacious interior with its divine smell of laundered sheets, she hung up her jacket, took out the vacuum and the bucket full of the tools of her trade, rolled up the sleeves of her cardigan and set off for a morning of work. She found herself humming in contentment at the prospect of the next couple of hours.

By mid-morning, while the curtains covering Tyke's windows remained resolutely closed, most of the other houses in the Low Mill cul-de-sac were showing signs of life. From his position beneath a laurel hedge in the back garden, Samson could hear a car engine starting further along the street, the distant bark of a dog excited to be out walking, and the sound of rapid footsteps heading off up the road as someone went for a jog. All of which meant it was time for him to leave, the residential area not offering the best of concealment even in the dark, and he really didn't want a report going in to Sergeant Clayton about a suspected prowler.

Feeling like every muscle in his body had been put through a mangle, he crawled from his hiding place, stretched his arms above his head and tried to ease the pain in his back. He was also regretting his choice of clothing. Not for the first time since he'd returned to his hometown, he'd been caught out by a dramatic change in the weather.

What had been a beautiful May day had metamorphosed at some point in the night, a blast of cold air whistling down into the town from the hills which surrounded it and sending the temperature into free fall. Close on its heels, a low-lying mist had formed, leaving its damp touch on every surface. Including Samson. Having travelled light on the motorbike, he hadn't had the luxury of putting on extra layers or even a waterproof and so had found himself shivering inside his thin jacket, wishing he'd thought to wear thermals as he would normally have done for an overnighter, and seriously contemplating turning on the hot tub in Tyke's back garden and jumping in.

He was getting too old for this, he decided as he jogged on the spot in an attempt to get the circulation going in his numb feet. Too old for spending consecutive nights on watch, crouched down in bushes or behind a wall, doing his best to stay alert while everyone else slept. Eating meagre cold rations and craving a coffee or a cuppa just for the chance of getting warm. Even one of Ida's industrial-strength brews would have been welcome as the dark hours crawled past.

Then the arrival of dawn, the light coming, forcing him to seek better cover. As he'd found himself squeezed into the small enclosure designed to screen the unsightly rubbish bins, the air far from perfumed, he'd heaped curses on the blasted Mini with its unique paintjob which rendered it unusable for such a covert operation. The confined quarters of its front seats would have felt like luxury in comparison to what he'd had to endure.

And as was often the way with such work, when it failed to produce anything it felt like a complete and utter waste of time.

While he knew he should be grateful that his surveillance had been peaceful, thus meaning that the threat against Tyke hadn't materialised, Samson couldn't help feeling frustrated. But at least he'd established that no one was keeping the house under watch, scoping it out for a potential attack.

He checked his phone, putting it on for the first time since he'd started his shift the evening before. No messages. Not even from Delilah. Not wanting to dwell on that, he sent

Tyke a quick text to verify that the fashion designer was sticking to the schedule he'd outlined for Samson the day before, and was staying at home that morning. The reply came back affirmative.

Satisfied that his client would be out of danger for the next few hours, he sent him a quick reminder about the need for extra vigilance should anyone come calling. Then he clambered over the stone wall into the field beyond, cutting across it to the track where he'd left the Enfield tucked away behind a derelict barn. A quick break. A chance to dry off, warm up and recharge his batteries, before returning to shadow Tyke over to Fellside Court to see his uncle later that day.

Feeling grubby and soaked through, Samson rode away, aware that he'd carried some of the pungent odours from his hiding place with him.

Delilah was at a dead end. Every trick she'd tried had turned up blanks. Every manoeuvre resulting in nothing but a headache.

She pushed back from her desk and stretched her arms above her head, worn out by the concentration required for the task and by yet another night without any sleep. While she couldn't seem to do anything about the latter, she could at least try approaching the former from a different angle.

Tyke's threatening messages – Delilah had spent all of Friday and now most of Saturday morning trying to get some hint of where they'd originated, but so far she'd been unsuccessful. Whoever was sending them was being careful to cover their tracks. The Twitter account was under the enigmatic username *TabithaTattles*. Delilah had scoured the internet using every search string she could think of but hadn't turned up anything other than the fact that St Tabitha was considered by some to be the patron saint of seamstresses and tailors. Which tied in with the faintly menacing dress-making scissors serving as an avatar on the social media account, the angled blades glinting sharply. From this, Delilah could deduce nothing more than that there might be a connection between the author of the tweets and Tyke's own profession, which was already a line of enquiry they were pursuing. Again without much success, the list of names Eloise had provided yet to yield any answers.

So while she knew it was probably unethical, Delilah found herself hoping there'd be news of another menacing communication appearing in Tyke's timeline or personal messages, and that this time the sender might not have been so circumspect about concealing their identity. She really needed something to give her more to go on.

With her eyes starting to droop and her mind clouding, what she also needed to do was get some fresh air.

'Time for a run?' she asked.

From the corner of her office came a bark, Tolpuddle rising from his basket, tail wagging.

It would do them both good, she reasoned as she plugged her mobile into its charger and pulled on the running kit she kept in her desk drawer. The hound had been showing signs of anxiety lately, picking up on her uncertainty when it came to Samson and their future. If she wasn't careful, he'd be back to chewing on shoes and tattering cushions, displaying the behaviour he'd exhibited when her marriage had broken down four years ago.

She patted his head, amazed at how different he was to the dog he'd been when she'd split from Neil Taylor. Gone were the siren-like whining, the tail biting, the inability to be apart from her for the merest moment. Now Tolpuddle was confident, happy to be left with people he trusted – a list of names which was growing all the time – and often more socially adjusted than Delilah was!

But the last couple of weeks there'd been a few signs that he was starting to regress to old habits. She'd come downstairs one morning to a running shoe which had been the recipient of the Weimaraner's attentions, his expression one of mournful accusation as she'd picked up the pieces and placed them in the bin. Then there had been the episode in the Spar a couple of days ago. She'd tied him up outside as had become the norm, but only a few minutes into her shop she'd had to dump her basket and rush outside as the sound of a high-pitched wail carried all the way to the tinned-food aisle.

She'd emerged into the marketplace to find a group of concerned people gathered around the distraught hound, all of them looking at her with reproach as she'd hurried forward to untie him and give him a hug. As she'd led him home, her shopping abandoned, she'd been filled with remorse that her own troubles were having such an effect on her dog. Her dog, who had been nothing but a rock for her when life had been so tough after her brother Ryan was killed in Afghanistan and her marriage fell apart.

He deserved better. She knew that. But until she could sort out the mess in her head, she didn't see how she could prevent him from picking up on her tension.

Opening her office door, she ushered him out ahead of her and heard the back door closing below. Tolpuddle went down the stairs like a rocket, barking, joyous. He reached the tiled hallway and came to an abrupt halt as Samson appeared.

A bemused bark. A lot of sniffing. And then the dog was bounding into Samson's embrace.

'He's braver than I am,' said Delilah, descending with a grin as the smell of rotten fruit floated up to her. 'What's the fragrance?'

'Eau de Wheelie Bin,' said Samson, smiling, his clothes damp, bits of greenery tangled in his hair, his face smudged with dirt and a weariness to him that made her want to hug him despite the odour. 'I had to get shelter where I could.'

'Any sign of Tyke's attacker?'

'Not a jot. Which we should be grateful for but . . .' He sighed. Ran a hand through his hair, a few leaves drifting to the floor. 'You?'

'No joy here either, I'm sorry to report. I can't get a grasp on where the messages originated. I hate to say it but I'm praying he gets another one so I've got more to work on.'

He nodded. 'I know what you mean.' He shrugged, sending a waft of mildew her way. 'Perhaps we're wasting our time? Maybe the accident on Thursday was nothing more than that?'

She shook her head. 'That's just the tiredness talking. We need to give it a couple more days at least. Besides, Tyke can afford it.' She winked at him and he smiled. Then he gestured at her clothes.

'Off for a run?'

'Thinking time. Figured I might get inspired up on the fells and this fella needs some exercise.' She bent down to pat Tolpuddle, the dog still leaning contentedly against Samson's legs.

'I'd offer to join you but I just about have time to grab a shower and forty winks before I'm back on duty. And besides,' he added with a grin, 'in the state I'm in, you'd make mincemeat of me.'

She laughed. 'I make mincemeat of you every time.' Then she stood up on tiptoes and kissed his cheek.

He stilled. An alertness to him that had been missing moments before.

'Delilah,' he said, catching her wrist as she made to go, 'can we talk—?'

She dropped her gaze, feeling tears in her eyes. Not wanting to see the pain and confusion in his. 'Yes,' she murmured. 'Just not now.'

She felt his fingers slip from her wrist, his hand brush across her cheek, then he kissed her forehead and made for the stairs, each weary tread accompanied by Tolpuddle's whines.

She loved him. She loved him not.

Samson found his mind as fragmented as a daisy in the hands of a lovesick teen as he made his way up the stairs to the first floor.

He was too tired to think about it. Plus he smelled like a sewer. No one was capable of loving him in this state, apart from Tolpuddle.

Although . . .

She'd kissed him. Despite the state of him, she'd planted a kiss on his cheek. That had to count for something?

He paused on the landing, grinning. It was true. Only someone who loved him would have been willing to endure the stench emanating from him right now. And Delilah had. Ergo—

The ping of a mobile came from within Delilah's office. Samson pushed the door open and spotted her phone on the desk, plugged in and charging.

He hurried to the window overlooking the back yard and the ginnel but she was already out of sight. As was the top of the Crag, the mass of limestone obscured by the mist which seemed to have dropped even lower.

Damn. She'd forgotten her mobile, not ideal when she was heading up onto the fells in this weather. She'd also be off-grid in terms of the app they both used to track each other when running, something they'd started doing to motivate each other when he was down in London. But her smartwatch was incapable of sending the data without a Bluetooth connection.

He held the phone in his hand. Telling himself not to be concerned. She'd be fine, and Tolpuddle was with her. Besides, she'd run many times before without such technological backup. And she'd be furious if she knew he was worrying about her, fussing over her welfare like her oldest brother.

Another ping, vibrating the phone, a photo of Tolpuddle fast asleep with legs in the air appearing on the screen. Along with a notification.

Samson blinked. Hoped he was seeing things with fatigue. But no. The name was still there along with the first few words of a message.

Tyke: ♥ *Can't wait to see—*

The world dipped and swayed, Samson having to reach out to the desk to steady himself as he stared at the love heart. It was innocuous. It had to be. Maybe a typo? But who hit an emoji by mistake?

He was doing it before he realised. Tapping on the notification, expecting it to open up. Expecting to see the rest of the incriminating text. But the screen remained fixed on Tolpuddle and the tantalising four words. And that love heart.

For a few seconds Samson wrestled with his conscience. It didn't take long. Then his fingers were putting in Delilah's pin, the date she'd got Tolpuddle, all the time aware that this was a massive breach of her privacy but driven on by that twist of panic in his gut.

Six digits. Entered correctly. The phone remained locked. He tried again. Same six numbers, pressed more carefully this time, no error made.

Incorrect pin entered.

Samson didn't dare try a third time and run the risk of locking the phone, alerting Delilah to his snooping. Anyhow, it was a waste of time. He knew he'd put the right code in. Which meant Delilah had changed her pin and not told him. Recently too as he'd accessed it at her request only the week before.

Unsure which was the most perturbing, the love heart from Tyke or Delilah's sudden desire for secrecy, Samson dropped the mobile back on the desk and headed upstairs to shower, the daisy in his head torn to shreds.

It appeared she loved him not.

9

Three down. Two to go.

Although as she headed to her next appointment, Ida didn't feel as though she was achieving much, given how the morning was taking shape.

One of her favourite positions of the many she now held, Ida's time at Fellside Court was normally an oasis of calm in the midst of what had become a busy life since Samson's return to Bruncliffe. Alongside the communal areas, she also cleaned for a select number of the residents and always found her work appreciated by those who were less agile than they had once been. But on this particular Saturday, it was as though the entire place had been beset with bad humour.

While Eric Bradley's grumpiness could be explained by a poor night's sleep owing to his breathing difficulties – and at least he'd been apologetic for his lack of zest as she wiped down his bathroom and vacuumed his bedrooms – Arty Robinson had no such excuse. Ida had arrived at the corner apartment he now shared with Edith to find him alone, unshaven and still in his dressing gown. For the duration of her time cleaning, he sat at the table nursing a cup of coffee, his mood as sour as an early picked gooseberry. Ida hadn't lingered.

Next, she'd walked down the corridor past the huge wall

of glass to Joseph O'Brien's smaller flat. Here she was greeted as normal with a warm smile and the offer of a cuppa. But when she'd seen the state of his lounge, her desire for refreshments had evaporated. Every surface was covered in clutter, sideboard drawers open, photos strewn across the floor. She'd turned to him with a despairing glance and he'd given that cheeky grin which his son had inherited, and shrugged.

'I was looking for something,' was all he'd said.

She'd done her best to work round the mess but as she crossed the corridor to the first flat in the far wing of the building, she couldn't help feeling disgruntled at having had to do a half-hearted job for the Irishman.

Hoping things would pick up, she rang Clarissa Ralph's bell. There was a shuffling sound from inside, then a hacking cough. When the door opened, Clarissa peered round, pale and clearly not at her best.

'Not today, Ida, if you don't mind. I don't think I could bear the dust or the noise.'

How could Ida mind? The poor thing was still struggling to get over an awful chest infection. Last thing she needed was a vacuum cleaner humming around the place, even if Ida held the view that good health sprang from a clean home.

'I'll catch thee next time,' said Ida. 'Just make sure tha drinks plenty. Hot brandy with lemon and honey – tha can't beat it.'

Promising she would try Ida's home remedy, Clarissa closed the door.

And so it was, with her brisk efficiency and hampered efforts, Ida was a full thirty minutes ahead of schedule for her final client, who just happened to be Clarissa's neighbour, Vinny King.

Almost as soon as he'd moved in, Vinny had approached

Ida one Saturday morning as she was leaving Clarissa's and asked if she would add him to her roster. Already stretched to the limit in terms of work, Ida had wanted to refuse. But the man had been so charming, sensing perhaps that she was about to turn him down, and had started promising her the moon. More per hour than she could dream of and, what clinched the deal, a cordless vacuum which she could leave in the cleaning cupboard and use in all the apartments, plus the communal areas.

Since she'd tried one of the new-fangled vacuums last autumn while on a case, Ida had become a convert. No bending down to plug them in. No faff with a cord always in danger of tripping someone. And so light to use.

She'd agreed and had had no reason to regret her decision. So it was with an expectation of ending her shambles of a Saturday morning on a high that she knocked brusquely on the door and began to open it, preparing to walk in as Vinny had advised her to do on her visits. When she heard the sound of voices, she paused on the threshold.

Vinny talking to a woman. Something intimate about the way they were speaking.

'This isn't a good idea, Vinny—'

'I won't take no for an answer—!'

'Hello?' called out Ida.

The voices fell quiet and Vinny appeared in the hall, hurrying towards her, charm personified.

'Ida! You're early!' He smiled.

'Is that a problem?' she demanded. Impatient now for this chaotic visit to Fellside Court to be at an end.

'Well, actually . . .' He tipped his head back towards the lounge, lowering his voice. 'I've got company.' He added a wink. 'Any chance you could come back on Tuesday?'

She nodded. Too shaken to produce any other response. He closed the door and she turned towards the stairs. Putting her bucket and vacuum back in the cupboard, she pulled on her jacket and headed down to the ground floor. Processing what had just happened.

That wink. That's what was bothering her. The suggestiveness of it.

Not that Ida was a prude. Or a busybody. What people did in their own time and who with was their own business, as long as it wasn't hurting anyone.

But that was the problem. Because whatever Vinny was doing, it *was* hurting someone: Arty Robinson. Ida knew that for sure because from the few words she'd overheard, she'd recognised the voice of Vinny's female companion.

It was Edith Hird.

It was one of those days when, looking out of the office window, going for a run seemed like the daftest idea in the world. But once you got up on the tops, the exhilaration of being outside took over. Even when there was mist swirling around, leaving droplets of moisture on everything and shifting the view from one minute to the next.

As she followed the narrow track that led from the back of the Crag along the ridge of the fell, Delilah hit her stride. Legs recovering from the brutal climb, breathing steadying and her heart rate settling to a more sustainable pace. Ahead of her, Tolpuddle was almost invisible, his grey form camouflaged by the conditions. Every so often he disappeared completely and then she'd hear a panicked bark, before he turned round and raced back to her side.

Daft dog. Seeing Samson had unsettled him. Made her realise how little the pair had seen of each other of late.

Given the work the Dales Detective Agency had just taken on, that wasn't going to be rectified any time soon, with Samson out on surveillance and her locked up in the office trying to unearth the source of Tyke's threats.

With the gloom of her thoughts threatening to descend as quickly as the mist around her, Delilah forced herself to concentrate. One slip up here in these conditions and she'd be in trouble. Especially as she'd forgotten her phone, an omission she'd only noticed when she reached the top of the steep path up to the Crag. Not inclined to turn back and have to run it a second time, she'd decided to carry on. The lack of a mobile didn't worry her. She was used to the terrain and had a basic safety kit in her rucksack. If anything, it felt liberating to be out of reach, to be away from the incessant messages her businesses necessitated.

She checked her watch. Her pace was good. It boded well for the race in a week's time. She grinned. Feeling that competitive urge which had lain dormant for so long. She'd already been looking forward to the Bruncliffe Hills event, wanting a chance to really test herself now that she was almost back to peak fitness. But the added spice of having Tyke competing too was a bonus. A chance to set the record straight.

Twelve years on and his behaviour the last time they'd raced against each other still rankled. Even despite the fact that Delilah, at the tender age of eighteen, had won not only her age category that day, but also the women's senior title. What she hadn't managed was to place in the top ten overall, because of Tyke. He'd taken that tenth spot, leaving her to come in a close eleventh.

He'd cheated. Pure and simple. An action which went against the very ethos of fell running. And while Delilah liked him as a person and found his company charming, she would be going all out to beat him.

Which is why she was up on the fells in this weather, following part of the route. She knew the course like the back of her hand but she just wanted to remind herself of some of the more difficult parts. And to reassure herself that this time, with the organisers from the Bruncliffe Harriers now using electronic checks to keep tabs on entrants, at least she'd know that whoever came home first out of her and Tyke, it would be an honest result.

She picked up the pace. Her feet skipping over the undulating terrain, her movements confident. This was the easy bit. The long ridge which wound back on itself before depositing the entrants back above Bruncliffe, and one of the toughest descents in the area. A mixture of limestone and scree, it was a brave heart or a fool who went down it at full speed.

Delilah had a bit of both in her DNA. Hopefully, though, she wouldn't have to resort to such tactics this year and could have Tyke beaten before they even reached the downhill.

A gust of wind pushed against her back, stronger than before. Lifting the mist ahead like curtains to reveal Tolpuddle, standing still, head tipped to one side. She stopped. Barely daring to breathe. On the track beyond Tolpuddle was a beautiful roe deer and her fawn. The doe watched them with wary eyes while the youngster didn't look as if it had fully mastered the use of its long legs, wobbling unsteadily as it tucked into its mother's side.

Delilah edged slowly towards Tolpuddle, placing a hand on his collar. Not that the softie would go on the attack, more like he'd be spooked and run the other way. But just to be on the safe side she slipped his lead on, every move-ment careful and cautious, not wanting to frighten the animals.

They stood there for a few heartbeats, the four of them watching each other. Delilah wishing she had her phone so she could record this magical moment. Then a roar from the dale below carried up the fellside and in a flash of white rump, doe and fawn were gone, running down the rocks and scree on the opposite side with an agility Delilah could only envy.

She watched them disappear in the distance and then turned to see what had triggered their flight. A black shape racing along one of the tracks on the valley floor, an offroad motorbike, its engine tearing into the silence.

It was a rare enough sight to hold her attention. And it was illegal, the tracks in the area all bridleways, not open to traffic. But the rider didn't seem to care, the bike bucking and kicking beneath him. It took her a few seconds and then the penny dropped.

A black trail bike. Too far away to see the make, but the rider dressed entirely in black. Coincidence? Delilah didn't think so. She was pretty sure she was watching the person who'd tried to run Tyke over in the marketplace.

Cursing her lack of mobile for the second time, she took off running. No plan. Just determined to keep it in sight. Hurtling along the ridge, Tolpuddle beside her on the lead, she kept her focus on the bike below. And so when it veered off towards the south, she went to follow, over the edge of the ledge.

One moment she was standing. The next she was on her back, slipping and sliding to a painful halt, her hand wrapped around the lead which was now taut. Up above, Tolpuddle was panting, legs braced, having baulked at following her, his jerk on the lead the reason for her fall.

She shuffled to a sitting position, stared at the terrain she'd been about to throw herself down and swore softly.

'Thanks,' she murmured back at the dog. Knowing he'd saved her life. Because she was at the top of Delilah's Descent, the fellside falling away in a steepness that made her dizzy.

She got to her feet slowly, and cautiously pulled herself back up onto safer ground beside the Weimaraner.

'Think those days are gone,' she muttered, looking down at the crazy route she'd once taken, not surprised that no one had taken it since. She lifted her gaze, tracking the motorbike as it faded into the distance.

She didn't have a photo. She didn't have the registration number. But what she did have was proof that whatever the nature of the threat against Tyke, the perpetrator was still in the area.

10

After years of surveillance, Samson wasn't convinced there was much difference between daytime or night-time operations. Sure, the former generally meant more temperate conditions, but daylight also meant even more need for concealment. Even more need for crawling around in bushes, as was presently the case. And to make matters worse in his current situation, the dramatic change in the weather hadn't even granted him the usual bonus which came with the waking hours – that of being warm.

He rubbed his hands together, glad of the dry clothes he'd put on at the office building but wishing he'd thought to add gloves. Wishing too that he'd had time to get more than the meagre twenty minutes of sleep he'd snatched on Delilah's office couch. As it was, he'd risen from the soft cushions in what felt like seconds after he'd lain down. Eyes gritty and sore, and with his back protesting more than ever, he'd made a quick sandwich to shove in his pocket before heading back out on the Enfield for Tyke's home.

Tyke had been late leaving his house and Samson – too tired for more hiding – had chosen instead to sit astride his motorbike at the end of the cul-de-sac, trying to look natural as he waited for the fashion designer to appear. Finally, he'd heard a door slam from behind the high wall and a few minutes later, he caught a glimpse of Tyke through the gate, crossing the drive in yet another eye-catching puffer-jacket and tracksuit-bottoms ensemble – this one covered in zigzags in vibrant red and orange, kind of like Samson imagined a migraine would feel. Baseball cap pulled low, the fashion designer had thrown a wave in Samson's direction before getting into the Porsche and starting the throaty engine.

No more walking around town. No matter how short the journey.

It had been one of the guidelines Samson had lain down for his client in an attempt to reduce the time Tyke spent out in the open as a target. As he'd followed the red car on the five-minute drive through town, however, Samson had to admit it did feel like overkill. Particularly as the last forty-eight hours had failed to reveal either a potential aggressor or any further threats.

Lying in the shrubs at the back of Fellside Court while Tyke was installed in the much warmer surrounds of his uncle's flat, Samson found himself wondering yet again if he was wasting his time. Or had Delilah been right – was it just the sleep deprivation over the past few days catching up with him and making him cynical?

He glanced up through the surrounding greenery to see a watery sun up in the sky, trying in vain to break through the persistent wisps of cloud. He lowered his gaze to the glass wall of Fellside Court. And the courtyard, where the sound of the back door slamming shut made him refocus his attentions.

Ida Capstick was stomping across the paving stones, muttering to herself, looking very put-out. He wondered what had happened to bring on such a mood. He was half tempted to jump out and surprise her, see if that could brighten her day. But knowing Ida, it was as likely to make her even more vexed. He left her to turn the corner with her ill humour as the door opened once more.

The same two women as before were crossing towards him, heading for the outside gym. Chatting away, as oblivious to his presence as last time.

Thinking that he'd never conducted surveillance quite so boring, and possibly quite so pointless, Samson turned his focus back to the first-floor window of Vinny King's flat.

Delilah tried texting Samson with her big news, even though she knew it was a waste of time. He always turned his phone off when carrying out the more covert parts of his business. Even when he was just in Bruncliffe.

But the messages which had been waiting for her on her mobile in the office meant she could deduce his whereabouts. So after a quick shower she headed across town to Fellside Court, Tolpuddle pulling on the lead the entire way, as though sensing where they were going and who they were going to meet.

With the sun not quite warm enough to burn off all the mist, there was a distinct chill to the air and Delilah's heart went out to Samson for having to endure such conditions after the night he'd just spent. At least now, though, she had a lead. Something to reassure him that their efforts weren't futile.

If only she'd had her mobile with her! With a photo she'd have been able to capture the number-plate, which would have been an incredible leap forward in the investigation.

Rueing her forgetfulness, she rounded the corner of Fell Lane and began walking up the hill to the retirement complex. She had just reached the drive which led round the back of the building when she met Ida, coming at her with an even more ferocious expression than usual.

'Is everything all right, Ida?' she asked.

'Folk should know better than to muck around with other folk's feelings,' snapped Ida, not even pausing as she strode on past, lips pursed in a stern line of disapproval.

Delilah stood, open-mouthed. Had it been that blatant, the way she was treating Samson? She hadn't thought so. But something must have given the game away because what else could have prompted Ida's typically direct outburst?

Face burning with a shame she knew was justified, Delilah carried on across the car park towards the courtyard. She was still mulling over the exchange when the outdoor gym came into view, two women exercising on the tandem air-walker.

Tolpuddle barked, as he had the other day when he'd seen them. But this time he pulled on his lead with such force that it slipped through Delilah's hand and he was off, tearing across the gravel, heading straight for them.

'Tolpuddle!' she shouted, as the ladies paused mid-stride, watching with alarm as forty kilograms of Weimaraner raced their way.

But Tolpuddle went straight past them. Diving into the bushes to their rear. Tail wagging. Barking joyous.

'What the hell?!' An exclamation of annoyance and a figure shot up out of the shrubbery and started hopping around, making one of the women yelp in surprise and sending Delilah into a fit of laughter.

Ousted from his hiding place by an over-exuberant canine, Samson didn't see the funny side. For a start, his right calf muscle was cramping thanks to the sudden action, pain shooting up his leg and leaving him hopping in agony.

Furthermore, the same ladies as the other day had suffered yet another near mishap with the exercise machine, his sudden appearance out of nowhere causing them to lose their balance and almost fall off.

Delilah, however, was doubled over laughing.

She tried to speak, got overcome by another burst of mirth, waved a hand in defeat and simply gave up trying to communicate. The sight of her caught in such a fit of laughter, tears running down her cheeks, made the two elderly ladies start laughing too. Meanwhile, Tolpuddle was nudging Samson's aching leg with demented affection . . .

Samson shook his head. Hobbled over to the helpless Delilah and gathered her into his arms.

'You absolute nutter,' he muttered into her hair as he held her against his chest.

'It wasn't my fault!' she managed to protest. She leaned back to look at him, the laughter subsiding into smiles now. 'It wasn't me who blew your cover. Besides, you just looked so funny . . .'

He grinned down at her. Happy for what felt like the first time in weeks.

'Did I now? Wracked by pain and with a perfect surveillance spot ruined. I'm glad you find that so amusing.' He reached down to pat Tolpuddle. 'What brings you and the hound to Fellside Court anyway?'

The change was dramatic, all levity abandoned as Delilah pulled away from him, a spark of excitement in her eyes.

'I saw the trail bike! The one that went for Tyke!'

'What? Where?'

'Up above the Crag while I was out running. There was this deer and her fawn and . . . anyway, this bike roared past on the track below. I swear it was the same one.'

'Did you get the registration?'

She shook her head. 'It was too far away. I didn't get a photo either as I forgot my phone.'

Samson frowned, distracted by the memory of her mobile on her desk, that blasted message—

'But seriously,' she continued, taking his silence for scepticism, 'it was black, about the same size as a Triumph. And the rider was all dressed in black, too. Just like Carol said. I doubt it's a coincidence.'

He nodded. Agreeing with her. Forcing himself to concentrate on the case and not his private life. 'You could be right. In which case . . .'

'In which case Tyke really is in danger,' murmured Delilah. 'And we're not wasting our time, no matter how fruitless it feels.'

Samson looked up towards the first floor of the building, to Vinny King's apartment where his client was safely secured. A love-heart emoji rising unbidden into his thoughts—

'How did you know I was here?' he asked.

The sudden shift of topic caught Delilah off guard. 'I . . . er . . . lucky guess?' She shrugged. Caught hold of Tolpuddle's lead and prepared to go. 'I'd best be getting back. The faster I can identify where those threats are coming from, the faster we can identify whoever is menacing Tyke.'

She gave him a kiss on the cheek. Then she was walking away, Tolpuddle looking back in confusion as Samson stayed behind.

'Ah,' sighed one of the women on the air-walkers. 'True love!'

'Hope the wedding plans are all going well, young O'Brien!' added the other. 'Sorted out your best man yet?'

Samson knew from their laughter that they were in on

the betting being organised by Troy at the Fleece. Had probably laid a few quid on the outcome.

In no mood for thinking about love or weddings, he looked back up at the window above. And saw Tyke there, watching the departing Delilah with a frown. The fashion designer checked his watch and then pulled out his phone and started texting.

Samson switched his gaze, just in time to see Delilah take her own phone out of her pocket, reading the screen before she disappeared around the corner.

'Everything all right, son?' A light tap on his elbow had him turning to see his father, a mobile in his hand, too.

'Yeah, fine,' he lied.

'Was that Delilah I saw there with you? Is she coming in?'

'She had to go. Work,' he murmured.

His father tipped his head to one side. Studying him. 'You look a bit out of sorts. Come in yourself and have a cuppa. There's no point lurking around out here in the bushes when everyone knows you're there anyway. And besides, Tyke's just about to join us in the lounge so you may as well catch a break and get warm while you can.'

In the need of creature comforts, Samson allowed his father to lead him inside the building.

She was the worst kind of traitor. Lying to his face about how she knew he was there. And then getting that message as she left. An invitation to betray him.

Even worse, she fully intended to take up the invitation some point soon. She needed to. It was the only way she could think of to sort out the mess in her mind. But to do that so blatantly, while he was outside on guard, seemed so wrong.

Date with Destiny

Shoving the phone back in her pocket, message unanswered, Delilah walked down Fell Lane, a sulking Tolpuddle beside her.

While Delilah was walking home in despair, Mrs Pettiford was strolling through town with the air of contentment that seemed to be her permanent state these days.

Some of this contentment had to be credited to her new working hours with the bank. With the establishment undergoing numerous changes to accommodate the technological age they were living in – changes she had to admit she'd once feared – she'd been able to make the most of the new flexible working patterns offered to all colleagues. Taking what felt like a drastic step, she'd reduced her hours to twenty-five a week, working nine until three Monday, Tuesday, Thursday and Friday, and alternate Saturday mornings.

The difference had been amazing. So much more time to herself. And for her companion currently trotting along next to her.

As if knowing she was the subject of warm thoughts, Lady glanced up and gave a satisfied yap. Once Mrs Pettiford's sister's dog, the cocker spaniel had settled in well to her new life in Bruncliffe, no longer a mere visitor to the Pettiford home but a permanent presence and a proper resident of the town. Mrs Pettiford couldn't believe the difference it had made. The daily walks. The way folk stopped to chat . . .

That had been the unexpected bonus.

When she'd given up some of her hours at the bank, Mrs Pettiford had been aware that it would reduce her capacity for gathering news, something she'd accepted with reluctance. Because make no mistake, although she'd found happiness, her appetite to know what was going on – and disseminate it – hadn't been diminished. Some folk called it gossip. In her mind, it was a public service. She'd found to her surprise, however, that the regular dog walks had presented other opportunities.

Like now. Walking down the cul-de-sac where Bruncliffe's most expensive homes were situated. Once she would have only done so under cover of dusk, not wanting her curiosity – as she termed it – on show for all to see. Today, Lady on her lead, Mrs Pettiford strode down the exclusive road. Looked through gateways, took her time walking past drives, all in the name of good citizenship. For it had been on a walk with Lady down this very road a year ago that she'd seen something which had helped save Delilah Metcalfe's life.

Rick Procter, welcoming Delilah into his home. Right before he tried to kill her.

Reaching the spot where it happened, the very end of the road where the tarmac swept round in a wide circle, two houses set back off it, Mrs Pettiford glanced to her right, taking in the unoccupied property behind the stone wall, the FOR SALE sign outside. Not Nancy Taylor's agency selling it. The woman had refused to have anything to do with the transaction, a stance one had to respect. Mrs Pettiford issued a silent curse on the man who'd plagued the town, as she always did at this point, then turned. Just as a shriek of pure terror split the air.

11

Another shriek. Mrs Pettiford hastening towards the sound, Lady already ahead, pulling on the lead.

The wail had originated from behind the high wall of the house which shared the seclusion offered by the end of the cul-de-sac with Procter's property. The gates were closed, but that didn't stop Mrs Pettiford. Unlatching them, she scurried up the drive to where a tall young woman was standing in the doorway of the opulent home, one hand over her mouth, the other clutching her stomach.

She was staring down at the doorstep in distress, and looking like she was going to be sick.

'Whatever's the matter?' asked Mrs Pettiford as she drew close.

The woman looked up and Mrs Pettiford recognised her – the lass who worked with Tyke, his secretary, PA or whatever it was they were called these days. With deathlike pallor, she was pointing at the doorstep.

A baseball cap and a bundle of rags dumped there.

Rags which Lady was finding very interesting, the cocker spaniel really tugging at the lead now.

'Honestly,' began Mrs Pettiford, not one to condone a commotion, 'all that fuss over a few scraps of cloth—'

'It's not cloth,' whispered the lass, turning away, hand back over her mouth.

So Mrs Pettiford went closer. And a small yelp of horror escaped her.

'What . . . why . . . ?' She blinked. Controlled herself and Lady, and looked again. 'I presume it's dead?'

The lass nodded.

'An accident maybe? The poor thing got caught in a trap or attacked by a dog and managed to make it here to die?'

The comment provoked a bitter sound from the young woman. 'And left that for good measure?' A shaking hand was now pointing at the rectangle of card pinned to the open door, just above the knocker.

Despite her advancing years, Mrs Pettiford had yet to need reading glasses. But as she leaned across the unfortunate bundle on the step to take in the message written in an uneven hand across the cardboard, she found herself wishing her sight was less acute.

NEXT TIME I WON'T MISS.

She glanced down at the step. At the baseball cap with that familiar logo.

Mrs Pettiford found herself shivering.

'Bruncliffe's answer to a horse's head,' muttered Sergeant Clayton as he carefully lifted the dead rabbit into a plastic bag and Constable Bradley took photographs.

Danny Bradley glanced at his boss. Not having a clue what he was talking about.

'*The Godfather*,' came the reply. 'A film. Before your time, no doubt. A horse's head was used to send a message.'

Date with Destiny

'A death threat?'

The sergeant gave a sombre nod. Eyes still on the bloodied doorstep and the macabre note pinned to the door.

Danny shuddered. It all seemed a bit out of the usual for Bruncliffe, notwithstanding the goings on over the last twelve months which had brought more than enough mayhem to the small town.

When the call had come in from an agitated Mrs Pettiford, both the sergeant and the constable had just got back to the police station on Church Street. A kettle had been boiled and a bag of Lucy Metcalfe's lemon and ginger scones had just been opened. The pair had looked at each other, not wanting to abandon the first chance to have a break since early that morning, a case of suspected hare coursing having kept Danny out the other side of Horton and a follow-up visit to read the riot act to a young lad who'd turned his parents' home into an impromptu rave the night before having tied up the sergeant.

Neither was in the mood for Mrs Pettiford and her capacity for exaggeration.

The sarge had offered to go. Feeling bad at remaining, Danny had pulled his helmet back on and left the station with him. Primarily because no one should have to deal with Mrs Pettiford unaccompanied.

He was glad he had. Because there was nothing exaggerated about the scene they'd found. A dead rabbit left on the doorstep of one of the homes in Bruncliffe's executive development. Not just any home, but that being rented by renowned fashion designer and TV personality Tyke.

Just in case the message wasn't clear enough, someone had gone to the trouble of adding a note to spell it out and leaving a baseball cap with Tyke's logo on it next to the dead animal.

Danny let his gaze lift to the fells in the background, the sun having finally broken cover and now bathing the green hillside in late-afternoon light. As always, he found the incongruity between the beauty of the landscape he'd been born in and the gruesome nature of the crime he had to investigate hard to reconcile.

'Who'd want to do such a thing?' he asked, turning to his sergeant.

'Price of being famous, lad. Attracts all kinds.' The sarge rubbed his chin. Then nodded at the note. 'Anything strike you as interesting? I mean, apart from the bizarreness of it all?'

Danny looked at the note again. '"Next time"!' he exclaimed. 'It says "next time"!'

Sergeant Clayton nodded. 'Aye, lad. Which has me wondering – if this isn't the first time Mr Tyke has been threatened, how come we haven't heard of it before now?'

'Happen as he didn't feel the need to tell you.' Mrs Pettiford had wandered over to join them. Having been surprisingly succinct in giving her evidence, she'd remained on the scene offering comfort to the young woman, Eloise Morgan, who'd found the poor critter and, by comparison, was barely able to string two words together.

'Tell us what?' the sergeant demanded, a steeliness to his tone.

'Why, about that hit-and-run incident on Thursday.' Seeing the confused looks of the policemen, she continued. 'In the marketplace. Tyke was crossing the road and a motorbike came out of nowhere and almost ran him over. But for Clive Knowles tackling him to the ground in time, it would have killed him. I think he would have written it off as a mere accident, despite the threats he's been receiving, but

Carol Kirby – sorry, Knowles – was adamant the bike swerved deliberately. You know, to hit him. So it's hardly surprising he sought help—'

'Did you know about any of this?' Sergeant Clayton demanded of his subordinate, cutting Mrs Pettiford off mid-stride.

'Not a word,' said Danny, truthfully.

'Jesus!' The sergeant ran a hand over his face. 'A prominent celebrity getting threats and almost being killed on our patch and we're only just learning about it?' Then he turned back to Mrs Pettiford, his face darkening. 'What do you mean he sought help? From where—?'

From the road came a throaty roar, a red Porsche Cayenne pulling onto the drive. The man who leaped out was wearing a riot of colourful clothing, enough to suggest his identity even if Danny hadn't recognised him from the TV.

'Tyke,' he murmured to his sarge.

'You don't say!' muttered the sergeant dryly, watching as the fashion designer jogged across the drive to put his arm around a very pale Eloise Morgan.

Danny noted the cuts and vivid bruising on the man's right cheek, no doubt the result of the incident Mrs Pettiford had mentioned. The constable also noted that Ms Morgan wasn't overly receptive to the comfort on offer, shrugging off the man's arm and bursting into tears. The poor woman had really been shaken by the incident. He was about to go over and offer some official reassurance, but Tyke was already walking purposefully towards them.

'Sorry for taking up your time,' he said, smiling apologetically as he gestured towards the plastic bag in the sergeant's hand. 'But this really doesn't merit a police investigation. It's just a prank.'

'And how can you be so sure of that,' asked Sergeant Clayton, bristling at being told what was and wasn't his business, 'seeing as you've already had death threats and an apparent near miss with a motorbike?'

There was a blink of silence, the fashion designer clearly wrong-footed by the local police being so well informed. Danny had to turn away to hide a grin at his sergeant's ability to bluff.

'Aye, lad. Not much passes us by in Bruncliffe,' continued the sergeant. 'So perhaps you'd best leave it up to us to decide what is and isn't worth pursuing.'

The smile returned, Tyke nodding now. 'You're right. Far be it from me to tell you how to do your job, but honestly, it's nothing. And I think you can appreciate that I really don't need the media attention something like this would bring.'

'What about these threats you've been receiving?'

'I've got that in hand. I've hired someone to—'

This time it was the distinctive sound of a motorbike approaching which cut through the conversation. Danny knew what it was before he even turned around.

A 1960 Royal Enfield Bullet 500.

The scarlet-and-chrome bike pulled up behind the Porsche and a low groan came from the sergeant.

'I might have bloody known,' he muttered as they watched the rider get off the bike and remove his helmet, releasing a mane of black hair. 'Of course he's involved in this. How could he not be?'

Samson O'Brien walked towards them. 'Afternoon,' he said, shaking hands before gesturing towards the doorstep. 'Mind if I take a look around?'

'Actually,' growled Sergeant Clayton, 'I do mind. Very

much so. Especially as you've been concealing a possible crime. My office, now, O'Brien. You've got some explaining to do. And bring Delilah with you.'

An hour later, sitting behind his desk in the back office of the police station, Sergeant Clayton's head was hurting and his stomach had begun to gurgle, both symptoms he recognised as resulting from being in the vicinity of the Dales Detective Agency team when there was a case ongoing.

'So, more than forty-eight hours since someone tried to run over one of the most recognised men in the country, you two have got zero leads?' he growled.

Samson shrugged while Delilah at least had the grace to look abashed.

'And on top of that, by failing to come to myself or Constable Bradley with what was going on, you've denied us the opportunity to set up a proper investigation while the leads were fresh.'

'To be fair, our client didn't want—'

'To be fair,' snapped the sergeant, cutting across Samson, 'your client's wishes count for bugger all when it comes to a crime being committed. And that's what this is.'

Sitting to one side, Danny Bradley looked uncomfortable as his boss ranted. But Sergeant Clayton didn't care if he was making the lad feel awkward by tearing a strip off the duo he idolised. While Gavin Clayton had learned to value the insight O'Brien and the Metcalfe lass had brought to numerous cases over the past year and a half, he took it as a personal affront that, in this instance, the pair had left him out in the cold.

'Who the hell do you think the press will make mincemeat of if this lad is killed in Bruncliffe?' he muttered across the desk at them. He thrust a thick thumb at his own chest. 'Muggins, that's who!'

'Sorry,' said Samson. 'You're right. We should have pressured Tyke more to involve you.'

The sergeant grunted. His constable pushed the plate containing the scones they hadn't had a chance to eat earlier towards him. He picked one up and wagged it at Samson.

'Tell me again. Everything you've got. And I mean *everything*.'

As Samson outlined the Dales Detective Agency's investigation once more, Sergeant Clayton began eating, Lucy Metcalfe's delicious creation going some way to calming his agitation, the amazing combination of lemon and ginger helping to soothe the acid gurgling in his guts. But by the time Samson had finished recapping the events of the past two days, the police officer was still troubled by the lack of progress in identifying the person who was targeting Tyke.

'This motorbike you saw from the fells,' he said, turning to Delilah. 'You didn't get any footage of it?'

She shook her head.

'So we can't even be sure it's the same one.'

'No but what are the chances —?'

'Let's deal in facts, not chances,' he grunted. 'I reckon that'll be a better way to keep this Tyke lad alive. Which means the only concrete evidence we have so far is the handful of threats that came through social media and then this.' He tapped the plastic bag on the table in front of him, the card which had been pinned to the door of Tyke's house contained within it.

'Can we ask forensics to work some magic on it?' asked Danny. 'Maybe tell us where the paper was from, or something about the handwriting?'

'You've been watching too much TV, Constable Bradley,' muttered the sergeant. 'Even if they could tell us all that, a case like this isn't going to be at the front of the queue.'

'Is the rabbit worth a closer look?' Delilah turned to Samson.

'Not sure DNA would reveal anything,' said Samson wryly. 'There's an awful lot of rabbits in these parts.'

'But what about how it was killed?'

Danny opened his mouth to speak but the sergeant pre-empted him.

'Don't even suggest it, lad. If I put in a request to have a post-mortem on that poor bunny we'll be the laughing stock of the force. I've marked it as an exhibit for now and stored it in the freezer. We need something else to go on.'

Danny gave a resigned nod. 'In that case, what about the doorbell?'

'What about it?'

'Is it a video one?'

Samson was shaking his head. 'No. I suggested Tyke get one fitted but unfortunately it hasn't arrived yet.'

'Damn.'

'What about Rick's?' Everyone turned to Delilah. 'Rick Procter. He had a video doorbell. I remember noticing it the day . . .' She paused, grimaced, memories still too vivid to contemplate. Samson laid a hand over hers, fingers inter-lacing, steadying her. 'If it's still active,' she continued, 'maybe it's pointed in such a way it could have caught something? Someone going up Tyke's drive maybe?'

The sergeant finally felt a spike of excitement. 'Danny, chase that up. Get onto the fancy estate agent the house is listed with and let's hope we get lucky.'

'I thought we didn't deal in chance and luck,' quipped the constable.

The sergeant shot him a glare. Then he turned back to Samson and Delilah.

'And as for you two, I'm afraid you're going to have to stop working on this case. This is an official investigation as of now and I can't have the pair of you muddying the waters.'

He could see Delilah about to protest, that flush of colour on her cheeks which presaged her hot-headed temper. But Samson squeezed her hand.

'Okay, it's all yours,' he said, catching the sergeant by surprise. 'We'll head back to the office and put together everything we have so far and bring it over to you.'

'What?' Delilah stared at him in shock, while Danny's eyebrows were up in his hairline.

'That's very gracious of you, O'Brien,' said the sergeant, nonplussed by this unexpected acquiescence.

O'Brien shrugged. 'To be honest, you're right. We weren't getting anywhere and with the fashion show looming, town is soon going to be filled with hundreds of fashionistas and fans from social media, not to mention reporters and the like. It's only going to get harder to identify and isolate the threat against Tyke – one we have to take as credible and dangerous after today. I'd rather not have the responsibility of looking after him in those circumstances.'

He stood to go.

'Not so fast, son!' Sergeant Clayton motioned to the chair, aware that the twinge in his stomach had set up again. 'Sit yourself back down.'

Samson sat. A look of complete innocence on his face.

'This fashion show. When is it?'

'In ten days.'

Ten days. Not long to run an investigation but an age to try to keep a man alive if someone was dead set on killing him. Even harder in a town overrun with offcumden, removing the natural advantage the local police officers normally had. They'd be left looking for someone suspicious in a sea of unrecognised faces.

It was a nightmare.

Sergeant Clayton let out a soft groan, shaking his head.

'You bugger,' he muttered.

'What?' Samson asked, eyes wide. While Danny was doing his best to hide the start of a grin.

'Don't play me for a fool, O'Brien. You know well that we need to crack this case before Bruncliffe becomes so busy with folk, we won't be able to protect the lad.'

'So what do you propose?'

The sergeant rubbed a hand across the wedge of his belly under the desk, part apology part warning for the trauma he was about to put it through. 'I propose,' he said through gritted teeth, 'we combine forces and catch this rabbit killer before he moves onto a bigger target and it all blows up in our faces.'

He was aware of his constable pushing the sole remaining scone in front of him. And of the look of delight the lad was struggling to hide. Delilah too, head down, lips curved.

'But before you get too smug the lot of you, there are a few provisos attached to this joint effort,' continued the sergeant. He leaned back in his chair with a grin of his own, knowing that the jaunty smile currently gracing O'Brien's face was about to disappear.

12

The sergeant had been right. As dawn broke on Tuesday morning, the jauntiness had left Samson O'Brien. In fact, it hadn't even taken that long.

'Time to go,' he murmured wearily.

Danny Bradley nodded and the pair crawled out of the bushes in the field behind Tyke's house, the light beginning to seep across the sky, the haunting call of a curlew coming from somewhere in the distance. With the dark shadows of the fells rising up around them, it was idyllic. Unless you'd spent the night on watch.

Limbs stiff and his body heavy with fatigue, Samson was aware of his back protesting as he stood. Aware also that Danny didn't seem to be so afflicted. Three consecutive nights on surveillance and, while the younger man carried the drawn features and ripe odour of someone who'd spent a long time skulking around in undergrowth when normal folk were sleeping, he looked eager for more.

'I hope Ida's got the bacon on,' the constable whispered, stuffing the notebook he'd been using to record the night's events into his back pocket. Watching the youngster diligently logging every hour, despite there being nothing to log, Samson hadn't been sure whether to be impressed or amused. 'This stakeout business makes me starving!'

Samson grunted. Almost too tired to think about food as they clambered over a wall onto the track that ran behind it.

They walked to the derelict barn, its door sagging on its hinges, roof partially caved in, and went round the back to where the Enfield was hidden. If Samson was suffering because of the demands of the case, so was his precious bike. After several days being ridden up and down what was little more than a dirt track, its chrome was dull and the brilliant scarlet was smeared with mud – and worse, given the track led to a dairy farm. It desperately needed a clean but Samson just didn't have the time.

Sergeant Clayton's price for the Dales Detective Agency being able to stay on the investigation into Tyke's death threats had been steep. He'd insisted that the surveillance Samson was currently carrying out would have to be shared with Danny. Which meant the constable was to have a crash course in tailing Tyke unseen before taking over some of Samson's duties, thus freeing the more experienced former detective for just that. Detecting.

'No point having someone of your calibre creeping around at all hours being a glorified babysitter when we could do with your investigative skills on the case,' the sergeant had pointed out. 'Let young Danny do the grunt work and let's get you concentrating on the background to the threats. We've more chance of finding this bugger that way than waiting for him to pop up in front of us.'

It had been an observation difficult to dispute. Particularly as the 'bugger', as the sergeant had termed the perpetrator, had managed to circumvent all efforts at security to leave a very visible threat on Tyke's doorstep.

So Samson had to admit, even though the last two days had been draining as he tutored Danny in the basics, he was relieved on several counts to have someone taking up the strain when it came to Tyke's insistence on what was pretty much twenty-four-hour covert surveillance. Not only was Samson still unsure it was the best way to prevent an attack on the fashion designer, he was also exhausted from trying to fulfil those wishes.

And frustrated. Because Sergeant Clayton had hit the nail on the head. Samson was desperate to do some proper investigating, sensing – like the sergeant – that merely providing protection for Tyke wouldn't solve the case and could even result in the threat being made real. As had been promised in the note above the dead rabbit.

Luckily, Danny had been over the moon about the sergeant's suggestion, holding a glamorous misconception about the realities of such work. Samson had been sure that after hours out in the open, sleepless nights and a distinct lack of proper food, the shine would wear off. So far, that didn't seem to be the case.

'You feel confident taking over from tonight, then?' Samson asked as he passed a helmet to the lad.

Danny nodded. 'Can't wait. And I won't let you down, I promise.'

'Just make sure you stay out of sight. Especially from Tyke. I don't want him knowing about the switch.'

The fashion designer had already declared that he didn't want any official investigation into the latest threat, no matter how grisly it had been, and seemed annoyed that the police had been called at all. It was hard to see him taking kindly to the concept of Danny now being his shadow. In which case, by going against Tyke's wishes and signing up to Sergeant Clayton's deal, the detective agency could be placing any payment for their efforts in jeopardy. Something they could ill afford.

So Samson had laid down a stipulation of his own when he agreed to unite forces. The sergeant and Danny weren't allowed to breathe a word about being involved with the Dales Detective Agency on the case. As far as Tyke was concerned, Samson would be the only one watching him.

'He won't have a clue I'm there, boss!' Danny snapped out a mock salute before putting on his helmet and climbing onto the Enfield behind Samson.

Due to a combination of tiredness and a lack of progress in the Tyke investigation, breakfast at the Dales Detective Agency was a subdued affair. And rather crowded.

With Samson, Delilah and Gareth all seated at the small kitchen table, and Danny Bradley perched on the window-sill, there was barely room for Ida at the stove, let alone Tolpuddle and Bounty, Gareth's springer spaniel. The two dogs were squashed into a corner, both sets of eyes on the frying pan Ida was wielding.

'Any news on getting video footage from Rick's doorbell, Danny?' Delilah asked. She'd given the team a chance to eat in peace, but was now anxious to get started on the day's work. Especially as her own appetite was lacking, half a bacon butty left on her plate.

Danny shook his head, wiping a smear of ketchup from his chin. The poor lad looked shattered after his brutal intro-duction to the world of surveillance. Judging by the way his eyes lingered momentarily on Ida's frying pan before he turned to Delilah, he was also very hungry.

'I left a message with the estate agents late afternoon on Saturday,' he said, 'but they haven't got back to me, so it probably needs chasing today. I'll give them another call if I get the time.'

Delilah nodded and got to her feet, reaching for the pen clipped to the whiteboard above the table. Normally the board listed all of the ongoing investigations for the Dales Detective Agency. Right now, it was being used solely to coordinate Tyke's case, such were the complicated logistics involved. In a neat hand, she added Danny's update.

'From my perspective,' she said, 'there's not much to report. I'm still drawing blanks on the source of the social media threats, I'm afraid. And I've chased up every name bar one on the list Eloise provided – the former contestants of *The Nines* who might have a grudge against Tyke. So far no joy. They all have watertight alibis for the days when Tyke was targeted and, to be frank, have moved on in terms of their own careers. I don't see any of them being our guy.'

'What about the outstanding name?' asked Gareth.

'A young woman called Holly Campbell who was on the programme three years ago and was eliminated in the penultimate round. She was very disgruntled at the time and posted a few rants aimed at Tyke, claiming he was biased because she'd worked as an intern for a rival designer. But since then she's disappeared – no social media presence to speak of and no online trace that I can find. I'll keep digging, though.'

'Definitely sounds like that could be worth sticking with,' said Samson. He took a swig of tea and gave a reflexive grimace. Eighteen months in and he still hadn't become accustomed to the strength of Ida's tea. Seeing Delilah watching him, he winked.

She felt the heat on her cheeks. The confusion in her heart. Relieved that everyone else was too busy eating or cooking to notice.

'But in the meantime,' he continued, 'perhaps we need to switch our focus.'

'Switch to the motorbike, tha means?' asked Ida, flipping bacon onto bread with practised efficiency before passing a second serving to Danny, whose expression of gratitude was close to worship.

'Exactly,' said Samson. 'We know the make and the colour. We also know there's a good chance it's still in the area, given what Delilah saw on the fells. So we put out an alert.'

'On the WhatsApp group?' Gareth had finished eating and was leaning back in his chair, his long limbs taking up even more of the kitchen's limited space.

'WhatsApp, Facebook, let's get all those folk around here who love to mind other people's business working for us. If the bike is in the vicinity, someone will have seen it.'

Danny was nodding. 'Like an APB, Bruncliffe style,' he grinned.

'Nowt as effective as the Bruncliffe grapevine,' muttered Ida. She turned to thump a second sandwich down in front of Samson. 'Eat. Tha's looking peaky and there's a wedding coming up.'

Samson laughed, but the look he gave Delilah was wary.

'Right,' she said, trying to mask her inner turmoil with efficiency as she faced the whiteboard and began writing. 'WhatsApp, Facebook . . . anything else?'

'I could follow up on Rick's doorbell,' volunteered Gareth. 'I've set up hidden cameras in the stock-room out at the dairy and a couple in the office as well, so it's just a waiting game now to see if the thief strikes again. Which means I've got a bit of down time today.'

Delilah glanced at Danny. 'Okay with you?'

'That would be great,' said Danny around a mouthful of food. He swallowed. Looked at Delilah's half-eaten sandwich and raised an eyebrow. 'Is that going spare?'

'Be my guest,' she murmured, aware that Ida had turned and was taking it all in. Feeling the intensity of the gaze on her.

'Tha's not dieting before the wedding, lass?' Ida snapped, more instruction than question. 'Because there's nowt so sad as a half-starved bride!'

'Don't be daft,' muttered Delilah, cheeks truly ablaze now.

Ida let her stare linger, Delilah doing her best to meet it as it lasered into her. It was Tolpuddle who came to the rescue. A bark so loud they all jumped, followed by an insistent paw tap on Ida's thigh.

'Sorry lad!' murmured Ida, breaking off her optical interrogation of Delilah to put a hand on the dog's head. 'Did I forget about thee and tha friend?'

Samson, meanwhile, had switched his attention to the whiteboard, taking in the paucity of new information Delilah had added after another twenty-four hours of hard work by the team. He shook his head and ran a hand over his face, looking bone weary.

'An attempted hit-and-run. A dead rabbit delivered in daylight. Not to mention a slew of threats. And yet we have zilch. Anyone else feel like we're getting nowhere with this?' he asked.

Ida grunted. 'Be faster running backwards in treacle,' she muttered.

'I still think the sarge should have ordered a post-mortem on the rabbit,' grumbled Danny.

But Samson was shaking his head. 'The sarge was right. There's no way he'd get one authorised given current budget constraints. And even if he did, it would take forever – the lab have far more pressing things on their plate.'

'I'd be happy to oblige,' said Gareth.

The others all turned to him and he shrugged.

'I'm no forensic scientist but I've dealt with enough dead

animals in a lifetime gamekeeping to be able to tell you how something was killed. Snare, shot, poison . . .'

Samson looked at Delilah. 'What do you think?'

'Worth a go.' She turned to Danny. 'Can you get Gareth access to the rabbit?'

'I'll have a word with the sarge.'

'Great,' said Samson. 'I don't know how much we'll gain from it but at least it feels like we're doing something proactive.'

'I just wish I'd been able to get a photo of that damn trail bike,' muttered Delilah. 'I can't help feeling like that was a missed opportunity.'

'Don't beat yourself up about it. There are always elements of bad luck in cases. What we need is some good luck to balance it out.'

From below came the noise of excited voices, followed by the thump of feet on the stairs. Nina was first to the top, Nathan right behind her.

'We've got something!' she exclaimed, rushing towards the kitchen with her laptop under her arm.

If Nina's demeanour wasn't a clue, the fact that Delilah's nephew – just turned sixteen and not known for emerging at such an early hour, especially during half-term – was grinning from ear to ear made Delilah cross her fingers.

Perhaps the good luck they so desperately needed had just arrived.

'Bloody hell! Is that—?'

Gareth broke off to peer closer at the laptop, his profanity going unchecked by Ida as they all crowded round, eyes on the black figure which cut across the far edge of the screen as Nina's video played out.

Nina was nodding, grinning. Danny giving Nathan a high five.

'Play it again,' said Samson.

A few taps of the screen and the video rolled once more, and there was Barry Dawson, standing proudly outside his bookshop in the marketplace while an out-of-shot voice interviewed him. Then the commotion, a blast of horn, the shouts from behind the camera. A vertiginous moment as the lens swung round rapidly towards the disturbance, providing a blurred snapshot of a passing van and irate driver. Focus all over the place, the image settled on the prostrate figures on the tarmac, Carol Knowles hurrying towards them, the shocked faces of bystanders. And at the edge of the screen, a black motorbike racing across the square towards Church Street.

Just a fleeting glance. And out of focus. But it was something, Samson was sure of it.

'How did you get this?' he asked, a familiar spark of excitement coursing through him.

Nina shrugged. 'Someone at school. We decided to ask around to see if anyone was in the square when Tyke was almost run over, just on the off chance.'

'And a mate on my Creative iMedia course happened to mention they knew someone making a video for their Enterprise and Marketing module,' explained Nathan. 'Turns out they'd interviewed Barry about his new business on Thursday, so we thought it was worth chasing up.'

'It took a while, though,' Nina added, with an exasperated shake of her head, 'as the lad who made the video had a house party Friday night when his folks were away. It got a bit out of hand and Sergeant Clayton was called out and, to cut a long story short, the lad's parents had to return early from their weekend away. As part of his punishment, they confiscated his phone. You can't imagine what a nightmare it was trying to contact him. We had to go round his house in person in the end!'

Samson laughed at her indignation at having to use such an outdated method of communication.

'Well, your efforts have paid off,' he said, patting Nathan on the back. 'I reckon we might be able to get something from this.'

'We?' Delilah was looking at him with a grin.

He grinned back. Suddenly feeling like the cloud above him had lifted. 'Fair enough. *Delilah* might be able to get something from this.'

'Don't hold your breath,' she said, gesturing at the screen where the disappearing motorbike was frozen in time. 'There's only so much magic I can work, but I'll do my best.'

She was already moving towards the office with Nina's laptop, heading for her computer. They followed her like sheep, the two dogs included. Watched as she connected the laptop to her PC and then sat down, fingers working the keyboard. The video on the screen, focus zooming in and out, bits of the footage being clipped and put into an app . . .

Fifteen minutes later, she leaned back. 'Best I can do,' she declared.

A much-truncated clip started playing, this time the motorbike the only star. It was still blurred. Still impossible to make out anything about the rider other than that they were wearing black. But the number-plate . . .

Delilah had somehow managed to isolate it and enlarge it, and, despite the muck covering the majority of the yellow rectangle, three fuzzy letters and a couple of digits had emerged.

13DWT

'You genius!' said Samson, planting a kiss on her head as he leaned in over her chair, eyes on the screen.

'It's only a partial,' Delilah cautioned, pointing at the lump of mud blocking the view of the initial two letters. 'I'm not sure what good it will do us.'

'Plenty!' said Gareth. He bent down to the keyboard. 'May I?'

'Go ahead.'

Thick fingers thumping keys, he entered a website address. 'WhatPlate,' he said. 'I used to use this all the time when I was chasing poachers. Quite often they'd be stupid enough to leave their vehicles close by and I'd sometimes get a glimpse of the registration number. Often not the full details. This site proved invaluable.'

He stood back and beamed as the screen starting throwing up variations of the partial number-plate, alongside the make of the vehicle connected to each one.

'Wow!' exclaimed Nathan as more options scrolled in front of them. 'All we need to do is find a Triumph and we've got him!'

'There!' said Nina, pointing at the laptop excitedly.

YK13DWT   Triumph

'That's got to be it,' said Delilah as the scrolling list of possibles came to a halt. 'It's the only Triumph.'

Danny was already photographing the screen. 'I'll get this to the sarge and get an address.'

'We've got the bugger!' declared Ida.

Samson nodded. Grinning at the equally excited group clustered around Delilah's desk. 'I'd say we've got our first big breakthrough!'

13

With a renewed sense of purpose among the team, the Dales Detective Agency became a hive of industry. Nathan and Nina were allocated more admin duties, while Gareth set about chasing up the possibility of video footage from Rick Procter's doorbell. Danny was entrusted with returning to the police station to run the registration number through the national database and securing authorisation for Gareth's access to the dead rabbit. He was also going to get his head down so he was fresh for the night's upcoming solo surveillance.

Which left Samson and Delilah with Ida in the kitchen. And Tolpuddle, who was standing next to Samson, nudging his thigh, emitting the occasional low whine.

Under the guise of clearing up the breakfast dishes, Ida watched the three of them, Samson and Delilah discussing their plans for the day like they were nothing more than colleagues, the way they weren't really relaxed around each other. The anxiety being displayed by the Weimaraner.

'Have fun at Barry's,' Samson was saying, a wariness to his smile.

Delilah nodded. Head dipped down. Not quite catching his eye. 'Good luck with Tyke.'

'He's running a rehearsal for the fashion show later this morning after he's been to see his uncle, so I'll need it. It's the first time he'll have really been out in the open since the attempted hit-and-run.'

'Be careful,' she said. She stretched up and left a kiss which could only be described as sisterly on his cheek as she prepared to leave.

It was enough to put Ida back in the sour mood that had remained with her since her calamitous visit to Fellside Court on Saturday. What was up with folk? Samson and Delilah. Edith and Arty. Why were they making such hard work of things?

Having been immersed in the Dales Dating Agency for the past few days, Ida had spent hours working with clients new and old and could testify to the eagerness – even desperation – with which most of them approached the quest to find a partner. From Ida's uninitiated perspective, considering the amount of effort folk spent looking for love, happen they'd be of a mind to put a similar amount of effort into looking after it once they found it.

Lacking the most basic qualification when it came to relationships of the heart, however, she kept her lips closed and her counsel to herself, although the strength with which she banged the clean frying pan back on the stove might have betrayed some of her disquiet. It certainly made Tolpuddle jump and Delilah turn round in the doorway in surprise.

'Sorry. It slipped,' muttered Ida, her apology addressed pointedly to the dog.

Delilah's gaze dropped to the floor. As though she could sense the disapproval radiating out from Ida. Then she simply nodded and left, Tolpuddle reluctantly trailing behind her. Samson followed a few minutes later, face like a wet winter's day in Morecambe. With the tide out.

All of this meant that by the time Ida got to Fellside Court, she was in a foul humour. Frustration mostly, not having a clue what was going on and not having a clue how to fix it, but able to see the damage the situation was having on those she cared about. So when she reached Vinny King's apartment, her lips were pursed and her hollow cheeks were even more gaunt, making her expression formidable.

The TV host opened the door full of welcome.

'Come in!' he said, not blinking at her ferocious glare as she stomped past him. 'Can I make you a brew?'

'No thanks. Got a lot on,' she muttered, before promptly switching on the vacuum, for once wishing she still had her old Hoover which had made such a racket that no conversation could be attempted.

But Vinny got the hint, and retreated to his armchair, allowing her to work undisturbed.

Only she was disturbed. Greatly. Because as she manoeuvred the vacuum around the bedroom, all she could think of was Edith's voice, those low murmurs. And poor Arty, sitting at the table in their flat looking like a broken man.

By the time she got to the bathroom, Ida was frothing internally. Her cloth whipped over surfaces, the spray doused ceramic and the toilet seat crashed shut despite its soft-close mechanism. She entered the lounge in a ferment of annoyance.

Which is why it happened.

One moment she was dusting the items cluttering the wall of Vinny's lounge and the next, she was aware of something falling. Of a loud noise as something hit the ground. Of Vinny jumping out of his chair, shouting.

She stared at the floor in shock. At the painting which lay there, the green water and the white diving board glistening in the morning light, mocking her with the suggestion of relaxation and enjoyment.

'You clumsy woman!' Vinny was saying as Ida bent to pick it up. Her heart thundering.

There was no visible damage. Just the painting a bit lopsided within the frame. She turned it over, preparing to open it up and adjust it, but paused when she saw that the back was sealed with tape, a sticker bearing the name of an art gallery at the top.

Vinny snatched it from her hands. 'Don't be stupid! It needs an expert to do that.' He stood there, glaring at her. 'Do you have any idea what this is worth? Bad enough you knocked it off the wall without devaluing it completely by trying to fix it.'

He turned round and hung it back up, the diving board now tipped to a precipitous angle.

'I'll have to take it back to the gallery,' he was muttering. 'Get them to sort it.'

Ida felt herself starting to shake. Her hands. Her legs. An excess of emotion in her chest.

Without saying a word, she gathered together her cleaning equipment, and moved towards the hallway. As she reached the front door and yanked it open, there was Edith, hand raised to knock.

'Ida!' she exclaimed. 'Is everything okay?'

Ida couldn't speak. She simply pushed past into the corridor. Heading for the cleaning cupboard. She'd almost reached it when the final straw snapped her resolve. The door to the stairs opened and Delilah emerged into the bright light spilling through the wall of glass beside them.

Delilah, who was supposed to be at Barry's . . .

'Oh! Ida. I didn't expect to see you here.' She blushed. Furtive-looking in the spotlight of sunshine.

Ida didn't reply. Just walked towards the cupboard, pulled

it open, stepped inside and firmly closed the door behind her. Surrounded by the comforting smell of polish and clean linen, she sat on an upturned bucket, overwhelmed with misery.

It wasn't just the painting that seemed tipped on its head at the moment. Everything was skew-whiff and, as Vinny had so brutally pointed out, Ida didn't have the expertise to fix any of it.

She pulled the rudimentary betting slip Troy had given her out of her pocket, fingers rubbing over it like a talisman, trying to ease the burning angst in her chest. He'd been right to caution her about placing a wager. Because the way things were going, there was little chance of the wedding ever taking place.

As unexpected tears slid down her cheeks, Ida found herself thinking that if this was the price of caring about folk, she wasn't sure she wanted to have friends any more.

Tyke was looking frustrated. Perhaps it was the sudden change of itinerary, Samson getting a text at short notice to say they weren't heading for Fellside Court as planned but direct to Bruncliffe Community Hall. Or maybe the weight of having someone threatening to kill him was taking its toll. As he'd pulled out from the drive that morning, he'd seemed relieved to see Samson waiting in the cul-de-sac on the Enfield, and had been fully on board when Samson suggested that it might be worthwhile having his protection a bit more visible for the next few days. Just as an added deterrent.

Of course, it was also possible that Tyke's current exasperation was simply the stress of his job.

Standing at the side of a raised platform running the length of the hall, the fashion designer was barking out instructions in a language Samson could barely understand. But he could appreciate the intensity the man was bringing to his work. And the aura he was creating about him.

It was an aura which suited the old Victorian music hall. A majestic building with a large main room and balcony, capable of hosting over three hundred people, it was somewhere Samson had always associated with light and laughter. Pantomimes, magic shows, Saturday matinees – he had fond memories of the place from his childhood, his parents always as excited as he was as they entered the hall and took their seats. He hadn't visited it much after his mother died, his father losing all interest in entertainment, apart from that which came out of a bottle and carried a potent kick. But despite having hosted almost two centuries of performances, it was doubtful the hall had ever seen the like of Tyke and his flamboyant clothing.

Or of the models currently slouching and prowling up and down the catwalk, their Tyke-creations vibrant under the spotlights, almost alive even, a spectrum of colours flashing from the fabrics as the men moved, a huge Retro Reversibles sign in neon hanging behind them.

Tyke was watching on with a critical eye, Eloise by his side, notebook in hand and taking furious notes.

'No no!' he shouted as the focus of the spotlights suddenly shifted. 'Too much bleed. We want the focal point on the clothing, not the audience!'

'Let's go with followspots,' said Eloise over her shoulder, addressing the light technician standing at the back of the hall behind a large control box. 'And backlights for the entry point.'

The man grunted, looking miserable. 'Not sure this antiquated kit won't blow up if we ask too much of it,' he muttered.

But Tyke had no time for the man's qualms. 'More intensity! Jesus! Everything looks washed out!'

'Maybe work on the triads,' Eloise suggested to the tech. 'More cyan, less magenta and dial down on the yellow.'

The lighting changed subtly, but the effect was dramatic, suddenly the models and the clothes they were wearing almost pulsing with energy. The technician was nodding, thumbs up to Eloise, Samson getting the sense that she was more than good at what she did. A confidence to her which he hadn't seen before.

Meanwhile, Tyke was striding around the base of the catwalk, taking in all the angles.

'The ending!' he shouted.

There was a twirl of bodies on the platform, about fifteen young men up there now, the lights dancing on them, the music booming out. Then on a clash of cymbals, they all snapped off their jackets and flipped them back on, inside out, the effect like a rainbow suddenly being inverted.

It was startling. Electrifying.

Samson was about to start clapping, impressed, when the young men parted dramatically, bodies taking up various poses to create a corridor as another figure appeared at the back of the platform. Larger. Bulkier. Older. Looking less confident in the baggy tracksuit bottoms and puffed-up jacket, the electric-blue fleurs-de-lis which covered them accentuating his size.

'Chin up!' said Tyke, voice encouraging as the man started hesitantly down the catwalk. 'Wear it like you're a king!'

The model lifted his chin, baseball cap rising, face visible—

'Clive!' said Samson, the name bursting from him in shock at the sight of the farmer so far from his usual context.

Clive Knowles glanced his way and gave a shy grin. A lift of the hand. Then a wolf whistle cut through the hall and everyone started laughing.

'Thanks, lass,' Clive said, peering through the spotlights at Carol, who was standing in the doorway, fingers in mouth.

'That's brilliant,' exclaimed Eloise, nodding appreciatively at Carol. 'Let's keep the whistle in for the actual event. A real sense of the fun Tyke is bringing with this collection.'

Tyke nodded. Then clapped his hands. 'Right! The whole thing again! We've got an hour before we're getting kicked out and only a week before the show. Let's make the time count.'

As his team started shifting into positions, the fashion designer came over to Samson.

'Sorry for putting you through this,' he said, casting a hand at the commotion behind him with a rueful smile. 'One fashion show is enough for most mortals; watching lots of rehearsals of one must be pure hell.'

Samson shook his head. 'It's fascinating. Such attention to detail. I don't think I'll ever look at the fashion world the same.'

'Be honest,' said Tyke with a laugh, 'you'll never look at the fashion world ever again once I'm out of your hair.' The laugh died, his right hand reaching up to his cheek, grazing and bruise still visible. 'Let's just hope me being out of your hair is for the right reasons. That damn rabbit . . . I'm doing my best to put on a brave face but I'm a nervous wreck. And Eloise is barely holding it together. It feels like things have gone up a whole other level since Saturday.'

'I've got the entire team on it,' said Samson, trying to reassure the man while hiding his own frustration at the lack of progress they were making in the investigation. 'We'll get there. I promise.'

Tyke nodded. 'I know you will. You're the best.' He went to turn away and paused, turning back. 'You will be there, won't you? Outside the house at night? I know we said it was temporary but it would be a real comfort to know you've got me covered.'

'Don't worry. I'll be there.'

The fashion designer walked back towards the catwalk, calling the models into order and leaving Samson to his guilty conscience at the blatant lie he'd just told. For it wouldn't be him in the undergrowth guarding Tyke's house that night. It would be the less experienced Danny.

The change of personnel wasn't something Samson was apprehensive about from an operational viewpoint, having come to the conclusion that the attack on Tyke, when it came, would be during the day. Out in the open, like the attempted hit-and-run. Or even the dead rabbit. He just wasn't comfortable telling lies, which was ironic, given his entire working life had been built on subterfuge.

It didn't help that the man he was lying to was trusting him to solve a case which currently was going nowhere.

'Samson!' Gareth Towler was coming through the door, his shock of russet hair and beard and the sheer size of him causing more than a few appreciative murmurs from the fashion show participants. 'News!'

As she stood with her back literally against the wall, the bricks of Fellside Court cool through her T-shirt, Delilah was taking stock after being forced back from the brink of treachery.

That blasted encounter with Ida had left her shaken. She could tell from the look her colleague had subjected her to that Ida sensed something was up. Exposed to such scrutiny, Delilah's courage had failed and she'd been seized by a sudden fear that if she let her concerns out into the open, they would become magnified. Uncontrollable. And all too real.

So she'd sent a text to cancel her rendezvous, hurried down the back stairs of the retirement complex, which emerged by the cafe, and walked brazenly through the kitchen, saying hello to the cook and murmuring something about checking the internet connections. Delilah knew from experience that those who didn't work in IT rarely questioned such statements. Slipping out the fire exit, she now found herself on the far side of the building, away from the all-seeing wall of glass and the busy residents' lounge.

She leaned against the bricks a bit longer, pondering which way offered the best cover. With the cafe situated on the front corner, she couldn't risk heading towards the road in full view of anyone treating themselves to a morning coffee, which meant she'd have to go cross-country, along the wall and then through the copse at the back.

Only problem was there were three ground-floor flats on this side, all with long windows and Juliet balconies overlooking the narrow path which separated the building from the thicket of trees and shrubs in front of her. She'd have to go past each window to escape unseen.

Sensing this was some kind of divine punishment, she dropped to her knees and began crawling along the path. She passed the first window, almost on her stomach as she wiggled underneath it, then the second. But as she approached the third, her heart sank.

It was open. Net curtains blowing out in a gentle breeze.

Damn.

Speed was the only solution.

She hurried forward, scampering along beneath the wrought iron of the decorative balustrade, palms on the rough slabs to hasten her progress. She'd just reached the other side when a stab of pain made her yelp loudly.

Hand throbbing, she threw herself flat against the wall, fearing she'd be discovered.

A few seconds of silence, no one appearing at the window to ask what she was doing. She risked a glance down at her hand. There was blood trickling from her palm, a shard of glass sticking out of the soft flesh. Teeth gritted, she pulled it out. And from above heard the slam of a door.

She looked up. The windows of the first-floor flat were also open, voile curtains in a soft shade of pink fluttering through the gap. The sound of a man's voice carried down to her. Raised. A few indistinct words then louder, as he approached the Juliet balcony.

Feeling like she was intruding, Delilah was about to leave. But then she recognised the voice. It was Vinny King. For some reason, she froze. Intrigued.

'I warned you that wouldn't be happening!' he snapped.

A female voice, from further inside the room, distressed. Delilah found herself straining to hear.

Then Vinny, sounding angry. 'Don't threaten me!'

Above, an arm appeared through the curtains, a woman's, a delicate silver watch on the wrist as the hand pulled the window closed.

Delilah waited a minute, making sure it was safe before she made a dash across the path and into the cover of the trees. As she jogged down through the copse and out into the library car park, she wasn't thinking about her own problems any more. She was thinking about Edith Hird.

And wondering what on earth had happened to make the mild-mannered former headmistress get into such a heated argument with Vinny King. For the flat on the first floor Delilah had been crouching under was the one where Edith lived.

14

'That's it? A dead end?'

Samson couldn't help letting his frustration show. He'd had a lot of hope pinned on the number-plate they'd managed to decipher from the video Nina and Nathan had brought to the office that morning. While he wasn't naive enough to think the case would be all done and dusted with one search of the DVLA database, he'd at least expected more than Gareth had just relayed.

'The guy said he sold the Triumph two months ago. Cash.' Gareth shrugged. 'Sergeant Clayton checked it out and it sounds legit.'

'And the new owner hasn't registered the bike with the DVLA yet?'

'Nope. No insurance either,' added Gareth, tone wry. 'Plus they gave the guy a fake name and address. Makes you think they didn't want to be traced.'

'What about a description?'

'Apparently it was a young man, hoodie, glasses, pretty nondescript according to the seller. Certainly nothing that raised suspicions. He just thought it was a lad getting into off-roading for the first time.'

In the background, Tyke and his team were dismantling

the catwalk, while Eloise was hanging the clothes back onto racks. Everyone busy. Everyone making progress.

Apart from Samson and this confounded case!

'So where was the bloke anyway?' he asked, out of idle curiosity.

'The one who sold it? Leeds.'

'Leeds?' Samson swung round to face Gareth. Feeling that tingle, the sense of something discordant.

'You think that's relevant?'

'God knows. But you have to ask why someone stalking a person living in London would travel to Leeds to buy a bike.'

'Perhaps it was handy? I wouldn't fancy riding a trail bike all the way up here from the south.'

Samson shook his head. 'I'm not buying that. Besides, how did he even know he'd need a motorbike that could go off road? Not much call for that in downtown Shoreditch, where Tyke is based.'

Gareth's eyes narrowed. Head nodding. 'Good point.' Then he gave a start. Gesturing at the activity all around them. 'Hang on a minute! Didn't Tyke say this whole thing was spontaneous? A sudden whim to reveal his collection in Bruncliffe now his uncle's moved back here? In which case . . .'

'In which case, how did the person buying the bike know *two months ago* that Tyke would be in the Yorkshire Dales?'

'We need a list of the people Tyke told,' said Gareth, taking out his phone and making notes. 'Anyone who might have had an inkling what his plans were.'

Samson nodded. Energised. It was a small lead. But it was a lead. The person threatening Tyke had known he was coming to Bruncliffe, which narrowed down the number of potential suspects. And anything which helped focus the investigation was a bonus.

'What about Rick's doorbell?' he asked, as Gareth finished typing. 'Any joy with that?'

'Yes and no. The estate agent let me view the footage from Saturday and while there's a perfect view of Tyke's gateway, there's nothing doing. No one walking down the cul-de-sac with a dead rabbit, anyway.'

'Huh,' Samson grunted. 'You said "yes and no". I'm failing to see how there's a "yes" in there.'

Gareth grinned. 'Well, way I see it, if the rabbit wasn't on the doorstep when Tyke left the house and it didn't arrive up the drive, there's only one way it could have got there.'

'Of course! Round the back!' Samson slapped him on the shoulder. 'They must have come across the fields from the track, like we've been doing.'

'Want me to check it out after I've had a look over our dead bunny with Sergeant Clayton?'

Samson shook his head. 'You've got enough to be going on with. I'll give Danny a call – get him in early to take over shadowing Tyke and I'll ride out there to have a look. Let's hope we get lucky and find something.'

Gareth crossed his fingers and turned to go. 'Oh,' he said, turning back, 'one thing that bloke over in Leeds did say was that he knew he was wrong about the kid the minute he got on the bike.'

'In what way?'

'He wasn't a rookie motorcyclist. He hopped on and started it up first time and rode off like a pro.'

Another nugget. Another bit of evidence which would

help close the net. Samson could sense that the case was finally beginning to turn their way.

'Thanks,' he said. 'And good work. We'll make a detective of you yet!'

Cheeks beaming as bright as his hair, Gareth headed out into the sunlight.

Only hours until the organised visit to Bruncliffe Community Hall for the live stream of *Romeo and Juliet*, and the atmosphere in the lounge of Fellside Court was close to fever pitch.

'What a great idea this was,' Ana said, stopping by Arty Robinson and Eric Bradley, who were sitting near the window enjoying a post-lunch cuppa.

Arty slouched in his chair and grunted. 'All credit owed to Vinny King, I suppose.'

Ana shrugged. 'It may have been his suggestion but it was the residents' committee who organised everything. Aren't you both looking forward to it?'

'I am. First time I'll have been out in days,' said Eric. 'But killjoy here has decided he's not coming.'

'Why on earth not?'

'Not my thing,' muttered Arty. 'Star-crossed lovers and all that.' There was a weariness to him that worried Ana.

'What about the others?' she asked.

'No doubt Edith will be going.' Arty's voice was rich with irony. 'She wouldn't miss it for the world.'

'What wouldn't I miss?' Edith had joined them, a distracted look on her face.

'The play,' said Eric on a wheeze, Ana sensing he was hurrying to fill the space in the conversation before Arty did.

Edith nodded. 'I'll be there, but I've just come from Clarissa's. Poor thing is back in bed and doesn't feel up to it.

I offered to stay with her but she's insisting we *all* go.' She looked at Arty as she said it.

'Does she want me to call Dr Naylor?' offered Ana, concerned to hear Clarissa was no better.

'She's already called him. He said he'd be out later this afternoon.'

'What about Joseph?' Eric asked, looking from Arty to Edith. 'Is he coming with us?'

Arty shrugged. 'Don't know. Haven't seen much of him *either* the last couple of days—'

'Speak of the devil,' said Edith, ignoring the pointed comment to wave towards the doorway where Joseph was looking around him, searching for his friends.

'Where the hell have you been all morning?' demanded Arty as he approached.

Joseph smiled and tapped the side of his nose. 'Some of us have private lives, you know.'

'Huh. Don't I know it.'

'Never mind all that,' said Eric, brushing over Arty's petulance, 'are you coming with us tonight?'

'Of course!' Joseph rubbed his hands in anticipation. 'Only a fool would miss the chance of a night out on the tiles.'

'Many a true word spoken in jest,' murmured Edith, gaze resting on Arty.

At which Arty rose from his chair with a huff and walked away, heading for the door.

Eric looked at Joseph. Joseph looked at Edith. And Edith, expression troubled, hurried after Arty.

'What's going on?' asked Ana, watching them both exit the lounge.

Joseph shook his head. 'Search me, but the pair of them are out of sorts.'

Date with Destiny

'That's putting it mildly,' wheezed Eric, reaching for his oxygen. 'All this tension is doing me no good at all!'

Ana glanced out of the long row of windows which lined the lounge, at the sunshine and the trees in the courtyard, and wondered what could possibly be making two of her favourite people so upset on such a beautiful day.

The thought had barely formed when she saw the door below the wall of glass crash open and Ida Capstick stomped out onto the patio, face set as though walking into a storm rather than a balmy May day full of birdsong and blossom.

Hoping the gloom which seemed to be besetting Fellside Court could be dispelled by the evening's outing, Ana left the lounge to check on Clarissa Ralph.

The afternoon was well established before Samson managed to work the switch with Danny. At Tyke's insistence, he'd joined the fashion designer and Eloise for lunch at their house, glad of the chance to refuel and more than happy to have second helpings of Lucy Metcalfe's leek and ricotta tart, which they'd picked up from Peaks Patisserie on the way. He'd also had one of the huge slices of lemon and elderflower cake Lucy had insisted on giving them. With his stomach full for what felt like the first time in days, he'd followed Tyke's Porsche back to Fellside Court and watched the fashion designer enter the building. No question about it, the man's style was unique – even the bright orange messenger bag slung across his shoulder had been chosen to complement his creative clothing. As Tyke disappeared from view on the first-floor corridor, Samson retraced his steps and met up with Danny around the side by the kitchen entrance.

'You all set?' he asked.

The constable nodded, dressed like Samson in dark jeans and

a dark hoodie, looking even younger than usual without the formality of his uniform. He patted the small rucksack slung over his shoulder, and held up the notebook in his hand. 'All ready,' he said, a hum of excitement about him. 'And thanks for the opportunity to do this. For trusting me with it.'

Samson nodded. Not sure how thankful the lad would be once the tedium set in from hours of doing nothing. 'Just make sure you stay out of sight and you'll be fine. I told Tyke that I'd be flying under the radar for the rest of the day so he's not expecting me to be visible until he's ready to leave his house tomorrow morning. We'll do the reverse swap before then.'

'And the motorbike?' The light in Danny's eyes suggested that at least some of his enthusiasm was stemming from the chance to ride the Enfield.

'Here.' Samson handed over the keys and a helmet, the visor dark. 'Keep a good distance back and he won't suspect a thing.'

'Right. Thanks.' The grin Danny gave him was one of joy.

'And mine?' asked Samson.

Danny's grin grew wider. He held out a small key and pointed towards the copse. 'Locked outside the library. And don't worry, I won't let you down.'

'I know you won't. Just stay alert and if anything happens, call me. Anything at all.'

With a confident nod, Danny headed off towards the bushes at the back of Fellside Court, leaving Samson to cut down through the trees and into the library car park. Sure enough, locked to a rack near the library's entrance was Danny's mode of transport. A mountain bike.

Thinking the lad had got the best of the deal, Samson cycled out onto Church Street, turning right to go under the huge viaduct which spanned the road and then left towards the industrial estate. It was the same route he'd ridden on the Enfield for the past five evenings, one which led to the rough farm track he'd used to get to the back of Tyke's rental property. Today, on Danny's bike, it seemed to take a lot longer. And demanded a lot more effort from a body crying out for sleep.

Breathing hard, he rode up the small incline past the cricket club, wondering how he'd never noticed how hilly Bruncliffe was before, and with some relief, turned onto the track. He paused at the entrance, getting off the bike to inspect the grass verge to the side, trying to see if there was any evidence of someone having parked up there in recent days.

But the spell of dry weather had made it almost impossible to tell, the mist on Saturday not enough to dampen conditions and enable tyre tracks. Plus, he reasoned, as he watched a couple of cars go past on the road, it wasn't exactly out of sight. If someone was intent on nefarious deeds, they'd hardly have left their vehicle in full view while they committed them.

He got back on the bike and began cycling along the track, the surface deteriorating the further he went, every rock and stone jarring his bones. It didn't take long to feel remote, the track cutting a narrow path between stone walls, lumpen fields full of sheep on both sides, outcrops of limestone breaking up the green. Just when he didn't feel he could pedal any further, he saw the derelict barn with its sagging roof where he'd left the Enfield during his surveillance.

Relieved to be able to rest, he pulled open the ramshackle gate into the field, wheeled the mountain bike through and propped it against the stone wall. He stood there, looking at the grass as it stretched up the hill, seeing nothing that would suggest a trail bike had been ridden over it recently. Which meant whoever had delivered the rabbit must have done what he'd been doing the last few nights: parked up here and hiked across the field to Tyke's back wall.

He turned back to the barn and began walking around it, eyes glued to the ground. When he reached the far side, the one most shielded from sight of anyone passing by, he saw a couple of indentations from the Enfield's kickstand. But nothing else. No tyre tracks. No obvious sign that someone else had parked here.

Not convinced he wasn't wasting his time, Samson moved to go, and the dipping sun sparked a flash of colour on the ground. Right where he'd left his bike every night. Intrigued, he bent down and dipped his finger in the drop of moisture which had caught the light. He didn't need to smell it. He could tell from the texture what it was.

Oil.

While the Royal Enfield had many quirks, leaking oil wasn't one of them. Not at the moment, anyway. He looked again at the marks in the ground. Four. Except . . .

He leaned forward and ran a hand over them. *There.* One of the impressions was blurred, as though the weight had been shifted partway through. Or used a second time on a different occasion . . .

Hands on his thighs, he remained on his haunches and looked back over the field. This was it. This was how the rabbit had been brought to Tyke's front door. The very same route Samson had been using to operate surveillance. And the cheeky bugger had even parked his trail bike right where the Enfield had been left.

Whoever this was, they were clever. And brazen. Which, in Samson's experience, was a dangerous combination.

Date with Destiny

With heightened concern, he got back on the mountain bike and headed towards town. He'd see if Delilah was up for a quick get-together to discuss the day's developments, then he'd grab a couple of hours' sleep before retracing his footsteps back here to relieve Danny of his night-time surveillance. Because whatever doubts Samson had held about the viability of the threats against Tyke, the cold, calculated delivering of the dead rabbit had changed his mind. This was someone who had his prey under observation. And possibly the Dales Detective team too. Which meant the inexperienced Danny wasn't the right person to be protecting Tyke, no matter what Sergeant Clayton wanted.

15

What Sergeant Clayton wanted at that precise moment was to be anywhere but where he was.

'Nearly done,' said Gareth, tone pragmatic as he leaned over the examination table and the inert form upon it.

'I think that's the key,' said Herriot, the local vet, who'd been given his nickname the moment he landed in the Dales town and announced his name was James. He was pointing, but at what, Sergeant Clayton had no desire to see.

'Is it me, or is it hot in here?' he murmured, keeping his gaze averted while running a hand around the collar of his uniform and fanning his face, wishing that the sausage roll he'd had just before leaving his desk would feel a bit more settled in his stomach.

The two men either side of the table didn't respond, too engrossed in their inspection, talking quietly to each other.

When Gareth arrived at the police station to carry out an informal post-mortem on the dead rabbit, the former game-keeper and the sergeant had both agreed that the veterinary practice across town would be a more suitable environment for what they needed to do. A quick call to Herriot and it had been arranged, the vet curious enough to join them in the examination room.

Perhaps that was it, thought the sergeant, as he shuffled

a bit further from the centre of the action, his back up against the metal cabinets by the door. The small space was overcrowded, Gareth's hulking frame and Herriot, not to mention his own substantial girth. There were too many folk in here. That's what was making him feel a bit . . .

The word 'faint' came to mind, but he dismissed the idea. Him, a police officer of several decades, having witnessed more than his share of trauma and distressing scenes. He wasn't about to keel over at the sight of a dead rabbit—

'So there we have it,' said Gareth, straightening up and moving towards the sink to wash his hands, affording Sergeant Clayton a good view of the small shape on the table. 'Agreed, Herriot?'

Herriot was nodding, moving too, nothing blocking the sergeant's line of sight now. 'Definitely. We can say without doubt that this rabbit was—'

The sergeant heard not a word more. Not until the darkness lifted and he opened his eyes to see Gareth and Herriot leaning over him.

'What—? How did—?' He struggled to sit up, confusion befuddling his brain.

'You passed out,' said Gareth, lips twitching.

Herriot too had a twinkle in his eye. 'Not the first time I've had someone keel over in here.'

'I didn't faint,' protested the sergeant. 'I just . . .'

'Fell over head first?' Gareth laughed, helping him to his feet. 'Did you at least hear our news before you took your forty winks?'

The sergeant shook his head. 'What have you found?' he asked gruffly.

'The rabbit was farmed. It's bigger than a wild rabbit and also it was killed humanely—'

'If there is such a thing,' muttered Herriot.

'—with a bolt. We found the marks on its skull.' Gareth was pointing at the evidence but the sergeant didn't risk a look, not wanting a repeat performance of whatever had just occurred. He focused on the facts instead.

'Which means,' he said, staring at the wall, 'whoever left this on Tyke's doorstep, didn't kill it himself.'

'I'd say that's a certainty.'

'So the next question is, where would you get your hands on a farmed rabbit?'

'Easy,' said Herriot. 'Online. There are butchers who specialise in game. Or even reptile centres that sell them as—'

'Right!' The sergeant didn't need the details, still feeling queasy. 'So that's our line of enquiry. I'll get Delilah to start doing some digital legwork and see if we can get a lead on whatever macabre bugger delivered this poor creature to Tyke's house.'

He turned to go, rubbing his forehead where he could already feel a bruise forming.

'Are you sure you're okay?' Herriot asked, his concern genuine.

'I'm fine. I just got too hot, that's all.'

Now the smile emerged, devilment dancing in the vet's eyes. 'That must be it,' he said. 'Because while I've seen many a student pass out during autopsies, it's usually because of all the blood. I've never seen one do it when the corpse is like this.' He lifted the rabbit's leg, the limb stiff, frozen solid. Not a drop of blood on the table.

Gavin Clayton shook his head and left the room. Knowing with all certainty that he would never live this down.

*

Across town, hiding in the undergrowth outside Fellside Court, Danny would have appreciated even a fraction of the excitement which had been experienced at Herriot's surgery. Instead, he was fighting to keep his eyes open, the overnight vigil catching up with him despite the couple of hours' sleep he'd managed in between.

He rubbed his hand across his face and yawned widely, rolling his shoulders at the same time. Trying to get the blood pumping and his energy levels up while remaining sequestered in the thick vegetation. He was beginning to think that being on surveillance wasn't half as exciting as it was made out to be on TV.

As he shifted position, a stinging sensation set in across his left calf. Pins and needles. They didn't tell you about that in police dramas either, he mused as he gently rubbed the numbed muscle, biting his lip against the pain.

'Come on, Tyke, time to head home,' he muttered, looking up at the windows to Vinny King's apartment, desperate for something, anything, to relieve his discomfort. And his boredom.

'Dr Naylor!' Ana Stoyanovic had appeared in the courtyard, walking across the cobbles as a man came around the corner from the car park, medical bag in hand. 'I didn't expect you to come—'

She broke off, a hand going out to touch his shoulder. Empathy in her expression.

'You heard?' he said, face drawn.

She nodded. 'I just called the hospice to see how she was and they told me. I'm so sorry for your loss . . .'

Danny didn't need an explanation. Like everyone in the town, he'd known about Liz Naylor's diagnosis and had heard she'd entered a hospice. Still, he felt shock at her passing. She'd been one of the teaching assistants in his primary school, a lovely lady. And here he was eavesdropping on her husband in his hour of grief.

'She went peacefully this morning,' said Dr Naylor.

From above came a clap of laughter, Vinny King and Tyke audible through the open window. Dr Naylor looked up, expression darkening, as though the humour was irreverent. Then, jaw set, he simply nodded at Ana and continued towards the entrance.

'You can't be serious?' Ana said, reaching out to stop him. 'No one expects you to work. Not today. One of the locums can come and look at Clarissa.'

He gave a forlorn smile. 'I find work takes my mind off things. Besides, what else would I do?'

Sensing she wasn't going to win the argument, Ana turned back with him and together they entered the building. Danny watched their progress through the wall of glass, towards the stairs. They disappeared momentarily then emerged on the floor above, turning down the wing towards Clarissa's apartment. Another bout of laughter, sounding unintentionally disrespectful in light of what Danny had just heard.

He caught himself wanting to run up to the first floor to tell Vinny and Tyke to pipe down, to alert them to the loss being suffered by someone in their vicinity. But he couldn't. He was under strict instructions to keep out of Tyke's sight. So he was left there, in the bushes, logging the doctor's visit in his notebook and hoping that the walls of Fellside Court were good and thick – at least then, as he treated Clarissa Ralph, Dr Naylor might be spared the levity emanating from the flat next door.

*

Delilah and Tolpuddle got back from a run to an empty office building. Samson had asked her to meet him there for a catch-up but as she listened to the silence from the floors above, she guessed he was running late.

Probably stopped for a breather on his way back, cycling not being his forte. She grinned at the thought.

At least they had something to catch up about at last, the investigation finally showing signs of going somewhere. A message from Sergeant Clayton had come through while she was on the fells to say that the rabbit had been farmed, and outlining how this should be followed up. Delilah had wasted no time in calling Nathan and Nina, who had left the office and were in Peaks Patisserie, and the pair were now on the case, contacting online game suppliers and reptile centres to see if they could find some kind of link. Something that would be useful in breaking the deadlock.

Aware that there was an element of needle and haystack to the task, Delilah had instructed the teens to only concentrate on deliveries made from companies within a fifteen-mile radius to begin with – as far as Kirkby Lonsdale to the north-west, Nelson to the south and Skipton to the south-east. With the rest of the area in between being taken up by the Forest of Bowland and the more remote parts of the Yorkshire Dales National Park, she was confident this was a manageable undertaking.

If they drew blanks, they could widen out the search area. But Delilah figured that whoever was behind the threats was staying close by. There was that glimpse she'd caught of the trail bike from up above the Crag, for a start. There was also the rabbit itself, not exactly the kind of cargo you'd want to be bringing over all the way from Leeds. Plus she had a sense that the culprit was keeping an eye on Tyke. Perhaps was even aware that the Dales Detective Agency was providing surveillance and security. Or was it just coincidence that the latest threat had been delivered while Samson was away from Tyke's rental property?

Since she'd started working with Samson eighteen months ago, Delilah had learned to doubt the existence of such a thing as coincidence. It wasn't the only thing she had doubts about, as she walked up the stairs towards her office.

She was dreading this meeting. Just the two of them alone, something she'd been doing her best to avoid for a week now. The turmoil she was suffering only getting worse with each passing day as the wedding date got ever closer.

If she was going to act, she needed to do it soon. It was only fair.

She reached the landing, intending to go and put the kettle on in anticipation of Samson's arrival, but Tolpuddle had other ideas. Padding softly towards her office, he nudged the door open and walked in. Coming to an abrupt stop by the couch.

He looked back at her, surprise on his face.

Not as surprised as she was. Samson was lying there, full length on his back, an arm thrown above his head, and the sweetest expression on his face as his chest rose and fell in long steady breaths.

He was fast asleep.

Delilah felt her heart swoop. Wondered how she could harbour any reservations when it came to this amazing man. It was a thought which found her creeping backwards out of the office, whispering at Tolpuddle to follow her. The meeting could wait. After his days on surveillance, Samson had earned an undisturbed sleep.

The Weimaraner, however, was having none of it. Worn

out from his run on the fells, he jumped up onto the couch
and squeezed himself into a space by Samson's legs, curled
up and laid his head on his paws, regarding Delilah with a
defiant gaze.

Samson hadn't moved as the dog muscled in on his nap.
Not even a murmur. But Delilah knew if she insisted on
Tolpuddle accompanying her, the hound was capable of
letting out a wail which would drag the dead from their
slumber.

'Okay,' she muttered, 'you win!'

With Tolpuddle's eyes already closing, she turned around
and hurried back down the stairs. If she was quick, she could
do what she'd been trying to do for days and finally give
voice to her misgivings.

16

Danny was struggling to stay awake. Head nodding. Then the snap back to consciousness and the cramped position in the bushes behind Fellside Court. As he forced his eyes wide, yawned, and stretched what he could of his limbs given the conditions, he found his respect for Samson O'Brien growing exponentially.

As a detective with the Met and then the NCA, Samson had spent the majority of his career working undercover and on surveillance. Creeping around like Danny was now, like they'd done the night before. It was a career Danny had aspired to. The romance he'd attributed to this side of policing, however, was fast evaporating – it was one of the hardest things he'd done since he joined the force. Yet Samson had excelled at it.

Kudos, thought Danny. No wonder the man was a legend.

A movement from the far corner of the courtyard caught his eye. Delilah, on her own, striding towards the entrance in the wall of glass. She must know he was there, watching her. Yet she didn't let on, not even the slightest glimpse to see where he could be. A total professional.

Another one the young constable had on a pedestal. A successful businesswoman who'd overcome the twin tragedies of losing her brother and a disastrous marriage collapsed by infidelity, she was also a phenomenal runner. A fell runner, like Danny. Someone who could have won every race in the area if she'd kept it up. Might still do if her current form was anything to go on. She was every bit as much a legend as the man she was set to marry.

He watched her walk into the reception area, wondering idly where she was heading. She turned right, towards the stairs, appearing a minute later on the first floor, the expanse of glass allowing Danny full view. She paused. Looked out, straight at the bushes where he was crouching, making the constable duck, even though he knew he was well hidden. Then she placed a finger on her lips.

What on earth . . . ? Was she sending him a message? Asking for his silence? About what?

With a nod of her head, as though deciding on a difficult course of action, she turned and knocked on the door of the apartment nearest her.

Danny watched on in bewilderment, pen poised above his notepad, wondering if he ought to log this. Then the door opened, a familiar face appeared and the penny dropped . . . The best man! It had to be. Elated at the scoop, he checked his watch, trying to work out how soon he'd be able to get to the Fleece and get a bet on. And what odds tight-fisted Troy Murgatroyd would give him.

'You made it this time!'

Delilah blushed. 'I'm so sorry for all the last-minute cancellations. It's just . . . I didn't want anyone knowing . . .'

'That you're hanging out with a reprobate?' Joseph O'Brien laughed and gestured her inside. 'Come on in quick, before someone sees you. I'd hate to ruin your reputation.'

She entered the flat, a tight smile appearing at his attempt to lighten the atmosphere. The strain she was under visible on her face. As he followed her into the lounge, he wondered whether he'd be up to the task. Whether he'd be able to rescue a relationship which was heading off the rails.

'I'm more than a little worried that you're not on the mend,' Dr Naylor said, putting away his stethoscope and giving Clarissa a concerned look as she lay back on the bed. Exhausted from simply sitting up.

It had a fierce grip on her, this chest infection. Making her breathing laboured, causing her to cough continually, which was draining in itself, and leaving her as weak as a kitten.

'Do I need putting down?' she asked, smiling up at him.

He smiled back, shaking his head. 'Not just yet. But I think we monitor you closely for the next couple of days and if there's no improvement, then the next step will be to get you into hospital.'

She did her best to restrain the shudder that went through her at the suggestion. Hospital. She could barely believe she'd reached the age where what had started out as a mere cold could result in such a thing. How had that happened? Surely it was only yesterday she was a young woman with her life ahead of her.

'Let's try to make sure it doesn't come to that,' the doctor said softly, understanding her apprehension with his usual empathy.

He began packing his bag when a burst of laughter from Vinny's next door came through the open window. Annoyance flickered across his face before he looked at her.

'Want me to close the window?' he asked.

'Oh no,' she said, 'they're not disturbing me. It's nice to hear folk enjoying themselves.'

'As long as it's not at someone else's expense,' muttered the doctor.

'Do you mean Vinny?' said Clarissa, thrown by this uncharacteristic churlishness. 'Why, he wouldn't hurt a soul!'

The doctor paused, one eyebrow raised. 'I'm surprised you hold that view, given what he did to Edith.'

It took Clarissa a moment to process the statement. Another moment to try to work out what it meant. She was on the verge of requesting the clarification she needed when Dr Naylor suddenly looked abashed, mistaking her silence for reprobation.

'Sorry. Ignore me. I'm not myself today and I spoke out of turn.' He snapped his bag shut, nodded at her and headed for the door. 'I'll drop by in the morning, but I want you to promise me you'll call straight away if you feel yourself getting any worse during the night. Now, try to get some rest.'

And with that, he was gone, the door closing softly behind him. Another loud laugh carried through the window like a postscript to his departure. Clarissa lay back on the pillows, puzzled. And perturbed.

What had Dr Naylor meant? He'd never been one to gossip, so this slip of the tongue must have been provoked by something of consequence. Something which involved Edith and Vinny King and had led the doctor to form an unfavourable opinion of the latter.

Clarissa cast her mind back through the years, to the morning her sister had broken the news that her engagement to Vinny was off. Edith had been her usual pragmatic self, scoffing at the more emotional reaction from her tender-hearted sister.

'It was a mutual decision. We wouldn't have worked out,' Edith had finally said, exasperated by Clarissa's tears. 'We weren't compatible on so many levels. That's all there is to it.'

Clarissa had taken her at her word, believing that Edith's excess of common sense had overcome any romantic attachment. But here was Dr Naylor, five decades on, implying that there was way more to the failed betrothal than that. Which begged the question, how had the doctor come into that knowledge when Clarissa – who had lived cheek by jowl with Edith all their lives – had never heard so much of a whisper about it?

Glancing at the carriage clock on her bedside table, Clarissa realised she was going to have to wait until the following morning before she got any answers, because in less than half an hour the residents of Fellside Court would be heading off to watch *Romeo and Juliet*. Feeling frustrated at missing out on the play and equally frustrated at not being able to talk to her sister, Clarissa knew the rest the doctor had prescribed was going to be hard to attain.

'I'm having second thoughts.' Sitting in the comfort of his lounge, mug of tea in hand, if Delilah had expected her confession to shock the man who, in a few weeks' time, was supposed to become her father-in-law, she was wrong.

Joseph simply nodded. 'I suspected as much.'

'Was it that obvious?' she asked, tone wry.

He smiled. 'No, love. I recognised the signs.' He gestured at the photo album lying open on the coffee table between them. 'That's why I dug this out.'

Delilah leaned forward and picked up the album, a glorious shot of a young couple on display. They were standing by a stone wall in a field, the man wearing a suit, the woman in a simple knee-length white dress, smiles wide, the fells rising up behind them in late summer colour.

Bride and groom.

'We got married after the hay harvest,' said Joseph. 'That was on the way back from Richmond registry office – we took the scenic route to Reeth, where we were renting. Nearly burned out the clutch on my old Allegro coming over the tops. Then Kathleen spotted a farmer by the side of the road, so we pulled over and she got him to take this. He did a good job considering how nervous he was!'

'It's stunning,' said Delilah.

'It's the only photo we have of the day. Kathleen didn't want fuss, no church wedding, nothing, not after the commotion with her family—'

'What commotion?'

'Samson's never said?'

Delilah shook her head.

'Ah well, perhaps he wasn't wanting to stir up a past he had no part of. Thing is, Kathleen's family were strict Wesleyans and they weren't that keen on her marrying an itinerant farm labourer over from Ireland. Not even one that was willing to convert. They thought she was too young and my prospects were too limited.'

'How old was she?' asked Delilah, looking closer at the photograph, recognising the strength in Kathleen's features as that shared by Samson.

'Nineteen. I was only a bit older myself. But we were certain.' He shrugged. 'Until I wasn't.'

Delilah looked up, surprised. 'You were the one to get cold feet?'

'Aye,' he laughed. 'Mad, when you think of it. She was way too good for me. But that was the problem.' He took the album from Delilah and flicked through a few pages, coming to rest on an earlier photograph, Kathleen sitting on the edge of some limestone pavement, laughing into the camera, her vibrancy tangible. 'I mean, just look at her. Why would someone that special want to spend their life with me? And to go against her family in order to do so?' He shook his head. 'It just didn't make sense.'

'What happened to change your mind?'

'Ha! I was too much of a coward, that's what happened.' He turned back to the wedding photo. 'It was just us. No family. A couple of witnesses the registrar provided. So I went along that day fully intending to tell her before we went in. To halt the whole thing before she made a huge mistake and sacrificed her family for something that she might regret.

'But then I saw her, standing outside the registrar's, and I just couldn't do it. Not because I was being noble or anything.' He snorted. 'No, I was being entirely selfish. I took one look at her, and put my love for her before any thoughts about mistakes or possible problems down the line.' He shrugged, smiled. 'It worked out for the best.'

'Did her family come round to the idea once you were married?' asked Delilah.

A sadness descended on Joseph. 'Never. Not even when Samson was born. Kathleen sent over some photos, hoping a newborn baby would melt hearts which we couldn't, but to no avail. And I tried again when Kathleen got her diagnosis but . . .' He sighed. 'We might as well have emigrated to New Zealand when we left Arkengarthdale.'

Delilah looked at the wedding photo again, the scene made more poignant by the knowledge of what a sacrifice Kathleen had made for the man she loved. She glanced up at Joseph, his eyes on her, anxious.

'Has it helped any?' he asked. 'With whatever it is that's making you nervous?'

She nodded. 'Kind of. But there's still the root question.'

'Which is?'

'How do I know this is the right thing to do? I mean, it was all so sudden. The proposal out of the blue and in public, all set against the euphoria of the auction . . . How do I know that Samson meant it? That it wasn't just a result of the occasion? And how can I be sure of my own response in return?'

A slow smile spread across Joseph's face. 'Trust,' he said gently. 'Trust that you know Samson. And most of all, trust yourself.'

'But that's the problem,' said Delilah, finally airing out loud the fear she'd been carrying for months. 'How can I trust myself when I've already proved that I can't make a marriage work?'

As the tears started down her cheeks, Joseph came and sat next to her, putting an arm around her shaking shoulders.

17

Arty had gone for a walk through the town to clear his head but arrived back at the apartment no less troubled than when he'd left. And to find Edith sitting on the couch, hands clenched, the sunlight streaming over her shoulders and the gentle breeze through the open windows making the curtains flutter.

'We need to talk.' She gestured to the armchair opposite.

He sat down slowly, his instinct to stall. To put off what felt like the inevitable. He gestured at the antique school clock on the wall. 'Have you got time? Aren't you leaving for the play soon?'

'What I've got to say won't take long.'

There was something contradictory in the scene, Arty noted, a disparity between the seriousness of Edith's face, the tone of her voice and the gentleness of the day around them. At least, he thought, he was about to get his heart broken when it was sunny. Better that than on a miserable grey day.

Maybe.

'You want me to move out?' he said. No recrimination. Just acceptance.

She jerked backwards, eyes wide. 'Why ever would you think that?'

He shrugged. 'Things haven't been right. Not since . . . not since . . . well, you know.'

Her head dipped. She nodded. 'Vinny.'

'Yeah, Vinny. You're still in love with him?'

A loud snort issued from her, her head snapping up, a look of disbelief, possibly even humour. 'Don't be daft. It's impossible for anyone to love Vinny King – apart from Vinny King himself. He doesn't exist. He's a creation of the world he chose when he left here.'

Arty was puzzled now, feeling wrong-footed, like the one time he'd boxed against a southpaw and hadn't known which way to send his jabs. Hoping he wasn't about to be knocked out like he had been back then, he reached across the coffee table and took Edith's hand.

'So what the hell is going on between you two?' he asked.

She looked at him, a tension about her that he'd never seen before. Then she gave that nod she always gave before she did or said something that needed doing but wasn't going to be pleasant.

'I should have told you before, but there never seemed to be an appropriate moment. Vinny and I were engaged, as you know. But what you don't know – what no one knows, not even Clarissa – is that we didn't break it off in mutual agreement.'

'And? After all these years, why does it matter who jilted who?' he asked.

'Whom,' she said, smiling.

He laughed at the instinctive correction, squeezed her hand. But her smile had already faded.

'It matters because of why we separated. Vinny King – or Vinny Ramsbottom as I knew him – always wanted the bright lights, to head off to London and find fame. I've always been much more of a homebird and I loved my job working in the primary school, hated the idea of giving it up. It was a constant bone of contention between us. But when he proposed, I thought he'd accepted that his dream of a life in showbusiness would never happen. That he'd knuckle down and make something of his position at the paper mill.' She gave a sardonic laugh. 'More fool I. He left me six months later on a Sunday night. Just popped a note through the door of the house. Thank goodness I was downstairs first and found it before Father.'

'Vinny didn't tell you face to face?'

She shook her head. 'But at least he waited for half-term so I didn't have to go into school and face a class of students. He also left it up to me to tell everyone else, so I got to put my spin on it. To say it was mutual, when it had been anything but.'

Arty shrugged. 'So why is this causing problems now? Surely it's ancient history.'

'Not quite.' Edith let go of his hand. Sat upright. Face pained. 'There's more to it. Vinny didn't just break my heart. He took all of my money, too.'

Arty felt his jaw drop. Blood rushing around his body. 'The bastard!'

'For once, I wholeheartedly agree with your profanity.'

'How much?'

'Does it matter now? Suffice to say, I'd been saving up for quite a few years, putting money in an account, planning to buy somewhere to live, so it was a substantial amount.'

'But how did he get the money? Wasn't it in your name?'

'He persuaded me to open a joint account after we got engaged . . .' Edith lifted her shoulders, a shrug of incomprehension as though she still didn't understand why she'd gone along with it. 'That's what makes me mad after all this time – that I was stupid enough to do as he asked. That I didn't suspect a thing. The only consolation – and it wasn't much of one – was that I was pretty sure I wasn't the only one fooled by him. But of course, because I never breathed a word about this to anyone, I could never be certain.' She looked at him. 'So there you have it. I'm an idiot of the first order and I've been covering it up all my life.'

Arty stood, stepped round the coffee table and sat next to her on the sofa, his arm going round her. 'You're the smartest person I've ever met, Edith Hird. Shrewd. Honest. Still willing to see the best in people despite that experience. Me living here is evidence of that! So don't be so hard on yourself. It's all in the past and there's little you can do about it now.' He winked, lifting both hands up into fists in front of him. 'Unless you want me to go round and show him some bright lights of a more painful kind?'

She gave a small smile, patted his knee. 'Thing is, it's not all in the past. I thought I could cope with him moving back, living here in the place I call home. And I have been able to, better than I thought. But he keeps pestering me.'

'To start a relationship with him again?'

'No. Not at all. He wants to make amends.'

Arty blinked. 'What? How?'

'He wants to leave me the Hockney in his will.'

There was a stunned moment of silence. Then Arty found himself laughing. And laughing. And laughing. So gripped by the irony of it all that he couldn't break off to explain to the woman he loved quite what was so hilarious.

Another gale of laughter filtered down to Danny's hiding place from one of the apartments, this time from somewhere off to his left, towards the front of the building.

Whatever else he took away from this long afternoon of surveillance, he would be leaving with an even greater appreciation for how happy the residents were in Fellside Court. An afternoon which was about to – thankfully – come to a close, judging by the growing number of people gathering in the foyer and the arrival of a Bruncliffe Taxis minibus in the car park.

The door to the courtyard opened and a pensive Delilah emerged, some of the group heading to see the play taking that as a cue for their departure, following her out like a flock of parrots, all sound and colour. While Delilah walked away from them, they milled around on the patio, Danny doing his best to see if Vinny King was among them. Because if he was, then Tyke must surely be about to head home.

He spotted the former talk-show host, debonair in a tweed suit, crimson handkerchief in his jacket pocket, moving through the chattering group. Beside him was Geraldine Mortimer, equally resplendent in a shimmering silver dress more suited to a night at the opera than Bruncliffe Community Hall. And behind them, Danny's grandad, Eric, flanked by Edith Hird and Joseph O'Brien, the three of them looking up at the window of the flat above where Clarissa was waving. Joseph blew her a kiss and she pretended to catch it while Eric rolled his eyes, and Danny was so caught up in watching them that he almost messed up.

Almost. What saved him was the flash of orange and lime. Baseball cap low, a messenger bag across his body and wearing one of his loudest ensembles yet, Tyke was moving around the back of the pensioners, cutting down the side of the building at speed, clearly not wanting to get waylaid.

Thrusting his notebook in his rucksack, Danny went to jump up and his numb leg collapsed under him, tipping him out of the bushes and into full view of those gathered in the courtyard. There was a moment of startled silence from the residents and then laughter as the constable staggered to his feet.

'You taken up birdwatching like your grandfather, young Danny?' came one amused shout.

'Happen as he's forgotten his binoculars,' quipped Eric.

'Aye, more like Sergeant Clayton's got him watching us because of all our drug habits!' joked another.

With more good-natured abuse following him, Danny did his best to hobble after his target. But the vibrant figure of Tyke was already out of sight around the front of the complex. Cursing the pins and needles which were now sending fire along the nerves of his left calf, the constable made his way towards the Enfield, praying he'd be able to ride it.

Silence reigned in the office building as, with somewhat lighter steps than when she'd left it earlier that afternoon, Delilah quietly climbed the stairs. She was met at the top by a sleepy Weimaraner. Sleepy and hungry, judging by the way Tolpuddle was gazing longingly towards the kitchen.

She led him into the narrow room, the day lingering softly outside as it gave its typically slow summer goodbye, casting a mellow lustre across the town. She shook a small helping of food into Tolpuddle's bowl – just enough to get him up the hill to home – and then, taking a big breath, headed for her office. It was time to confess.

To confess everything she'd just told her future father-in-law. Because that's what she was hoping Joseph would be. Only trouble was, as she'd explained to him through her tears, she'd messed everything up. So unnerved by her doubts, she'd let everything slide. The wedding venue unconfirmed.

The celebrant not organised. She didn't even have a dress! Every time Samson had asked her how the planning was going or offered to help with it, she'd insisted he left it to her. And now none of it was done and it was too late.

In short, there would be no wedding.

Dreading the conversation to come, she headed for the office. A loud snore greeted her as she crossed the threshold, her fiancé still dead to the world on the sofa. She brushed a hand across his hair, saw a flicker of a dreamy smile in response. Nothing more.

Deciding to let him sleep while he had the chance, she bent down to leave a light kiss on his forehead, collected Tolpuddle, who'd already inhaled his snack, and went back down the stairs. As she stepped out into the yard, she was too far away to hear the buzz of the mobile up on her desk.

Not hers, but Samson's, the alarm he'd set going off unheard. It buzzed for ten minutes then fell silent. Samson failed to wake. Failed to head off and relieve the inexperienced Danny Bradley of his surveillance duties as planned.

18

The frantic departure in Tyke's wake, followed by a very painful ride on the Enfield as sensation returned to his sleeping leg, had left Danny with an appetite. He was ravenous. Which was a slight problem as, thanks to the sheer boredom that had set in as he sat outside Fellside Court, he'd been dipping into his rucksack on a regular basis. Now, with the entire night still stretching ahead of him, he had nothing left of his provisions bar a couple of bruised bananas.

He peeled one and bit into it, wishing he could swap it for a Rice N Spice lamb desi. Or one of Kay Murgatroyd's mouth-watering steak and ale pies from the Fleece. Followed by a couple of Lucy Metcalfe's blueberry and almond tarts.

In protest at such cruel imaginings, his stomach let out a low growl. Danny finished the banana and switched his focus to the house he was supposed to be guarding.

Nothing was happening. Just as nothing had been happening for the last half an hour since he'd started his surveillance. He'd taken the back route out of town and left the Enfield parked up at the derelict barn as Samson had shown him, then he'd trekked across the field and arrived at the back of Tyke's property just as the fashion designer crossed in front of the kitchen window in a blur of orange and lime zigzags.

Julia Chapman

At least the man was easy to keep track of.

In the far corner of the house, a lamp near a window suddenly spilled light through the glass. Early, given the sky was still blue, albeit the sun was slanting low across the fields behind Danny. He saw Tyke disappear from view into an armchair, the television going on in the background. From the floor above, the room Samson had said was Eloise's studio, came the soft sound of music through the open sash.

Suspecting it was all a bit futile, Danny made a few sparse notes on the limited action in the household. Time, location, nature of activity.

Another rumble of hunger and he let out a groan, sensing it was going to be a very dull and very long night. He found himself wishing something would happen. Something which would relieve this boredom and stop him from thinking about food all the time.

In Bruncliffe Community Hall the evening was in full swing. With the live broadcast of *Romeo and Juliet* still fifteen minutes away, the main hall was resonant with chat and laughter, the residents of Fellside Court taking up the majority of the tables which were laid out in cabaret style around the large room.

'These pre-show cocktails were a great idea!' said Eric Bradley, holding up what Ana Stoyanovic suspected was his third Martini.

Ana had decided to accompany the group at the last minute, Grigore having persuaded her he was capable of looking after Luka. She'd left the pair of them playing football in the garden as Grigore's homemade *mici* sizzled on the barbecue, the delicious smells coming from the Romanian sausages almost tempting her back. But when she arrived at the hall, she'd been invited to join Eric, Joseph and Edith at their table and so far was enjoying herself immensely. And unless she was mistaken, she wasn't the only one, a much lighter mood prevailing among those she was sitting with compared to earlier. Certainly Edith seemed in better form, a sparkle to her eyes which had been missing for a while.

'Let's hope you're still saying that tomorrow morning,' the former headmistress retorted to Eric with a benevolent smile as she sipped at her daiquiri.

'Mocktails too,' said Joseph O'Brien, raising his glass to clink with his friends.

A loud clap of hands from a table at the front brought a hush to the audience, everyone turning to see Vinny King, who was standing, his own cocktail raised high, his flushed complexion suggesting he wasn't on his first drink either.

'To the phenomenal folk of Fellside Court!' he said, getting a rousing cheer in response. 'And,' he added with a wink, 'here's to all the star-crossed lovers out there!'

More cheering as he sat down and the volume of noise rose around him, conversations resumed, drinks consumed.

'Got to give it to your ex-boyfriend, Edith,' said Eric, nudging her playfully, 'this was a brilliant idea.'

Edith hmphed in response and Ana looked at her, surprised.

'I didn't know you and Vinny had a history,' she said.

A smile twisted Edith's lips. 'Oh yes. We go way back.'

'Is that why Arty—?' Ana broke off, realising she could be overstepping a line. But Edith just shrugged.

'Doesn't care for Vinny?' she said, eyebrow arched as she finished Ana's question. 'Yes. Among other things.'

'Is that why he didn't come tonight?'

Edith laughed. 'Goodness, no. Arty would never let something so trivial prevent him from enjoying himself. Truth is, he's not a fan of the theatre. He finds it too intense, especially if it's a bad production. So he decided he'd rather stay in and watch television. Plus he's offered to keep an eye on Clarissa.'

'Is she any better?' Eric asked.

'She doesn't seem to be,' said Edith, frowning. 'Dr Naylor has mentioned the possibility of her going to hospital.'

Joseph leaned over and patted her hand. 'I'm sure it won't come to that. Clarissa is a tough cookie, she'll get over this.'

'Joseph's right,' said Ana, sensing Edith's understandable concern. 'But I'll drop by on my way home and check in on her.'

'Oh,' said Edith, looking grateful, 'that would put my mind at rest. Thank you.'

The lights started to dim and an expectant murmur went around the room as the screen suddenly blazed into life and the play began. For a few minutes silence settled on the audience. Until there was a disruption of voices from the front.

Vinny King, standing up, patting his pockets. Muttering. Geraldine Mortimer standing too, flapping about something.

'Sit down!' called out a voice impatiently from behind. 'You're blocking my view!'

'Sorry. Sorry,' Vinny was mumbling, then he was threading his way through tables, Geraldine trailing him.

'Is everything okay?' Ana leaned over as Vinny went by, touching his arm to get his attention. She wasn't officially at work but the truth was, she felt a duty of care that never switched off.

'I've brought the wrong blasted glasses,' Vinny murmured. 'I'm going to ask the minibus driver to drop me back to get my others.'

'I'm going with him,' whispered Geraldine, a proprietorial hand on his elbow.

There was a subdued snort from Edith, sitting next to Ana. But she didn't volunteer anything beyond that.

Ana nodded. Satisfied it was nothing serious, she settled back to enjoy the play as the doors at the back of the hall clattered closed in the wake of Vinny and Geraldine's departure.

Clarissa wasn't feeling very well. Thoroughly fed up at missing a night out to the theatre, she'd got up from her sick bed, slipped her dressing gown over her pyjamas and headed into the kitchen to make a hot chocolate, hoping that the treat would both help her feel better and compensate in some way for not being able to participate in what she was sure would be an excellent evening's entertainment.

But the hot chocolate had failed to hit the spot, making her stomach a bit unsettled instead. And then she'd been struck with a coughing fit which had seen her stagger into the lounge and collapse on the sofa, breath coming in short pants, a searing pain in her head.

She sat there now, waiting for her heart to stop pattering, and for her breathing to calm, while wondering if she should give Dr Naylor a call. She glanced at the clock above the television. Almost eight. It wasn't too late. But she hated to be a nuisance, and besides, the coughing had eased. If only the throbbing in her temples would subside, too.

What would Edith do?

It was a question Clarissa had found herself asking many times during her life, like when she was in danger of being sunk by the grief which followed her husband's death in a car accident. The mantra focusing on her pragmatic older sister had got her through the toughest of moments back then. And right now, Clarissa knew exactly what Edith would prescribe.

She took her mobile from the coffee table and made the call. It rang several times before voicemail kicked in, Dr Naylor's calm tones asking her to leave a message. Apologising profusely, she did as she was bid, her voice rasping at the effort of speaking, then she ended the call, already feeling guilty at having disturbed the man. A few more minutes sitting and she would be right as rain. She was sure of it.

From outside, filtering through the open window, came the sound of voices. A man and a woman, crossing the courtyard, high heels clicking on the patio slabs.

Wondering who it could be, given that pretty much everyone had gone to Bruncliffe Community Hall, Clarissa got to her feet, sending her head reeling. She paused for a second to get her balance and then moved gingerly to the window. She peered out just in time to see Vinny King and Geraldine Mortimer reach the entrance below.

'Stop following me like a lap dog,' Vinny snapped over his shoulder, jerking the door open and letting it slam behind him as he headed inside.

Geraldine was left out in the courtyard, looking furious at the rebuke. She stood for a few moments before going over to one of the wrought-iron chairs which decorated the patio and sitting heavily onto it, her back to the entrance. She rubbed her feet, flexing them, fiddling with the straps on her stiletto sandals. Clarissa was about to move away, tired from standing and her head thumping, when something caught her eye. Someone on the same floor as her, looking down on Geraldine from behind the sheer glass.

It was Arty, at the far end of the main corridor. He pulled back from the window and turned, facing towards the lift outside Clarissa's flat. He nodded down the corridor at someone she couldn't see. Jaw set. As though the greeting had been begrudgingly given. For a few seconds he stood there, seemingly debating with himself. Then he started walking purposely along the length of the glass wall towards her side of the building.

From down below came a scrape of metal. Geraldine on her feet, turning, moving towards the entrance.

The insatiable curiosity she had for drama would normally have kept Clarissa in her post, watching Geraldine and Arty, waiting to see what happened. But the pain in her head was bad now, as was the dizziness. Feeling an urgent need to lie down, she crossed the room, a hand going out to steady herself on the armchair as she passed it. She got no further than the sofa before collapsing onto its cushions and into oblivion.

Danny had just peeled his last banana when he saw movement within the house. A flash of orange and lime. Tyke, leaving the lounge. Even across the distance of the large back garden, there was a visible sense of haste. Danny made a note of it. And continued eating. Trying to savour what could be his last food for a while.

Several minutes later a door slammed and Tyke emerged, running across the gravel to the Porsche in a change of outfit, his jacket and tracksuit bottoms now festooned with huge orchids in fuchsia against a deep purple background, his trade-mark baseball cap the only constant.

Caught unawares, Danny had no time to admire the latest get-up. Or to finish his banana.

'Shit!' he exclaimed into the bushes surrounding him as he leaped up. Then he was off over the back wall as the Porsche pulled away from the house at speed. Phone in his hand, heart rate skyrocketing, he ran across the field towards the motor-bike. Their target had just gone AWOL.

The phone finally woke him.

Lifting a groggy head from the couch, Samson blinked a few times, saw the time on his watch, cursed, and then recognised the sound. He reached for his mobile.

'Danny?'

There was a stream of indecipherable panic from the other end, all overlaid by heavy breathing.

'Slow down, Danny! I can't understand a word you're saying!' Samson was already rising, moving. Knowing something bad was happening.

'It's Tyke!' came an exclamation. 'He's left the house and I don't know where he's going! I've lost him! I'm so sorry!'

Samson was at the landing, heading down the stairs two at a time as he assessed the situation.

'Okay, let's not overreact,' he said. 'I'll call him and get an idea of where he's heading and go after him.' Then he remembered he didn't have transport. 'The Enfield!'

'I'm just at it,' Danny was saying over the roar of the engine starting up in the background. 'I'll come and drop it off.'

The buzz of a text interrupted the call. Tyke's name on the screen. Relief flooding through Samson as he read it.

'It's okay, Danny. Panic over,' he said. 'Tyke's gone to his uncle's flat, something about returning a pair of glasses he took by mistake. I'll jog over there now, so if you park up at the library, we can make the switch and he'll never know it wasn't me on his tail all evening.'

'Thank God,' muttered Danny. 'I'll see you there.'

The call ended and Samson was left in the hall of the office building, lamenting the excessive sleep which had scuppered his plans to relieve Danny. For while it seemed a harmless lapse on his part, there was still the fact that the subject of his surveillance, the man who had tasked Samson with keeping him safe, was out in the wild without protection.

The thought had Samson running out the back door and up the ginnel towards the marketplace and Fellside Court beyond it.

Caught in the grip of her illness, Clarissa was in a world of jumbled dreams and wild imaginings. She heard voices. A couple of exclamations. All embroidered by her fevered mind into a tapestry of nightmares. Even the loud thud failing to pierce her sleep. Afterwards, she wasn't able to say how long she was out of things. All she knew was that she was woken by the shrill sound of screaming.

And that it was coming from outside her front door.

19

The scream was like an alarm, pulling Clarissa back to consciousness and driving her to her feet with a primordial fear.

Death. That was the only thing which could have triggered such a harrowing sound.

She stumbled across the lounge and into the hall, hands on the walls to steady her progress, head spinning. With a monumental effort she pulled open her front door, the scream even louder, nerve-shredding.

Geraldine Mortimer was in the corridor, both hands at her mouth as if trying to capture her deathly wail, eyes wide with shock, her focus on something inside the neighbouring flat to the right, beyond Clarissa's line of sight.

'What's happening?' Clarissa rasped, making her way to her neighbour's open door, leaning forward to see around the door jamb.

A lamp smashed on the floor in the hall, shards of glass everywhere. Beyond it, a pair of legs. Stretching out from the lounge. Someone lying face down. Confused, Clarissa took an unsteady step inside, wishing Geraldine would stop screaming.

'Call a bloody ambulance,' came a rough command.

Arty. Crouched down in the archway to the lounge over whoever it was. Then another voice from the stairwell by the lift.

'What's going on?' Dr Naylor running along the corridor towards them, bag in his hand, the shock of his appearance making Geraldine's screams subside into tears.

'In here!' shouted Arty. 'He needs help.'

Dr Naylor ran past Clarissa and into the flat where he dropped to his knees, shoving Arty aside as he started checking the prostrate figure. Then he was rolling him over and Clarissa saw a glasses case. And blood.

She had to look away, the floor tilting dramatically beneath her feet.

'We need an ambulance,' Arty was saying into his mobile, eyes fixed on the doctor and his patient, his own shirt and hands smeared with red. 'Fellside Court, Bruncliffe. Quickly.'

But the doctor was shaking his head. Grim-faced.

From out in the corridor Geraldine let out another wail. High-pitched and agonised. Clarissa turned, too quickly. Was aware of the stair door banging, of feet running towards them. Then her legs gave way and she slid down the wall to the floor.

Arriving at Fellside Court out of breath and heart pounding, Samson headed straight for the car park, relieved to see Tyke's Porsche there, bonnet warm to the touch. The relief didn't last long.

Parked next to it at an angle that suggested haste was a police car. Blue lights still flashing.

Samson hurried round the back of the building and almost collided with Danny, coming from the far side, motorcycle helmet in hand. Eyes wide.

'What's going on?' he asked. 'Sarge went roaring past me at the viaduct, lights going. I saw him pull in here.'

'Search me, but it can't be good,' muttered Samson. He looked up, the glass wall above the courtyard ablaze with light and every window in Clarissa and Vinny's flats illuminated. Something definitely wasn't right. 'Come on. Let's see what's happening.'

He started moving towards the entrance but Danny was hesitant.

'Won't it blow our cover if we both go in?'

The question was punctuated by a loud hammering from above, a strained Sergeant Clayton looking down at them, fist thumping the glass. He beckoned them inside.

'I think,' said Samson with growing trepidation, 'that the time for worrying about being covert is long since past.'

Samson and Danny ran up the stairs and arrived on the first-floor corridor into a tense silence.

Arty Robinson, shirt stained red, was leaning against the cupboard by the stairs, his face as white as the linen Ida kept within it. Geraldine Mortimer was sitting in one of the armchairs in the main corridor that looked out over the courtyard, eyes unfocused, deep in shock as her hands worked in her lap, twisting a handkerchief into tight knots. Meanwhile, Clarissa Ralph was slumped in another armchair, Dr Naylor kneeling by her side, frowning, her wrist in his hand as he took her pulse.

Standing at the start of the spur which led down towards the four apartments in the north wing of the building was a strained-looking Sergeant Clayton. And Tyke. Very much alive, if distressed, the gaiety of the pink orchids decorating his clothing striking a discordant note with the shock etched into his face.

'Is everything okay?' Samson asked his client, his reassurance about Tyke's safety turning to puzzlement as to the cause of the tension. 'What's going on?'

'Thank God you're here,' said the fashion designer, starting to move forward.

'We've no time for emotional reunions,' snapped the sergeant, fixing Tyke to the spot with a glare before gesturing at the wing of the building behind him. 'Danny, lad, I need this corridor roped off. No one in or out. Not even residents. When you've got that done, I'll give you a quick debrief and then we'll need statements from this lot. All of them. As for you, O'Brien. With me. And look sharp.'

Samson gave Danny a shrug of incomprehension before starting to follow the sergeant down the corridor. But Dr Naylor intervened.

'Sergeant, I'm sorry, but I'm going to have to pull rank here.' He got to his feet and crossed towards them in quick strides. When he spoke it was quietly but insistently. 'Clarissa Ralph needs to be taken to hospital. Immediately.'

The sergeant glanced over the doctor's shoulder to where Clarissa was listing to one side in her chair, skin waxen, breath coming in rasps. Sensing his indecision, the doctor pressed on.

'I realise you have procedure to follow but if she doesn't get proper medical care promptly then I suspect you will have two deaths to deal with.'

'*Two* deaths?' Samson's head snapped towards the sergeant, who held up a hand to silence him.

'Okay, Doc,' he murmured. 'But she'll need to be interviewed as soon as she's able. You too.'

The doctor nodded. 'I'll report to the police station the minute I'm back from the hospital.'

'You're taking her yourself?' asked Samson.

'I have to. I can't risk waiting for an ambulance.' Without seeking any further corroboration, the doctor went back to

Clarissa and gently began guiding her towards the lift. In the distance came the sound of sirens. Multiple.

'Come on, O'Brien,' snapped the sergeant, setting off down the corridor. 'We don't have all day.'

They went past Clarissa's flat and on to her neighbour's. The door wide open.

'Now listen up.' Sergeant Clayton stopped at the doorway and laid a wide hand on Samson's chest. 'I'll be skinned alive for letting you in here now you're not on the force, but I value your input in cases and this one looks set to be nasty. So let's get in and out as fast as we can before the big boys arrive and take over. And don't forget, this is a crime scene, so act accordingly.'

He stepped aside and Samson could see glass scattered across the floor just inside the door, and a pair of legs protruding through the archway of the lounge. Careful to keep his steps to the far edge of the tiles, he walked along the hallway to get a better view.

A man, lying on his back, dressed in an elegant tweed suit and smart shoes, crimson handkerchief in his jacket pocket, a green glasses case by his side. A man who was very dead.

'Vinny?' Shocked, Samson looked back at the sergeant, who'd remained in the doorway.

'None other,' muttered the sergeant. 'Thoughts?'

Samson squatted down, not touching anything, assessing the situation. Noticing the blood soaking into the carpet under the dead talk-show host's head, the same colour as his handkerchief. Noticing the object on the floor just beyond the body.

A long silver twist of metal, topped by a small globe and descending to a heavy base bearing some sort of inscription. A trophy. The globe stained red. More blotches on the base.

He lifted his focus up, onto the small sideboard, noticing

other trophies. Noticing a gap between them. And above, arrayed all over the wall, photos of Vinny King in his heyday and a painting of a swimming pool, oddly serene amidst the carnage of the room.

He turned back for another look at the dead man.

'Was he found like this?' he asked.

'No, he was face down. The doc turned him over, checking for signs of life.'

Face down. Samson leaned lower, seeing it now, just about discernible from this angle. The edge of a wound on the back of Vinny's head.

He straightened up, retracing his steps as closely as he could, and paused in the hall. The glass was from a lamp, smashed and on the floor. Presumably fallen from the console table to the left of the front door which now only held a small ceramic bowl. He peered into it. Spare change and a key on a keyring. On the wall above were three hooks, two empty, a set of car keys hanging from the third.

He was about to step back out into the corridor when he spotted a second glasses case by the skirting board just inside the flat, this one navy blue.

'Tyke dropped that when he arrived,' said the sergeant, following his gaze. 'Said he was bringing it back to his uncle. Seems there was some mix-up which was what brought Vinny back here.'

'What do you mean brought him back?'

'From the play.' At Samson's raised eyebrow, Sergeant Clayton continued. 'Pretty much all the residents have gone down to Bruncliffe Community Hall to watch a live stream of *Romeo and Juliet*. Apparently, Vinny took the wrong glasses with him and came back to swap them.' He gestured back towards the body. 'Any chance it was an accident?'

The question was filled with hope. Hope Samson couldn't fulfil.

'Not unless that trophy jumped up and hit him of its own accord.'

'So we're talking a deliberate attack?'

'Looks that way. And whoever it was, I'd say Vinny knew them. There's no sign of a forced entry or of the lock being picked. So unless someone had a key—'

'I think we can rule that out. I asked Geraldine Mortimer about the chances of anyone having a spare and she said Vinny wouldn't hear of it. He said it would invalidate his contents insurance . . .' The sergeant shrugged and nodded towards the bowl on the console table and the key within it. 'She said that's the only spare in there.'

Samson glanced again at the key and then towards the lounge, playing through the sequence of events in his mind. 'In which case, we're looking at two possibilities. Either Vinny was already in his flat and someone knocked at the door. He opened it, let them in, they followed him inside and then attacked him. Or he met them in the corridor as he returned from the play and they entered the flat together. But either way, the fact that Vinny wasn't supposed to be here suggests this wasn't premeditated. And that's before we even consider the choice of weapon.'

'An argument that got out of hand, then? Someone reaches for the nearest object . . .'

'Possibly.'

'Christ! The irony of it. The poor bloke organises some outing, comes back early because of a simple mistake and gets killed.'

Samson felt something shift and settle in his consciousness. A rustle of thought like a fieldmouse scurrying under fallen leaves and out of sight. He knew better than to chase it.

'Who found him?' he asked instead.

Sergeant Clayton glanced along the corridor towards where the others were gathered, Danny standing by them, bright tape strung across the hallway in a grim barrier. 'That,' he said, 'is what we need to find out.'

From the car park below came the sound of car doors slamming. Feet on the patio.

'Come on,' muttered the sergeant. 'Let's get you out of here. The detectives will already be wanting my guts for garters for letting two witnesses leave without being debriefed. Last thing I need is them knowing I let you inspect the crime scene, too.'

They hurried up the corridor together, ducking under the tape just as the door to the stairs flew open and a tall man walked through, thick fair hair cropped above a face which looked too young to be in authority.

'DS Benson,' said Sergeant Clayton with something close to relief, recognising the detective who'd overseen the last major case in the town eight months before. He held out a hand in welcome. 'Can't stay away from us?'

Benson grimaced. His astute glance taking in Samson, the nod he sent him half greeting half warning. 'What have we got?' he asked, pointedly turning back to the sergeant.

'I'm afraid it's looking like murder,' said Sergeant Clayton, as the door behind the detective opened again and a team of crime scene technicians appeared.

Whether it was the dramatic impact of the white suits, hoods pulled up, overshoes on, or the bleak assertion about the nature of the crime, Geraldine Mortimer suddenly stood up, roused from the stupor she'd been in. Handkerchief fluttering to the floor, she raised a hand and pointed at Arty.

'It was him! He killed him! He killed the only man I ever loved!'

20

Fellside Court was in turmoil. When Ana Stoyanovic's mobile rang in the darkened auditorium – a device she never turned off, given the responsibility of her position – it drew noises of disapproval from the audience around her as she left the room, phone to her ear. When she returned moments later and held an urgent whispered conversation with Edith Hird, she provoked even more criticism. But when Edith stood, along with Eric, Joseph and pretty much the entire contingent from the retirement complex, and hustled up the aisle, the rebukes turned to curiosity. Concern even. For what could possibly have happened to occasion the mass exodus of such a large group of people from an event they'd been so looking forward to?

Already the murder of Vinny King was having repercussions around the town.

For Delilah Metcalfe, the news – delivered in a rushed call from Samson – had brought her haring down from her cottage, Tolpuddle running beside her on his lead. When she arrived at the car park and saw the quantity of official vehicles and what looked like a local TV crew setting up cameras, the enormity of what had occurred hit home.

Hurrying across the courtyard, she reached the entrance,

Danny standing at the door looking hastily attired in his uniform.

'It's supposed to be residents only,' he muttered as she approached. He glanced over his shoulder and then gestured her in with his head. 'Quick, before you're seen.'

'Thanks, Danny.'

Inside the large entrance hall were clusters of pensioners, all sharing the same expression of disbelief. Horror even. Joseph O'Brien broke away from the nearest group and came over.

'Here,' he said, holding out a hand for Tolpuddle's lead, 'leave the big fella with me. You're going to have your work cut out. Besides, we could do with the distraction.' He ruffled the dog's ears.

'How's it going?' she asked as several figures in white oversuits came down the stairs and out into the courtyard, while Ana started gently herding the residents towards the communal lounge.

Joseph grimaced. 'They're still going over Vinny's apartment. But they're about to start interviewing the folk who were here when it happened. They're using the cafe.'

'And Samson?' she asked.

He pointed towards the closed kitchen door and raised a finger to his lips. 'Sergeant Clayton pulled a blinder.'

Not sure what he meant, she hurried across the hallway and saw Tyke sitting in an armchair to one side, head in his hands, Eloise perched on the arm of the chair, leaning against him, an air of vulnerability about the pair of them. In all the commotion of Vinny King's death, Delilah had completely forgotten about their client and the need to have him protected.

'Tyke,' she said, approaching him. 'I'm so sorry about your uncle. Let me call Gareth and ask him to come by and escort you both back home.'

Tyke looked up, the bruising from his impact with the tarmac in the marketplace five days before vivid against the ghostly pallor of his skin. He shook his head in dismissal. 'Don't worry about it. I'm hardly at risk here with all the police around and besides, I've got to wait to speak to them anyway. We can sort something out after that. For now, I want everyone focusing on catching whoever killed Uncle Vinny.'

Eloise shuddered, eyes closing. Tyke placed a hand over hers and murmured something in her ear. She nodded. A tear slipping out from under her closed eyelids. In that moment Delilah realised their relationship was significantly more than just employer and assistant. Tyke caught her glance and gave an apologetic shrug.

'I guess I should have been more up front about me and Eloise,' he said, 'but we don't care to advertise that we're a couple. The media knows enough about my life without giving them that as well.'

'That's totally understandable,' murmured Delilah. 'Just give Gareth a call when you're ready to leave.'

'Will do.'

Glad that at least Tyke had someone to comfort him in such shocking times, Delilah headed for the kitchen. She slipped inside and found Samson leaning against the counter on the right-hand side, facing the wall.

He turned, raised a finger to his lips in a replica of his father, and beckoned her over.

'Benson wouldn't let me sit in on the interviews,' he whispered, 'so Sergeant Clayton showed me in here and suggested I make a cup of tea and take my time about it. Didn't know what he meant until I saw these.'

He was gesturing in front of him at the glass serving hatches which led to the cafe next door. On the other side,

Date with Destiny

DS Benson was sitting at a table across from Geraldine Mortimer, Sergeant Clayton next to him. The sergeant glanced towards the hatch, Delilah instinctively jerking back, out of sight.

'No need,' whispered Samson with a grin. 'One-way mirror! Benson has no idea we're here.'

He gently slid the left side of the hatch open a crack, just as DS Benson began speaking.

'So, Mrs Mortimer,' the detective said, 'perhaps you could start with why you came back from the play early with Vinny King?'

Delilah reached into her bag and pulled out a notepad.

'He forgot his glasses.'

Geraldine Mortimer's voice quavered and DS Josh Benson knew, even without having met the woman before, that she was a long way from her usual self. Her hair was tousled, stray wisps sticking to her face, which was damp with tears. And there was an air of despair to her which was at variance with the shimmering fabric of her silver dress.

Hand shaking, she took a drink of water the sergeant had been thoughtful enough to provide, and continued.

'Or rather, he brought the wrong ones with him. Somehow he had his reading glasses in his distance glasses case. I offered to come back with him to get the right pair. Just for the company, you know.'

'Do you have any idea what time it was when you arrived back here?' asked Sergeant Clayton.

'Eight o'clock on the dot.' Geraldine indicated the watch on her wrist. 'I remember checking the time as we got out of the minibus and thinking we'd be lucky to get back to the play before the balcony scene.'

Benson nodded. 'So what happened then?'

'We came across the courtyard and then . . .' Geraldine bit her lip, a smear of lipstick left on her teeth. 'Then Vinny went up to his flat and I stayed outside.'

'You didn't go up with him?'

'No.'

'Why not?'

'He didn't want to wait for the lift and I didn't fancy climbing the stairs in these heels.' She gestured down at her feet to the pair of strappy stilettos she was wearing. 'So I left him to it. I nipped inside to the ladies' but then sat back on the patio to wait—' A sob broke from her, full of remorse. 'I should have gone with him. I could have saved him.'

Benson pushed a packet of tissues across the table. Geraldine took one, used it to wipe her eyes.

'Then what happened?' Benson asked gently. Restraining the urge to tell her to get to the point, aware of the pressure this case brought with it, even so early in the investigation.

'I . . . I felt he'd been a while. Ten minutes at least. So I thought I'd go up . . . see what was keeping him. I got the lift.' She stopped. Dabbed at her eyes again, composure barely holding. 'I didn't realise at first. When I saw the door open to his flat. I just thought he'd nipped in and . . . but then I saw the glass. The tiles covered in it. And that's when . . .' A ripple of shock went through her.

'Take your time, Mrs Mortimer,' said Sergeant Clayton. 'We're in no hurry.'

Geraldine nodded. Glanced down at her lap. 'I could see Vinny's legs on the floor, so I rushed in and I saw Arty Robinson.' She lifted her gaze. 'He'd killed him.'

The two officers shared a glance.

'What makes you so certain?' asked Benson.

'He was leaning over him, holding that blasted trophy, that's what. He killed Vinny, and I know why!'

DS Benson pushed his chair back from the table and rubbed his temples. Only a few hours into the case and already his head was pounding. That's what Bruncliffe did to you. He'd hoped he'd seen the back of the town from a professional point of view when they wrapped up that dreadful affair in the autumn. Yet here he was again, investigating another death.

'Coffee?' Sergeant Clayton had returned from escorting their first witness back into the communal lounge and was carrying two mugs, the sweet scent of roasted beans coming from them.

'You saint.' The detective took a mug, sipped it, hoped the caffeine would ease some of the tension.

Because this was tension of the highest level. A national treasure murdered in his own retirement apartment, with his own National Television Awards trophy. And if that wasn't bad enough, it was looking very likely the murderer had been a fellow resident. Benson had already had some of his team go through the CCTV footage from the onsite cameras, one situated above the front entrance and the other over the courtyard door, and so far they'd found nothing to raise the least suspicion that the attack on Vinny King had been perpetrated by an unknown intruder.

Vinny King. Dead.

Josh Benson couldn't get his head round it. While Vinny had been a star in a generation of television a bit older than his own tastes, his parents adored the man. The nation adored the man. Not only that but he was the uncle to yet another celebrity who was also held with great affection by the public – Tyke.

The same man who'd been one of the first on the scene to find his uncle dead.

The fact that Josh's superiors had already been on the phone promising him whatever he needed – extra manpower, expedited forensics, even access to the cloud-based digital fingerprint service which could turn results round in hours rather than days – testified to just how high-profile this case was. And to the pressure he was going to be under to find the killer. All while under incredible scrutiny.

Some of that scrutiny would come from the growing number of journalists starting to gather by the entrance to the car park outside, Constable Danny Bradley having moved the cordon out that far to keep them at bay. The murder of Vinny King was destined to sell newspapers. Add in the theory just advanced by Geraldine Mortimer – that the roots of the crime lay in a broken tryst from the past arousing jealousy in the present, all among a cast well advanced in years – and the media was going to go into a frenzy.

There was absolutely no room for mistakes.

'We need to get this right,' muttered the sergeant, as though reading Benson's thoughts. 'Not go jumping to conclusions or building our case on hearsay.'

'You don't think Mrs Mortimer is telling the truth?'

A heavy shrug came in response. 'I'm not doubting as to what she says she saw or her reasoning for motive. All I'm saying is, let's hear everyone out before we go making any moves. There's going to be a lot of eyes on us. You in particular.'

'Thanks.' Benson let the sarcasm show.

He got another shrug in return.

He'd taken the unusual step of having Gavin Clayton sit in on the informal statement-taking with him, knowing the man's presence would be a reassuring one for the residents of the complex. But he'd also wanted the sergeant's insight, having worked with him before and respecting his opinions.

Even if Clayton's local loyalties had led him to go behind Benson's back on occasion during that last case. Passing on inside information . . .

'Has O'Brien gone home?' Benson asked, casually.

'I suspect so.' The sergeant studied his mug. A mulishness to him which had first surfaced when Benson explained that, as Samson O'Brien was no longer a serving officer, it wouldn't be appropriate for him to be part of the interview process. In an investigation this high-profile, things had to be done by the book. Especially as the detective was well aware that the book would be stopping with him if things went pear-shaped.

It was a shame about O'Brien, though. The man was an excellent investigator. And his team at the Dales Detective Agency had proven themselves more than adept at solving crimes. But Benson had no choice but to sacrifice that additional input when there was so much at stake.

He rubbed the back of his neck, the stress tightening the tendons, already reaching down into his shoulders with spikes of pain. He also felt a strange sense of being under scrutiny. Literally. A tingling in his spine as though there was someone spying on him.

He looked towards the wall to his right, the counter in front of it, sauces and condiments arrayed neatly, teapots and mugs on shelves behind. In the mirror of the serving hatch, he saw the reflection of the crimson sky outside as the day slowly slid to a close. Silhouetted against the fiery backdrop, he appeared as a worried and weary man. One who already looked like things were going wrong.

Shrugging off the paranoia and pessimism, he consulted the notes he'd made. 'Right. Who's next on our list?'

'We've got someone with Clarissa Ralph out at the hospital and your DC is interviewing Tyke in the manager's office . . .' The sergeant paused, as though debating saying something more. He glanced towards the wall separating the cafe from the kitchen – perhaps sensing the same pressure, feeling the same paranoia – before continuing. 'There's something you should know. We've been . . . unofficially . . . keeping an eye on Tyke the last couple of days. There was an incident out at the house he's rented for his stay here – a dead rabbit left on the doorstep along with a threatening note. He didn't want to take it any further but in light of the fact there was a possible attempt on his life a few days before, well . . . I thought it wouldn't hurt to monitor the situation.'

Benson's interest was piqued. 'Define unofficially.'

'Young Danny has been secretly included as part of a surveillance team the lad hired—'

'Don't tell me,' said Benson, groaning. 'O'Brien's mob?'

The sergeant nodded, cheeks reddening. 'I couldn't insist on Tyke letting us take over and I wasn't prepared to walk away from what could be a credible risk to his life, so I thought combining forces was the best option.'

'And you think this could have some bearing on this case? A man who was threatened now finds his own uncle killed? That's a rapid escalation from a dead rabbit on a doorstep.'

'Agreed. But look at it another way – Tyke was on his way here when the murder happened. From what he said when I arrived, he was bringing back his uncle's glasses which he'd taken by mistake.'

'Wait!' Benson held up a hand, the pain in his head thumping now. 'You're suggesting that Vinny might not have been the target? That this could have been intended for Tyke and Vinny just happened to come home at the wrong time?'

Date with Destiny

'It's a possibility we need to consider. Or the entire Tyke death-threat thing could just be a horrible coincidence.' The sergeant sat back in his seat, arms folded across his chest. 'I thought you should see the bigger picture, that's all.'

The picture was crystal clear for the detective, along with the carnage it could bring to his career. The idea that Vinny King's death was the result of a love triangle gone wrong suddenly held appeal.

'What is it about this damn place?' he muttered. 'Nothing is ever straightforward. Not even murder.'

'Welcome to my life,' retorted the sergeant, getting to his feet. 'I'll fetch in the next witness – Arty Robinson.'

'Bring some more coffee with you, too, please,' said the detective. 'And cake if you can find any. I've a feeling this will be a long night.'

'Jealous of Vinny King?!' Arty spluttered the words out, incredulity in every syllable. 'What the hell have I got to be jealous about?'

DS Benson leaned forward, the change in his demeanour marked even through the glass of the serving hatch as Samson and Delilah watched on. The detective was definitely showing less compassion than he had with Geraldine Mortimer.

'Because, of course, Mr King's incredible wealth wouldn't be something you'd envy,' he said sardonically. 'Or how about the fact that he was Edith Hird's fiancé once upon a time and, according to some, seemed keen to rekindle that romance.'

Arty thrust himself towards the detective, face florid, a hair's breadth away from losing his temper.

'Careful, tiger,' murmured Samson, recognising Benson's tactics. 'He's trying to bait you.'

'Succeeding too,' muttered Delilah.

'I'll have you know,' snapped Arty, 'I've got nothing to fear when it comes to that man. Alive or dead, he was no threat to me.'

Delilah let out a small gasp. Samson saw her look down at her palms, to the plaster taped across one of them as though it had significance. When she looked back up, her expression was one of consternation.

'You okay?' Samson whispered.

She placed a finger on her lips, her gaze fixed back on Arty.

'So tell me again, what brought you to his apartment?' DS Benson was asking.

'Like I said, I went to check on Clarissa. I got to her door and noticed Vinny's was open. I knew he was out at the play so I went to see what was going on. That's when I found him.'

'And he was already dead?'

'Very much so.'

'And how much time elapsed before Mrs Mortimer arrived?'

A snort of exasperation came from the other side of the table. 'I was too bloody busy trying to see if the man was dead or not to check the time!'

'Is it me,' murmured Samson to Delilah, 'or is Arty rather wound up considering he's simply being asked to clarify details?'

He was expecting the usual passionate defence – albeit in a whisper – which Delilah had mustered for previous Bruncliffe locals who'd been caught in the crosshairs of an investigation, but she didn't reply. Lip caught between her teeth, she was watching the interview anxiously.

'Just a rough estimate, Arty,' Sergeant Clayton was saying calmly on the other side of the glass. 'That's all we're asking for.'

'A minute? Two at most. Not that Geraldine was much use. Set up wailing in the hallway and didn't make a move to call an ambulance.'

DS Benson nodded as though in sympathy and, just as he had back in the autumn, Samson found himself admiring the man's interviewing technique. The ability to switch moods, to lull those he was questioning into a false sense of security.

'I can see how that would have been irritating,' he continued. 'Thing is though, despite her wailing, as you put it, Mrs Mortimer was able to observe that when she arrived you were holding what we are pretty sure is the murder weapon in what she described as a very threatening manner. Can you explain to me why that was?'

'That trophy? It was right next to Vinny! I just moved it to check his pulse!'

'Convenient,' said Benson.

Arty slapped his hands on the table and stood up. 'I don't have to take this. I'm not under arrest—'

The door to the cafe swung open in the background, a female detective gesturing urgently for Benson to join her in the hallway. He exited the room and Arty slumped back into his seat, breathing hard.

'What the hell is he playing at?' Samson whispered, perplexed by the behaviour of the former bookie. 'If Arty wants to get taken down to the station, he's going the right way about it.'

Delilah glanced at him, worried. 'Do you think Geraldine Mortimer's tittle-tattle is enough to provide a motive for murder?'

'I've come across cases built on weaker foundations. But thankfully, so far Benson is lacking concrete evidence.'

A small groan came from Delilah and she gripped the ledge below the hatches, knuckles white. If Samson was puzzled by what was going on in the cafe, he was equally puzzled by his companion, unusually muted even given their clandestine circumstances.

'Is everything okay?' he murmured.

She turned to him, took a deep breath and opened her mouth to speak but then Benson re-entered the cafe. Purposeful. Energised. He resumed his seat, allowing the taut silence to stretch while he leafed through his notes. When he looked up at Arty it was with feigned confusion. Samson felt Delilah tense up next to him. They'd both seen the detective go through this routine before and it meant trouble.

'It seems we have a problem with our timings,' he said benignly, as though discussing the latest timetable for the Bruncliffe to Skipton bus.

Arty shrugged. Folded his arms across his chest.

'You've told us that Mrs Mortimer arrived no more than two minutes after you reached Vinny King's flat and found him deceased.' Benson waited for corroboration and got a sullen nod. 'Thing is, we've just been informed by another witness that you were seen walking along the first-floor corridor towards Mr King's flat some ten minutes before that. While Mrs Mortimer was still sitting outside on the patio.'

Arty's arms unfolded, as if of their own accord. His cheeks drained of colour. 'What—? Who—?'

'Are you denying this to be the case?'

'I didn't . . . I mean I was going to but then . . .' Arty stuttered to a halt.

'A full *ten* minutes before Mrs Mortimer arrived,' Benson reiterated. The words heavy with accusation. 'That's substantially more than you originally told us. Want to tell us what you were doing in Vinny King's flat for those ten minutes?'

'I was in my own flat!' Arty looked from Benson to Sergeant Clayton, panic in his voice. 'I'm telling the truth. I was going to go and see Vinny but I changed my mind. So I went back to mine instead.'

'You admit, then, that you knew Mr King had returned unexpectedly?'

Arty's nod was glum. 'I was heading to check in on Clarissa and he appeared out of the stairwell at the far end of the corridor. I went to follow him but then thought better of it.'

'What were you going to see him about?'

Arty's mouth opened. Closed. He shook his head.

Samson felt Delilah's hand reach for his, her face almost as ashen as Arty's.

'Mr Robinson, I'm asking you again.' Benson was leaning forward across the table, sensing he was onto something. 'What did you need to talk to Vinny King about?'

'I was going to ask him to back off,' muttered Arty. 'To leave Edith alone.'

Sergeant Clayton let out a long sigh. Looking strained while his colleague was all excitement now.

'So instead of doing that,' proposed DS Benson, 'you went back to your flat. Waited ten minutes and then went to see him?'

'No. Yes. I mean, not quite. I went back, paced around, calmed down and then, when I thought Vinny would be inside his flat and the coast was clear, I went to see Clarissa. That's when I found him.' Arty looked from one officer to the other. Saw their scepticism. 'It's the truth!'

Benson nodded, seemingly in full agreement. Then sat back. And Samson knew the killer blow was coming.

'Problem I have with that, Mr Robinson, is that we only have your word for it. Whereas we have a witness who places you in the vicinity of Mr King's flat at a time which fits with a different scenario altogether. Combine that with your previous conviction for actual bodily harm—'

'That was half a century ago!' protested Arty. 'And there were mitigating circumstances!'

'—a conviction which handily gave us a record of your fingerprints,' continued Benson as though Arty hadn't interrupted, 'and I'm less inclined to accept your version of events. You see, I've just been informed by a colleague that your fingerprints are all over the trophy which we believe was used to kill Mr King.'

'Of course they bloody are! I had to lift it up to see if he was dead!'

Benson nodded. 'Okay. But perhaps you could explain why yours are the *only* fingerprints we found on it?'

The air seemed to leave Arty's chest in a rush as he stared at the detective in shock.

'I think, Mr Robinson, it's probably best if we continue this conversation over at the station,' said DS Benson as Sergeant Clayton got to his feet and crossed to Arty's side of the table.

'I'm telling the truth!' Arty murmured. Stunned.

Behind the glass, Delilah had her hand over her mouth, while tears had formed in her eyes.

'Don't worry, it's all supposition,' murmured Samson. 'I'm sure there's some explanation. There's no way Arty did this.'

But Delilah was shaking her head. Eyes on his now, wide with horror.

'I think Benson could be right. I think Arty might have killed Vinny King.'

21

It made the front page of all the national newspapers.

TV STAR KILLED. OLD FLAME'S LOVER ARRESTED.

Wednesday morning and Mike Whitaker, owner of Whitaker's newsagents situated proudly on the marketplace, had already sold out of the *Yorkshire Post*, with the other dailies flying off the shelves. Business had been brisk. Well, the buying aspect of it had been. But there'd been a marked increase in the number of people lingering in the shop to talk, or gathering outside in small groups, the warm sunshine at odds with the cold shadow of such dark news.

Bruncliffe was in deep shock. There was a sense of collective guilt that a son of the town had returned to spend his twilight years there, only to meet an untimely and brutal death. Possibly at the hands of another local – one who was beloved of everyone. As Seth Thistlethwaite observed when he purchased his usual paper, it was like the whole place had gone into mourning.

Just as the rest of the population were trying to get to grips with the horrific events of the night before, so too were the members of the Dales Detective Agency as they gathered for a debrief. With the entire team present, they'd abandoned the kitchen as their usual meeting space and had adjourned to Delilah's more spacious office instead, Nina and Gareth on the couch, Nathan perched on the arm next to Nina, and Samson on a chair opposite Delilah, Tolpuddle and Bounty sprawled at his feet. Propped against the wall was the whiteboard containing all the details of Tyke's case and from the kitchen came the whistle of the kettle, Ida busy making tea, her go-to activity in times of stress.

For it was stressful. Vinny King dead and Arty Robinson – lovely, cheerful Arty, a man Delilah had always thought wouldn't hurt a fly – accused of murder. And now, fresh from Sergeant Clayton that morning, a message informing them that DS Benson was on the verge of making the charges formal.

'That clown is about to make another mistake,' muttered Nathan as Ida entered the room with a tray of mugs. 'You'd think he'd have learned his lesson last time he was here.'

'DS Benson is just doing his job,' said Samson.

'Looks like he's not doing it that well from where I'm sitting,' said Gareth, shaking his head. 'What reason would Arty have for killing Vinny? This supposed jealousy – there's no evidence that anything was going on between Edith and Vinny.'

A loud crash punctuated his speech, Ida setting the tray down heavily on the coffee table.

'Happen we don't know the half of what's going on in folks' heads,' she muttered.

'Do you think Arty did it?' Nina asked, surprised.

'Not my place to comment.' Ida's lips closed with a snap and she began distributing mugs, leaving Nina to turn to Samson and Delilah.

'What about you two?'

'Best to keep an open mind,' said Samson.

Delilah simply nodded, not trusting herself to speak.

'But we are going to be helping Arty prove his innocence, aren't we?' Nathan asked, looking from his aunt to Samson.

Heart thumping, Delilah could feel the heat on her cheeks, her mind like sludge. She glanced at Samson.

'I think it's best if we stay out of it for now,' he said, his composure something she could only admire. 'We've got enough on our plates trying to keep Tyke safe.'

'Aunt Delilah?' Nathan swung round to her.

She gave a shrug. A shake of her head. 'Sorry, Nathan, I agree with Samson.'

'But Benson is screwing things up. Again!' exclaimed Nathan with the full passion of a sixteen-year-old. 'I can't believe you're going to stand by and do nothing!'

Delilah gave another shrug and pretended preoccupation with her mobile, her palms so sweaty, she was struggling not to drop it. All the while aware of Ida's fierce regard upon her. Ida who was also being unusually muted.

Unsure what Ida's reasons were for keeping her normally strident opinions to herself, Delilah knew her own. And that she wasn't cut out for blatant deception. For pretending she supported the prevailing local sentiment that DS Benson had got it all wrong and that Arty Robinson couldn't possibly be a killer.

She picked at the edge of the plaster on her palm. In the mayhem of yesterday evening, she'd forgotten all about the cut on her hand. And how she'd got it. It was only as she was in the kitchen, watching Arty protest his innocence, that she'd remembered. The argument – or whatever it had been – she'd overheard while she'd been under Edith Hird's apartment earlier that day.

An angry Vinny King, accusing Edith of threatening him.

It hadn't meant anything at the time. But in the context of Vinny's death, with DS Benson pointing out that Arty had had ample opportunity to commit the crime, suddenly the heated words had taken on another meaning.

One which gave Arty motive.

A disagreement between Vinny and Edith which had spiralled out of control. A concerned Arty going round to confront the talk-show host, both men provoked into violence. Watching Arty being interviewed, Delilah had seen all too easily how it might have happened.

She'd also realised that what she'd witnessed would be of vital interest to the police. And that her evidence could possibly condemn Arty – something she didn't want to bear responsibility for. Plus she'd have to explain how she'd come to be underneath that open window and why she'd been trying to sneak out of Fellside Court without being seen. Bad enough that she was going to have to tell Samson about her wedding jitters at some point; having the whole of Bruncliffe hear about it was an outcome she'd rather avoid.

So, as they'd watched Arty being led away by Sergeant Clayton, she'd offered Samson no further explanation as to why she was so convinced of their friend's guilt. Perhaps sensing her inner conflict, he hadn't pressed her for one. Instead, he'd headed off to Tyke's on the Enfield to check up on their client and on Gareth, who'd taken over night-time surveillance duties, leaving Delilah to walk back to her cottage with Tolpuddle.

An hour later she'd been still sitting at the kitchen table trying to decide what she should do, when the back door opened and Samson appeared, a bag of takeaway in one hand

and a bottle of wine in the other. He'd placed the food on the worktop, gathered her into an embrace, and then simply murmured, 'Tell me about Arty.'

So she'd told him. Noticing the flicker of surprise when she explained where she'd been. Sensing he was aware she was editing the story, offering no reason for why she'd ended up under Edith's flat.

He'd let her finish without interrupting and then they'd talked while they ate. Trying to find some justification for what Delilah had heard which wouldn't make things worse for Arty. Trying to come up with a good excuse for why she shouldn't take such information to the police. Not once did Samson ask her to give him the details she'd omitted.

The discussion had finally ended in the small hours of the morning when Delilah returned to the lounge with another round of tea only to find an exhausted Samson fast asleep on the sofa, Tolpuddle lying on his legs like a canine blanket.

She'd gone to bed alone and had awoken after a fitful sleep with daylight streaming in the window and the smell of toast drifting up the stairs. Samson, operating a lot better than she did on such meagre rest, had outlined a plan as they had their breakfast. They would keep what Delilah had overheard to themselves for now, not even sharing it with the rest of the DDA team. And they would leave the investigation into Vinny King's murder to the police.

Easier said than done when their colleagues felt otherwise.

'Nathan's right,' Gareth said, Nina nodding beside him. 'There's got to be something we can do and besides, there could be a connection between our investigation and the murder of Tyke's uncle. Have you thought of that?'

His question got a murmur of support from the teenagers but Samson was shaking his head.

'Thought about it and dismissed it,' he said. 'There are way too many variables to make it a feasible theory.'

'Like what?' challenged Gareth, looking surprised at the flat rejection.

'For starters, the fact that it looks like Vinny was killed by someone he knew, someone he welcomed into his flat. There were no signs of a forced entry so the killer wasn't waiting for him. And before you ask, no lock-picking either. What's more, if you're suggesting that Tyke was the intended victim, there would have to have been a string of ridiculous coincidences for someone to have known Tyke would be at Fellside Court yesterday evening when he didn't know himself that he would be heading there.'

'But you said after the rabbit incident that you thought the person behind it could have had Tyke's place under surveillance, perhaps even us as well,' protested Nathan. 'In which case, couldn't they have followed Tyke when he left the house?'

Samson nodded. 'Fair enough. So how did they get to Fellside Court ahead of him? Because Vinny was already dead when he got there.'

'Maybe it is connected, but Tyke was never the intended target?' Nina's suggestion was voiced quietly but it drew the attention of the entire room.

Ida turned to her. 'Tha means Vinny might have been?'

'It's just a thought.'

'A bloody good one,' said Gareth. 'A message to Tyke. Letting him know the danger he's in.'

They were all looking at Samson now, almost daring him to counter their arguments.

He shrugged. 'I've considered that too. In my experience, those who intend to carry out a murder come prepared with a weapon. They don't just pick up the nearest, heaviest object and use that. And then we come back to coincidences – just like with Tyke, no one could have known that Vinny would be in his flat at that time. Unless you're suggesting the killer was the one who swapped his glasses over?'

It was an irony which made the death of Vinny King even more bizarre. And one which the media would have a field day with when it was uncovered. The TV host had walked into a terrible situation all because he'd unwittingly got his glasses confused and put his readers in the wrong case.

Silence met Samson's question. Nathan still looking defiant. Gareth and Nina also looking less than convinced. Even Ida seemed to be in turmoil, murmuring away to herself. Delilah understood the reason for their disquiet – if Vinny's murder could be tied to Tyke's death threats, then Arty was innocent. For residents of Bruncliffe, this would be the best of all possible outcomes.

'I'm sorry to be a naysayer,' said Samson, sensing the prevailing mood. 'Believe me, I'd love nothing more than for some unknown assailant to have killed Vinny and for Arty to be off the hook. But we have to be realistic—' He broke off, looking down at the mug from which he'd just taken a sip, the contents a pale imitation of what was usually served. 'Good tea, Ida!' he said, surprised.

She grunted in contempt. 'Weak as dishwater! I should know better than to make a brew when distracted.'

Samson waited, giving her the space to enlarge on whatever was occupying her thoughts, but when Ida offered nothing more, he took another drink of tea and then continued.

'So, as I was saying, we have to be realistic. You've all worked enough cases in the last year to know that detective work mostly consists of applying basic logic to a series of events. It's basic logic which has got DS Benson looking hard at Arty Robinson, and it's difficult to argue with that.'

'Tha shares that opinion, lass?' Ida was addressing Delilah, who'd remained quiet throughout.

Delilah's shrug was non-committal. 'The facts are compelling. Arty was seen going to Vinny's and he's admitted himself that he wanted to confront him. Not to mention his fingerprints on the trophy, the only ones on it—'

'The killer probably wiped it,' said Gareth.

'Pah!' Ida gave a snort, arms folding across her chest. 'That weren't no killer. That were me. There were no other prints on that blasted trophy because I cleaned the place yesterday morning. So that doesn't help Arty any.'

'But the killer could have worn gloves!' insisted Nathan.

'Aye, and by sticking our noses into all this we could be more of a hindrance than a help, lad,' said Ida with uncharacteristic sharpness.

Samson gave her a puzzled look before raising a hand and bringing the room to quiet.

'Okay!' he said. 'I understand the passion Arty's situation is provoking and this loyalty to a friend, but I think the best thing we can do right now is to focus on the case we have in hand. Way I see it, if I'm right and Arty is guilty, then we still have someone out there trying to kill Tyke. And if I'm wrong and you lot are right about a possible connection between what's happening with Tyke and his uncle's murder, then even more reason for us to knuckle down and find whoever it is that's terrorising our client.'

'Solve one and we might solve both, tha means?' Ida asked, giving Samson a look of grudging respect.

'Exactly. So let's recap. Where are we with the Tyke investigation?'

The answer to Samson's question was sobering. After half an hour of collating the latest developments from their various strands of enquiry, precious little new information had been added to the whiteboard.

Despite posting details of the trail bike and its registration on local social media groups, so far nothing had come of it. No sightings. No further details. As for the two people who had known ahead of time that Tyke was going to be heading to Bruncliffe, Gareth had checked them out. And was in the process of discounting them.

'His agent was in Paris on Thursday when the attempt was made on Tyke's life,' he explained, 'and the photographer who's coming up to shoot the show is in Milan at the moment. She got there last Wednesday and isn't due back until next weekend. So neither of them could have been involved. Not in person, anyway.'

Ida grunted at the caveat, pen poised by the board. 'Don't need to be here in person to have someone killed, as we know full well,' she muttered, casting a glance at Samson.

He grinned at her, knowing she was thinking of the attempt on his life by a hitman twelve months ago. 'In which case, you'd best get knitting, Ida. Get Tyke in a yellow jumper and he'll have nothing to fear.'

He was relieved to hear laughter erupt around the room, the tension which had developed during the discussion about Vinny King's murder having lingered like a low cloud on Pen-y-ghent. He hadn't relished withholding information from the others, information which would probably have them agreeing with his take on things, but after Delilah's revelation the night before, he had no choice.

'Happen I've not seen thee wear that jumper since,' muttered Ida, provoking more laughter.

'Moving swiftly on,' he said, still grinning, 'while we make light of the subject, Ida's right – we shouldn't rule out the possibility of a professional having been hired, no matter how ludicrous that might seem. In which case, Gareth, did you find any indications that Tyke's agent or this photographer might have a grudge against him?'

'Just the opposite. They both stand to lose financially if he's not around. And for the record, I also did a bit of probing into the background of the lighting engineer who was at the rehearsals yesterday. Again, nothing jumped out. He's worked with Tyke for the last four years and also on the TV programme. No disputes with him and nothing to gain from Tyke being dead.'

'Good work,' Samson acknowledged, while Ida added the three names to the board and promptly put a red line through them.

'What about the former contestant from *The Nines* you were chasing, Delilah?' Samson turned to her, taking in the grey tinge to her skin, the tiredness in her eyes. She was always an open book, even when she was trying her hardest to be deceitful. That business with Edith's apartment and the conversation she'd overheard . . . She wasn't just concealing it from the team, she was also concealing her reasons for being at Fellside Court from him. And the strain was showing.

'Holly Campbell,' she said. 'No joy in locating her but I did manage to unearth an interesting article published six months after she was ousted from Tyke's TV programme. It was on a website devoted to gossip in the fashion world called Loose Threads and basically she accuses Tyke of being a fraud. I'll pass it round.'

Delilah clicked on her phone and a succession of beeps sounded, eyes going to screens. Samson glanced at his own mobile and saw the article there, accompanied by a photograph of a young woman, her severe expression contrasting with the sweetness of her face and her halo of blonde hair.

Fraud was putting it mildly. In a strongly worded attack on Tyke and his company, Holly Campbell claimed that the fashion designer had stolen his designs from others and lacked any creative talent.

'Blimey!' said Nina, looking up. 'She didn't hold back! How come Tyke didn't take her to court over this?'

Delilah shook her head. 'I don't know. It certainly seems libellous. But I have to say, finding that article took a lot of digital digging. My gut instinct says Loose Threads attempted to bury it.'

'So Tyke might have put pressure on them?' asked Gareth.

'Possibly. I can't say for sure. Maybe we could ask Tyke about it? See if we can shed a bit more light on her accusations?'

Samson nodded. 'Definitely worth following up.'

'So that just leaves us with the dead rabbit,' said Ida, tapping her pen against the whiteboard and looking at the teenagers.

'Sorry,' said Nina, grimacing as she stood up to place her laptop on Delilah's desk, a spreadsheet displayed on the screen. 'We didn't get very far. We called every game supplier in the radius Delilah gave us, but either they didn't make any deliveries in this area or they refused to divulge information for data protection reasons.'

Delilah sighed. 'It was a long shot. We'll have to resort to old-fashioned methods and circulate the names of the possible suppliers on the WhatsApp group, see if anyone remembers seeing one of their vans in the area. We might get lucky.'

'We might already be lucky,' said Samson, looking at the list. Feeling an itch of recognition. 'Yorkshire Wild,' he murmured, reading out one of the names before looking around the group. 'Is that ringing bells with anyone else?'

There was a succession of shaking heads.

'They're based just outside Kirkby Lonsdale,' said Nina. 'Perhaps that's how you know of them?'

'No, it's not that. I feel I've seen the name somewhere lately.'

Ida was squinting at him. 'Aye, happen tha could be right.' Then her head snapped round to Nathan. 'That video. Of the trail bike and the hit-and-run. Has tha got it?'

Nathan nodded while Nina's fingers flashed across the keyboard of her laptop.

'Easier to watch on here,' she said, standing back to let Ida get closer as the facade of Barry's Books came into view.

The video scrolled by, Barry talking, the sudden commotion off screen, the blare of a horn—

'There!' Ida exclaimed, and Nina pressed pause just before the camera swung round to focus on Tyke and Clive Knowles. 'What's that?'

Ida was pointing at a transit van in the background, the source of the irate blast of horn. The image was blurred but even so, the logo on the side was clear. A rabbit. The words 'Yorkshire Wild' arched over it.

'Good one, Ida!' said Nathan, throwing an arm around her shoulders. Something close to a smile curved her lips.

'This is brilliant!' said Gareth, on his feet, energy radiating from him. 'A proper breakthrough.'

Samson nodded. Feeling the same thrill that was being reflected on the faces around him. Delilah, however, was still staring at the screen, deep in thought.

'Have you spotted something else?' asked Samson.

She went to speak, paused, then looked up, shocked. 'I think we need to increase Tyke's protection,' she said.

'What makes you say that?' asked Gareth.

'The person behind all this. I think they're in Bruncliffe. I think they've been here all the time.'

22

Fellside Court was more like a funeral home than the lively place Ana Stoyanovic was used to overseeing. Outside the sun was beaming down, the sky a shade of blue rarely seen in Bruncliffe, clouds no more than mere afterthoughts dotted above the hills, and yet, within the walls of the retirement complex, there was none of the joy which such glorious weather usually inspired.

This morning's Stretch and Smile class had seen a significant drop in numbers and when Ana had popped her head around the lounge door, she'd seen very few smiles on the faces of those who had turned up. Likewise, the cafe had been ghostly quiet, the cook complaining that she was going to end up with a surfeit of cake if things didn't pick up. As for the corridors, they echoed in their emptiness. No laughter. No animated conversations. It was as if a dark cloud had settled over the U-shaped building and its occupants, blotting out the sunshine.

It was hardly surprising. Less than twenty-four hours ago, a man – friend and neighbour to many – had been killed inside his own apartment. A place where he should have been safe. That alone was enough to make the residents nervous. But combined with the arrest of Arty Robinson, it was little wonder that everyone was out of sorts. Not to mention that the prevailing view being expressed within Fellside Court was that the police had got it wrong – this being Yorkshire, it was expressed in more forthright terms by many – and that Arty couldn't possibly have committed murder. Which meant Vinny King's killer was still on the loose.

Thus, Vinny's death was having ramifications far beyond the inconvenience of the police tape still strung across the corridor on the first floor. Or the trail of dirty footprints up and down the stairs from the multitude of officials visiting the crime scene.

Perturbed by the silence, Ana left her office in the reception area and walked along the corridor, looking through the glass wall across the courtyard and into the lounge. Not a soul in it. And outside on the patio, which was usually crowded with people on such a stunning day, the chairs were empty, the tables unoccupied. Beyond them, two lone figures were sitting on a bench by the outdoor gym, the equipment lying idle.

As she stared out of the window, Ana began to feel the darkness touch her own soul. After all, it wasn't the first time violent death had visited Fellside Court on her watch. And while she hadn't been responsible for events eighteen months ago, she still felt residual guilt. A sense that she had let down the people she was supposed to be looking after.

Now here she was again in a situation where she'd failed the residents of Fellside Court. Allowed something awful to take place in the premises she was supposed to make safe. And this time she had a feeling that if she didn't do something soon to pull people together and out of this malaise which was affecting them all, the delicate fabric of the close-knit community could come unravelled. Permanently.

The flash of light on metal caught her eye. Eric's portable

oxygen cannister. That's who was on the bench. Guessing who his companion would be, she stepped outside, crossed the paving and walked onto the grass, towards the two men.

'Morning, Ana,' Joseph O'Brien greeted her, his words lacking their usual energy. 'Sorry I didn't make Stretch and Smile. I just didn't feel in the mood.'

'You weren't the only one,' said Eric morosely. 'It was like a morgue in there today.' He winced. 'Sorry. Bad choice of phrase.'

'No need for apologies,' said Ana. Thinking how strange it was to see them without the others. 'How's Edith doing?'

Joseph grimaced. 'Not so good. She went off to the hospital early this morning to see Clarissa.'

'Can't imagine that'll go so well,' muttered Eric.

'What makes you say that?' Ana asked.

The two men looked at each other and then Eric shrugged. 'It'll be common knowledge soon enough,' he said, turning back to Ana, 'so I don't suppose there's any harm in telling you. The witness who saw Arty heading for Vinny's flat last night? It was Clarissa.'

Clarissa. Edith's own sister, who had been too ill to attend the play and so found herself providing the evidence which had helped have Arty arrested. It was a mess of gigantic proportions.

'Have a seat,' Joseph murmured, patting the empty bit of bench next to him. 'Kind of hard to take in.'

Ana sat. Letting the sun warm her. Wondering how she could pull the community back from the brink of this terrible tragedy.

'Do you think he did it?' she asked, unaware of the words until they'd slipped from her lips.

The men didn't recoil, just considered her question as

though it was all they'd been considering for the entire time they'd been sitting on the bench.

'He certainly didn't like Vinny,' muttered Eric. 'But I can't see him killing him.'

Ana noted the uncertainty in the words. 'What about this previous conviction the police mentioned?'

Joseph waved a hand in dismissal. 'It was something and nothing. Arty used to moonlight as a nightclub bouncer back in the day. One night he stepped in to have words with a bloke who was getting a bit too hands-on with a lass, clearly against her wishes, and it turned into a fight. The bloke found out the hard way that Arty was a nifty boxer. It ended up in court, Arty got a slap on the wrists and a fine, and a permanent record for actual bodily harm.'

'That sounds so like Arty,' murmured Ana with a smile. 'Always riding to the rescue.'

'He doesn't have time for tyrants, true enough. But as for Vinny King's murder,' continued Joseph, 'he wouldn't have stooped that low. He knew how Edith felt about the man. More importantly, he knew how Edith felt about him. I'm sure it's all just a mistake and the police will release him soon.'

Eric glanced at Ana. 'And this is why I'm friends with Joseph O'Brien. His eternal optimism in human nature. Although I've a horrible feeling that's about to be tested by this case.'

'What about Samson and Delilah?' asked Ana. 'Are they going to be helping with the investigation?'

Joseph shook his head. 'Not this time. I asked Samson last night before they left and he said something about it being too complicated. I think DS Benson isn't keen to have them involved.'

'Huh, never stopped them before,' muttered Eric.

It was a valid point. The Dales Detective Agency had handled several cases over the last eighteen months where their participation hadn't been officially approved. Ana couldn't help thinking that their decision to rule themselves out of this one wasn't a good sign for Arty. Nor would it provide a much-needed distraction for the rest of the residents of Fellside Court, well accustomed to being part of the agency's investigations.

'I just feel so useless,' sighed Eric, echoing her concerns.

Joseph patted his shoulder. 'Me too.'

'Well,' said Ana, getting to her feet with forced enthusiasm, 'sitting around feeling sorry for yourselves isn't going to help. Even if it is in the sunshine.'

Eric squinted up at her. 'What else is there for us to do? Eat cake on our own in the cafe all day?'

She shrugged. 'Do something to lift everyone's spirits. Something nice. Something we can all get involved in to take our minds off things until this mess gets sorted.'

'Easier said than done! Besides, it's normally Clarissa who comes up with stuff like that. Us two aren't exactly the creative types, are we Joseph?'

But Joseph wasn't listening. He was pulling out his wallet, taking out a piece of paper inside and looking up at Ana, his sunlit face reminding her of the beatific expressions of the saints who'd graced the walls in her childhood church back in Serbia.

'I think,' he said, beaming, 'we might be able to do just that!'

They were all standing around the desk, an OS map of Bruncliffe and the surrounding area laid out across it.

'The Yorkshire Wild van was here,' said Delilah, placing

a finger on the marketplace, 'heading up High Street when it was captured on the video.' She turned to Nina. 'You said the company is based out by Kirkby Lonsdale?'

Nina nodded. Delilah tapped the map again, this time to the north-west of the town.

'So we can reasonably assume that the van came in from this direction, which means it probably left the A65 at Gunnerstang Brow and entered town that way. It then came along under the viaduct, up Church Street and into the market square, where it had a near collision with the trail bike attempting to run Tyke over before heading off down High Street.' She glanced up from the map and at her colleagues. 'Which means it must have been delivering to somewhere in Bruncliffe.'

'How do you figure that?' asked Gareth, frowning.

Samson, however, was nodding, gesturing at the route the van had taken and at the curve of the A65 as it looped around the south-west of the town. 'Because no delivery driver would come off the main road at Gunnerstang Brow to meander through the streets, only to go straight down High Street and back onto the A65 again. It wouldn't make sense.'

'And as the van had already passed the roads up to Horton and Thorpdale before it got to the marketplace, we can assume it wasn't delivering up there,' added Ida.

'Couldn't it have been coming back from there?' Nathan asked.

Delilah felt her certainty wane. Her nephew's question was a good one.

'Damn it,' she muttered. 'I thought I might have narrowed down our options.'

'I still think you might have!' Nina had turned back to her laptop, letting the video run. Tyke and Clive Knowles

Julia Chapman

on the ground. The motorbike disappearing along Church Street. She didn't pause it there as she had done before, but let it keep rolling. The camera swinging back to focus on a shocked Barry and there, visible over his shoulder in the distance, was the van. An orange light blinking. 'Look! It's turning right!'

Delilah was already on her mobile, pulling up a more detailed map of the town centre. 'This area here,' she said, drawing a vague grid on the screen. An area flanked by High Street on one side and the straight line of the railway tracks to the other, with the rugby ground to the south. 'This has to be where they were delivering to!'

'What about the other side of the tracks?' Ida pointed towards the industrial estate and the dairy.

'The van wouldn't have come through the centre of town if it was going that way,' said Nathan. 'It would have come off Gunnerstang Brow and immediately turned right at the Crown.'

Samson was grinning now, looking across the desk at Delilah, making her feel dizzy. 'You're a star!' he said, as a buzz went around the room, everyone seeing the significance of what they'd found. 'Reckon you might have identified where our mystery threat-maker is hanging out, Delilah!'

'So what next?' asked Gareth. 'How do we follow up on this?'

'Before you ask,' said Nina, 'there's no point in calling Yorkshire Wild. They were one of the companies which refused to answer our questions. Although I guess Danny or Sergeant Clayton might have more luck?'

Samson nodded. 'I'll mention it to Danny but I'm not sure finding out the delivery details for a dead rabbit will be high on their list of priorities right at the moment. In the meantime, we need to identify every property in that area which might be a rental. Holiday lets, folk renting out rooms, anything like that. Then we need to contact each one and find out if they've got tenants and, if so, who they are.'

'We're on it,' said Nathan, glancing at Nina, who was nodding.

'Of course, the downside to this is exactly what Delilah said earlier. Now we suspect the threat to Tyke is this close, we'll have to increase our protection of him. Seeing as we no longer have the luxury of Danny's services, Gareth, you okay to do split-shifts with me? You take the overnight one?'

The former gamekeeper yawned, scratched his beard and grinned. 'Definitely. Just don't expect me to contribute much at morning meetings.'

The laughter which met his comment was giddy with excitement, Delilah feeling it too. That swell of energy which came when an investigation made an unexpected lurch forward. The mood in the room was a lot lighter than it had been earlier when they'd been discussing taking on Vinny's case.

'And we'll probably need some cover from Delilah, too,' continued Samson, addressing the others. 'I spoke to Tyke last night and he's agreed to dispense with his demand for covert surveillance – with the story about his uncle breaking, he thinks the journalists pouring into town will be more concerned with that than with him. Plus I think he'll be glad to have visible eyes on him. He's feeling a bit jittery, understandably.'

Delilah nodded. 'He also feels responsible for Vinny returning to the flat. Seems yesterday afternoon, when Tyke had finished showing his uncle some designs Eloise has sketched for the fashion show, he gathered the drawings into his bag and somehow managed to sweep a glasses case in there along with them. The case for Vinny's reading glasses which, as we now know, actually contained his distance glasses. Tyke only noticed he had it when he got home that night.'

'The lad's daft to be blaming himself,' murmured Ida. 'That had nowt to do with his uncle's murder. If Vinny hadn't got his glasses mixed up, he'd have had no cause to return to his flat, even with Tyke's honest mistake.'

'I agree. Anyway, we had a message from Tyke earlier saying he needs time to process what's happened, plus he wants to keep out of the public eye. So he's staying home all morning with no need for cover, which is a relief given how stretched we are. That said,' she added, glancing at her phone, 'he texted a few moments ago and suggested I go for a run with him this afternoon. He wants to speak to me about a website he's asked me to put together—'

'First I've heard about this,' said Samson, an edge to his tone.

Delilah shrugged, not sure why something so mundane had caught his ire. 'He mentioned it the other day when I bumped into him at Fellside Court. He wants a dedicated site linking the show and his new collection and the whole homecoming thing – "a tribute to his roots" was how he termed it. Which is why he wants a local designer to take it on. So we discussed it over coffee and he's been messaging me about it non-stop, but I just haven't had time to put any proposals together. A trot up on the fells will give us a chance to go over it.'

'Is that wise?' asked Gareth, glancing from Delilah to Samson and back again. 'Going for a run just the two of you? If we're right about whoever is threatening Tyke being here in Bruncliffe, then isn't this playing into their hands? And I don't mean that because you're a lass, Delilah,' he added hastily. 'I respect that right hook of yours as much as everyone else around here. But heading off out of range like that . . .' He shrugged. 'We could be putting our client in danger.'

'Happen he's got a point,' said Ida. 'Going up on the tops alone with Tyke might not be the most prudent thing.'

Delilah looked at Samson. Expecting him to echo the misgivings being expressed. But he shook his head.

'I think it's a great idea. Delilah is as capable of keeping Tyke safe as any of us, even more so up there. And as we're at our limits in terms of manpower, having her spend time with him will free up the rest of us.' He turned to her. 'Just make sure you keep your tracker on so we know where you are at all times.'

She nodded. 'I'll stick to the fells, off the beaten track. I don't see how anyone could predict that we'll be up there.'

'They predicted that the coast was clear when they delivered the dead rabbit,' said Gareth in grave tones. 'And until we've categorically ruled out any chance of a link between Vinny's death and Tyke's case, we'd be sensible to consider all options.'

There was a rumble of support from those still not convinced by Samson and Delilah's stance on Vinny's murder.

'Point taken,' said Samson. He paused, looked down at his mug of tea and back up. 'But we also have to accept that the case against Arty is looking pretty solid.'

'Haven't you heard of innocent until proven guilty?' Nathan muttered caustically.

Samson took the rebuke with good humour. 'I merely think that we can't afford to let what's going on in the Vinny

King case make us lose sight of our real focus, which is keeping his nephew safe and alive.'

'Along with the multitude of other jobs we have on,' said Delilah. 'Seems we've gone from famine to feast when it comes to work.'

'Aye,' muttered Ida. 'Next person who asks for help is going to be told to bugger off.'

'I hope that doesn't apply to me.' The tired voice from the doorway made them all leap round.

Edith Hird was standing there, handbag in her grasp, cane in her other hand, and looking a decade older than she had the day before.

'I've come to hire you,' she said. 'Arty's innocent and I want you to prove it.'

23

Ida was the first to react, rounding up the teenagers and Gareth and herding them out of the office like a sheepdog at a trial. Almost as if she was relieved to have an excuse to leave, too.

'Tha'll want privacy,' she said over her shoulder as she was closing the door behind her. 'And strong tea.'

'Thanks, Ida,' said Samson, gesturing Edith towards the now vacant couch while Delilah pulled up two chairs to the other side of the small coffee table.

Edith sat slowly, as though every movement was painful. Her face drawn and pale. But still there was something stoic in the way she was carrying herself, despite the evident turmoil she was going through.

'I know it looks bad,' she said. 'And some of what I'm going to tell you will make it look worse. But Arty didn't do this. I'd bet my life on it.'

Despite his reservations about Arty's innocence and – given Delilah's revelations – his concerns about Edith's possible involvement in what had happened, Samson reached over and put his hand on hers, feeling the cold of the skin, the fine bones under it. 'Tell us what you know, Edith, and we'll do what we can. But we can't make any promises.'

'Fair enough. In that case, I'll start in the past. Because I'm sure that's where we'll find the reason for Vinny's murder. But first I have to ask that you both promise to keep the confidences I'm about to disclose. At least until we decide whether I should take them to the police.'

Delilah nodded, Samson too, and at that moment the door opened and Ida came in, bringing the supplies she considered essential for any drama – a pot of tea, two mugs, milk, sugar and biscuits. And, unusually, a mug of coffee.

'The coffee's for thee, lad,' she said with an expression Samson could only describe as sympathetic as she passed it to him. As though she knew how awkward the interview was going to be.

She turned to go but Edith shook her head.

'Stay, please, Ida. I'd value your input as a member of the Dales Detective Agency.'

A look of panic flashed across Ida's face, then she blinked a couple of times, gave a sharp nod and sat on the couch. Samson watched her as she busied herself pouring the tea. She seemed . . . rattled. It was the only word for it.

The unflappable Ida Capstick was behaving like someone with something to hide. In fact, she'd been behaving that way all morning – the unusual reticence to air her views, the tea that wasn't up to its usual strength. There was something bothering her. Something major.

He tried to catch her eye, wondering if she somehow had inside knowledge about Vinny's death. If that's why she had been reluctant to join the others in championing Arty's cause. When Edith began speaking, however, he soon forgot about Ida's odd behaviour.

Voice strong, chin up, for the next fifteen minutes, the former headmistress laid bare the skeletons from a closet she'd kept closed for decades. The broken-off engagement, the embezzled money, right up to Vinny's return to Fellside Court and the jealousy it had provoked in Arty. Her audience listened in shocked silence.

'So,' she finally said, 'that's the backdrop to this sordid tale and a true reflection of the person Vinny King was.'

'The bast—'

'Happen we're all inclined to share that view,' muttered Ida, cutting short Delilah's exclamation.

Samson, however, was processing it from the perspective of DS Benson. 'Did Arty know about this?'

Edith gave a fatalistic nod, but held up a hand before he could speak again. 'I'm fully aware this could be seen as further motive to hang on him. And I'm also sure that this is what he was going to speak to Vinny about when he happened to see him in the corridor. But I believe Arty when he says he turned back and made himself calm down.'

'Even though it's your own sister who places him in the hallway ten minutes earlier than he claimed?' said Samson gently, hesitant to raise the fact that it was Clarissa's testimony, delivered from her hospital bed, which had helped seal Arty's fate.

'Clarissa was running a temperature and befuddled,' said Edith, unruffled by the challenge. 'I've come straight from the hospital and she said herself that she's confused about what happened. But even if she is right and she did see Arty at just gone eight o'clock, she admits that she then collapsed on the couch and can't really remember much after that. So both Clarissa *and* Arty could be telling the truth.'

Samson nodded, thinking what a brilliant lawyer Edith would have made, her clarity of thought impressive. 'Have you told the police any of this?'

'Not yet. I wanted to run it past you first. Plus there's

more . . .' She paused, took a deep breath. 'Vinny King told me he was leaving his Hockney to me in his will.'

'Hockney?' spluttered Delilah. 'Vinny King had a Hockney?'

'Aye, lass. Picture of a green pool,' grunted Ida, not noticeably impressed. 'And by goodness did he like everyone knowing about it.'

'But they're worth a fortune!'

'Two million for that particular painting,' said Edith.

Ida just stared at her in shock. Delilah, meanwhile, was looking at Samson, even more concerned. For Edith had just hammered another nail into Arty's coffin.

'Before you ask, yes, Arty knew,' Edith said softly. 'He laughed so hard when I told him, I thought he'd rupture something. But unfortunately, I can't tell you why he found it so funny as I had to rush off to the play and he said it would wait until I was back.' She sighed. 'But now I'm here and he's in a cell in Harrogate, and I'm afraid DS Benson will view it differently, won't he?'

'It doesn't look good,' admitted Samson. He glanced at Delilah, thinking of what she'd told him about Edith and Vinny. She caught his eye and gave the smallest of nods.

He cleared his throat, suddenly nervous. Suddenly hyperconscious that this woman sitting opposite him was once his teacher, a woman with an impeccable reputation for propriety, yet he was about to accuse her of something terrible.

'Thing is, Edith,' he said, 'there's something we need to clear up before we go any further. It's about the argument you had with Vinny King the day he died.'

Ida's head swivelled round, eyes locking onto him, lips drawn tight. There was something bothering her, that was for sure. But Samson kept his focus on Edith.

'An argument?' she said, eyebrows arched in query. 'You

mean about the Hockney? I refused his offer in the clearest of terms but I'd hardly call that an argument . . .'

Samson shook his head. 'No, this was a bit more robust. Vinny was overheard getting irate in your apartment. He said something about you threatening him.'

'Well,' said Edith, folding her arms, tone severe and taking Samson right back to his childhood, 'I have no idea whom your source is, but I regret to tell you they are misinformed. I never made any such threats, and besides, Vinny King has never set foot in my apartment. I wouldn't do Arty such a disservice.'

Heat radiating across his neck and face, Samson glanced at Delilah but she was studying the table, cheeks pink. With no help from that quarter, he persisted.

'So you can categorically confirm that this isn't true? Because you must understand, Edith, how, if it were true, it would place both you and Arty in a difficult position. And myself as well as I'd be duty bound to pass this knowledge on to the police.'

Ida gave a soft humph. Looking from Samson to Delilah and back again. No doubt working out the reason for their reluctance to discuss Arty's case earlier. But Edith was just staring at Samson.

'I can only reiterate what I have just said. Whomever your source overheard, it wasn't me. I spoke to Vinny twice about the Hockney, both times to reinforce my opinion that it wasn't a good idea. Both times he told me he wouldn't take no for an answer—'

Ida jerked forward in her seat, almost knocking the milk jug off the coffee table. 'That were Saturday morning! In Vinny's apartment!'

'Saturday morning, yes, and then again yesterday morning. Why? What relevance does that have?'

'Then tha wasn't . . . tha and Vinny weren't . . . ?' It was Ida's turn to squirm under the forceful gaze of Edith Hird. 'Intimate?' she finally blurted out.

'Intimate?! I can assure you, we most definitely were not!'

If Edith was lying, she was a master of the art. Face severe, lips pursed, indignation radiating from her, Samson would have bet that she was telling the truth. And would have hated to be on the end of that formidable stare. Ida, however, was made of equally robust material. Nodding her head, she met Edith's eyes, something resembling her normal demeanour finally returning.

'Happen Vinny insinuated something of the kind,' she said. 'When I called round to clean on Saturday I heard thee and Vinny talking – Vinny stopped me coming in. He winked, said he had company.' Ida shrugged. 'Tha's a decent woman, Edith Hird, so that fair shook me. Made me wonder if perhaps—'

'Arty had motive?' asked Edith.

'Aye. I'm ashamed to say tha's right. It's had me out of sorts all morning.'

'But why would Vinny have suggested such a thing?' asked Delilah.

Edith gave a small smile. 'Because he couldn't resist making his life more dramatic than it was. Irony is, he ended up being the biggest drama ever to hit Bruncliffe. But I had nothing to do with it and neither did Arty. As for this argument someone overheard,' she continued, laser-like focus back on Samson, 'I can only reiterate what I stated earlier – you have your facts all wrong. But perhaps,' she added, 'we could clarify this right now if you were to reveal the source of your erroneous information.'

She reached forward for her drink with an icy calmness.

In contrast, Samson's palms were sweating and he felt far from composed.

'Delilah?' he said, turning to her in desperation. Hoping she was ready to explain all.

Instead she was staring at Edith's arm, where the sleeve of her lacey blue cardigan had fallen away from her wrist as she sipped her tea.

'Is that your watch?' Delilah asked.

The abrupt change of subject made Edith frown. 'Who else's would it be?' She glanced down at the watch, as did Samson, noting the leather strap, the large face and the clear numerals. Not seeing anything remarkable about it. When Edith looked back at Delilah, there was a light laugh to her tone. 'You're not going to accuse me of stealing as well as being an adulterer and an accessory to murder, are you?'

'No . . . I mean . . . is that the one you always wear?'

There was something in Delilah's tone, an urgency Samson recognised from previous cases when she'd got the scent of something. But for the life of him, he couldn't see where she was going with this particular line of questioning.

'Yes, for the past forty years. Granted, it's not the most attractive piece of jewellery,' said Edith, placing her mug back on the table and touching the leather strap, as though protecting it from Delilah's intense regard, 'but I didn't choose it for its looks. I chose it because it was easy to see when I was teaching.'

Gaze still on Edith's arm, Delilah made no further effort to speak, her face contorted as though she was working something out. Edith looked at Samson. Who, at a complete loss as to how to continue, looked at Ida.

'So,' said Ida, stepping into the silence and rescuing her colleagues, 'how's about we leave the issue of the argument someone possibly overheard to one side for now. Is there anything tha can tell us, Edith, which would help exonerate Arty?'

'You mean point the finger in other directions?' asked Edith with a wan smile. She nodded. 'I fear so. You see, I always suspected that I wasn't the only woman to fall foul of Vinny King back then.'

'He duped someone else?' asked Samson.

Edith shrugged. 'I can't be a hundred per cent sure, but there were certain clues. We had a blazing argument before he left for London – and yes, I'll admit to *that* argument! It should have been a red flag to me really, but I was young and in love. At least I thought I was. Anyway, things got heated and, in the course of our row, Vinny said something about having other irons in the fire. I thought at the time that he meant opportunities for work but on reflection . . .'

'Tha thinks he meant another woman?'

'Exactly so. Or more precisely, another woman's money.'

Ida gasped while Samson's mind was whirring. 'So someone else in the area may have been swindled by him?'

Edith nodded. 'Possibly more than one.'

'I don't suppose you have any names?'

She opened her mouth to speak but before she could, Delilah bolted up out of her chair and declared, 'Pink curtains!'

'What's tha wittering on about, lass?' demanded Ida, a hand on her heart in shock at the sudden interjection, while Edith was just staring at Delilah as though she'd gone insane.

Samson wasn't sure she hadn't as she turned to him, a manic look in her eyes. 'Care to explain?' he said.

'When I overheard the argument below Edith's flat,' she said breathlessly, forgetting about any attempt to conceal the identity of their source, 'there was a woman there. All I saw was her watch – it had a dainty silver band with a small face. And there were pink curtains.'

'I don't have pink curtains,' said Edith, bemused by this digression.

Delilah nodded. 'I know that. Of course I do. But I got the layout all confused. I was trying to sneak out . . . I mean, I came out of the kitchen and turned left. I thought I was under your flat but I wasn't. I was at the other end of that wing.'

'So whose blasted flat was it?' demanded Ida, exasperated.

'Geraldine Mortimer's.'

Edith gasped. A hand going to her mouth. Delilah nodded, grimly.

'Is Geraldine one of them, Edith?' she asked. 'One of the other women you think might have been a victim of Vinny?'

'Yes,' came the whispered reply.

Delilah looked at Samson, eyebrow raised, a look of determination to her that he knew well. 'That,' she said, 'changes everything.'

If the rest of the Dales Detective Agency team were surprised by the complete about-turn from their colleagues, they didn't gloat about the capitulation. At least not in front of their new client.

'I told you Arty was innocent!' stated Nathan after Edith had left the building and Samson had brought the teenagers and Gareth up to speed with developments, the kitchen thrumming with excitement.

'Aye, lad, and tha was right to stick to tha convictions,' said Ida, patting his arm.

'So we're taking the case?' asked Nina.

'Yes,' said Samson. 'Which means we'll have to rejig the schedule, which in turn means there's going to be more work for all of us.'

'Fine by me,' said Gareth. 'Are we starting with Geraldine Mortimer?'

Delilah nodded. 'Definitely. I suggest some discreet scrutiny of her background – let's see if we can corroborate Edith's suspicion that Geraldine was another of Vinny's scam victims.'

'This Vinny bloke is coming across as a right sleazeball,' muttered Nathan.

'Tha's not wrong there,' muttered Ida. She was leaning against the worktop, Samson noting that she looked a lot less flustered, a weight lifted off her shoulders following the meeting and its revelations. Her conscience now cleared to throw her full support behind Arty. 'And the argument Delilah overheard? Is tha going to DS Benson with that?'

'Difficult to see how we can justify doing otherwise,' said Samson. 'Given that Geraldine proclaimed her love for Vinny in front of several of us the day he died and the tears she shed for him in her interview with Benson, she clearly had a relationship of some sort with him in the past. So there's a possibility that Edith is right about the rest. All of which gives Geraldine a strong motive for wanting Vinny dead.'

'She also had opportunity,' added Delilah. 'If Arty is telling the truth and he went back to his apartment after Clarissa saw him, Geraldine could have gone upstairs and killed Vinny before Arty arrived.'

'Tha'd need to be shifting some to get up and down in that time, mind,' cautioned Ida. 'The lift takes forever and while Geraldine is fit for her age, she'd have to have run up those stairs at a fair pace to commit the deed and be back downstairs before Arty arrived at Vinny's.'

'And in those shoes . . .' murmured Samson, remembering the strappy stilettos. 'Maybe that is asking a bit much?'

'Unless she only went one way.' Nathan's comment drew everyone's focus.

'How do you mean?' asked Nina.

Nathan shrugged. 'She only had to go upstairs to kill Vinny. She didn't need to go back down again.'

'But Arty would have seen her when he came along the corridor.'

'Not if she hid in the stairwell.'

'That's right!' Samson looked at Nathan, nodding. 'Geraldine didn't need to go back outside. She only needed to be seen arriving after someone else. And by kicking up a racket outside Vinny's door when she did, she ensured that both Arty and Clarissa gave her an alibi.'

'Nice one!' said Gareth, slapping Nathan on the back and almost making the teenager fall over.

'So what's next?' asked Nina.

'Edith has a doctor's appointment but then she's heading straight to the police station to tell Sergeant Clayton everything she's just told us,' said Samson.

'That's brave,' murmured Gareth. 'The entire town is going to find out what happened to her back then.'

'Happen she's happy for folk to think her a fool as long as it helps get Arty out of this mess,' said Ida. 'There's no doubting her feelings for him, that's for sure.'

'Agreed on all counts,' said Samson.

Edith Hird was one of the bravest people he knew. Before she'd left, not only had she waived her initial request for her past to be kept secret, she'd also insisted on seeing some of the photos taken at the scene of the crime, which Sergeant

Clayton had made sure reached the Dales Detective team. Samson had tried to persuade her otherwise, not wanting her final memory of Vinny King to be so brutal, but she'd overridden his objections, stating bluntly that she'd been one of the last people in that apartment and maybe she'd see something out of place which could help. Glancing through the photographs, she'd kept her emotions in check, but he'd noticed the tremor in her hand as she passed him back his mobile.

A woman made of stellar stuff. And one they now had a chance to help.

'Anyway,' he resumed, 'in light of these developments, I thought it might be a good idea for Delilah and I to nip over to Fellside Court and have a chat with Geraldine before Benson beats us to it.'

'What about this other woman who could have been a victim of Vinny's scam, too?' asked Nina. 'Do we have anything more to go on as to who she is?'

Delilah shook her head. 'Edith wasn't even certain there was a third person. It was more of a gut feeling. So, for now, we're going to concentrate on Geraldine.'

'And the rest of us?' Gareth asked.

'As we discussed before – full focus on Tyke's case for the time being, until we unearth anything new which could help us put Arty in the clear.'

'Let's hope that happens soon,' muttered Ida. 'I hate to think of him sitting in a prison cell over in Harrogate.'

It was said in such a way that the object of Ida's concern was unclear – the idea of a prison cell being Arty's current lodging or it being in Harrogate, so far from Bruncliffe and the fells. Then she gestured towards the wall with a glimmer of a smile.

'Happen we're going to need a bigger whiteboard.'

The ensuing burst of laughter was a welcome relief to the entire Dales Detective team.

Under normal circumstances, the brisk walk through the town and along the secluded riverside path which ran behind the dairy and the industrial estate would have been a delight. Blossom on the overhanging trees. Birds singing. The gentle burble of the water and the promise of a blue sky stretching overhead. Enough to soothe the most troubled of souls.

Today was an exception. By the time she entered the doctor's surgery and crossed to the reception, Edith Hird was no calmer than she had been when she left the Dales Detective Agency.

'I'm sorry, Miss Hird, but Dr Naylor is running a bit late,' said the receptionist, a middle-aged woman Edith had taught many moons ago who had never learned to cope with calling the former headmistress by her first name. And whose married name Edith could never remember in return, the woman forever being Nicky Ferris in her mind. Cousin of the unfortunate Pete Ferris and mother of two children, both of whom had also passed through Edith's school at some point. 'He's in with someone and then there's two other people before you. Are you okay to wait?'

'Dr Naylor? He's working?' Edith was surprised.

Around the edges of yesterday's drama concerning Vinny King's murder had seeped the sad news that Liz Naylor had passed away earlier in the day. Someone else Edith had known in her working life, Liz being one of the best classroom assistants Bruncliffe Primary had ever had. Quiet and unassuming, she'd come to the school just after Edith had taken on the role of headmistress, worried that her time working in accounts at the papermill before she got married might not be enough to qualify her for such a position. But Liz had been a natural, possessing a manner with the children which was guaranteed to calm the most fractious pupil or engage the most distracted mind.

Edith knew which of the two recently deceased deserved the town's mourning. And she certainly hadn't expected Liz's husband to be the doctor seeing her today.

'Surely he should be at home?' she queried.

Nicky nodded, equally concerned. 'I agree. We've all tried to tell him that but he said he prefers to be busy.' Then she reached across the desk and squeezed Edith's hand. 'And just so you know,' she murmured, 'we all think . . . know . . . we all know Arty couldn't have done what they're saying.'

'Thank you,' Edith said. Fighting the rush of tears brought on by the unexpected show of support.

She turned towards the waiting area, the bright light streaming down through the skylights making her squint. A young woman and a teenage lad were in the only occupied chairs, sitting at opposite ends of the room. Edith nodded a general greeting, not recognising either of them, the lass smiling back, her long blonde hair lit up like a halo in the sunshine. It was only as she moved out of the direct sunlight that Edith realised the other patient was also a young woman, an elfin look about her Edith recognised.

Tyke's friend. She'd been at Fellside Court last night, comforting him. Face drawn and pale, she looked what Edith would call peaky, sitting with her hands clasped tightly in her lap. Sensing Edith's regard, she raised her head and nodded a belated hello. Then she picked up a magazine and began leafing through it.

Date with Destiny

Never one for forcing her company on others, Edith took the hint and sat on a chair in the middle, glad not to have to make small talk.

It wasn't the best of days to be getting her regular checkup, her blood pressure no doubt elevated. But she was hoping the routine of it would help keep her mind off things. Things like Arty being locked up in a cell for something he didn't do.

Because not even a scintilla of doubt existed in Edith's mind about Arty's innocence.

Feeling the stress building up again, Edith reached for the nearest magazine, an old copy of a celebrity-obsessed publication which she wouldn't normally give a second glance. Idly she began flicking through the pages, barely seeing the text. Until she turned to a double page feature article.

King of Talk Returns Home

Vinny King, smiling out at her from the glossy photo, standing in his apartment in Fellside Court next to his wall of fame, that blasted painting behind him. And beside him on the sideboard, the National Television Awards trophy, destined to become a murder weapon.

Edith must have made a noise. Possibly even gone a bit pale. Because Nicky was looking over, asking if she was okay.

'Fine, fine,' she said, forcing her voice to be firm. Making her lips curve in a reassuring smile until Nicky turned back to her monitor.

But the shock of it, seeing him there like that and so soon after the crime scene photos – the horrible juxtaposition sent Edith's heart thumping. She ran an eye over the article, lots of words, so little content. Not unlike Vinny's life. Then she looked again at the photograph.

It had been taken not long after he'd moved in, the residents of Fellside Court delighted at the arrival of the photographer and the journalist from the magazine. Edith had stayed out of the way, still getting accustomed to Vinny being back in her life, but she remembered the fuss of it all. And now here it was, the printed version of that day lying in a doctor's waiting room while the man it featured was lying dead in a morgue.

All that fame. All that vanity. And for what—?

She blinked. Looked again at the photo. She stared at it. Stared harder. A memory coming, thumping into her consciousness. Then she was on her feet, saying something to Nicky, and hurrying towards the door.

24

Nicky Parker (née Ferris) had known Miss Hird all her life. And in those forty-some years, she had never seen her former headmistress agitated. Or upset.

So when Miss Hird suddenly got to her feet, the magazine she'd been reading falling to the floor, Nicky looked over fearing the worst. But it wasn't a heart attack. Or any recognisable ailment. Instead, Miss Hird was heading for the door, stick in hand.

'I've got to go back to Fellside Court,' she exclaimed over her shoulder.

Then the door was closing behind her just as Dr Naylor emerged from his office, preparing to call the next patient.

'Is everything all right, Nicky?' he asked, taking in the receptionist's shocked expression.

'Miss Hird,' she said, gesturing towards the departing figure through the glass doors. 'She just suddenly left.'

Dr Naylor glanced towards the exit and back at Nicky. 'Did she get a call or something?'

'Nothing of the sort. One minute she was reading that magazine and the next, she was hotfooting it out of here like her house was on fire.'

The doctor walked over to the now empty chair and picked up the magazine which was spine up on the floor. He turned it over, his face darkening as he glanced at the open page. Then he slapped it closed and dropped it on the low table.

Running a hand over his face, he walked back towards her.

'Actually, Nicky,' he murmured across the desk, 'I don't feel so good myself. Can you give Dr Varley a call and get her in to take over?'

'What, now? Immediately?'

'Yes. Sorry. I should have listened to you. I'm not in any fit state to be working.'

She nodded, reaching for the phone. Thinking of all the things she'd have to rejuggle to accommodate this sudden change of plan.

'No worries, Doctor. Just get yourself home and try to get some rest.'

Dr Naylor was already heading down the corridor towards the car park at the back as she began speaking to Dr Varley, explaining to the locum why her shift was about to begin a couple of hours earlier than she'd anticipated.

When Nicky hung up, she remembered the other patients. Neither of them local, their names didn't spring to mind.

'I'm awfully sorry,' she said, looking out into the reception area, 'but there's been an emergency. Are you both okay to wait a bit longer?'

One of the women was sitting, head down, phone in hand. She glanced up. 'Yes, of course. No problem.'

But the blonde one was standing, heading for the door. 'Sorry, but I've got to go. I'm meeting someone.'

'Can I reschedule you for tomorrow?'

'I'm going home tomorrow. But don't worry, it wasn't serious. Thanks anyway.' With a warm smile, she left.

Grateful for such understanding, the receptionist stepped out from behind her desk and crossed the room, curious to see what had triggered Edith Hird's departure. When she reached the table she picked up the magazine and flicked through the pages and found herself staring at the recently deceased Vinny King.

That must be it. No wonder the poor woman had been shocked. Not even twenty-four hours after the violent death of a man she'd once held a torch for and there she was, confronted by a double-page spread on him. It must have torn her grief wide open.

Annoyed with herself for not having remembered the article was in there, Nicky carried the magazine back to her desk and stuck it in her bag. At least that way no other unsuspecting patient could come across it unawares.

'You don't deny that you were having a relationship with Vinny King, then?' asked Delilah.

'It's a bit late for that, don't you think?' As she sat on the edge of the couch in her apartment, framed by the soft-pink curtains behind her, there was something subdued about Geraldine Mortimer. If Samson had been asked to put a name to it, he'd have said it was akin to grief.

The Dales Detective duo had arrived at Fellside Court after lunch and as they entered the building, they'd seen Geraldine leaving the cafe. She hadn't seemed surprised by their request to speak to her. As if their involvement in the investigation of Vinny King's death was a foregone conclusion. She'd invited them up to her apartment and had insisted on making tea before taking a seat opposite them.

Sitting with the delicate cup and saucer in his hands, Samson couldn't help wondering if their host would have been as hospitable if she'd known the direction their questions would take.

'The entire town is aware of it now,' she continued, giving a twisted smile. 'Which is ironic, really.'

'How's that?' asked Samson.

'Vinny didn't want anyone knowing about it. About us.'

'So your relationship wasn't just in the past?'

Her gaze sharpened. 'Ah,' she said, nodding, 'you've been doing your research. Or Edith Hird has been telling tales. Saint Edith, the epitome of discretion.' The laugh she gave was devoid of humour. 'All these years spinning that yarn about a mutual break-up. It was anything but. Vinny couldn't wait to be shot of her and her constant demands that he forsake a career in showbusiness and settle down in Bruncliffe.'

'And you?' asked Delilah. 'Didn't he leave you behind, too?'

Geraldine tossed her head, some of her customary confidence returning. 'It wasn't the same. We had an understanding. I would never have stood in the way of Vinny achieving his dreams.'

'Even though he stole your money to do so?'

It was a stab in the dark, based on Edith's hunch, but Delilah's question had hit the mark. Geraldine jerked backwards, face flushing.

'It was a loan,' she said.

'Did he pay you back? Or is that why you were overheard arguing with him yesterday morning? Was it over the money?'

'No . . . it wasn't . . . how did you know . . . ?' Thrown off balance, Geraldine looked at Samson as if for help. But he wasn't about to intervene. Delilah was handling the interview like a seasoned investigator.

'Vinny mentioned something about you threatening him,'

Delilah continued, her tone suddenly sympathetic. 'What was going on, Geraldine?'

'He didn't want to go public,' she snapped. 'We'd re-kindled our relationship but Vinny wanted to keep it quiet. He said I wasn't ready for the media attention it would bring. He was protecting me.'

'So you gave him an ultimatum? Is that what happened?'

'No! I just told him I thought it was time we opened up about it. And that I wasn't prepared to sneak around this place like a teenage girl, meeting up in secret. I had enough sneaking around the first time.'

'When you were having an affair with a man engaged to be married?'

Another dry laugh. 'That engagement was a sham. Even Edith knew it in her heart of hearts. She was never the right woman for him.'

'But yet her lifetime's savings were good enough for him.'

Geraldine's cup clattered against its saucer, her eyes widening at Delilah's revelation.

'Ah,' said Delilah. 'You weren't aware of that.'

'Edith loaned him money as well?'

'Not a loan. He stole it. Just like he stole yours, no matter how you choose to term it.' Delilah looked at Samson, eyebrow raised. 'What do you think? A man running off with all that hard-earned cash. Motive enough for murder, I'd say.'

'So that's what this is?' Geraldine's gaze flicked between the pair of them. Confusion mixed with pain. 'You're not here to have my eyewitness account of what happened. You're here to try to pin Vinny's murder on me?'

Samson shrugged. 'The facts fit, Geraldine. You definitely had the motive and, if Arty is to be believed, you also had the opportunity. I think once the police know a bit more about your background with Vinny King, they might be as interested as we are in your movements yesterday evening.'

'There's nothing new to know! I came back with Vinny in the minibus, I waited outside and then finally went up to his apartment and found Arty Robinson leaning over him, murder weapon in hand. It's an open and shut case.'

'So the threats and the fact Vinny took your money, that didn't leave you hating him?'

'Hate him?' Geraldine was incredulous. 'I loved him. Can't you see that? Enough to put up with being kept at the periphery of his life. Enough to forgive him for everything back then. Enough that even my marriage to someone else couldn't smother that flame.' She stopped, tears on her cheeks now. 'I could never have killed him.'

Then she lifted her head, some of her usual fire returning. 'Besides, that row yesterday – whoever was listening in clearly didn't stay to the end. Vinny agreed to stop hiding what was between us. And as for the money which he borrowed all those years ago,' she added, triumphant now, 'he told me he'd left me the Hockney in his will. I reckon that will more than cover it, don't you?'

It was only when they reached the door of their destination that Joseph began to feel stupid.

'What the hell are we doing here?' asked Eric, staring at the sign in disbelief. Bruncliffe Bright Whites. Tucked away on the industrial estate, the dry cleaners wasn't somewhere either man had cause to visit ordinarily.

'Just trust me,' muttered Joseph. He pushed the door open, a bell clanging somewhere in the depths of the place, the warm smell of detergent enveloping them.

'Can I help you?' A young woman had appeared at the

counter, a long rail fixed to the wall behind her, plastic-covered garments hanging from it.

Now he really felt stupid. But there was no going back.

'Yes . . . at least I hope so . . . the thing is . . .' He was all fingers and thumbs, pulling out his wallet, mumbling away while she smiled patiently. 'This,' he finally said, passing the piece of paper over the counter.

It felt like grief. That slip of paper which he'd carried in his pocket for ten years, the creases and faded type giving testament to its longevity. He was letting it go. Letting go of the hope it had held for him all that time.

What if he had left it too late and that hope was about to be shattered?

'Oh!' She looked at the receipt. Shook her head, doubtful. 'I'm not sure . . . it's been a while!' She gave a tentative smile. 'I'll have to check out back.'

She disappeared through the beaded curtains, leaving Joseph standing there like a deluded fool. Meanwhile, Eric was prowling the small waiting area, his oxygen canister rattling behind him. 'I don't see how picking up your clean laundry is going to weave a magic wand of happiness over everyone,' he was muttering.

The minutes ticked by. Eric finally collapsing onto the only seat in the place. Pointedly looking at his watch. All the while, Joseph's faith was fading.

He was daft. There was no way, after all these years—

A rustle of movement beyond the beaded curtains and the woman reappeared, this time with an older woman as well.

'Mr O'Brien,' the older woman said, smile warm. 'I always knew you'd come back!'

And then she was passing him a parcel across the counter, patting his hand, telling him how she'd kept it safe for him.

He didn't really hear the words. He was staring too hard at that parcel. The precious possession he'd had the foresight to protect in a rare moment of lucidity while in the depths of drink. Knowing it would be better off here than with him out at Twistleton Farm, where alcohol had removed the value from everything but the next bottle.

'Thank you!' he said. Tears forming.

'Bloody hell, Joseph,' muttered Eric as they left the building, Joseph dabbing at his eyes with his handkerchief. 'I thought we were on a mission to cheer folk up!'

Clutching his package to his chest, Joseph just smiled. 'We are, my friend,' he said. 'We are.'

'Well, in that case,' came the response, 'let's cut across into town and go to Peaks. Reckon Edith will appreciate a bit of cake when she gets back.'

'Good idea. I need to talk to Lucy anyway.'

'About this mysterious plan of yours?' said Eric. 'Are you going to tell me what it is?'

Joseph gave him a sideways glance, suddenly unsure again. Wondering if Eric would pour scorn on his madcap idea. But the package in his hands gave him strength, its mere existence an auspicious sign that he was doing the right thing.

'So,' he began, 'this is what I was thinking . . .'

With the sun warming their backs, and Joseph relating his clandestine scheme, the two friends began making their way through the industrial estate towards the river path.

The river path was secluded. A blessing Edith was grateful for as she walked as fast as her bad hip would allow, her stick tapping at the ground in a frantic rhythm. She didn't have time to dally. She'd texted Ana as soon as she'd set off from the doctor's, asking to meet at Vinny's apartment. It was imperative that she got inside. Because she was sure the clue to Arty's innocence lay in there.

And perhaps even the answer to who killed Vinny.

Spurred on by her urgency, Edith didn't take in the trees around her. The river flowing fast to her right. The path ahead, shielded from the town beyond, not another soul on it. When the figure rushed out from the bushes, she didn't even have the wherewithal to scream.

A sharp pain in her head. Instant dizziness. Edith was aware she was falling, her stick flying out from under her, her handbag dropping from her grasp. Then there was the rough impact of the ground. All her breath escaping in one whoosh. The sound of something breaking.

An accident. Someone running into her. But no.

She looked up, vision blurring, and saw the figure, dressed in black. Arm raised in a menacing silhouette against that ludicrously blue sky. About to hit her again.

Consciousness slipping, her last thought was of Arty. Sweet Arty. And how she wouldn't be able to save him now.

25

Much to Joseph's relief, Eric loved his idea.

'Wait till the lasses hear about this!' he exclaimed, a huge smile splitting his face. 'It's the perfect pick-me-up.'

They turned onto the river path, the blissful sunshine and the picturesque setting so sublime, it was almost easy to forget the terrible events of the evening before. To have Arty's plight slip the mind. They lapsed into a companionable silence until Eric halted abruptly, a hand on Joseph's arm.

'What the hell—?' He was staring up ahead, along the path through the trees.

Joseph followed his gaze, squinting in the bright light, struggling to make out what he was seeing. A shape on the ground, a person leaning over it.

'Looks like somebody's fallen,' he said. 'And someone's helping them—' He broke off. The pair of them watching, the strain of arms against the body, moving it off the path. The intent in it—

Eric was the first to work it out.

'They're not helping!' he yelped. 'They're trying to push them in the river! Oi! You!' He started running, taking gulps of breath. The oxygen cart thumping against his side.

Joseph ran too. A motion so alien to him now. Outpacing

Eric. But up ahead the attacker had frozen, twisted towards them, and then was off, through the trees. A blur of black.

'Go after them, Joseph!' gasped Eric from behind.

Joseph didn't give it a second thought. Just veered off the path and into the trees. Trying to keep his focus on the black-clad figure in the distance as branches pulled and tore at his clothes and limbs. Ripping the package from his hands. He kept going. A pain in his ribs. Stitch. Letting him know that this wasn't what he normally did, this hectic flight through the shrubs.

'Hey!' he tried shouting, his voice coming on a rasp of air. Higher pitched. 'Hey! Stop!'

They didn't. They just ran faster, the gap between them too big now. Had always been too big for a man whose body was aged beyond his years by decades of abuse.

He pulled up when he broke out onto a back street in the industrial estate. He looked left. Right. No movement. No one around.

Whoever it was, they were gone.

Samson would have caught them. Delilah even more so.

Dejected at his failure, Joseph turned and jogged his way back to the river, picking up his parcel on the way. Mud all over it. Trying to brush the worst of it off, he emerged onto the path where he found Eric kneeling on the ground, mobile at his ear, panic on his face. The prostrate form of the victim the far side of him, perilously close to the fast-flowing water of the river. A handbag and walking stick to one side. Both triggering some kind of recognition in Joseph.

'Ambulance,' Eric was saying. 'Urgently. Someone's been mugged.'

Joseph shifted his position and felt his heart rattle with fear, the parcel falling from his grasp for a second time.

The woman lying on the ground bleeding profusely was Edith Hird. And she really didn't look good.

'Thoughts?' murmured Samson as they walked down the stairs to the foyer of Fellside Court.

Delilah grimaced. 'My brain is telling me Geraldine had motive in abundance – the fact Vinny took her money for starters. Plus we know she had opportunity, as much so as Arty. But . . .'

'You think her love for Vinny was genuine.'

'Yes. And while I don't think loving someone necessarily rules out being capable of killing them,' she said, throwing Samson a devilish grin that made him want to hug her, 'there's something in her story which just rings true. I mean, who the hell would admit to forgiving a creep like Vinny King after he made a fool of them? Geraldine didn't just do it once – she's doing it again now. Making out that Vinny leaving her the Hockney balances everything out. Even when we told her he'd made the same promise to Edith.' Delilah shrugged.

It had been startling to watch the way Geraldine Mortimer had assimilated the revelation about the Hockney and Vinny's duplicate gifting of it. She'd simply fallen silent. Shrugged. Then declared that Edith must be lying.

Because Vinny, the man with the past history of deception, couldn't possibly be hoodwinking her once more.

That was love of the blind, unquestioning, forbearing type.

'Maybe it wasn't the money,' mused Samson. 'Maybe it was jealousy?'

Delilah paused at the bottom step. 'Of Edith, you mean?'

'It's possible. Geraldine was holding out hope that this time Vinny would be hers, all out in the open and official. But from all accounts, Vinny liked spending time with Edith.

Sought her out so much, in fact, that Arty got jealous. Perhaps that jealousy cut both ways?'

'In which case Geraldine would still be a viable suspect—'

'Delilah! Samson!' Ana Stoyanovic had burst out of her office and was running across the entrance hall towards them. The normally calm and measured manager of Fellside Court was looking and sounding desperate. 'Thank God you're here!'

Her cries had brought residents out of the lounge and the cafe. A gathering of pensioners, all alarmed by her distress.

'What's going on?' asked Delilah, moving forward, grasping Ana's hands in hers.

'It's Edith! She's been mugged!'

Ana drove Samson and Delilah down to the car park at the end of the riverside path, filling them in on the scant details she had as they went. The attack Eric and Joseph had witnessed. Their frantic call to her as they waited for the ambulance. When the trio arrived at the scene they found Joseph and Eric sitting on a bench with Danny Bradley standing in front of them, taking notes. There was a smear of blood on the dust of the path and Edith's bag and stick were lying beyond it.

'Are you both okay?' Samson asked, taking in the shock on their faces. The rumpled look of his father, bits of dirt and greenery sticking to his cardigan and a grubby Bruncliffe Bright Whites' bag on the bench next to him.

'We are,' said Eric gravely. 'Edith not so much.'

'They've taken her to Airedale. She was unconscious. A nasty wound on her head and a suspected broken hip—' Joseph's voice faltered. 'And I couldn't catch the bastard! I wasn't fast enough.'

Samson squeezed his shoulder. 'You did what you could, Dad.'

'Did you manage to get a look at whoever it was?' asked Danny.

'Not really. It was all a blur. Average height. Average build. Dressed in black.' Joseph shrugged. 'Sorry. I know that's not enough to go on.'

'If only we'd come along earlier,' said Eric bitterly. 'We could have prevented it.'

Ana sat next to him, took his hand in hers. 'You can't blame yourself, Eric. No one could have predicted this would happen.'

'And in broad daylight, too!' said Joseph, shaking his head. 'So brazen.'

'Drugs will do that to folk, unfortunately,' said Danny. 'Someone needing a fix. Driven to desperate measures.'

'Except,' said Delilah, pointing to the path, 'they didn't take what they came for.'

They all looked at the handbag, lying there in full view.

'Did Edith fall on it, perhaps?' asked Samson. 'Making it hard to snatch? Or was she wearing it across her body and the paramedics took it off when they were treating her?'

Eric shrugged. 'I couldn't say for sure. I was so panicked.'

'I can.' Joseph was looking at his son. 'The bag was lying there like that when I came back from the chase . . .' He paused. Frowning. 'Funny thing is, when we first saw what was happening, it looked like the attacker was trying to push Edith into the river, even though she was down and had dropped her bag. Isn't that right, Eric?'

'Horrible, it was,' shuddered Eric. 'Something determined about it. If we hadn't have been here . . .' He stuttered to a halt, face grey with shock.

'Good job we were,' muttered Joseph, putting an arm around his friend.

'Which brings us back to the question – why would a mugger continue attacking a victim once they had access to what they wanted?' asked Delilah.

'You think there could be more to this?' Danny was looking from Delilah to Samson.

'God knows,' muttered Samson. 'But it does seem a bit bizarre if it was just a random snatch and run.'

'But that would mean . . .' Eric faltered, blinking.

'That Edith was targeted,' said Delilah grimly. 'Could it be connected to her visit to us this morning?'

Her question, addressed to Samson, caught the attention of both Danny and Joseph.

'Did she hire you to clear Arty?' asked Danny.

'More importantly, did you take the case?' demanded Joseph.

Samson nodded. 'Yes to both. But I fail to see how that could be the link here.'

'Perhaps this might be,' said Ana, frowning. She was holding out her phone, a text showing on the screen. 'I've only just seen it. It's from Edith, sent a short while ago. "Walking back to FSC. Meet me at Vinny's. Bring your keys. Urgent."'

'Christ!' muttered Samson. 'That seems to make the link clear-cut. Somehow Edith discovered something which made her want to revisit the crime scene.'

'And this attack prevented her from doing that,' murmured Delilah.

'Bloody hell!' Danny shook his head. 'Where was she coming from when she was attacked?'

'The doctor's,' said Samson. 'She said she was going straight to the surgery when she left us.'

'Right, I'll need to corroborate that. Perhaps head over there and see if anything happened to trigger this.'

'We'll come with you,' said Samson.

'Much appreciated,' said Danny. 'If this is connected to Vinny King's murder, then the more eyes the better.'

But Delilah was shaking her head. 'You'll have to go without me. I've got to get back to collect Tolpuddle from Ida and then I'm due to run with Tyke. But if you do unearth a connection,' she added, looking at Samson, 'then this could put Geraldine Mortimer in the clear. She was with us when this happened.'

'Geraldine Mortimer?' asked Danny, puzzled. 'You think she could've killed Vinny King?'

'I'll fill you in on the way,' said Samson. 'But whatever the outcome from this, I suspect Benson is going to have to revise his opinion of Arty as the culprit.'

Danny threw him a wry look. 'He isn't going to like that!'

Danny was right. When he sent through his update on the suspected mugging of Edith Hird to Sergeant Clayton, the sergeant read it out to DS Benson sitting across the office from him at the back of the police station.

'You're joking,' muttered the detective. 'Danny's barking up the wrong tree if he thinks someone taking a swipe at a pensioner is somehow connected to the murder of Vinny King. Just because both victims are elderly, doesn't mean there's a link.'

'Doesn't mean there isn't either,' countered the sergeant, feeling belligerent in the face of the fact that he hadn't had time for a coffee all morning, let alone a cake, the murder case taking all their time. 'Edith Hird's supposed relationship with Vinny is the hook we're hanging Arty Robinson on.

It's a bit of a coincidence that she's then attacked the next day, in a town not known for its muggings. So maybe we'd best keep an open mind until young Danny has reported back in full.'

The detective grumbled something about 'typical Bruncliffe overthinking' before his mobile started ringing and he turned away to answer it. Sergeant Clayton decided it was probably best not to bother him further by telling him Samson O'Brien was with Constable Bradley and had requested an urgent meeting with the detective when they were done at the doctor's surgery.

Instead he got up, put on his helmet and headed out the door. Time to get some refreshments in. He had a feeling DS Benson was going to need the sugar to sweeten whatever it was that had got O'Brien's nose twitching.

Half an hour later, Delilah was running up the fellside behind Bruncliffe with Tolpuddle and Tyke. Or rather, she was chasing the pair of them up the steep landscape, a blur of grey canine and fluorescent lime green pulling away from her.

He was good, this lad from the city. Even if his kit was as over the top as his everyday clothing – a swirl of orange cutting through the green of his top, his shorts matching – he ran like a natural with an easy stride, a lightness to his footfall as he almost bounded up the incline. She'd been impressed with him twelve years ago, seeing him as a credible opponent, one who had pushed her to run at her limits. But then he'd gone and cheated, and, while she liked him as a person, she had never forgiven him for that.

Never would.

So that made the current situation even harder to bear,

lagging behind him like this. When she had unlimited access to the fells for training and he barely had a hill to run up where he lived.

'Come on, slacker!' he called back down at her as he crested the rise and came to a halt, Tolpuddle jumping excited circles around him.

She reached the pair of them, breathing hard. 'Good running!' she said.

'Got a lot of adrenalin to burn off. Been a slow morning and what with Uncle Vinny . . .' Tyke tailed off, staring out across the fells, the town a smudge of grey roofs and chimneys below them.

'Are you still intending to enter the Bruncliffe Hills at the weekend?' she asked. 'Because I'd say you're more than ready.'

'That's the plan. It'll take my mind off what's going on, if nothing else. Things were bad enough with those blasted threats but this murder has thrown me completely.' He shook his head. Then he sighed. 'At least the police seem to be on top of it – I have to confess, I wasn't holding out much hope for the abilities of DS Benson, given he's just a provincial copper, but he's come through. Getting an arrest that quickly is impressive.'

Delilah dipped her head, turning away from him, but not quickly enough.

'What? What is it?' he demanded, staring at her.

'Nothing,' she said, cursing her ridiculous inability to maintain a poker face.

'Delilah, if there's been a development, don't you think I deserve to know?'

It was a fair point. He was Vinny's nephew. And also the agency's client.

'Okay, but this isn't verified so it goes no further,' she warned.

'You have my word.'

'Right, well, there has been a development as you say. We have reason to believe that Arty might not be the only potential suspect.'

'You mean he might be innocent?' Tyke asked, frowning. 'Even with his fingerprints all over that trophy?'

Delilah nodded. 'Yes. There are other factors which we're investigating—'

'"We're"?'

'Edith Hird has hired the Dales Detective Agency to look into your uncle's murder.'

He spun away, clearly shocked. 'Christ! I thought it was all sorted . . .'

She placed a hand on his arm. 'It's good that Samson's on the case. He'll make sure the real culprit is caught.'

'Yeah. You're right. I couldn't ask for more. But . . .' Tyke shook his head. 'I feel selfish for even thinking this, but won't that make you overstretched? I mean, Uncle Vinny's investigation and mine?'

'It's a totally reasonable question given the circumstances,' Delilah reassured him. 'But don't worry. We'll still have your back. Plus we've got a couple of leads which are looking solid – we're pretty sure we've identified the supplier of the dead rabbit left on your doorstep so it's only a matter of time until we have a delivery address. And we've got the licence plate for the motorbike that almost ran you over. It's not much of a help in that it's not registered or insured but at least there's a chance of it being spotted if it's used on the roads. So trust me, we are still focusing on your case.'

Not wanting to spook him unnecessarily, she decided not

to mention that the person responsible for the death threats could be staying in Bruncliffe. A decision that seemed the right one when he gave her a relieved grin.

'Crikey! You have been busy! What about who's behind it all? Are you any closer to finding that out?'

'Nothing definite at the moment but we're certainly having a long hard look at Holly Campbell.'

The name brought a grimace to Tyke's face. 'Ah,' he said.

'Can you tell me what you know about her?'

He stared down at the ground, Delilah getting the sense he was choosing how to respond. Then he sighed. 'I don't like to speak ill of people, but Holly . . . she had a problem with me from the moment we met on set for *The Nines*. She didn't respond well to criticism, no matter how gently it was worded. And once she was eliminated, she took it personally. Started accusing me of all sorts.' He shrugged. 'I tried to tell myself it would all blow over but she kept it up. Getting more and more vindictive, writing articles attacking my credibility as a designer, turning up at events where I was scheduled to appear and hurling abuse. It got to the point where I even considered taking out an injunction against her but I knew how that would look. And then about a year ago it all went quiet. She just disappeared from my life.'

'Do you think she could be capable of what's going on now?'

The thought brought a worried frown to his face. 'Possibly . . . I don't know. The whole thing just feels like a bad dream.'

'Believe me,' said Delilah, 'we're doing everything we can to make it end.'

He nodded. 'I know. Thanks.' He took a deep breath and

then gestured towards the far side of the fell, managing a smile. 'Last one gets the coffees?'

She didn't answer. Just took off running, Tolpuddle along-side her, a yelp of protest coming from behind them. Tyke wasn't the only one capable of cheating.

'You can't be serious?' DS Benson looked up in disbelief from the magazine on his desk, and regarded Samson O'Brien with a frown. 'You barge in here, tell me some story about Vinny King swindling two women out of their savings – one of whom is connected to our current suspect and the other of whom, given this news, could have the potential to be a suspect herself – and then you say that none of that matters and that I should derail the entire investigation because of this?' He gestured at the article in front of him. 'A fluff piece in a gossip mag?'

'Yes.'

Give O'Brien his due, he had courage behind his convictions. Still, even Sergeant Clayton, watching on from his chair, thought that this time the former Met officer was completely off target. He'd entered the office with Constable Bradley, the youngster wearing that eager look he always possessed when things got exciting, and had promptly instructed the detective to reconsider the Vinny King case.

All based on a double-page spread on the talk-show host.

'It's not just that,' interjected Danny, pointing at the magazine. 'It's what happened afterwards. Edith Hird abruptly left the doctor's after seeing it and was then attacked in what – according to eyewitnesses – was an attempted murder.'

Benson shook his head. 'We don't know for sure that this

was the catalyst which made Miss Hird leave the surgery – you said yourselves that the receptionist didn't actually see her reading it—'

'It would be a hell of a coincidence if it wasn't.' Danny's tone was verging on insubordinate. Sergeant Clayton gave him a gentle kick under the table, making the lad flush.

'Not necessarily,' DS Benson continued, fixing Danny with a stern eye before turning to address O'Brien as well. 'But even if you do manage to confirm what Miss Hird was reading, there's still the matter of what happened next. No disrespect to either of you or your relatives, but your witnesses are hardly reliable when it comes to eyesight. They're not exactly in the first flush of youth and could easily have misunderstood the situation over that distance.'

'You mean the attacker was simply making sure Edith was okay when he was seen leaning over her, pushing her towards the river?' There was a bite to O'Brien's words.

'I mean, it was a mugging. Brutal. Shocking. But nothing more. Everything else is conjecture.'

O'Brien threw up his hands in exasperation. 'Conjecture is exactly how we solve cases. Aren't you at least curious as to why this feature on Vinny King might have precipitated the chain of events which has left Edith Hird in hospital, fighting for her life?'

A sombre pall descended on the room. Ana Stoyanovic had just called to update them on developments and had brought the worrying news about Edith's condition. Still unconscious, she wasn't in good shape and it was touch and go as to whether she'd make it.

'O'Brien has a point.' Sergeant Clayton finally spoke. 'We have nothing to lose by putting a bit of manpower into this possible link. Happen as Danny and I could take it on, leave you clear to concentrate on Arty Robinson. And perhaps have a chat with Geraldine Mortimer, given what we've just learned. If you're right and this magazine business has no relevance to the murder, it could be worth looking into Mrs Mortimer's past. No harm in covering all bases in a case like this.'

There was a loud sigh from across the desk. DS Benson nodding. 'Okay. So what do you propose?'

'That we have another look around Vinny's apartment, for starters,' said Samson.

'There's no "we" in this instance,' said the detective, brusquely. 'Sorry, O'Brien, but you're no longer on the job and we can't risk fouling up a prosecution because of your involvement. You shouldn't even have accompanied Constable Bradley to the doctor's surgery.'

Danny Bradley gazed at the floor. A stubborn set to his jaw. Sensing rebellion – and the chance of getting to eat the delicious-looking brownies he'd brought back from Peaks being delayed even longer – the sergeant stepped in.

'DS Benson is right, lads. You'll have to sit this one out, O'Brien. Danny and I will head over to Vinny's apartment first thing tomorrow and give it a look over.'

'Tomorrow?' Constable Bradley asked, head whipping round to look at his sergeant. 'Why not today?'

'Because we've got a lot on and the apartment and its contents aren't going anywhere,' snapped Benson. 'Now if you'll excuse us, O'Brien, we've got an investigation to run.'

'As you wish.' With an air of indifference the sergeant wasn't buying, Samson leaned forward to pick up the magazine but Benson slapped his hand flat across it.

'Oh no you don't,' muttered the detective. 'That stays with us.'

Samson O'Brien merely nodded, smiled and headed for the door. Looking like butter wouldn't melt.

Hiding a smile of his own, Sergeant Clayton reached forward and took one of the brownies from the plate. He needed the energy. It was going to be an interesting night.

They waited until it was dark, which took a while given it was May, when the sun set reluctantly, leaving streaks of light in the sky long after it had sunk below the horizon. Finally Samson gave the nod, and they crept out of the bushes and along the side of the building towards the emergency exit.

'What if she's not there?' whispered Delilah, her face a pale blur against her dark clothing. Fellside Court looming over her, a black silhouette against a black sky.

'She'll be there.' He tapped the door lightly and it opened immediately.

'Hurry,' murmured Ana Stoyanovic, ushering them into the unlit kitchen and closing the door behind them. With a torch shielded by her hand, she led them silently across the room, the stainless-steel counters glinting in the stray beams escaping through her fingers. Pausing by the door that led out into the foyer, she handed Samson a key.

'Be quick. And be ultra quiet,' she warned. 'I know from experience how lightly older people sleep. And how curious they are. The slightest sound and you'll have a posse of them on you before you know it.'

'Understood,' said Samson.

'And whatever you do, don't get caught in the apartment. My spare keys are for emergencies only and that doesn't cover breaking into a crime scene. I'll lose my job for sure.'

'We'll be careful,' Delilah assured her. 'All we need is a quick look.'

Ana nodded. Then she eased the door open to peer out. Seeing no one there, she motioned them past her into the entrance hall.

The large area was a different place at this time of night. Security lights provided a minimum of illumination and, without the sunshine streaming through it, the high wall of glass took on a sinister aspect, making Samson feel like a hundred eyes were on him as he hurried after Delilah. Reaching the far side, they slipped through the door into the stairwell, and were suddenly spotlit in a blaze of light.

'Damn it!' muttered Samson, pulling Delilah against the wall beside him.

Motion-sensor lights. He should have expected that on the stairs. Not a place you wanted the residents wandering around in the dark.

They stood there, like statues, until the lights went back out.

'How do we get up the stairs without triggering them again?' whispered Delilah.

'We don't,' he muttered. 'We just have to go fast and hope no one is in the corridor up there and sees the light. Ready?'

'Totally!' He could tell she was grinning. Excited to be doing something illicit.

'Go!' he whispered.

They took the stairs two at a time but even so, the lights flared above them before they had even reached the dogleg. Up the remaining stairs and then flat against the wall once more, touching distance from the door.

A few seconds, which felt like forever, and darkness returned, Samson aware of his heart thudding in his chest. A steal of movement, Delilah's hand reaching for his. Squeezing it. The little devil was enjoying this.

'Let's give it a minute,' he murmured, lips close to her ear. 'Just to make sure no one is wandering around who shouldn't be.'

'Happy to take all night,' she whispered back. Laughter in the words.

He fought the urge to kiss her. Wondering how Ana's job would be affected if they were discovered being, in Ida's words, intimate in the stairwell.

'Ready?' he asked, not trusting himself to linger in the dark with this woman any longer.

'Always.'

He pulled open the door and they hustled onto the first-floor landing, a spike of light behind them now, making them totally visible even in the darkened corridor. And then they heard the rattle of a lock. The squeak of hinges.

Someone was coming out of one of the apartments.

'In here!' Samson was moving, towards the door next to the stairwell. Ida's cleaning cupboard. Praying it was unlocked. He yanked the door towards him, twisting as it opened and pushing Delilah ahead of him into the cupboard. The door closing. Complete dark.

'That was close!' he whispered, aware of her breathing, as rapid as his.

'Sure was.'

'Well, isn't this cosy!' A third murmured voice from the inky depths. Making Delilah yelp and sending Samson's heart rate through the roof.

26

A light, splitting the darkness. Delilah had managed to acti-
vate the torch on her phone, the beam fluctuating in her
shaking hand. She aimed it at the back of the cupboard where
it came to rest on a face leering out of the darkness.

'I've been expecting you, O'Brien!' Sergeant Clayton,
sitting on an upturned bucket, and clearly enjoying himself.
'Might have known you'd bring reinforcements.'

'What the hell!' muttered Samson, looking as shocked as
Delilah felt.

The sergeant shrugged. 'You're not the only one capable
of creeping around unobserved. Thought I'd let myself in
and wait for you. A one-man welcoming committee.'

'But how did you know . . . ?'

'Elementary, dear Watson.' The sergeant's grin was wide
now. 'Seeing as you've never been able to take no for an
answer, I figured you'd want a look around Vinny's apartment unofficially, before our flat feet trampled all over it. I
came along to keep you out of trouble. I presume,' he said,
standing up, 'you have a set of keys?'

Samson laughed. Dangled the keys from his fingers. 'You
presume right. Shall we go?'

They eased open the cupboard and crept out into the unlit
corridor, down towards Vinny King's front door, police tape

still forming a stark barrier across the wood. Showing no attempt to hide their trespass, the sergeant yanked it off and stood aside for Samson to unlock. Once the three of them were inside, he closed the door and they turned on the torches on their mobiles.

Standing there in the hallway, it was no different to any of the other apartments Delilah had visited in Fellside Court. The same tiles on the floor. The same inoffensive cream tones on the wall. The same smell of Ida's favoured brand of polish.

And then the torch beam caught on the jagged edges of glass.

She shivered. Aware that this was a place where someone had met a violent death.

'What are we looking for, exactly?' asked Sergeant Clayton as he moved towards the lounge, a pool of light sweeping the room before him.

'I've no idea. I'm hoping this might give us a clue, though.' Samson was holding out his mobile, a photo of the article which had triggered Edith Hird's rapid departure from the doctor's showing on the screen.

'You sly bugger,' laughed the sergeant. 'No wonder you weren't bothered when Benson kept the original.'

Samson grinned. 'I suspected he might do something like that, so I took a copy. There has to be something in this which made Edith react like she did. And having read it through several times, I can't see anything in the text, so it must be in the photo.'

He zoomed in, Vinny King before his vanity wall, something poignant about his beaming smile. The ignorance of the fate which awaited him.

Delilah and the sergeant stood either side of Samson, the

photo before them, and beyond it, the very setting where it had been taken.

'It's like spot the difference,' murmured Delilah, skimming her eyes from screen to room, back and forth, trying to see what could be out of place.

The famous faces looking down from the wall. The Hockney, supposedly bequeathed to two separate women. The sideboard with its display of commendations.

The reality before them was all exactly the same as that displayed in the magazine, apart from three key items. The distinctive trophy was gone from the sideboard. Vinny wasn't standing by the wall. And there was now a large stain on the carpet.

Another shudder went down Delilah's spine.

'Don't know about you two,' said the sergeant, 'but apart from the obvious, I don't see anything untoward.'

'Me neither,' muttered Samson.

'Maybe we've got it wrong,' said Delilah. 'Maybe this had nothing whatsoever to do with Edith leaving the doctor's.'

Samson shook his head. 'It's too much of a coincidence. A woman known for her calmness suddenly spooks and heads off at a pace. Texts Ana on the way to meet her here, using the word "urgent". And on her way to that urgent meeting, she's mugged in a manner that bears the hallmarks of being a targeted attack rather than a random bag snatch.' He gestured towards the photo. 'This had to be the spark that caused all that.'

'Well, if it is, I'm buggered if I can see how,' sighed Sergeant Clayton, glancing at his watch and stifling a yawn. 'And as it's way past my bedtime, I suggest we leave it here tonight.'

He turned as if to go and then paused. Turned back. Frowning.

'Of course, there's another way of looking at all this,' he said. 'Happen we can't tell what Edith saw in that magazine, but if your theory is right, O'Brien, and that mugging wasn't the work of some opportunist, then someone else also knew this photo was important.'

'And that Edith had discovered it!' said Delilah excitedly, seeing where he was heading. 'So even if we can't solve the problem of the photo, we could try to work out who could possibly have known that she'd stumbled upon it.'

'Someone who had the opportunity to act upon that information, too.' Samson was nodding. 'I'll drop by the surgery as soon as it opens tomorrow morning and speak to the receptionist again. See what she can tell us.'

'Take Danny with you,' said Sergeant Clayton, dryly. 'Let's keep it somewhat official – stop Benson having a heart attack. And keep me abreast of any developments. Edith Hird is a good woman, one of the rocks this town rests on. It's only right we work together on this and get a result, for her sake.'

'I'm not going to argue with that,' murmured Samson.

'Good. In the meantime, we'd best call it a night before we disturb the good folk asleep around us.'

They headed into the hall, turned off their torches and quietly opened the front door. Only to see the corridor beyond fully illuminated and a group of pensioners in night attire assembled there wielding walking sticks, golf clubs, even an ancient tennis racket. Joseph O'Brien was at the front of them, a hurley stick raised and ready for action.

'Samson! It's you!' he exclaimed, relieved, lowering his arm. 'We heard noises. Thought the killer might be back!'

Eyes wide, Sergeant Clayton took in the range of weapons. 'Seriously?! And you didn't think to just call the police?'

He shook his head in disbelief, glancing over his shoulder at Samson. 'I'll leave you to sort out these Magnificent Seventies. I'm going home to bed.'

When the last of the lights went off in Fellside Court, it having taken some time for the residents to calm down after their nocturnal adventures, the night was at its darkest. That hour when, even in summer, the skies finally yield to the stars and silence descends.

In the small cottage at the back of town, sleep had overtaken the residents. Samson and Delilah were spark out, the sprawled shape of Tolpuddle lying across the bottom of the bed, the lonesome hoot of a barn owl outside not enough to stir them as it flew over the roof.

Down in town, at the back of the large house in the Low Mill development, Gareth heard the owl moments later as it continued its journey to the fields beyond. Sitting in the bushes, he was fighting the cobwebs as fatigue tried to claim him. He yawned, doing his best to stretch his long limbs in the confined space. He felt the nudge of a nose on his leg, Bounty, letting him know she was there. That he wasn't alone in his surveillance.

He stroked her soft ears, marvelling at how far they'd both come since the dark days a year ago. Marvelling at the fact he'd made a decision about their future. One which was going to be exciting for both of them. All he had to do now was break the news to Samson and Delilah.

Gareth wasn't the only native of Bruncliffe still awake. Across the dales and down to the south, Clarissa Ralph was lying in a hospital bed and wishing she was back in her apartment. Sleep was evading her. It wasn't the unaccustomed noises of the ward, the occasional groan and snore from the other patients, which were keeping her awake. It was the grave news of her sister, who, a mere twist of corridors and a flight of stairs away, was in the intensive care unit, battling for her life.

Edith was oblivious to the lights around her, or the beeping of the machines. Unaware of the prayers being said on her behalf by a town which was reeling after this second shock. Unaware too, that across the country to the east, in a small room with basic comforts, Arty Robinson was crying. Head in his hands, he was sobbing his heart out.

They'd been good enough to tell him about what had happened. About how Edith's life was hanging in the balance. They'd even sent in a chaplain to be with him, the poor lass sitting there holding his hand while he cried like a baby. She'd talked to him about faith. About hope. Thinking, no doubt, that his tears were born out of fear.

But they weren't. They were out of frustration. And anger. Because Arty couldn't help thinking that if he'd been with her, Edith wouldn't be in this situation. And that if Vinny King had never come back to Bruncliffe, the world would have been a better place.

27

Thursday started with a bang. Literally.

Arriving at the office, Samson, Delilah and Tolpuddle went upstairs to the kitchen to find Nathan and Nina already standing by the window and Ida spooning tea into the pot. She had just turned to greet the new arrivals when there was an almighty crash below. The front door. Slammed in temper.

It was followed by the angry thump of feet – large given the noise – coming up the stairs.

Gareth Towler appeared on the landing, russet hair sticking out in tufts, beard bushy and a furious expression on his sleep-deprived face.

'He bloody sacked me!' he exclaimed.

Behind him, head down and looking morose, trailed Bounty.

Six puzzled faces stared back at the pair, Ida's spoon left in mid-air over the teapot, its load undelivered.

'Tyke!' said Gareth as still no one spoke. 'That runt sacked me!'

'What do you mean?' asked Delilah, finding her voice.

'I mean, he wandered out into the back yard in one of those fancy creations of his about half an hour ago and beckoned me over. I was leaning against a wall, eating a banana. Didn't know what he wanted. Thought it might be an emergency, except he didn't look stressed. And then when I walk up to him, he just says "Sorry, Gareth, but I won't be needing your services any more."' Gareth shrugged. 'That was it. Short and sweet.'

Samson looked at Delilah. 'What the hell?'

'Search me!' she said. 'He didn't say anything else?'

Gareth shook his head. 'Just said to tell you he'd be in touch.'

'Call him,' muttered Ida. 'And tell the lad, no matter the reason, he's making a big mistake. He needs protecting.'

Samson was pulling out his phone, moving into the hall, while Gareth flopped down onto a seat at the table, the legs squeaking in protest at the sudden weight.

'Sorry, Delilah,' he sighed, the anger leaving him as exhaustion took its place. The look he gave her was anguished. 'I must have screwed up somehow. And I know how much you need the money from that job, so if Tyke doesn't pay, I'll make it up to you, I promise.'

'Don't be daft,' murmured Delilah, while trying not to think about what a sudden termination of their contract with Tyke would do to the agency's already shaky bottom line.

Ida, meanwhile, was at her pragmatic best, reaching into a cupboard and pulling out the frying pan.

'Happen life always looks worse on an empty stomach and no sleep,' she said, placing it on the cooker, the two dogs suddenly showing an interest.

Gareth managed a weary grin. 'Thanks, Ida. I wouldn't say no to one of your fine butties.'

'Make that two,' muttered Samson, re-entering the kitchen. He ran a hand through his hair and forced a smile. 'So the good news is you didn't do anything wrong, Gareth.'

There was an audible sigh of relief from the former game-keeper.

'And the bad news?' Delilah was watching Samson, a knot in her stomach.

'Bad news is Tyke has let us go.'

'Did he give a reason?' asked Nina.

'Yeah – a valid one in a way. He wants all our energies focused on catching the person who killed his uncle.' Samson turned to Delilah. 'He's offered to pay us for our efforts.'

She nodded, knowing it would be churlish to point out that Edith was already covering their costs and, even if they took Tyke up on his offer, they could hardly bill two clients for the same work. No matter how you looked at it, their finances had just taken a huge hit.

'Huh!' said Ida as the bacon hit the pan. 'All good and well, but like as not we'll then be needed to catch whoever kills *him*!'

Samson nodded. 'I tried to tell him about the danger he could be in but he wasn't listening. He just kept saying that he couldn't live with himself if our work for him prevented us from identifying Vinny's murderer. Seems his guilt over the glasses mix-up has really taken hold.'

Delilah felt a pang of guilt herself, because so far she'd only been thinking about the commercial implications of losing their client. 'Did you tell him our thoughts about the threat-maker possibly being in Bruncliffe?'

'Yep.' Samson shrugged. 'He just said he'd take extra precautions. He seems to think that the swarm of journalists who've descended on the town will offer him some protection. Safety in numbers and all that.'

'The lad's a fool,' murmured Ida, placing the first lot of

bacon into bread and passing it to Gareth, who bit into it hungrily.

'So what do we do?' Nina asked.

'What Tyke's asked us to do,' said Delilah. 'We walk away from it.'

'After all the hard work we've put in?' protested Nathan. 'Nina and I have spent hours contacting rentals in the town. We're so close to getting somewhere with it, I just know we are. We can't quit now!'

'It's not quitting, Nathan,' said Samson, draping an arm around the lad's hunched shoulders. 'We've been told to drop it and that's what we have to do. It's the client's decision, not ours.'

'And if he gets killed?' asked Ida quietly. 'This client of ours?'

Samson gave a helpless shrug. 'Let's just pray it doesn't come to that.'

Ida turned wordlessly back to her frying pan.

'Full steam ahead on Vinny's murder, then,' said Gareth, sitting back in his chair, the plate in front of him empty. 'What's the plan for today?'

Clarissa Ralph had never been so happy to be home. Still a little breathless as she entered her flat, nevertheless, she felt a million times better than she had done when she left.

'Come on in and get your feet up,' said Joseph, gesturing to her armchair, a cuppa on the coffee table ready and waiting.

'It's so good to see you,' said Eric. 'And we've been out for essentials – milk, butter, eggs, chocolate . . .' He smiled.

She tried to smile in return but the sadness weighing heavily in her heart made short work of it, turning her lips back down before they'd really lifted. For while she was physically better, mentally she was in torment.

'Sorry,' she said. 'I'm not much fun to be around. I just keep worrying about Edith and Arty.'

'You're not the only one,' said Joseph, sitting down on the sofa with a sigh. 'We've been beating ourselves up since yesterday afternoon for not being quicker on the scene. For not having walked that bit faster so we could have saved her.'

Eric tapped the oxygen cylinder beside him. 'My fault,' he muttered.

'Rubbish!' said Clarissa, an uncustomary sharpness to her words. 'No one is to blame but the fiend who attacked Edith. And I'm sure Samson and Delilah are on the case by now.'

Joseph nodded. 'They were here last night, looking over Vinny's apartment.'

'So they really think there's a link between the two incidents?'

'Seems so. Which would mean that Arty would be in the clear.'

Clarissa nodded. Feeling again the smart of pain which came from knowing it was her statement to the police which had helped place poor Arty in a cell.

'And did they find anything?' she asked.

'Not a thing,' muttered Eric. 'Although I think the welcoming committee when they came out was a surprise.'

Joseph grinned as Clarissa looked to him for an explanation. 'Suffice to say, they weren't expecting us lot to have the gumption to try to protect ourselves.'

She smiled. Picturing the scene. A mob of feisty pensioners, not afraid to have a go. And something shifted inside her. Moved the self-reproach aside and replaced it with something stronger. Fiercer.

'What would Edith do?' she murmured.

'Sorry?' Joseph was looking at her.

'I said . . .' Clarissa paused.

What *would* Edith do? In a situation where she'd made a mistake, she would be the first to try to rectify it. Whatever that took.

'Keys!' Clarissa exclaimed, the two men staring at her in bewilderment now. 'Where would we get a set of keys for Vinny King's apartment?'

'You want to have a look inside?' asked Eric.

'Yes. I was in and out of there more than most, apart from Edith and Geraldine. I might be able to spot something Samson and Delilah didn't.'

'Well, if we get a move on, we won't need any,' said Joseph, looking at his watch. 'Samson said Sergeant Clayton and Danny are coming over this morning for another inspection, official this time. They should be here any minute now.'

Sure enough, from outside the apartment came the sound of voices in the corridor.

Clarissa pulled herself up from her chair. 'Right lads, let's go and see if we can be of any help.'

Ida wouldn't allow them to wipe clean Tyke's whiteboard, insisting that they might have need of it should anything happen to him. And so it was taken down and stored in Delilah's office, a new one dedicated to Vinny King's murder put up in its place. While Samson and Delilah updated the team on developments following on from the terrible attack on Edith Hird, Ida had been rapidly making notes and the surface was now covered.

'Does this mean Geraldine Mortimer is ruled out then?' asked Nina, squinting at the mass of information on the board.

Samson nodded. 'For now, yes. But only if we unearth a link between Vinny's death and what happened yesterday. So far, we've had no joy. Here's hoping our trip back to the surgery will rectify that.'

'We should focus on the attacker, too,' said Gareth. 'See if we can get some idea of where he went when he ran off. I could ask the dairy for a look at their CCTV from yesterday – it covers a bit of the road where Joseph lost him.'

'Would they let you see it?' asked Delilah.

'It's worth a try. I forgot to tell you in all the mayhem that my hidden cameras came through in the pilfering case out there – caught the thief red-handed in the stock-room yesterday. The dairy manager was thrilled to have it sorted, so I'm sure he'll be happy to help us out with this.'

'Great. That would be brilliant.'

'What about us?' asked Nina, gesturing at Nathan with her thumb.

Delilah shrugged. 'Just admin for now. Although, if you wanted to take the day off and enjoy a bit of your half-term break—'

'A day off sounds good,' Nina agreed readily. 'We could take your lurchers out for a walk, Nathan. Or even better, do a bit of revision.'

Nathan looked about to protest, the lad having shown no enthusiasm for studying, despite still having some of his GCSE exams to come once half-term was over. But Nina shot him a glance and he simply nodded meekly.

'I suppose if I'm going to try to get into agricultural college, I need to get my head down.'

'You're going to college?' Delilah didn't even try to keep the shock from her voice.

For the past few years, Nathan had been declaring to

anyone who'd listen that he was leaving school the moment he was of age, that he had no use for classroom learning when his future lay on a farm. He took no heed when his mother, aunt and grandparents tried to persuade him otherwise, knowing the truth of how hard things could be for a youngster trying to make their way in agriculture when there was no family farm to take over. For while Nathan helped out on Ellershaw, the Metcalfe farm, there was no prospect of that becoming his when Will had a family of his own.

All their entreaties had fallen on deaf ears. Yet now Delilah's nephew had somehow seen the light.

'Yep.' He grinned, gesturing at Nina. 'She persuaded me.'

Delilah turned to Nina, eyebrows raised. 'How on earth did you do that?'

Nina shrugged. 'Told him he'd be an idiot not to get some qualifications under his belt. And sent him to talk to Jimmy Thornton. First thing Jimmy told him was that he'd need to be able to put together a business plan if he wanted to take on a tenancy.'

'Jimmy knows what he's talking about,' said Samson, the young tenant farmer up on Bowland Knotts having made quite an impression on him since he'd got to know him over the last year.

'Seems so,' said Nathan. He gave a bashful smile. 'All going well, I'll be off in September.'

'Good to see thee taking tha future seriously, lad,' said Ida, patting the teenager on the arm.

'Talking of futures,' said Gareth, clearing his throat, a sheepish look to him, 'Bounty and I have got a bit of news.'

Hearing her name, the springer spaniel picked her head up from where it had been resting on Tolpuddle's flank, the pair of them curled up in the corner.

'Bounty's been accepted onto a course to become a conservation detection dog – she passed the trials with flying colours.' The pride in Gareth's voice brought a lump to Delilah's throat, knowing everything the pair had been through in recent times. The freak accident that had left one of the best gun dogs in the area terrified of gunshot and cost her owner his career.

'That's fantastic,' said Samson, leaning over to pat Bounty.

'What does that mean, exactly?' asked Ida.

'She'll be trained up to find endangered or protected species—'

'Like the great crested newt she found up on the farm,' said Nathan, referring to their case in the autumn.

'Aye, exactly that. It was Sergeant Grewal, the wildlife officer, who gave me the idea,' admitted Gareth. 'But that's not all. I've realised, working here with you lot, how much I enjoy what we do. So I decided to go the whole hog. I've been accepted onto the training programme for North Yorkshire police.'

'Congratulations!' said Samson, shaking the large man's hand. 'That's just great!'

Nina was grinning at him. 'Keep a seat warm for me, then! I'll be applying as soon as I graduate.'

'So that'll make two of us in uniform,' said Gareth, beaming. Then he turned to Delilah. 'I'll still need a place to stay, so I'll stop on upstairs for now, if that's okay? Might even be able to pay you something towards it!'

She smiled. Nodded. Happy to see him so excited about the future. But aware that there was a sense of things coming to an end. Nathan about to go off to college. Nina not having long left in school. And now Gareth . . .

'Don't fret, lass,' Ida murmured in her ear while the others all peppered Gareth with excited questions. 'It's nowt but life moving on. There's plenty round here won't be changing. This is Bruncliffe, after all.'

Sergeant Clayton didn't have the heart to say no. Having just left a tense conversation with Geraldine Mortimer – in which she'd confirmed O'Brien's account of her past with Vinny but had bristled at attempts to verify her movements on the day of the man's murder – the sergeant and his constable had found themselves faced with Clarissa Ralph, a hand on her chest, wheezing dramatically at the door of Vinny King's flat as she asked if she could help with the investigation – almost in tears as she referenced her critically ill sister. He'd simply said yes. Noting out of the corner of his eye the surprised look of young Danny Bradley, standing beside him.

The sergeant hadn't realised, of course, that Clarissa's two sidekicks were loitering in her hallway and would promptly tag along as they entered the apartment.

Now, as they stood in the dead man's lounge, Clarissa's breathing markedly improved, not a wheeze to be heard, Eric Bradley and Joseph O'Brien mesmerised by the Hockney, the sergeant was at a loss as to how they had thought they could be of assistance. Clarissa in particular was looking crestfallen, as though she'd expected there to be some-thing dramatic, some kind of clue, which she would see when no one else had.

Mind you, his own constable had something of the same disappointed air about him, the magazine article in his hands, head rising and falling as he tried to compare the two scenes.

'I think we're probably all wasting our time,' said the sergeant gently, looking pointedly towards the door.

'Two million,' muttered Eric, tearing his gaze from the aquamarine pool. 'How can something be worth that much?'

'Didn't bring him any luck, mind, poor soul,' murmured Joseph, making the sign of the cross as he glanced down at the stain on the carpet.

'Thanks for humouring us, Sergeant.' Clarissa bestowed a smile on him as she walked past and into the hallway. 'It means a lot —' There was a pause. Then a small sound. 'Oh!'

He turned to see what had caught her attention. She was by the smashed lamp, but it wasn't the glass which had triggered the exclamation.

'That's not where he kept them,' she said, about to reach out towards the small dish on the console table.

'Don't touch anything!' The sergeant's exclamation was enough to make her snap her arm back, as though she'd placed her fingers in a fire. 'Sorry, didn't mean to make you jump, Clarissa. But best to keep fingerprints to a minimum, just in case. Can you tell me what's out of place?'

'Why, that, of course,' she said, pointing at the spare key in the bowl. She raised her hand, pointing now to the three hooks above the table. 'That's where he kept his keys. Car and two for the flat.'

'He didn't join in our safety-net scheme,' muttered Eric. 'Gave some tosh about it nullifying his insurance.'

'Safety-net scheme?' asked the sergeant.

'All the residents hold a spare for someone else's flat,' explained Danny. 'Isn't that right, Grandad?'

Eric nodded. 'Stops us getting locked out accidentally. And, as I can testify, also means other folk can get in if there's an emergency.' He glanced gratefully at Joseph and Clarissa, the spare key left with a friend having saved his life during his own emergency not that long ago.

'But Vinny wasn't a part of this?' the sergeant asked, more out of duty, not really seeing how any of this could have relevance.

'He point-blank refused,' said Clarissa. 'And was also very particular about keeping his keys on the hooks. So I'm surprised that was left in there.' She looked at him, eyes wide. 'Do you think it could be important?'

'We'll certainly make a note of it,' the sergeant said diplomatically as he ushered the pensioners out of the apartment. When he turned to his constable, Danny was staring at the console table.

'Do you think what Clarissa said could be relevant?' he asked.

'Doubt it. Our dead man got his glasses all muddled up, so no surprise if he popped his keys in a different place.'

'And the lamp? How did that get smashed? If we're working on the theory Vinny knew the person and let them in, why would there have been a struggle in the hall? Vinny wasn't attacked until he reached the lounge.'

Sergeant Clayton looked at the fragments of glass and felt that burn in his stomach which used to be only caused when in the company of Samson O'Brien. Of late, Constable Bradley had developed the knack of triggering it too.

'The killer must have knocked it over when he was running off,' he muttered. 'Now let's get on and do some proper police work. You need to head off to the surgery and I need to go to Peaks. It's gone nine thirty and I've not even had a coffee.'

28

'Do you think this is wise?' murmured Nathan, as he crouched behind Nina at the end of the ginnel while she checked it was safe to proceed. At his heels were his lurchers, silent as shadows, providing an excuse for the teenagers' outing should they be spotted. 'Samson said we weren't to work on it.'

She grinned over her shoulder at him. 'What would you rather be doing? This or revising?'

He grinned back. Heart somersaulting in the way it always did around her.

'There they are!' she murmured, eyes back on their target.

He peered round her into Back Street, Samson and Delilah walking away with Tolpuddle, en route to the surgery. With Ida having left already and Gareth at the dairy, the coast was finally clear.

'Come on!' Nina caught Nathan's hand and then the pair of them were moving rapidly across the street, lurchers loping after them, and down towards the recently renovated shop-front which was their destination.

Dales Homes.

It had been Nina's idea to carry on with their research into rental properties in the area, trying to locate the destination of the Yorkshire Wild van, despite orders to the contrary. As she'd rightly argued, it wouldn't harm anyone if they did a bit more digging and might even save Tyke's life. So they'd decamped to Peaks Patisserie and, under the guise of revising, had followed up the few remaining properties which offered potential.

They'd drawn a blank. And then Nathan had a brainwave. Which is why he was now tethering the lurchers to a lamp post and tucking in behind Nina as they entered the estate agents, knowing she was better at this than he was.

'Hello you two!' Nancy Taylor was sitting at a desk, smiling at them in welcome, no one else in there.

Nina glanced at Nathan. They'd been hoping to talk to either Julie or Stuart, the younger employees, rather than Nancy herself. Wife of the now deceased – and disgraced – mayor, Bernard Taylor, Nancy always came across so calm and collected, even through the turmoil her life had been thrown into. She was widely regarded as a good person and, since setting up Dales Homes, a formidable businesswoman.

She wasn't someone to be easily duped.

Nathan gave Nina a slight shake of his head, a signal to abort.

But Nina just walked across to the desk and sat in one of the chairs opposite Nancy, leaving him no option but to follow.

'I'm taking it you're not here to buy a house,' said Nancy with a laugh. 'So how can I help you.'

Nina took a deep breath. 'We're working on a case for Samson and Delilah—'

Nathan gave a start. This wasn't what they'd planned to say. What had happened to the geography project on residential patterns in the town?

'Anyway, we can't say much more than that, as I'm sure

you'll understand,' Nina continued, hitting her stride now, 'but we're trying to locate a rental address in this area of town.' She held out her mobile, circling the map on the screen with her finger. 'We've pretty much exhausted the possibility of it being a holiday let so we wondered if you had any short-term lets in that area which might fit the bill.'

Nancy studied the map. Furrowed her brow. And turned to her computer. 'Let me have a quick look at the records.'

She wasn't making any move to kick them out. She was taking them seriously, treating them like adults. Nathan felt the rigid cord that was his spine begin to relax.

'Sorry. Nothing doing I'm afraid,' Nancy said, turning back to them. 'Is it just this particular area you're interested in?'

Nina went to speak. Then looked at Nathan. Neither of them sure how to proceed.

'If it's discretion you're worried about,' said Nancy with a warm smile, 'you're safe with me. After everything Samson and Delilah have done for me over the past year and more, I'll help them any way I can and not tell a soul about it.'

'We're looking for a delivery address,' blurted Nathan.

'We know that something was delivered in this area and to someone who probably doesn't live here,' Nina clarified. 'So we thought holiday let, rental, temporary accommodation of some sort.' She shrugged.

'Good thinking,' said Nancy, sitting back, thoughtful. 'But you don't have to live in Bruncliffe to get something delivered here.'

Seeing their lack of comprehension, she leaned forward again and tapped on Nina's phone, zooming in on the far edge of their search zone.

'Here,' she said. 'The station. They had some of those lockers installed early last year – you know, where you can drop off or collect parcels. I remember because it caused a bit of fuss on the council, Bernard and a few others worried that it might ruin the historic features of the building.' She shook her head at the recollection. 'The planning was approved and the lockers have been a great success. Maybe that's where your mystery delivery was taken?'

Nathan felt the certainty in his bones. This was it. The route fitted. The van turning off High Street, down the road that led directly to the station.

'That's it,' murmured Nina, obviously feeling the same. She looked up at Nancy. 'You're a genius! You may well have just saved a man's life!'

Then they were both on their feet and heading for the door, the day certainly a lot more exciting than if they'd spent it revising.

Samson and Delilah reached the doctor's surgery to see Danny walking towards them from the direction of the river path. Leaving Tolpuddle to enjoy the sunshine, the trio entered the reception area, and Samson's heart sank. The woman behind the desk wasn't the same as the day before.

Thankfully Delilah knew her. Of course.

Samson watched with an amazement which – eighteen months in – had yet to diminish. The way she could simply walk up to someone and start chatting with that easy conviviality which came from a lifetime of living in the same place, among the same people. He stood to the side with Danny while the two women talked, Delilah a past master when it came to the unwritten codes of Bruncliffe interactions. For a population who wore their bluntness with pride, woe betide the outsider who cut to the chase before the necessary social interactions had been observed.

'So,' the woman said after a few minutes, a mischievous glance flicking to Samson, 'the big day is looming. Has he named the best man yet?'

Delilah laughed. As if the wedding wasn't an elephant in the room of their relationship. 'He hasn't told me – so if you're looking for insider information, I'm afraid you're asking the wrong person. Anyway,' she said, gesturing towards the computer screen in front of the receptionist, 'we mustn't keep you from your work any longer. We're looking into the attack on Edith Hird and were hoping to speak to Nicky about yesterday. Is she here?'

The smile fell from the woman's face. 'Yes, poor Edith. That was awful what happened. But I'm afraid Nicky isn't in. She went on holiday this morning – should be landing in Tenerife about now.'

'Bugger,' murmured Danny.

'Was there anything in particular you wanted to know?' the receptionist continued.

Samson stepped forward. 'We're just following up on events, really, and so were wondering if there were any other witnesses to Edith's sudden departure from here.'

The woman was shaking her head. 'I'm sorry, I can't help—'

'Dr Naylor might know.' A young woman was standing at the other end of the desk, mug of coffee in hand. 'Emma Varley,' she said, nodding towards the three of them. 'Locum. I'm covering for Paul while he's on compassionate leave.'

'Was Dr Naylor here yesterday?' asked Delilah, surprised.

'He wouldn't hear otherwise. Said he wanted to work to take his mind off things. Then I got a call from Nicky asking me to rush in because Paul wanted to go home. I think it all got too much for him. Judging by the timings, it's possible he was still here when Miss Hird left.'

'Thanks,' said Danny. 'We'll give him a call.'

The call to Dr Naylor went unanswered. As did the two further attempts Delilah made as she walked back to the town centre with Samson and Danny, the sunshine bathing the river path seeming almost indecent considering what had occurred in that location only the day before.

'He's got his mobile turned off,' she said, as they emerged at the viaduct on Church Street.

'Hardly surprising,' murmured Danny. 'Not sure I'd want to be bothered talking to folk if I'd just lost my wife. I couldn't believe it when he turned up at Fellside Court on Tuesday – Liz only died that morning.' The young officer shook his head. 'No one can accuse the doc of not being dedicated.'

'So what now?' Delilah looked at Samson.

'Seems Gareth has come up trumps at the dairy,' he said, checking his phone. 'He's unearthed some CCTV footage of what could be the attacker fleeing the scene. He's let Sergeant Clayton know.'

At that moment, Danny's phone beeped. 'That's the sarge,' he laughed. 'He's ordered me back to base to go through the footage with him.'

'Keep us posted,' said Samson.

'Likewise, if you get through to the doc,' said the constable over his shoulder, already walking off.

'And us?' Delilah was smiling up at Samson, sun on her face, Tolpuddle leaning gently against her.

Samson wished for all the world they could just disappear. Just for the day. Take a picnic up to Hawber Woods, see the last of the bluebells. But they owed Edith and Arty every ounce of effort.

'Clarissa has invited us round. She wants to give us her version of what happened Tuesday night.'

Delilah nodded. 'What are we waiting for, then?'

They passed under the viaduct and turned up Fell Lane towards Fellside Court.

Clarissa was holding court, sitting in her armchair, the coffee table in front of her bearing the weight of a teapot, cups, plates and a fine selection of finger sandwiches and small cakes. On the kitchen counter, an empty Peaks Patisserie bag gave the provenance of the spread. Already seated, like courtiers, were Eric and Joseph on the sofa and Ana on the other armchair, the four of them breaking off a huddled conversation as Samson and Delilah entered.

'Hope we're not interrupting,' said Delilah.

'Not at all! Come on in.' Clarissa beckoned them into the lounge, Samson pleased to note the colour in their host's cheeks, a vast improvement on how she'd looked Tuesday evening.

'Good to see you celebrating being home,' he said, as he took a seat on one of the chairs at the table in the corner, Delilah next to him. Tolpuddle, however, went straight to Clarissa, flopping his head on her lap and being rewarded with instant affection.

'Your father popped in to see Lucy about . . . something . . . and ended up splashing out,' she said, looking up from the dog and winking towards Joseph and Eric. Something conspiratorial in her smile.

'It's just a few things,' said Joseph, smiling back. 'Thought they might cheer us all up.'

'And goodness do we need cheering up.'

'Any word on Edith?' Delilah asked.

Clarissa's smile slipped and she shook her head, fingers scrunching up the handkerchief in her hand. 'It's still touch and go—' She broke off, tears in her eyes, lowering her gaze to concentrate on Tolpuddle for a few seconds.

'She'll pull through,' muttered Eric. 'She's as tough as old boots.'

A hiccup from Clarissa, as her tears became a strangled laugh. 'I'll tell her you said that.'

Eric grinned at her. 'I'll look forward to it. In the meantime, let's get started on this lot. Edith would be the first to tell us off if we let it go to waste.' He reached for one of the miniature red velvet cakes and ate it in two bites.

'What about you two?' Ana addressed Samson and Delilah. 'Have there been any developments in either case?'

Samson shook his head regretfully. 'Nothing major. But we've just heard that there's CCTV footage of what could be Edith's assailant running past the dairy. Sergeant Clayton is going over it as we speak.'

'Well, that's something,' Joseph said with a nod, Samson sensing his father's guilt at not catching the attacker was still lingering.

'And Vinny's death?' asked Ana. 'Is it definitely connected to what happened yesterday?'

'It's too early to say for sure, but we're working on it. We're trying to locate Dr Naylor, as there's a chance he might be able to shed more light on what actually happened before Edith left the surgery.'

'Try the allotments,' said Eric, a dainty carrot cake in his hand. 'He likes to escape down there for a bit of peace and quiet.'

'Of course,' murmured Samson, nodding, Dr Naylor's delight in the solitude of his vegetable garden something he'd mentioned to the Dales Detective duo only last year. 'We'll check it out when we leave here. In the meantime,' he continued, 'there's something else we need to talk to you about.'

He glanced at Delilah, happy to let her take over for what was going to be an awkward conversation. One which, on their walk over to the flat, they'd agreed needed to be had sooner rather than later. And one which, to Samson's relief, Delilah had offered to initiate.

'It concerns Edith,' she began. 'What I'm about to tell you is probably going to become public knowledge very soon, given that the police are looking at other angles to Vinny's death, and I know she would rather you heard it from us than from someone else.'

Delilah set about relating the history Edith had shared with them in confidence, adding to it Geraldine Mortimer's disclosures, the current audience listening with the same intensity Samson and Delilah had shown when they first heard the sordid tale. They wore the same shocked expressions at the conclusion.

For a moment there was silence, the enormity of what had been revealed sinking in.

'Poor Edith,' Eric finally murmured.

'Geraldine, too,' said Ana.

'And Arty?' Joseph was looking at Samson, his question displaying excellent investigative instincts. 'Did he know?'

'Yes.'

'That's not so good.' Joseph shook his head.

Clarissa, meanwhile, was just sitting there, staring at the floor, clearly distressed.

'Are you okay?' Delilah was reaching over, taking her

hand. 'I'm sorry you had to hear this from us rather than from your sister but under the circumstances, we thought it best.'

As if emerging from a dream, Clarissa blinked a couple of times and then nodded.

'Yes . . . it's just such a shock . . . all these years she carried the weight of that without telling me.'

'She didn't tell anyone. Not until she told Arty on Tuesday.'

'She told Dr Naylor,' said Clarissa, a hint of hurt in her words.

'Dr Naylor? What makes you think he knew?'

Clarissa flapped a hand towards her bedroom. 'When he came to see me on Tuesday afternoon, he mentioned something about Vinny and the terrible things he'd done to Edith in the past. I didn't have a clue what he was talking about, but I suppose this must be it.'

Something darted across Samson's consciousness, there and gone like the flash of a sparrowhawk after prey.

'She probably didn't want to burden you,' said Ana gently. 'You know what older siblings are like. Always trying to protect the younger ones.'

'You're right,' said Clarissa, with a bright smile which didn't quite reach her eyes. 'I'm being silly. The priority right now is to get Edith better and find out who committed these heinous acts.'

'I'm guessing you've considered the possibility that Geraldine could have been involved in Vinny's murder?' Joseph asked.

'We were talking to her while Edith was attacked,' said Delilah. 'So if we're right and there is a connection between the two incidents, then we can pretty much rule Geraldine out.'

'And if there isn't any connection?'

Delilah shrugged. 'I'd still say she's innocent. There was something very genuine about her love for Vinny.'

'Huh!' Eric snorted. 'Genuine and Geraldine don't often go together.'

Samson let the conversation continue around him while he sat quietly, allowing space for that elusive thought to reappear. It took a few minutes, but then as Eric reached for a miniature chocolate and cherry cake, it came back. Forceful. Nothing elusive whatsoever about it. And triggered by the slightest of things.

'Why, Eric,' said Clarissa, laughing, 'that's your third!'

Third.

Mind whirring, Samson stared at Eric's plate.

'Three is perfectly acceptable,' Eric was saying.

Three . . . what was it about that number—?

'That's it!' exclaimed Samson, propelled to his feet by the strength of the realisation. 'Of course!'

Ana went to speak but Clarissa laid a hand on her arm, eyes wide, shaking her head as Samson moved over to the patio door, staring out at the glass wall to his right. Thoughts tumbling now. Connections being made.

The corridor. He was seeing afresh the scenario on the night he'd arrived at the scene of Vinny's murder. That tableau of people already there, Clarissa among them, and standing next to her, taking care of her, had been—

'How did he know?' he asked, turning round, the fire of an investigation coming to life blazing through his veins. 'How did Dr Naylor know the truth about Edith and Vinny?'

'Why, she must have told him,' said Clarissa.

'No. Your sister doesn't lie, we all know that. And she was adamant that she never told a soul. So how did he know?'

'Geraldine?' offered Joseph.

Ana was shaking her head. 'I don't want to be unprofessional here, but I doubt that Geraldine and Dr Naylor had that kind of relationship. Dr Naylor wouldn't have been her confidant.'

'Third,' parroted Delilah, face going pale, seeing where Samson was going with this. 'Edith said there could be a third woman.'

Joseph and Eric were looking puzzled, Ana wide-eyed and Clarissa . . . She had a hand to her mouth.

'A third woman Vinny scammed?' she whispered.

'Possibly,' said Samson. 'Which suggests that if Dr Naylor knew what Vinny had done to Edith, yet didn't learn it from Edith or Geraldine then . . .' He shrugged. 'Dr Naylor knew the third woman.'

'Oh, Jesus!' It was Eric's turn to go pale. Lowering the uneaten cake to his plate. 'The paper mill. When I was working there, I used to see Vinny always hanging around one of the women in accounts . . .' He shook his head, as though trying to dispel the awful truth coming to his mind. But then he just looked at Samson. 'I think I know who Edith's third woman could have been.'

Samson was nodding. Already there. 'Liz Naylor,' he said.

29

Whatever qualms Nathan had been harbouring about carrying out an unauthorised investigation had evaporated in the heat of the excitement generated from the chat with Nancy Taylor. He was currently standing next to Nina on the forecourt of Bruncliffe Station with his lurchers sitting quietly at his feet. In front of them was the one-storey construction which was the station building, with its multiple gables and ornate bargeboards. They were facing the end wall, the entrance to the car park behind them and access to the platforms to their right. But they weren't bothered about any of that. Nor were they taking any heed of the people flowing around them, a train having just passed through.

Their focus was on a block of yellow doors of varying sizes situated against the stone wall, a touch screen with a scrolling welcome message set into the centre of them.

'This has to be it,' said Nina, gaze resting on the lockers Nancy had told them about. 'This was where the Yorkshire Wild van was heading.'

Nathan nodded, sensing that they'd just made a breakthrough in the search for Tyke's tormentor.

'Where do we go from here, though?' Nina continued. 'How do we find out who collected the rabbit?'

'We need footage from the day of the delivery,' said

Nathan. The bank of lockers had a small camera positioned above the touch screen, but only an official investigation would get access to that. He turned, looked up, seeking out any other CCTV equipment.

There. On the side of the station building, a camera pointing into the car park and another angled towards the platform. Neither had a view down onto the lockers but between them, anyone entering the station – whether from town or from a train – would have been captured on video.

'Not a chance,' said Nina, seeing where he was looking. 'We'll never get our hands on those.'

Nathan grinned. 'I think we know a man who might be able to help.'

Liz Naylor.

The name dropped into the room like a bomb, a blast wave of shock throwing those still seated back in their chairs, thoughts swirling like debris, only to be followed by a second wave, pulling them forward as the implications of the revelation finally hit them.

'You don't think . . . ?' Clarissa was the first to try to voice the impossible. 'You're not suggesting Dr Naylor might have been the one who . . . ?'

'We have to consider it, for sure,' said Samson. 'If Liz Naylor was a victim of one of Vinny's scams, then it's possible Dr Naylor might have taken revenge.'

'He certainly didn't like him,' Ana murmured, ashen. 'Dr Naylor was always diplomatic, even with the least likeable of patients, but he never made much effort to hide his disdain for Vinny.'

'It's a long way from disdain to murder, mind,' cautioned Joseph.

Samson nodded. 'Fair point, Dad, but we have to accept that avenging his wife would be a solid motive. And then we come to opportunity.'

'He was at the surgery yesterday morning,' said Delilah in a half whisper, barely believing what she was suggesting. 'Dr Varley told us Dr Naylor might have been there when Edith left.'

'You can't think Dr Naylor attacked Edith, too?' Clarissa's voice was weighed down with doubt.

'I don't want to think any of this,' said Samson, 'but we have to look at the facts. And they point to Dr Naylor having a possible role in both Vinny's murder *and* the attempted murder of Edith.'

'But how?' persisted Clarissa. 'Even if you're right about him being in the vicinity for yesterday's incident, he wasn't here on Tuesday evening when Vinny was killed.'

'He was here when I arrived,' countered Samson.

'Only because I'd called him out! And the murder was already committed by the time he got here – I witnessed that myself.'

'Okay, admittedly there are a few holes in this theory at the moment, but I'm convinced it's something we need to follow up.'

'He took Clarissa to the hospital.' It was almost said as an aside, Ana's voice so quiet they strained to hear.

'You think that could be important, Ana?' Delilah asked.

Ana started. Realised she had their attention and blushed. 'It could be. I don't know. And I don't want to cast stones but . . . I remember thinking it was unusual when the rest of us got back here and I was told Clarissa had been rushed to Airedale by Dr Naylor.'

'Why would that be unusual?'

'Because the ambulance was on its way—'

'That's right! It was almost here,' said Samson, nodding. 'I remember hearing sirens when we were in the corridor. Just as Dr Naylor was leaving with Clarissa.'

'Yes, in which case – and this is my opinion as a medical professional – it would have made more sense to wait for the ambulance to arrive. Dr Naylor would have known that Clarissa would get instant care from the paramedics which he couldn't provide in his car. It just seemed an unusual thing to have done.' She shrugged. 'Not that I can see how that links to any of this.'

'I can,' said Samson, gravely. 'It gave Dr Naylor an excuse to avoid being interviewed by the police straight away and, possibly more importantly, gave him an opportunity to change his clothes.'

'Getting rid of any evidence in the meantime,' said Delilah, a bad taste in her mouth as she said it. For how could she be contemplating that a man like Dr Naylor, who'd been a source of good to the town for his entire working life, had committed such crimes?

'You really think it could be him?' Joseph asked, Delilah not the only one struggling with the concept.

'I hope to God I'm wrong,' said Samson. 'But there's enough here to warrant us going straight to the police.'

Sergeant Clayton knew from the look of Samson and Delilah that this was business best conducted in the office at the back of the police station. Ushering them through, he gestured towards the desks where Danny and DS Benson were already seated, going over the latest feedback from the forensics team with dour expressions. It was making interesting reading.

If you counted a case being turned on its head interesting.

'Come to gloat, O'Brien?' muttered the detective, on looking up and seeing who the visitors were.

Samson glanced from Danny to the sergeant, puzzled.

'Forensics report from the scene of the crime,' said Danny. 'The technicians have managed to narrow down the relative positions of Vinny and his killer at the time of the attack and there's strong evidence to suggest the perpetrator was already waiting in the flat when Vinny arrived back there.'

Give O'Brien his due, he didn't need it explaining. Nor did Delilah.

'So Arty can't have done it!' she exclaimed. 'Clarissa's testimony places him in the corridor when Vinny came back.'

Benson gave a non-committal shrug. 'We're not ruling anything out at the moment, but we are looking into other angles. Which means we don't have time—'

'Even more reason you're going to want to hear this, then,' said Samson, taking a seat. There was something to his tone that made the detective pause. An authority that came from years of experience. 'We've reason to believe Dr Naylor could be our man.'

Sergeant Clayton had just taken a slurp of coffee and nearly coughed it all back up. The very idea of it. Paul Naylor as a killer. Someone capable of attacking old ladies.

Danny was looking equally dubious. 'The doc?' he asked. 'You've got to be joking!'

'I wish I was,' said Samson. 'We've uncovered new evidence that points in his direction – we've been trying to get hold of him to get his take on it but he's not answering his phone.'

'Not exactly unusual given the circumstances,' muttered the sergeant.

DS Benson was watching the exchange with the look of

a tourist in a land for which he didn't have a map. Sergeant Clayton took pity on him.

'The local doctor,' he explained. 'He lost his wife on Tuesday.'

The detective turned to Samson and raised an eyebrow. 'We're listening, so get explaining.'

So Samson did. In that measured way of his which made even something this outrageous seem worthy of consideration. When he'd finished, Benson sat back in his chair, rubbing his forehead as though he had an O'Brien-induced headache.

'Let me get this straight,' he said. 'The man you were seeking in order to corroborate whether or not Edith Hird's attack might have been triggered by a magazine article, is the man you now want to pin the blame on? For both the attack on her and the murder?'

'Yes.'

'And this is based on the unconfirmed suspicion that the doctor's recently deceased wife was a potential victim of Vinny King's scamming?'

'Yes.'

'Then we have a major problem.' The detective folded his arms. 'As a result of our investigation, Dr Naylor has already been discounted as a possible murder suspect.'

'How come?' asked Delilah.

'CCTV. The cameras at Fellside Court cover both entrances and we've been through all the footage for the evening in question and he doesn't appear on any of it at a time which would put him in the frame. In fact,' he continued, glancing at Danny, 'thanks to Constable Bradley's diligent surveillance notes, we can say with certainty exactly who entered Fellside Court in the run up to the murder of Vinny King, with time stamps to boot. Which means we've been able to conclude that there is no way Dr Naylor could have committed this crime. This forensic report only strengthens that summation.'

Delilah looked at Samson, who slumped in his chair.

'There has to be a mistake,' he murmured. 'Something we're missing.'

'Believe me, I went through the footage with a fine-tooth comb,' said Danny. 'Apart from his visit to Clarissa earlier in the afternoon, Dr Naylor didn't enter the building again until after Vinny had been found.'

'Which is backed up by testimony from both Clarissa and Geraldine, who saw him arrive at the scene,' added Sergeant Clayton.

'Looks like it's another dead end, O'Brien,' said DS Benson, rising from his chair, as if about to see the pair of them out. 'We can't magic up evidence to convict a man, no matter how much it might fit whichever theory you're floating today.'

Danny frowned at the jibe. 'To be fair, sir, once you get over the initial shock, Samson's idea does have legs. I can vouch for the fact Dr Naylor wasn't keen on Vinny King.' He pulled his notebook out of his pocket and flicked back through a few pages. 'Here.' He held it out for the detective to see. 'This was Tuesday afternoon when the doc called in to see Clarissa the first time. I thought he was on a short fuse because of his wife dying but maybe there was more to it.'

Benson skimmed over the text where Danny was pointing. 'Dr Naylor got cross when he overheard Vinny laughing?' he said dryly, before passing the notebook into the sergeant's outstretched hand. 'Hardly a hanging offence. Now if you don't mind, O'Brien, Delilah, I'm going to have to ask you to leave.'

Samson and Delilah stood to go while Sergeant Clayton

cast a glance over Danny's notes. They were a credit to the lad. Neat. Organised. Coherent. The sergeant felt a surge of pride in his constable, letting his eyes run back up the page, across times and names and detailed comments. And then down again, to the end of Danny's surveillance at Fellside Court and—

What was it? Something. A shift in the air around him. A current of awareness, recognition of something missing in Danny's meticulous reporting . . .

'Hold your horses, you two!'

The Dales Detective duo were already at the door, turning round at the sergeant's command. He tapped the notebook, looking at Danny now.

'What time did Dr Naylor leave Fellside Court that afternoon? Before he returned later on?'

Danny shook his head, gesturing at his notebook. 'It'll be in there.'

'Nope. It isn't. Do you remember seeing him leave?'

The lad frowned, concentrating hard. 'No,' he said. 'I can't say I did.'

'What are you suggesting, Sergeant?' asked DS Benson.

'I'm not suggesting. I'm saying. If Danny here didn't make a note of the doc leaving that building, then it didn't happen.'

A burst of disbelieving laughter from the detective met his reply. 'Come off it! We've got footage of the man going *back* in – we've got eyewitness accounts of him arriving that second time – so of course he bloody left! Your constable overlooked a detail, that's all.'

Samson was back at the desk, looking at the notebook now, giving a small start and then nodding. That fire coming to his eyes which Sergeant Clayton recognised and had grown to respect.

'And the CCTV? Does that show him leaving?' O'Brien asked.

Danny rifled through a stack of folders, pulling out a page of paper, more notes on it. He scanned down them. Shook his head, eyes wide. 'No. I'm happy to double check, but I don't have any record of him leaving. Two lots of entries but no exit.'

'But how . . . ?' Delilah sat back down, frowning. 'How can he have entered the building twice if he didn't leave?'

'And how did he get into Vinny's flat?' muttered Samson, gesturing at the forensics report in front of Benson. 'According to that, the killer was waiting inside, but there's no evidence of a break-in, so how did Dr Naylor get access?'

'A spare key?' offered the detective.

Samson shook his head. 'Vinny was notoriously cautious with his keys. He wouldn't have handed one out.'

'Maybe he didn't give one out,' said Danny, voice excited. 'What if someone helped themselves to one?'

'Any evidence of that?' asked the detective.

'Could be. When the sarge and I were in there this morning, Clarissa Ralph said—'

'She was in the crime scene with you?' DS Benson's tone was sharp.

'A minor detail,' intervened Sergeant Clayton, taking the heat off his constable. 'What Danny's trying to say is that Mrs Ralph pointed out a discrepancy with Vinny's keys. Apparently, the spare should have been hanging on a hook but it was in a bowl on the hall table.'

'That's it,' murmured Samson. 'The lamp! That's how it was broken!'

'Someone in a rush as they fled the flat,' said Danny, nodding animatedly. 'They had no time to hang the key they'd stolen back up where it should be, so they threw it at the bowl. And caught the lamp in the process, sending it to the floor.'

'Any fingerprint results from that key?' asked Delilah.

'Wiped clean,' said the sergeant.

'I doubt that was Ida's diligence,' Samson murmured.

'Okay, okay!' Benson was standing now, clearly feeling the energy in the room. Beginning to get on board. 'So we have a scenario where Dr Naylor helps himself to a spare key. When?'

'I'll check if he made a house call on Vinny in the last week,' said Danny, taking notes.

'He then calls in to see Clarissa on Tuesday,' continued the detective, 'and afterwards, lets himself into Vinny King's flat with the stolen key—'

Danny was shaking his head. 'It can't have been straight away. Vinny was still there. It must have been after everyone left for the play.'

'What kind of time span are we talking?' asked Samson, sending the constable back to his notebook.

'The doc arrived at ten to four; Vinny and the rest exited the building at six thirty, just as Tyke was leaving.'

'That's two and a half hours! Where did Dr Naylor go in that intervening time?' asked Delilah. 'He can't have hung around in the cafe. That would have been too obvious.'

It came to the sergeant in a blinding flash. A memory of a space smelling of laundry. Of waiting in the dark . . .

'Ida's cleaning cupboard!' he declared.

'Jesus!' Samson was nodding. 'That's it! He went to see Clarissa, nipped into the cupboard when no one was watching and then waited for everyone to leave. He let himself into Vinny's flat with the spare key, waited for him to return. And then killed him.'

'At which point he left the building, and then re-entered through the courtyard as though in response to Clarissa's call.'

'And by waiting until Vinny had been discovered, he provided himself with the perfect alibi in the process,' said Danny.

They all turned to DS Benson, who was looking a lot less sceptical. He raised both hands. 'Okay. I admit it's plausible. We have motive and opportunity. There's only one small problem. We still don't have a record of Dr Naylor leaving the building. How come?'

'Erm . . . I might know,' said Delilah, something confessional about her tone. 'He could have gone through the kitchen. The emergency exit in there opens from the inside – I used it myself that day. No CCTV or alarms on it, either.'

'Oh my God! Of course! CCTV!' Danny started clicking through folders on his computer, energy fizzing from him now. 'That footage Gareth sent through from the dairy the day of the attack on Edith? We saw someone running past. It was too far away for any detailed description, but look!' He twisted the screen so they could all see. 'The attacker was running away . . . in the direction of the surgery!'

'Right.' Benson nodded. 'Much as I can't believe I'm saying this, it's starting to sound like we should at least have a chat with Dr Naylor – maybe hear his side of the story before we start making any accusations.'

'And Arty Robinson?' asked Samson.

DS Benson gave a weary smile. 'Give me some credit, O'Brien. I called Harrogate as soon as we got that report in from forensics. Arty Robinson is no longer a suspect – he was released an hour ago.'

'Thank goodness,' murmured Delilah.

'In the meantime, any idea where we can find Dr Naylor?'

'Possibly.' Delilah looked at Samson and Sergeant Clayton knew how she was feeling.

Guilty.

Because he was feeling exactly the same. They had just denounced a man they'd known all their lives.

30

Neither of them having the stomach to see Paul Naylor taken in for questioning, Samson and Delilah chose not to accompany DS Benson and Sergeant Clayton to the allotments. Instead, after sending a text to Joseph with the good news about Arty's release, they made their way back to the office with a very hungry Tolpuddle. The afternoon was already heading towards evening and the Weimaraner was letting out the odd protest whine at having missed his midday meal, so they picked up some pies for the team from Mrs Hargreaves at the butchers before heading across the market square and down Back Street. They entered the building to the sound of laughter coming from the downstairs office, a sound out of keeping with their melancholic moods.

'Thought tha'd never come back,' said Ida, as they entered the room.

Megan Gifford was sitting at Samson's desk, a wide smile on her face as she stood up to greet them. Thick plait of blonde hair hanging down her back, face as guileless as it had been a year ago when they'd investigated the murder out at the auction mart, the young apprentice auctioneer hadn't aged a bit. Twenty years old now, she could have still passed for fifteen.

Samson, by comparison, felt he'd aged a decade in the past couple of hours.

'Poor lass popped in for a chat and had to put up with me,' continued Ida, while Megan made a fuss of Tolpuddle, the dog happily forgetting his stomach for a few minutes. 'Happen I'll feed the hound and,' she added, spotting the bag in Samson's hand which was emitting delicious odours, 'I'll bring plates and tea. Let thee catch up over a bite to eat.'

'Oh no, I couldn't possibly intrude—' Megan began.

'Hargreaves pies? The best in the Dales? You sure you want to leave?' Delilah was grinning at her cousin across the desk.

Megan laughed and resumed her seat.

'So what brings you to sunny Bruncliffe?'

'Uncle Vinny's will. Father was named as executor—'

'Your father?' queried Delilah, looking puzzled. 'I thought it was your mother who was related to Vinny.'

'Yeah, she was his niece. But it seems he was a bit of a misogynist,' said Megan, with a wry lift of an eyebrow, 'and thought his affairs would be better handled by a man. Which is why Father's over at Turpin's in a meeting. I've got the day off, so I said I'd come with him and call in to see you.'

'Wow,' said Samson, surprised. 'No disrespect, but I didn't take your uncle for someone who would be happy using a local solicitor to handle his will, no matter how good Matty is.'

'He didn't. He just lodged it there. He had it drawn up in London.'

A snort from the door as Ida entered with a pot of tea, four mugs and four plates.

'Fancy folk and their fancy ways,' she muttered, dishing up the pies and passing them around. 'Not many as accomplished as Matty Thistlethwaite when it comes to the law.'

'That's why Father's gone to see him. The will is a bit odd, to say the least.'

'In what way?' asked Delilah.

Megan paused, looking towards the office door behind Ida, which was slightly ajar.

'Don't worry, everything said between these walls is kept in confidence,' Samson assured her.

The youngster blushed. 'Sorry. I didn't mean to suggest . . . It's just that Father isn't supposed to divulge any of this, but he's worried it will be contested. Possibly on grounds of insanity.'

'What?!' Delilah had a pie halfway to her mouth, frozen in mid-air. 'Vinny was as sound in the head as any of us.'

'That's what we all thought. But he still left instructions for his Hockney to be burned.' Megan bit into her own pie with the nonchalance of the young, while the other three just stared at her.

'Two million pounds up in smoke?' muttered Ida, astounded.

Megan nodded. 'Like I said, Father's worried it'll put him in a difficult place if some of the family contest it.'

'You can kind of understand why they might,' said Delilah.

'What in heaven's name possessed Vinny to do that?' asked Samson, struggling to see any logical reason for the dead man's decision. And struggling to compute it with the fact he'd already promised the painting to two different women.

'God knows.' Megan shrugged. 'Mother reckons he was always tight, so she was surprised he forked out for a Hockney in the first place. And now this is even more out of character. So you can see why there could be challenges made.'

'Burning something that precious,' murmured Delilah, shaking her head. 'It's cultural vandalism.'

'Not to mention completely daft!' said Ida.

'What does Tyke make of this?' Samson's question triggered

a reaction, Megan's hand going to her mouth, eyes widening, a rush of panicked words coming from her.

'Oh! I forgot you were working for him! You have to promise me you won't say a word? I mean, he'll find out soon enough, but Father would kill me if he knew I'd been blabbing!'

Delilah reached out, putting an arm around her cousin's shoulders. 'Don't worry – we won't say anything. Besides, we're not working for him as of this morning.'

It was Megan's turn to look surprised. 'How come? Uncle Vinny told us there'd been an attempt on Tyke's life. We understood you were protecting him.'

'He asked us to focus our efforts on finding your uncle's killer,' said Delilah. 'A magnanimous gesture.'

'Let's hope it won't prove to be a reckless one,' murmured Ida.

It was a sentiment Samson found himself agreeing with. He'd been chafed by concern all morning, uneasy about how things had ended with their client and how vulnerable that might have left Tyke.

'Maybe it's for the best,' said Megan, a cheeky spark back in her eyes. 'Father's always said Tyke was cut from the same cloth as Uncle Vinny – he can be a bit slow to pay.'

Delilah managed a laugh, Samson knowing the effort it took her. Because money wasn't a joking matter in the agency of late.

They finished their meal with more general chat and it was only as Megan got up to go that her face turned sombre once more.

'Mother sends her love. She said to tell you we're all thinking of you. You know, over the Rick Procter thing.'

'Thanks.' Delilah nodded. Doing her best to look serene.

'Do you have a date for giving evidence yet?'

'Not yet. It'll be any day soon I suspect.'

Sensing her cousin's anxiety, Megan threw her arms around her, hugging her tight. 'My lot would do anything for you two, you know that, right?' she said, releasing Delilah from her hold and casting a glance at Samson. 'Father thinks you both walk on water for saving the auction mart and my job into the bargain. And Mother is just glad there's somewhere for him to go once a week to get him out of her hair.'

The words produced the desired effect, laughter bursting from Delilah. Samson grinning. Ida looking at the pair of them with something akin to pride.

'So if there's anything we can do,' Megan continued, 'just shout. Oh, and they said to drop a big hint about the wedding. They haven't had their invitations yet and neither have I! Luckily your mother told us the date, so we'll just gatecrash if none arrive.'

With a final grin and a big kiss on the cheek for Delilah, Megan was gone. Into the hall and out the front door. Leaving Ida staring at Delilah. And Samson trying not to panic about what he'd just heard.

No invitations. Delilah still hadn't sent them out. Perhaps it was just an oversight. Or maybe something worse . . .

'I'm going to get changed and go for a run,' said Delilah, smile brittle. 'Catch you later.'

The sound of her feet up the stairs was nowhere near as loud as the silence between Ida and Samson.

'Tha needs to sort this,' Ida finally murmured, gathering up plates and mugs. 'Whatever's going on between thee. Sort it soon, afore it's too late.'

'Reckon it might be too late already,' he muttered back.

'Hmph! No good ever came of feeling sorry for thyself. Stop tiptoeing around the lass like she's made of glass and talk to her.'

With that final word of advice, Ida stomped out of the office and left Samson alone with his worries.

What on earth was going on with Delilah? First the business with Tyke. Then the skulking around Fellside Court, leaving through discreet exits and stealing along under windows. Not to mention what he'd spotted earlier at the police station when he'd looked at Danny's detailed notes from the day Vinny King died.

Joseph O'Brien's name, leaping off the page at him. Alongside Delilah's.

Her secret visit to the retirement complex had been to see Samson's own father.

Samson sat there, staring at the tattered lino and the battered filing cabinet, feeling like his world was coming untethered. Ida was right. He needed to talk to Delilah. Tonight. It was time to sort out whatever was tearing their relationship apart.

'He's not here!' came a brusque shout from the other side of a greenhouse bursting with tomatoes.

A lean figure emerged into view, spade in hand, face cut from the same granite that formed the features of so many native to the town, and topped by the bushiest set of eyebrows DS Benson had ever seen. The eyes beneath those fine specimens were boring into him.

'The doc,' barked the man. 'He's not here.'

'We can see that, Seth,' said Sergeant Clayton, gesturing at the empty plastic chair and the straggle of a vegetable patch behind it. They'd walked the full length of the allotments, the

Date with Destiny

odd person looking up from their weeding or digging on well-tended plots, and had reached Dr Naylor's at the far end.

Samson had said they'd know it by sight. Looking at the cheerful profusion of dandelions peeking out from between the leeks and carrots, and the indentations in the ground where a deckchair had been used regularly, they hadn't needed their years of policing to know this was it.

'Happen you know where he's at?' continued the sergeant.

Seth's hostile regard flicked between the two policemen. 'This official, like?'

'We just want a chat with him, Mr . . . ?' Benson left the opening, hoping it would be filled. He got another bark in response.

'Seth'll do you fine. As for the doc, he's not been here in days. Not since his wife took a turn for the worse, God rest her soul.'

Sergeant Clayton looked at Benson, who had to restrain the shout of frustration threatening to burst from him.

'Right, thanks,' he murmured instead.

Seth nodded, the gesture sharp, like everything about him.

'If you do see him, Seth, can you tell him I was asking to speak to him,' said the sergeant, Benson noting the use of the singular. Knowing it was deliberate, an attempt to keep a local onside by excluding the outsider – him – from the conversation.

It worked, Seth nodding again. 'Will do.'

Leaning on his spade, he watched them walk away across the allotments. Others now pausing in their work to watch too, taking in the sergeant's uniform, the tall city detective, sensing the import of it.

'It'll be around town within the hour that we're looking for Dr Naylor,' said Sergeant Clayton, tipping his head back at their audience. 'Which could be a good thing.'

315

'Or it could scare him off and on the run,' muttered DS Benson, as they exited onto the pavement, the sergeant closing the gate firmly behind them, the gesture almost metaphoric for yet another avenue of enquiry cut off. 'Is it just me or is this case a bloody nightmare?'

'It's a bloody nightmare,' concurred the sergeant, before turning away, mobile to his ear.

Two possible suspects – one discounted; one nowhere to be found. No firm leads. Benson could feel the pressure on his shoulders, as tangible as the warmth from the sun overhead. He checked his phone. A stack of missed calls, the majority from his DI. Wanting to know what progress he'd made. Wanting to know why no one was in custody.

Forty-eight hours after the murder of a major celebrity and they were getting nowhere. Something the press had already taken delight in pointing out that morning.

And they couldn't even be sure Paul Naylor was their man.

'The doc's still not answering his phone and he's not at the surgery,' said Sergeant Clayton, putting his mobile back in his pocket. 'But a bit of news. Danny checked with Ana Stoyanovic at Fellside Court – she confirmed Dr Naylor visited Vinny in his flat on Thursday.'

'So he could have pocketed the spare key then?'

'Perhaps. Although Ana didn't see it happen if he did.'

'You don't sound convinced.'

The sergeant sighed. 'I've known Paul Naylor all my life. A good man. Now suddenly I have to see him as a possible murderer. It's the part of the job round here that brings you down. Seeing folk you know and like go wrong somehow, their life come off the rails because of one daft moment of anger or stupidity.' He shrugged. 'Happen that's the main difference between your experience as a copper and that of ours in Bruncliffe. We know most of the folk we have to put away. I doubt you know any of them.'

Josh Benson nodded, taking in what was being said. Seeing for the first time the differing pressures bearing down on the sergeant. It might not be Clayton's case, but he was going to have to live with the consequences of it long after Josh had shaken the dust of the town from his feet.

'So what would be your next step, in my shoes?' he asked.

From across the road came the sound of laughter, a pub called the Crown doing good business, the tables out front busy with people enjoying post-work drinks in the fine weather.

'Go for a pint,' said Sergeant Clayton, gesturing towards the pub. 'I'm off duty as of now and they've got a south-facing beer garden and pork scratchings to die for. We could discuss the case over a pint of Pheasant Plucker while young Danny holds the fort back at the station. Plus the landlord is Dr Naylor's brother-in-law. He might be able to give us an idea of where the doc's disappeared to.'

DS Benson opened his mouth to decline. Then shrugged. He was due some time off. And perhaps a bit of Dales sunshine might be just the ticket to help sort things out. Maybe even conjure up some inspiration in what seemed to be a dead-end investigation.

'Just the one,' he said.

'Great. You head over and get a round in, I'll nip back to the office and change.'

He watched the sergeant walk away, aware that he'd been left to pay for the beer in a cunning manoeuvre, but also aware that he didn't mind. Perhaps he was becoming a local after all.

With a world of stress weighing him down, Josh Benson crossed the road towards the pub.

Arty Robinson went straight to Edith's side from the police station. He knew he should probably have gone back home and washed away the stale smell of the cells, changed his clothes at the very least. But when the kind-hearted duty sergeant had said he was finishing his shift and heading in the direction of the hospital if Arty cared for a lift, he'd accepted immediately.

He was shown into her ward, part of the intensive care unit, Edith a small figure in a bed surrounded by instruments, her head wrapped in bandages, making the sharp bones of her cheeks even more pronounced.

It was a waiting game, the nurse had explained. Only time would tell if she was robust enough to come back from the trauma of her injuries.

Arty had barely heard a word. Just staggered across the room to the chair by the bed, sinking into it and taking Edith's hand. They brought him food – sandwiches which went untouched, cups of tea which went cold. All the while he talked to her. Tried to coax her back from the edge of death where she was balanced so precariously.

Heading back to the office building hadn't been part of Gareth's plans as his working day came towards a close. He'd been out at the dairy most of the afternoon, tying up the last few ends of the pilfering case and then staying on to have a chat with the manager, thanking him in person for granting the Dales Detective team access to the CCTV. The brief glimpse of what was probably Edith's attacker running away to the south of the industrial estate hadn't seemed much at the time. But once focus switched to Dr Naylor, it had proved informative. The surgery lay in that direction.

Paul Naylor. Gareth couldn't believe it. The doctor had been a regular visitor to the Towler household when Gareth was in his teens, checking in on Gareth's grandmother as her dementia worsened. That the same man was capable of murdering someone and then violently accosting – possibly even trying to kill – an elderly woman was hard to accept.

But that's the way the facts were pointing. And now it seemed the doc had gone missing – no sign of him at work, home or at his allotment. Samson had called with an update and the frustration had been apparent in his voice. Telling Gareth to call it a day, he'd hung up, leaving the former gamekeeper to contemplate a pint in the Fleece.

Just as he'd left the dairy, however, Bounty as happy as he was to be back out in the fresh air, his phone had pinged. A text from Nathan asking him if he knew anyone working at the station, preferably with access to the cameras on the forecourt. Intrigued, Gareth had texted back, asking what it was about. He'd got a one-word reply.

Tyke.

Along with an emoji of a finger placed across lips.

So they were still working that case, the teenagers, but on the sly.

Gareth was considering that as he walked along the road in the summer sunshine, Bounty tugging on the lead. With a day's reflection, his annoyance – and embarrassment – at having been kicked off the investigation had subsided, leaving behind embers of concern which the text from Nathan had rekindled.

Was it ethical to obey a client when they asked you to do something which might be placing them in danger? Should the Dales Detective Agency have acquiesced so readily when Tyke instructed them to stop searching for the person behind the death threats? And what about the surveillance? The lad had been left completely unprotected as of this morning.

But Samson had been in the game a long time. Who were Gareth and the youngsters to question his reading of the situation? And should he, Gareth, be encouraging Nathan and Nina to take matters into their own hands — ?

The roar of a motorbike sliced through his contemplations.

He turned, saw it coming along the road. Black. Raised at the rear. Rider all in black. And that badge on the side as it raced past him.

A Triumph trail bike. Heading out of town towards the fells.

Heart thudding, Gareth broke into a run.

31

'Tha's done what?'

Ida had in fact heard perfectly well what the two teenagers had been up to. And their justification for it. But she was using her question to give herself time to decide whether their actions should be condemned or commended.

Leaning against the kitchen windowsill, Nina shrugged. 'Tyke's in danger. It would be irresponsible of us to give up now. Especially as we're so close to cracking this.'

It was a justification which couldn't be faulted, not by Ida, who held a soft spot for the lad. There was a certain responsibility which came with the business after all. If Tyke's life was in danger, the Dales Detective Agency had a duty to protect it, even if he wasn't footing their bills.

'Tha thinks this could be a lead, then? This locker?' She gestured at Nathan's phone, the bright yellow boxes on it.

'Yeah,' he said. 'And we're hoping Gareth will help us prove that.'

'And Samson and Delilah? When was tha planning on telling them about tha exploits?'

Nathan looked at Nina, cheeks flushing.

'Soon,' said Nina. 'Honestly. We just thought we'd suss it out on our own first. They're so busy with the Vinny

King murder and what happened to Edith, we didn't want to disturb them until we have something concrete.'

'Huh.' Ida stared at the pair of them. Still undecided. Thinking about the other things which were making claims on Samson and Delilah, and how they'd benefit from a bit of time together this evening without being pestered about something which might be nothing.

She was also selfishly thinking about how much she'd missed investigating. Proper detective work, out in the field like the teenagers had been doing. After a week of working pretty much only on the Dales Dating Agency side of the business, Ida had to admit that she was far more interested in criminal affairs than those of the heart.

'Are you going to tell them?' asked Nina.

'No, lass. But I don't think tha should take this any further unless Gareth turns up something—'

'Nina? Nathan?' Gareth's voice was followed up the stairs by his large body moving at speed. He rounded the newel post, onto the landing, eyes wide, Bounty barking next to him, infected by the same excitement

'I saw the bike! The trail bike!' he exclaimed. 'Tyke's still in danger!'

The decision was made for Ida in that moment. The Dales Detective Agency was going into action – and it would be doing so behind Samson and Delilah's back.

Delilah had pushed herself more than she should have done, given she was only a couple of days out from a race. But the stress burning through her body had needed an outlet. The punishing climb out of town, past the Hoffmann kiln and up onto the tops had more than done the trick.

Well, almost. As she ran back down towards home,

Tolpuddle loping easily alongside her in the low-slung sunshine, she definitely felt lighter in her soul. Although she now felt anxious for a different reason.

The conversation she'd managed to put off for two days could be avoided no longer. Especially not after Megan's comment about the waylaid invitations. Delilah had seen the hurt and confusion on Samson's face her cousin's playful remarks had prompted. He was owed the truth. And an explanation as to why their wedding wasn't going to be happening.

Slowing up as the cottage came into sight, she felt the vibration of her watch on her wrist. An incoming call.

She didn't recognise the number on the screen as she pulled the mobile out of her pocket. But she knew the voice.

'Ms Metcalfe?' Those smooth vowels, the honeyed tones. It was the lawyer in charge of the prosecution case against Rick Procter. 'I've got news. And I'm afraid what I'm about to tell you might come as a bit of a shock . . .'

She listened in silence. Making a few responses once he'd stopped speaking. Not even aware of the words she was forming. Then she was moving forward, towards the cottage. Stumbling like a late-night drunk. Hoping and praying that Samson was already there.

Samson was walking up Crag Lane, the evening sunshine doing nothing to raise his spirits, which were at rock bottom. Word had come from Danny that Dr Naylor was nowhere to be found and now the news that the police were looking for him was spreading around the town like so many dandelion seeds carried on the wind. And sprouting as many weeds when it came to rumours and supposition.

He'd popped into the Spar to get a bottle of wine – hoping

that would give him the courage to have the conversation he needed with Delilah – and had been accosted by several people, Mrs Pettiford among them, all keen to tell him that the offcumden detective was making a big mistake. That only someone from out of town could believe Paul Naylor was capable of murder.

Samson had shuffled on by, mumbling promises that he'd have a word with DS Benson, not admitting that it was his theory which had set the detective on the doctor's trail.

He was feeling weary and guilty as he reached the cottage. But not so weary that he didn't notice the porch door was ajar.

'Delilah?' he called out, pushing it open, easing around it. Seeing the trainers, kicked off in haste. Tense now. He lowered the shopping to the ground, freeing up his hands. The instincts from years of working in dangerous situations still sharp.

From within came a sound that cut to his soul. A keening. Soft but distraught.

He hurried inside, and there she was, sitting on the kitchen floor in her running kit, knees drawn up to her chest, rocking, while tears flowed down her cheeks. Tolpuddle next to her, eyes wide, ears pricked, whining. Stressed. He turned towards Samson. Barked.

'Delilah!' Samson dropped to the floor, pulling her into his arms and against his chest, while Tolpuddle flopped against him. 'What is it? What's happened?'

She was shaking, shuddering sobs tearing from her now. Trying to form words.

'The fire . . . I was straight back in the fire and I couldn't get out . . .'

He stroked her head. Images of the inferno which had

engulfed the cafe up on Gunnerstang Brow stark in his mind. How she'd escaped from it, a miracle and nothing less. Over a year on and Delilah had come through the events leading up to Rick Procter's capture seemingly unaffected. The broken bones had healed. The smashed watch had been replaced. But not once had she talked about it.

What it had been like to be left for dead in a burning building.

He held her tight, wondering what had triggered the trauma now overwhelming her. He had no idea how long they sat there, one of his arms around Tolpuddle, the other around Delilah. But finally her cries fell silent. She lifted her head from his chest, sleeve rubbing her eyes dry.

'Sorry —'

'Don't even think about apologising,' he said softly, a hand brushing her hair back from her damp cheeks.

She nodded. Tried a smile. And then pulled out her phone.

'Here. He called me and then sent an email. It's all there.'

He saw the lawyer's name. Skimmed the text. And swore.

'Rick's pleaded guilty?' he breathed. Stunned.

'There's more.'

She was right. The words 'King's Evidence', with an explanation which Samson didn't need, having worked on enough drugs busts and seen enough criminal gangs taken down to know what it meant.

A deal. Plead guilty. Remove the need for a trial. Get a lesser sentence and, in return, help the prosecution catch the bigger fish which were still circling in the sea of crime. In this case, a Bulgarian criminal organisation run by the Karamanski brothers, ruthless and, so far, beyond capture.

He let the implications sink in. Rick Procter wasn't going to go on trial.

'You won't have to face him,' he said, taking her face in his hands. 'You won't have to relive it all.'

She nodded. 'I know. I should be happy. But the thought of him getting off lightly . . . it just triggered everything. All the stress of waiting to go to court and testify. The memories of last year . . . I managed to keep a lid on it all but then I heard this and it was like something snapped.'

Samson didn't say anything. But he was thinking about what DCI Frank Thistlethwaite had said when Procter was first arrested. How, having stolen a million pounds from the men he was working for, the disgraced property developer would be forever living with a target on his back.

Now, Procter was betraying the Karamanski brothers again, officially this time.

Whatever the sentence handed down to him, Rick Procter wasn't going to get off lightly. He'd be lucky to see his next birthday.

'I'm so sorry.' She was looking at him now. Full on. Like she hadn't done for weeks. 'Not just about this. I've made such a mess of things—'

He placed a finger on her lips. 'It's okay. This isn't the time for talking.'

Instead he got to his feet, took her hand and led her up the stairs.

Tolpuddle watched them go. Heard the bedroom door close. Fatigued but calm, he crossed the lounge, curled up in his bed and was soon fast asleep.

There would be no sleep for Gareth Towler that night. After a hurried consultation with Ida, Nathan and Nina, it had been agreed that the covert surveillance of Tyke needed to be resumed. Immediately. The lad was still in danger and none of them wanted his death on their hands, especially when it felt like they were so close to identifying who was behind the threats which had been menacing him.

For the teenagers had updated Gareth on their discovery, courtesy of Nancy Taylor. And had enlisted his help in getting access to the CCTV footage from the cameras overlooking the lockers at the station, Nathan knowing that one of those in charge of security was the older brother of Tommy, the lad who'd been Gareth's assistant back at Bruncliffe Hall.

Back when life had been about raising pheasants and stopping poachers.

When everything had gone so terribly wrong after Rick Procter's disastrous shooting party, Gareth had managed to keep young Tommy out of it all. While Gareth had lost his gun licence and his job, Tommy had managed to stay on at the hall and was now well on the way to becoming a gamekeeper himself.

His brother wouldn't hesitate to help Gareth if he could. So Gareth had sent a quick text, outlining the assistance he wanted. The reply had been almost immediate. Affirmative. They would have footage from the cameras within forty-eight hours.

Gareth didn't linger to celebrate with the others over a cup of tea. Instead, having opted to take the night shift, he'd grabbed a few essentials from his room and headed out with Bounty into the evening. As the skies darkened he was crouched deep in the bushes at the back of the house on Low Mill, watching the closed curtains on the bedroom windows, and hoping they could keep Tyke safe, at least until that video footage came through.

*

Gareth wasn't the only one keeping vigil.

Sitting at Edith's bedside in the hospital ward, night outside the windows, Arty could feel his stamina waning. He'd lost track of how many hours he'd been there – his voice cracking from overuse, his eyes starting to droop as the strain of the past few days caught up with him – when he felt the twitch of her fingers.

'Edith, love!' he said, instantly alert, adrenalin firing through him. 'Edith, it's me! Arty!'

Her lips moved. Her eyelids flickered. Then they were opening, and she was blinking. Her focus falling on him.

A murmur of sound came from her. He leaned in to better hear whatever she was trying to communicate as a nurse hustled into the ward, telling Edith not to fuss, to lie back and relax. Checking her statistics on the machines, plumping up her pillows and offering her a drink. Saying how lovely it was to see her awake.

Edith shook a hand at her, eyes fierce. Determined. And Arty watched on, so full of love. Amused that the nurse didn't know the strength of character of his lass. For there she was, looking at him. Trying to communicate with him. She took a sip of water from the beaker the nurse was holding out. Used it to wet her lips.

'The Hockney,' she managed, on a whispering breath.

Arty snapped back in his seat. What the hell? Just out of a coma, and she was thinking about that blasted painting. How he wished he'd had the chance to tell her the truth about it before she was attacked.

'What about it?' he asked.

She shook her head, energy fading. 'Something . . . wrong . . . Ida will know.'

He knew better than to patronise her by telling her to

rest. To not worry. Instead, he took her hand. 'I'll get onto it first thing in the morning,' he promised.

Her eyelids fluttered. Her lips curved into a part smile. Then she was drifting off.

'Is she okay?' he asked, panicked, looking at the nurse.

She smiled at him. 'She's fine. Just needs to sleep. I suggest you do the same.'

Arty leaned back in his chair and minutes later was sound out.

32

The call came from an unexpected source. And at an early hour.

Bleary-eyed, Samson rolled over and peered at the clock on the bedside table as he picked up his ringing mobile.

'Six thirty,' he grunted. 'Who calls at six thirty?'

Arty's name on the screen ripped the dregs of sleep from him. Edith. It had to be bad news about Edith.

'Is everything okay?' he asked, not bothering with a greeting.

'If you call having to walk a mile to catch a train in order to be here at this ungodly hour okay,' came Arty Robinson's gruff voice, 'then yeah, everything's fine. I'm just arriving at the station. I need you to meet me at Vinny's flat as soon as possible. Edith's come round and she's possibly onto something.'

He hung up before Samson could ask anything further.

'What's going on?' Delilah had surfaced from her own slumber and was raised up on her elbow, facing him, sensing something was happening. Behind her the blue sky offered a brilliant frame as birdsong filtered through the open window.

'We're needed,' he said, aware of the contradiction between the glorious promise of the day and the matter in hand. 'I think Arty might have information about the murder of Vinny King.'

They weren't the only ones Arty had got out of bed early. When Samson and Delilah arrived at the retirement complex, Ana was waiting for them in the foyer, keys in hand. None the wiser as to the reason for the summons, she led them up the stairs and along the corridor to Vinny's flat, where Ida Capstick was already standing. Along with Eric, Joseph and Clarissa, the pensioners looking like they'd dressed in haste as they clustered around Arty Robinson, their faces wreathed in smiles to see him finally home.

As for Arty, to say he'd looked better was an understatement. Several days of stubble had darkened his jawline and the lack of sleep had etched deep rings under his eyes. His clothes were rumpled and he was giving off a faint odour.

'Good to see you, Arty!' said Delilah, kissing his cheek while Samson held out a hand.

Arty shook it, nodded, animated despite what had clearly been a rough time.

'I was just telling everyone that Edith came round last night,' he explained, as Ana opened up the flat and they all filed inside.

'Oh, that's great news!' exclaimed Delilah. 'How is she?'

'Groggy. In a lot of pain. But you know Edith. The only thing she was bothered about was passing on what she discovered before she was attacked.'

'Which was?' Samson asked.

Arty walked through into the lounge, skirting the stain on the ground, to stand before the painting of the swimming pool. 'This.'

Everyone stared from the Hockney to Arty and back again, Eric finally breaking the puzzled silence.

'Anything in particular about it?' he asked.

Arty shrugged. 'All she said was there's something wrong with it. And that Ida would know.'

'Me!' Ida's eyebrows shot up.

'That's what she said. Then she fell asleep and was still out of it when I had to leave to catch the early train back this morning.' He gestured at the painting and then turned back to Ida. 'So? Any idea?'

She frowned. Shook her head. 'Not the foggiest.'

'Perhaps this might help,' said Samson, pulling out his mobile and showing her the photo from the magazine. 'This is what Edith saw before she left the surgery.'

Ida took the phone, letting her eyes run from the screen and up to the painting and back again. 'Why, there's nowt different about it at all,' she muttered.

'Maybe that's it,' offered Clarissa. 'Maybe there should be something different—'

It was like a fuse had been lit under Ida. Suddenly her head snapped up and her mouth dropped open.

'Tuesday! It were Tuesday.'

'What?' asked Samson.

'I knocked the painting off the wall when I was cleaning for Mr King. He threw a right strop.'

'Can't see why,' said Ana. 'There's no damage done.'

'But that's the thing,' said Ida. 'There was. Well, not damage exactly, but the painting slipped inside the frame. Made the whole thing look wonky. Now look at it!'

They did. En masse.

The green pool and the white diving board were perfectly aligned within the frame. Not a bit of wonkiness in sight.

'He must have fixed it before he went out that evening,' said Delilah.

'No.' Ida was shaking her head. 'Happen he went crazy when I went to sort it. Told me he'd have to return it to the art gallery – seems he couldn't open the back himself because it would invalidate his insurance.'

There was no denying it was curious. But still, Samson didn't think this justified the drama which had greeted the morning so far.

'I'm sure there's an innocent explanation,' he said, reaching forward and taking down the Hockney, turning it round to inspect the back. He rested it against the wall, rear side out. 'All looks above board. Vinny must have called them and got the okay to go ahead and reposition the painting himself.'

But Ida was staring at it, eyes wide. 'Tell me this, then – if Mr King fixed it himself, where did he get another one of those from?'

She was pointing at a sticker, the name and address of a London art gallery embossed into the small rectangle. It was positioned so it overlapped the tape which ran along the edges between backing and frame.

'Because,' she continued, 'that's the exact same sticker as was on the back of the painting Tuesday morning.'

It was a good point. In order to access the painting, the sticker would have to be cut in half. Yet it was completely intact.

'Maybe he had a spare,' said Joseph, sounding sleepy.

Ida snorted. 'Did he heck as like.'

'So how did Edith know about this?' asked Delilah.

'She arrived just as I was leaving. She'd have seen it all askew.'

'And then we showed her a couple of photos from the scene . . .' murmured Samson.

He worked it back through in his mind – Ida knocking the painting down, Edith arriving, noticing it was crooked, possibly even having Vinny moan about it to her. Then Vinny is killed that evening. The room is sealed. Yet somehow, the painting has been put right. Something which escapes Edith's notice until a day later, when she sees a photo in a magazine and recalls the photos from the crime scene. Photos that showed the Hockney inexplicably righted . . . In that instant, she'd spotted the anomaly Ida had just highlighted.

It all sounded plausible. But how it fitted into the murder, he had no idea. Unless they'd had it wrong all along.

'What if it was an attempted burglary?' he said. 'Vinny comes home unexpectedly and disturbs them.'

'What?' scoffed Eric. 'Disturbs them fixing his painting for him?'

'And how does Dr Naylor fit into all that?' asked Clarissa.

Samson shook his head, knowing it wasn't just the early hour which was obscuring his thinking. This case was like none other he'd ever worked. Twists and turns at every angle. Clues as substantial as the pockets of mist which hung over Pen-y-ghent even on fine days. And somehow, at the heart of it all, a painting, bequeathed to two women and now condemned to be burned.

'Funny thing is,' said Arty as Samson hung the Hockney back on the wall, 'I'm pretty sure Vinny was making a fuss over nothing.'

'What do you mean?' asked Samson, looking over his shoulder at him.

'The painting. So valuable he was leaving it to Edith to make amends.' Arty gave a bitter smile. 'When she told me, I couldn't stop laughing. See, I'm no art expert but I know a bit about Hockney. And that particular piece? There are fifteen of them. So I did a bit of research and it turns out all fifteen can be accounted for. Not one of them in the collection of Vinny King.'

'Tha means it's a fake?!' gasped Ida.

Arty nodded. And Samson felt yet another piece of the puzzle shift and shimmer, and disappear into nothing.

Sergeant Clayton's call had come about an hour later than Samson's, while the policeman was having breakfast.

'I hear you're looking for me,' had been Dr Naylor's dry greeting.

The sergeant had left the house in a hurry, slice of toast in one hand, mobile in the other as he called DS Benson. They met at the allotment gate and walked the same walk as the day before, through the well-tended vegetable patches to the far end where Dr Naylor was waiting, sitting in a sagging deckchair, an old bench and the plastic chair opposite and three cups of tea placed on an upturned crate between them. There was even a plate of biscuits.

'Courtesy of Seth,' said the doctor, gesturing at the refreshments as the policemen sat down. 'Clearly he sensed there was trouble brewing, as he rarely hands out his Hobnobs.'

The sergeant looked over towards the neighbouring plot, raising a hand in greeting to Seth Thistlethwaite, who was regarding them suspiciously from under his eyebrows.

'So,' the doctor continued, attention back on his visitors, 'Seth told me you called by yesterday. And then I switched on my phone this morning to a torrent of messages from concerned citizens. It seems you're inclined to think I may have had something to do with Vinny King's death?'

Sergeant Clayton shifted on the bench, uncomfortable at

the position he'd found himself in. It couldn't have been more incongruous. Accusing a man who healed people for a living of murder and attempted murder in such a bucolic setting. All around them were delicate tendrils of peas climbing stakes, vibrant heads of lettuce, fronds of carrots in neat rows, and potatoes drilled in a way the sergeant's father would have approved of. Thick red stalks of rhubarb too, only to be expected in a Yorkshire town, and even a large chicken coop with an enclosed run, four healthy-looking hens pecking at the ground contentedly in the early morning sunshine.

Behind it all rose the fellside of Gunnerstang Brow, a copse of mature trees spread across the lower slopes. With the high walls screening them from the road and the pub opposite, the place was a small piece of paradise. The kind of place a man would go to when nursing grief. A place where recovery might just be possible.

And here they were, tainting it.

'Well, I can tell you right now that you've got the wrong man,' Dr Naylor stated wearily. As though the mere effort of speaking was consuming the last of his resources. 'I didn't kill Vinny King. And I certainly didn't attack Edith Hird.'

Sergeant Clayton sensed there was greater outrage at being accused of the latter.

'Tell us more about Liz's history with Vinny,' he urged gently. 'We know they worked together at the paper mill before he left town. Did she lend him money?'

'Lend? Ha!' The doctor shook his head. 'It was worse than that. Liz was in the accounts department, in charge of payroll despite being so young. Then Vinny started working in the mill. He used to seek her out at the end of his shift, making time to chat to her, working his charm. She thought he was a mate. One day, Vinny asked her to let him take his wages early. A month early. Said he had need of money, what with the wedding to Edith coming up. Liz was always a soft touch for someone in desperate straits and Vinny knew even then how to work people. So she arranged for him to be paid in advance, and two days later he was gone. Down to London, the engagement to Edith broken off.'

'And the money?'

'Gone with him. Liz confessed to her boss what had happened and he made her pay it all back out of her own wages. It took her six months and when she paid the final instalment, they fired her. She lost her job, she lost her pride, she almost lost her sanity.' He gave a slight smile. 'Which is how we met. She had a breakdown and ended up as my patient.'

'You can see why this could be considered a motive,' suggested DS Benson, the man's tone less abrasive down here among the clucking hens and the vegetables, as though his city ways had been left the other side of the allotment walls. 'Perhaps you wanted to avenge your wife?'

'I can see that all right. And I'm happy to admit I detested everything about Vinny King. But I didn't kill him.' The doctor glanced over at Sergeant Clayton. 'Do you really think the two events are connected, then? Vinny and Edith?'

'We're working on that assumption, yes. Can you walk us through your version of events the morning Edith Hird was attacked?'

'I went to work. Which was a mistake. I was already feeling . . . fragile . . . when Nicky told me Edith had left suddenly. I saw the magazine on the floor and went over to pick it up and there he was. Blasted Vinny King staring out at me. I couldn't take it. So I had Nicky call in cover and I left.'

'Where did you go?' asked Sergeant Clayton.

'Back to the house to pick up my rucksack and bivvy bag. Then I caught the train to Ribblehead and spent the last two days up on the hills with my mobile off, walking home via Ingleborough. And before you accuse me of another crime,' he said with a small smile, 'I had the landowners' permission to sleep out.'

Benson was frowning. 'Did you see anyone on the way back to your house from the surgery? Anyone to speak to?'

The doctor chuckled. 'You clearly don't know anything about what it's like to be a rural GP. *Everyone* I see speaks to me. Usually to ask about an ailment, either of their own or of their livestock. On that particular day, I spoke to Harry Furness outside the rugby ground and Hannah Wilson, who was just getting into the mobile library as I walked past the primary school. I'm sure they'll be happy to vouch for me.'

Sergeant Clayton was making notes, knowing the locations tallied with the doctor's route home, which would have taken him away from the river path where Edith was attacked. If his movements could be verified, he would be in the clear. For one accusation, anyway.

'So I guess,' continued the doctor, reading the sergeant's mind, 'that just leaves the day of Vinny's murder.'

'Funny thing about that,' said DS Benson, 'is you're on CCTV entering Fellside Court twice. Yet we have no footage of you leaving the first time. Can you explain why that is?'

Another laugh. The doctor shaking his head. 'I left through the kitchen door. An avoidance tactic I sometimes deploy when I'm there.'

'What triggered it on Tuesday?'

'Geraldine Mortimer.' He looked at the detective. 'Have you met her?'

Benson nodded.

'Then perhaps you can understand why, on the day my wife died, I had no need of Geraldine or her hypochondria. I saw her coming along the corridor, blocking my exit, so I doubled back and went through the kitchen.' He gave an unapologetic shrug. 'If I'd known that would put me in the frame for a murder, I might have suffered her complaints about her bunions.'

DS Benson caught Sergeant Clayton's eye and gave a small nod. He was buying it.

'One last question,' said the sergeant. 'How did you know? About Edith and Vinny? She said she never told anyone.'

Dr Naylor's sigh was laden with grief. 'Liz spotted it. She'd always suspected there was more to the break-up between Edith and Vinny, given her own experience of the man. Then when she started working at the school, she got to know Edith well. By that time, Vinny was at the height of his fame, and yet Edith never passed comment, one way or the other, and removed herself from conversations about him. But what Liz noticed even more was the way Edith carried herself.' He paused, shaking his head at the memory. 'She once said to me that they shared the same air of caution, the mark of someone who's been badly deceived and forever bears the shame.'

They left the doctor sitting there, contemplating the past amidst the serenity of the allotments, and headed to the police station, where they found Samson O'Brien waiting in the back office with Danny.

'The doc's got an alibi?' said Danny, as soon as they walked in empty-handed.

Sergeant Clayton nodded, removed his helmet and gave a brief outline of what they'd learned in the summer sunshine.

'So we need statements from Hannah Wilson and Harry Furness,' he concluded, nodding towards his constable, who was taking notes. 'And it wouldn't harm to get the CCTV from the station. See if we can get actual footage of the doc heading for that train.'

'What about you?' DS Benson was looking at Samson. 'Anything you can share with us?'

O'Brien flicked the sergeant a look of surprise, the detective's attitude markedly less antagonistic than it had been.

'Couple of pints of Pheasant Plucker in the Crown,' murmured Sergeant Clayton. 'We'll get him in the Fleece tonight and by tomorrow he'll really be one of us.'

A grin split O'Brien's face. But quickly faded. 'Nothing except more confusion, I'm afraid.'

The three police officers listened in silence as he relayed the information Arty had brought back from Edith, and how that had led on to even more bizarre discoveries.

'Fake?' Sergeant Clayton scratched his chin. Tried to ignore the burn in his stomach. 'Reckon Vinny King knew it was?'

'God knows.' O'Brien shrugged. 'But seeing as he stipulated it should be burned after his death, I'm leaning towards saying yes.'

'Which would explain his reluctance to let Ida near it,' mused Danny.

'None of which tells us anything of use,' sighed Benson.

'I don't know.' Danny was frowning. 'Surely we have to accept that there is a link now between Vinny's death and Edith's attack, and that link is the Hockney.'

'Which means, we should go back to the line of questioning we were pursuing at the start,' said O'Brien. 'Who knew Edith had seen that magazine?'

Sergeant Clayton slapped his forehead. 'We didn't ask Dr Naylor who else was in the surgery that day.'

'I'm on it,' said Danny. He turned away, mobile to his ear.

'So we've ruled out revenge on the part of Arty, Geraldine Mortimer and the doc,' said O'Brien, pacing the room now. 'Which doesn't mean it can't have been someone else seeking retribution.'

'Someone who most likely gained access to the flat using that spare key,' added Benson.

'And, seeing as everyone who appears on the CCTV leading up to the murder has been accounted for, our perpetrator was possibly already in the building. Which throws the spotlight back on the handful of residents who didn't go to the play.'

'Or it could be an attempted theft gone wrong?' suggested the sergeant.

Samson nodded. 'We contemplated that, but nothing was taken.'

'They ran out of time? Vinny walked in the door and surprised them. Paying for it with his life.'

'There is another possibility,' murmured DS Benson. 'Something you mooted right at the beginning, Gavin.' The use of his first name caught the sergeant off guard, O'Brien grinning widely, but Benson carried on regardless. 'What if Vinny King's murder *is* somehow connected to the threats Tyke has been getting? You said yourself that Tyke was on his way to the flat when his uncle was killed. What if you're right? What if Tyke was the intended target? Or Vinny was, to send Tyke a message?'

'Hell of a message,' declared O'Brien. But Sergeant Clayton could tell by the knots forming on his forehead that he was contemplating the idea. Turning it over in that fine mind of his, one which the sergeant knew he could never match.

'Dr Naylor says there were two women in the surgery on Wednesday.' Danny had returned to the desks, notebook out. 'Both out-of-towners. He didn't recognise either of them, but he remembers Nicky making a fuss about one of them in particular. He seemed to think she might have been Tyke's assistant?'

'Eloise Morgan,' said Samson. 'According to Delilah she's a bit more than just his assistant.'

'And the other one?' asked Benson.

'Blonde. Here on holiday, staying in a lodge out at the campsite.'

Sergeant Clayton saw the stillness descend on O'Brien. Then he was fishing in his pocket, pulling out his mobile.

'What's Dr Naylor's mobile number,' he asked, tapping the screen. 'I need to send him something.'

The reply from the doctor was almost instantaneous. O'Brien looking at the message before holding out the phone to the others. On it was an article from a website entitled Loose Threads, a picture of a tense-looking woman below the text, long blonde hair curling around a cherubic face.

'Holly Campbell,' he explained. 'A line of enquiry in our investigation for Tyke. We've yet to locate her but we know that she does harbour a grudge against him. I asked the doc if she could have been the other woman in the surgery on Wednesday.'

Beneath the message was the doctor's reply.

Possibly.

33

It was enough to galvanise them into action. What had been growing despair had now turned into burgeoning hope.

A lead they could chase down.

Sergeant Clayton and DS Benson were heading out to the campsite to see if they could unearth the identity of the woman who was possibly Holly Campbell, while Danny was tasked with chasing up the statements which would help clear Dr Naylor. Benson also instructed him to start a deep mine into the backgrounds of both Tyke and Eloise Morgan, covering all bases in case something had been missed by the Dales Detective team.

Samson didn't say anything at the perceived slur on his agency, even as Danny threw him an apologetic look, the lad knowing how thorough Delilah was when it came to internet searches. At this point in the investigation, with everything thrown wide open again, egos had to take a back seat. And including Eloise in that scrutiny made sense. As DS Benson had pointed out – they'd been presuming the threat to Tyke originated from his own background. It was possible it was connected to hers instead.

As he walked back towards the office in what was now late-morning sunshine, stomach rumbling, Samson was contemplating the various threads which were somehow all connected to the death of Vinny King. Mulling over the possible scenarios – a robbery gone wrong, or a targeted killing?

He was just turning onto Back Street when it hit him.

If Vinny had indeed been killed simply to send a message to Tyke, then could Eloise be in danger, too? Was someone taunting the fashion designer by targeting those closest to him?

It was a worrying thought. Especially now Tyke had instructed the Dales Detective Agency to cease surveillance. Samson's only consolation as he entered the office building was that at least there had been no new threats made against the man. No dead rabbits. No sightings of the trail bike. Nothing to suggest that Tyke, or even Eloise, was in danger.

Plus Samson kept returning to the one thing which made a serious dent in the theory that the talk-show host had been an intended victim.

How had anyone known Vinny would be at home? Even Vinny himself hadn't known it. A chance mix-up involving his glasses and he'd returned back to the flat on spec, where his killer was waiting.

Because Samson was more and more convinced of that. The spare key, the broken lamp. They suggested someone already in the apartment. What they didn't provide the answer to was why that person had been there. And as for the improvised weapon, a trophy grabbed from a sideboard, that just muddied the waters even further.

Which brought him back full circle. Targeted killing or a robbery gone wrong? And where did the potentially fake Hockney fit into it all?

Head throbbing, he entered the building and made straight for the kitchen. He had time to have a quick sandwich before he had to meet Will Metcalfe at the rugby ground which would be the base for the Bruncliffe Hills race the following day. Will had roped him into helping prepare for the event, the fell race seemingly no longer the simple occasion it had been in Samson's youth, when it had consisted of nothing more than a run up and down treacherous terrain. Now there were stalls of local produce, a raffle, cakes and scones, and even a hog roast, all needing shelter in case the weather turned inclement. Samson was hoping that the physical activity of putting up marquees would help take his mind off the imponderable aspects of the Vinny King case.

Reaching the landing, he stuck his head around Delilah's door, not really expecting her to be back yet as she was dropping a freshly showered and shaved Arty Robinson over to the hospital and visiting Edith at the same time. Sure enough, the office was empty. As was the kitchen, no sound from Gareth's rooms above either.

Hopefully, thought Samson, putting the kettle on in an unaccustomed silence, the others were all doing what Delilah had suggested. Having a bit of time off.

Gareth was barely able to keep his eyes open.

Bone-tired from his shift on watch, he was walking back from Bruncliffe Station, a USB stick in his pocket. Tommy's brother had come up trumps and even faster than promised, securing the CCTV footage for the day the Yorkshire Wild van had been seen. The day Tyke had almost been run over. All Gareth had to do now was stay awake long enough to watch it through.

He was thinking about his bed, and how he'd just snatch a half hour's kip before commencing on the viewing, when his phone went.

A panicked text from Nina. Tyke had just left his home in his Porsche.

Working with scant resources and without authorisation, Gareth, Ida and the teenagers had drawn up a rough plan for surveillance. Gareth would do the nights, when the danger was possibly highest. Nathan and Nina would cover the morning, and Ida the afternoons. If Tyke left the house on foot, whoever was on duty would do their best to follow him unseen. Other than that, they would stay by the house. Watching. And hoping nothing happened.

If Tyke left the house by car, however, then their plans went to pot.

The only upside, as Ida had pointed out the night before when they'd spotted the shortcomings of their approach, was that Tyke was probably in the least danger when he was behind the wheel of his car.

Gareth was in the middle of composing a reply when there was a hoot of a horn and a red Cayenne pulled up alongside him. Tyke was leaning across the passenger seat, today's ensemble a mix of browns and oranges in geometric patterns that made Gareth's tired eyes ache. The fashion designer was living testimony to his own catchphrase, his clothing certainly getting him noticed.

'Gareth! I've been meaning to catch you,' said Tyke, a warm smile lighting up his handsome features, the dark bruise on his cheek standing out. 'Sorry for being so brusque yesterday morning. The stress of Uncle Vinny's murder is really getting to me.'

Gareth nodded. 'No worries,' he said.

'Any developments you can tell me about?'

'Sorry, I haven't touched base in a while. Been working on another case . . . out at the dairy,' he added rapidly. 'Check in with Samson. I'm sure he'll be happy to update you.' Then he gestured at the car. 'I thought you were keeping a low profile and staying at home. Where are you off to?'

'Just the community hall.' Tyke pulled a face. 'I've made the difficult decision to cancel the fashion show. Out of respect for my uncle as much as anything. I hate letting people down but I just don't have the heart to go through with it.'

'Folk will understand, under the circumstances. And don't take this the wrong way, seeing as you've already sacked us,' continued Gareth with a grin, 'but it's probably best that you're not going through with it given the outstanding threats against you.'

Tyke laughed. 'Fair point.'

'And the race tomorrow? You still planning on taking part?'

'Totally. Even if she's not there in an official capacity, Delilah will be right on my tail. I couldn't be safer.' He smiled again. 'No hard feelings?'

'None at all. Just watch yourself, okay? Anything at all out of the ordinary and you let us know.'

'Will do.' Tyke nodded one last time and with a roar of the mighty engine, he was gone.

Gareth hastily rewrote his message to Nina, updating her on what had occurred and telling her to hold her position, and then resumed his walk back home. His bed was calling him. The CCTV footage would have to wait.

Gareth was already sound asleep by the time Delilah got back to the office building in mid-afternoon. She'd ended up taking a Mini full of visitors to the hospital, Arty turning up in the Fellside Court car park alongside Eric, Joseph and Clarissa. With Tolpuddle as well, it had been a tight squeeze.

347

Fortunately, Edith had been overjoyed to see them all. And when her energy started to wane, she'd simply lain back in her bed and listened to her friends bringing her up to date with the Vinny King case, her hand held tightly in Arty's the entire time.

Delilah had watched the pair of them. Marvelling at the strength of their love. At how Edith was so willing to place her trust in someone wholeheartedly after all she'd been through. When Arty corralled his friends to accompany him to the cafeteria, Delilah found herself alone with Edith and had taken the chance to ask the question.

'You and Arty,' she'd said, as the voices of the others faded away down the corridor beyond the ward. 'Weren't you wary of making such a commitment at all? You know, after Vinny?'

Edith looked surprised. 'Why, Delilah, for someone who enjoys hurtling themself down fellsides as a pastime, you of all people should understand. What's the point in living if you don't take risks? Or, as my father always used to say, you'll never find gold if you don't venture down the mine.' She smiled. 'Arty is my gold.'

Then she'd regarded Delilah with that shrewd look for which she was famous.

'Cold feet?' she simply said.

'Not any more.' Delilah shook her head, amazed to find it was the truth. Wondering when her heart had stopped being fearful. Then she grimaced. 'But I may have messed up the wedding.'

And she'd found herself telling Edith all about it, how she'd put everything into jeopardy with her foolishness.

When she'd left the hospital a while later – Arty and the others opting to stay behind, Clarissa saying they had things to discuss with Edith in that impish way she had when she was planning something nice – Delilah had felt a lightness in her soul she hadn't felt in months. The Rick Procter trial, which had been hanging over her, was no longer an issue, and as for the botched nuptials? As Edith had said, it wasn't the end of the world. They could be rearranged.

All she had to do was tell Samson.

Tomorrow, she decided, as she let herself in the back door of the office building. She'd tell him tomorrow, after the race. The last thing she needed lining up for the start of the Bruncliffe Hills was a mind preoccupied with other things.

Checking her messages as she walked up the stairs, Tolpuddle already on the landing, heading for his food bowl, she saw a couple from Samson, bringing her up to speed with developments. And explaining that he'd be stopping over in the office tonight – he wanted to work late on a couple of things once he was done helping set up the marquees and he didn't want to disturb her sleep.

She grinned. Thinking that he'd disturbed it perfectly the night before. But she was also grateful. All she wanted to do for the rest of the day was put her feet up, eat and go to bed, making sure she was ready to give her best tomorrow. With that in mind, she was going to check through her emails and then head home. She'd just reached her office when her mobile went. Nancy Taylor's name on the screen.

'Hi Delilah! Just a quick call – I'm about to head off for the weekend but I thought I'd check up and see if Nathan and Nina had any joy with the station lockers?'

Delilah's puzzlement must have been apparent in her silence, Nancy continuing with an explanation.

'They came to see me, asking about rentals in the area?

Something to do with a delivery – reading between the lines, I'm guessing it was in relation to your work with Tyke?'

The Yorkshire Wild van. Of course. The teenagers had obviously got further than they'd admitted when the plug was pulled on the investigation.

'Oh, right,' said Delilah. 'Well actually, we're not working with him any more. He wants us to concentrate on catching his uncle's killer, so we've put that case on hold for now.'

'Ah!' There was a long pause. Then Nancy spoke again. 'Please don't think that I'm speaking out of turn or anything, but it might be for the best. I heard on the real-estate grapevine today that he's behind on his rent for the house in Low Mill. The agent wants to push the matter but the landlord is reluctant to, given the circumstances.'

'I'm sure it's just an oversight,' said Delilah, trying not to think of the outstanding invoice which she really ought to follow up. But, like Tyke's landlord, she didn't want to seem crass chasing her client – former client – for money when he was going through such a tough time. Even though it was putting a strain on the agency's cash flow. 'But good to know. Thanks.'

'No worries. And good luck for the race tomorrow. You'll do Bruncliffe proud!'

Nancy hung up. Delilah stared at her mobile for a second, thinking about what she'd heard. Then she looked at the invoices stacked on her desk. Tyke's was on top.

Was that the real reason he'd asked them to break off their surveillance? He was having money difficulties? Delilah knew all too well how easily financial problems could hit a business. How funds could be momentarily tied up or slow to arrive, causing issues further down the chain of payments. Even for someone as seemingly wealthy as Tyke.

So, faced with such an embarrassment – even more morti-
fying when he was so famous and in his family's hometown
– but anxious to bring his uncle's killer to justice, Tyke had
been forced into a difficult choice. Rather than confess he
couldn't afford to fund both investigations, he'd terminated
their contract to provide protection for him.

.If this was true, then it put a different light on things.
Perhaps Tyke wasn't so blasé about the threat to his life as
he'd made out. Even worse, he was now exposed and possibly
in danger, simply because he couldn't afford to pay for the
services of the Dales Detective Agency.

Fingers tapping her mobile, she sent Samson a message.
Maybe it was time the agency did a bit of voluntary work
and kept an eye on Tyke surreptitiously.

The back door slamming shut woke him, even up on the top
floor.

Gareth groaned, rolled over and checked his watch,
muttering a curse as he saw the time. He'd been asleep for
hours.

'You should have woken me, girl!' he murmured, reaching
across the bed to stroke Bounty's ears.

She raised a sleepy eyelid in response.

He rubbed his face with a large hand, trying to brush
away the fatigue, then swung his legs out of the bed and
reached for his laptop. The USB stick was lying next to it.

He didn't have to be at Tyke's house for another hour.
He had time to do an initial view of the CCTV footage.
Preferably over a cuppa and a decent meal. But first he needed
to know if the coast was clear – his co-conspirators would
never forgive him if he was caught working on the Tyke
investigation by Samson or Delilah.

Sticking his head round his bedroom door, he listened for a second or two, sensing the emptiness of the place. Then he whistled softly at Bounty, the spaniel leaping off the bed to accompany him down the stairs and into the kitchen.

The decent meal was ready-made lasagne. A portion which was supposed to feed two people but which Gareth knew would barely touch the sides of his hunger. There was something about working nightshifts which left him with an insatiable appetite.

While the microwave did its work, he inserted the USB stick in the laptop and began fast-forwarding through the video using the clock at the bottom of the screen. No point wasting hours watching it if the rabbit hadn't even been delivered to the station lockers. The attempted hit-and-run on Tyke had been late morning, so the drop off would have been shortly after that—

And there it was! The Yorkshire Wild van, pulling into the station car park. Nathan and Nina had been right.

Impressed by the teenagers and excited about what he might discover, Gareth sat down with his lasagne for a more careful scrutiny of the footage. He ate slowly, his meal interrupted by constantly having to tweak the settings, trying to get the speed right. One moment the images were scrolling past so fast, he couldn't see a thing. Next, they were unfolding in real time, which would take forever to watch.

After half an hour, he pressed pause, excitement waning and his head hurting. Wishing Delilah was here so he could get the benefit of her tech expertise. Not that he could tell her what he was doing.

It had been gnawing at him all day – the need for secrecy. The fact they hadn't told Samson and Delilah about what they were up to, nor about the sighting of that trail bike yesterday. Tyke was quite possibly in danger. Surely it would be better if they all pulled together on this. Easier to keep their former client safe.

The only thing that offered him some comfort was the knowledge that tomorrow morning, Tyke would be lining up for the start of the Bruncliffe Hills race and that meant Delilah would be by his side. But after that . . . ?

He turned his attention back to the video, letting it play, daunted by the amount there was to get through. Just one day's worth and there was so much. People coming and going all the time, a swell in numbers as trains arrived and departed. He needed to filter it down somehow. Approach the search in a more systematic way.

Because right now, he felt overwhelmed with the task. And he couldn't even be sure that this was the day when the parcel had been collected. Sure, it was when it had been delivered but the package contained a dead rabbit, one not intended for consumption. The person who'd ordered it didn't exactly have to worry about it going off. They could easily have delayed collecting it until the following day.

Aware of time ticking, he flipped the laptop closed, wolfed down the remains of the lasagne and stood to go. Another night on duty and then he'd come back to it. Hopefully with a better method of winnowing out the one person in all those images who really counted.

The one person who, even now, could be plotting to kill Tyke.

Another dead end.

Sergeant Clayton threw his helmet on the desk in despair and crossed to the kettle.

'No joy at the campsite, I take it?' Danny was looking

up from his computer, CCTV footage from the train station frozen on the screen.

'Not as such,' muttered the sarge. 'DS Benson showed the owner that photo Samson had of this Holly Campbell lass and they couldn't say for certain whether it was the same woman.'

'But they thought it could be?' Danny was looking excited.

'Aye. Only thing is, she checked out yesterday.'

'Do they have contact details for her?'

The sergeant nodded. 'Benson is following it up. Poor sod. Think he's feeling the pressure – his DI is never off the phone, checking on progress. And I thought that swarm of journalists might have buzzed off home by now but they're still hanging around, as welcome as wasps at a picnic.'

Danny leaned back in his chair, stretching his arms out wide, his neck cracking as he rolled his head.

DS Benson wasn't the only one feeling the strain. They all were. Young Danny was putting in hours beyond the normal. And Gavin Clayton couldn't remember when he'd last felt so tired. Weary. Disillusioned.

This wretched case was such a puzzle and now there was the added tension that Tyke could be in danger. The lass he lived with, too.

'How about you?' he asked, crossing to look at Danny's computer, a blurred figure captured walking towards the platform as a train came into sight. 'Is that the doc?'

'Sure is!' Danny grinned. 'Getting onto the Ribblehead train just as he said. Plus I got statements from Hannah Wilson and Harry Furness and both of their accounts tally with what Dr Naylor claimed. In which case, considering the timings, I don't see how he could possibly have been involved in the attack on Edith Hird.'

'Thank God for small mercies,' sighed the sergeant, placing a mug of tea on his desk and sinking into his chair.

'Where's my cuppa?' asked Danny, pointedly.

'At home.' Sergeant Clayton gestured towards the clock and then the door. 'Long past time for knocking off.'

'But I'm only just getting going on the search into Tyke and Eloise Morgan that DS Benson told me to do.'

'It'll wait. You can resume first thing before we head down to the race. Going to be a long enough day tomorrow without you burning the candle at both ends.'

He thought the lad was about to object. But then he just nodded, gathered up his rucksack and headed off. Sergeant Clayton had a bit of his tea, and then fired up his own computer.

Danny wasn't the only one who could conduct a search. After all his years on the force, the sergeant was well versed in negotiating his way around the labyrinth of police files. Plus he had a network of contacts he could call up, should the need arise. Tapping away at the keys, he commenced his work. Grimly determined that he wasn't going to have another death on his hands as a result of this case.

Two hours later, he was staring at the screen, wondering if this was it. The origins of everything that was going on. But he needed more information. The relevant file hadn't been digitised but that didn't deter him. He dialled the number, imagining the corresponding phone ringing out in a bustling London police station that worked around the clock, a world away from Bruncliffe. Thus he was caught somewhat off guard by the languid response, the lack of urgency and the frank explanation that the records department was closed for the day but that if he left a message, someone would get back to him during office hours.

Having ascertained that Saturdays were, thankfully, considered a working day in the capital, he gave his details and hung up. Disgruntled. But with those old nerves jangling.

He was onto something. Something which might help them conclude this infernal investigation and, if DS Benson's concerns were justified, keep Tyke and Eloise Morgan safe and well.

34

The sun rose over the Crag into a sky streaked dusty pink, alighting on the grey roofs of the town, turning Hawber Woods golden, and making the white of the marquees arranged around the outside of the rugby ground brilliant. For Gareth Towler, hunkered down behind the wheelie bins at the back of Tyke's house in Low Mill, it was the signal to move.

He placed a hand on Bounty, the dog knowing how to keep silent when needed from their years of tracking poachers together on the Bruncliffe Hall estate. She stretched, yawned and then followed him out from their hiding place, both of them using a well-placed garden bench to help them scramble over the wall and into the field beyond.

Relief was the overwhelming feeling consuming Gareth as he flexed his stiff limbs after what had felt like the longest night of his life. Relief at finishing his shift. Relief that it had been uneventful. And relief at having made the decision that it was time to bring Samson and Delilah in on what was happening.

While the morning ahead didn't pose any real logistical problems, Tyke's movements limited to a stroll down to the rugby ground to sign on and then the race itself, beyond that things would become strained. The team of four was stretched to breaking point, Nathan and Nina committed to helping

Lucy Metcalfe out on her stall at the race, and Ida having already cancelled some of her cleaning duties in order to cover the intervening hours. They couldn't keep it up.

He crept along the stone border, bent double, Bounty at his heels, until he reached the start of what had been Rick Procter's property. Picking the spaniel up, he placed her on the top of the wall and she leaped gracefully down into the garden on the other side. Gareth's own landing was more of a thump. He straightened up, the vacant house staring back at him, making him shudder. Judging by the fact it was still on the market, despite being priced competitively, he wasn't the only one who wanted nothing to do with the place. It was tainted, like everything Procter had touched.

And now there would be no trial. News had filtered through the town the day before that Procter was trying to get off lightly by turning on his former associates. While it saved poor Delilah from having to relive her nightmare, it meant folk would never really know the full extent of the damage the man had caused.

Although, having met those associates – in particular the quietly menacing Karamanski brothers – Gareth didn't rate Procter's chances of surviving his decision.

Still caught in the memories of that dreadful day up at Bruncliffe Hall, he started towards the side of the house and nearly jumped out of his skin when a dark figure emerged from behind the shed.

'Tha looks fair done in,' came a whisper. Ida, her black combats and black hoodie emphasising the angles of her face. 'There's tea in the pot and the makings of a fry-up in the fridge.'

'You're a saint,' he murmured, grinning.

'Any problems?'

'All good.' He paused. 'Although, I've been thinking it might be best if we let Samson and Delilah in on what we're up to. If this is as serious as we suspect it is, we really ought to tell them.'

'Happen we're of the same mind,' said Ida, nodding. 'Leave it with me. I'll sort it.'

'Thanks! See you at the rugby ground later.'

With a final nod, and an agility which surprised him, she slipped over the wall and disappeared.

Thinking that Ida Capstick was a woman of many talents, Gareth headed for the office building. Breakfast and another stint with the CCTV footage. Then, if he was lucky, while the rest of the town was watching the race, he might even get a kip.

Despite it being relatively early for a Saturday, the rugby ground was busy. Stallholders bustling between vans and marquees, setting up for the day. A few eager runners already hovering anxiously.

As she crossed the wide expanse of field, Delilah felt the familiar spike of adrenalin which accompanied the build-up to every race. A fizz of energy in her legs. A knot of tension in her stomach.

'You'll be fine,' muttered a brusque voice behind her and she turned to see the craggy face and bushy eyebrows of Seth Thistlethwaite, her coach from her younger days and now, on her return to the sport after a long absence, her mentor once more. 'Just don't set out like a lurcher off the leash at the start.'

She grinned at him. 'Yes, Coach.'

'And no running other folks' races either, mind.' He stared at her, knowing her so well. 'What happened with that Tyke was a long time ago. Focus on what you're doing today, not him. Even if we both know he cheated.'

Delilah blinked. All these years and Seth had never admitted to her that she'd been right. On the contrary, when she'd reached the end of the race in a blind rage and had marched up to Tyke and pushed him over, Seth had banned her from training for a month, for unsporting behaviour.

'You knew?' she said.

'Aye, lass. But all anyone remembers of that race is you coming down that fellside like a demon, not him taking tenth. You turned yourself into a legend that day. What he did is an irrelevance.' He placed a hand on her arm. 'So go and do me proud up there.'

She nodded, overcome with emotion that Seth still had such faith in her. He walked away towards the race tent where runners were beginning to line up for registration.

'Getting some last-minute advice?' Samson had found her, slipping an arm around her shoulders. 'Not that you need it.'

'Something like that. Did you get my message?' she asked, wanting to turn the topic off the race, her nerves starting to jangle. 'About resuming our personal protections services for Tyke?'

He nodded. 'I was just thinking the same yesterday. I'm not totally convinced by Benson's theory but in the light of things, it wouldn't hurt to keep a covert eye on Tyke for now. Thankfully you'll be doing that anyway this morning.'

'If I'm lucky. He's fast. I'll have to be at my best to keep up.'

'You're always at your best in my eyes,' Samson said, pulling her into his arms with a grin.

'Sorry to interrupt!' Danny Bradley had approached them, uniform on, looking like he was there on business. 'Got a bit of news,' he said, confirming Delilah's impression. 'The sarge pulled a late one last night and found something interesting. It seems Eloise Morgan had quite a difficult time in the past.' He pulled out his notebook, flipping to a marked page. 'She was arrested for vagrancy, not just rough sleeping but also begging. Not your usual sitting on a street corner, mind. Look at this.'

Danny held out his mobile, flicking through a selection of photographs all showing pavement art of an amazing quality. Van Gogh's *The Starry Night*, swirling up off the concrete, the lovers of Klimt's *The Kiss* embracing passionately beneath a street light and Hokusai's *The Great Wave off Kanagawa* crashing towards a postbox. All different styles. All brilliantly executed.

'Wow! She's talented,' said Delilah.

Samson was nodding. 'I saw some of her work when I went round to check the house out the first day.' He gestured at the photographs. 'And this kind of makes sense of something Eloise said about how she met Tyke. She said they bumped into each other on the street, which seemed to be an in-joke.'

'Do you think he was her turning point? She met him and he took her in off the streets?' asked Danny.

'It's possible. Eloise did mention something about owing him big style.'

'So how does this fit in with the investigation?' asked Delilah.

Danny shook his head. 'I'm not sure this bit does. But there was an older arrest on her record. One that hasn't been digitised yet. The sarge is chasing it up – analogue style,' he grinned. 'It could be something or nothing. But he wanted to keep you posted.'

'And Holly Campbell? Any luck locating her?'

'DS Benson is working on it. He got a name and address for the blonde woman at the surgery the day Edith was attacked but so far he's not had any luck making contact. The lack of progress is getting to him. He's like a caged bear this morning. I was glad to be ordered over here on duty.'

Samson laughed. 'You got the better deal. There's never any trouble at a fell race.'

'Unless they run out of hog roast too early,' quipped Danny. 'Anyway, good luck, Delilah. We'll all be down here cheering you on.'

With a tip of his helmet, he walked away, leaving Delilah to muse how much more mature he seemed these days. Like he'd finally grown into his uniform and the responsibility it brought with it.

'You ready?' asked Samson.

Delilah turned and looked up at the Crag looming over them. The steep sides. The rough terrain. 'I'm ready.'

Hunched over his laptop in the solitude of the office building, a mug of tea next to him and his empty plate pushed to the far end of the kitchen table, Gareth couldn't work out if it was his sluggish, sleep-deprived brain that was at fault or if the rough filtering system he'd devised simply wasn't very good.

Whatever it was, he was making no progress with the CCTV from the train station. And now his eyes were starting to cloud over, his head heavy on his shoulders as he tried to concentrate on the split-screen footage.

Two cameras. That was the problem. One overlooking the entrance to the car park and the other directed towards the platform. Neither of them offering a view of the block of yellow lockers. So while Gareth had got to grips with the technology, enabling him to watch at a comfortable speed, there was still way too much content to get through. It would take him hours.

And as for the idea he'd come up with to help him narrow down the range of potential suspects, it had seemed a good one while he was out on watch but now, as he attempted to apply it, he could see the flaws.

He'd decided to only focus on people carrying something, reasoning that a dead rabbit wasn't exactly the kind of thing you could stuff in a jacket pocket or inside a coat. Unfortunately, his rudimentary search parameters had only ruled out about two per cent of the folk passing the cameras. Bags. Rucksacks. Bike panniers. Supersize handbags.

Everyone pretty much carrying something which was large enough to fit Gareth's criteria.

He needed a better way of reducing his options.

Leaning back in his chair, he stretched out his arms, Bounty glancing up from the floor where she'd been dozing, wondering if they were on the move.

'As you were, lass,' he murmured, glad that at least one of the team was catching up on some missed sleep. Then he turned his neck to ease out the kinks and saw the whiteboard above the table.

Vinny King's case laid out in Ida's neat handwriting. Apart from a couple of additions . . .

Samson must have been in, for he'd added a few items. He was clearly considering some kind of link between Vinny's death and Tyke's case, judging by the sparse notes. Even more reason to speak to him. Let him know about the trail bike—

Gareth froze. Staring at the board. A name had been added to it, the words 'at doctor's surgery?' written underneath. A name Gareth recognised from Tyke's case.

Holly Campbell.

An image of her came to mind.

Gareth clicked on the laptop, starting the footage all over again. This time he was only looking for blondes.

There was no skill needed to tail the lad through town. In his bright orange kit, he was like a walking Belisha beacon.

Ida Capstick was able to keep her distance as she followed Tyke out of the Low Mill housing development, under the railway bridge and along the road to the rugby club. The mass of people heading in the same direction gave her ample cover. Runners, families, tourists, all pouring onto the fields, the marquees already thronging with customers.

Ida, however, only had eyes for one person. Well, three actually. She needed to have a word with Samson and Delilah, like she'd promised Gareth. But for now, keeping tabs on Tyke was her main priority.

Of course, while the crowd gave her ample cover and allowed her to follow her target with ease, this was Bruncliffe. An event of this magnitude drew the entire town out, and pretty much all of its inhabitants knew her. By the time she'd crossed the first third of the rugby ground Ida had been stopped multiple times – Barbara Hargreaves, Harry Furness, Seth Thistlethwaite, Herriot the vet, Annie Hardacre and even Mrs Pettiford, an unlikely alliance having been formed between the two women in the autumn.

Exasperated at these constant interruptions, Ida clamped her lips and creased her forehead, adopting her fiercest expression in the hope of dissuading any other friendly sorts from derailing her mission. A few yards on, it seemed her fiercest expression no longer held the power it once had.

'Ida! Lovely to see you taking a day off and enjoying the

festivities.' Joseph O'Brien was standing in front of her, Tolpuddle on a lead next to him and Eric Bradley the other side.

'Aye,' muttered Ida, not contradicting him, her focus on the registration tent in the background where Tyke was standing, signing autographs as a small crowd of fans formed around him. Could one of them be the threat? With Nathan and Nina on the other side of the ground, working on the Peaks Patisserie stall, and Gareth back at the office, Ida was getting concerned about their ability to keep Tyke safe.

'Of course, you're presuming Ida's on a day off, Joseph,' Eric was saying, with a knowing wink. He gestured at Ida's combat trousers. 'But she's wearing her undercover gear.'

Ida's gaze snapped onto him. Her surprised reaction telling the truth.

'You *are* working undercover!' breathed Eric, eyes widening, looking around, trying to see who she was watching. 'Tyke!' he exclaimed, his gaze landing on the fashion designer.

'Behave!' she hissed. 'Tha'll give the game away!'

'I thought he'd cancelled your contract,' said Joseph. 'Is there still a threat to his life?'

The bluntness of the question made Ida's already taut nerves stretch even further. She needed to find Samson and Delilah. And quick.

While the entirety of Bruncliffe had flocked to the rugby ground, Sergeant Clayton and DS Benson were working hard in the small office at the back of the police station. And making progress of sorts.

'It's not her,' said Benson, hanging up the phone and getting to his feet with a curse, shoulders tight with stress, head pounding. 'The blonde woman at the campsite. She's

---

not Holly Campbell. Just someone who was up here on holiday and happened to have need of a doctor.'

'She checks out? For when Vinny King was killed?'

Benson nodded. 'Iron-clad alibi. She was actually in Bruncliffe Community Hall watching the play. Saw him leave, too.'

'Bugger,' muttered the sergeant. He reached for his mug, saw it was already empty and thumped it back down. 'This blasted case.'

The sergeant had been at his desk when Benson arrived – judging by the shadows on his jaw and under his eyes, he hadn't spent long away from it overnight. Chasing up a will-o'-the-wisp lead from Eloise Morgan's past which the detective suspected would turn out to be nothing. Like everything in this investigation so far – a hall of mirrors, giving them glimpses of hope, only to find themselves staring back at their own inadequacies.

'No reply from the London lot, yet?' he asked.

The irritated shake of the head told him the answer. 'Too early. Office doesn't open until ten. Bloody slackers.'

Another thirty minutes to wait. The sergeant was sitting looking at him, sharing his despair.

'Get the kettle on and break out the biscuits,' said Benson, resuming his seat with determination. 'We've got the entire police service at our fingertips, access to information beyond the bounds of O'Brien and his team – there has to be a way to locate this Holly Campbell. Some kind of connection to Tyke.'

'On it!' said the sergeant, crossing towards the cupboard.

To the background sound of the boiling kettle and the clatter of crockery, DS Benson began his search.

35

It was almost time for the race. Runners gathering in shifting, nervous groups, wary smiles, a bit of forced laughter. Samson found himself picking up the vibes, thrown back to his teenage years when he'd been a competitive runner, lining up alongside Delilah. Knowing how hard she would be to beat. Towards the end of his time in the town, she'd surpassed him, becoming the phenomenal athlete Seth Thistlethwaite had always predicted she'd be.

Not once, in all the times they'd raced together, had she shown her nerves.

Today was a different matter.

She was standing next to Samson, kit on, ready to go. Looking more anxious than he'd ever seen her. And it was easy to see why. Pretty much the entire town had shown up, word getting around that Delilah Metcalfe was running the Bruncliffe Hills for the first time in a decade. While she'd dipped her toe back into the fell race circuit with the race at the Bruncliffe Show the previous summer, coming an admirable fourth, this was different.

The Hills was notorious for its brutality. A sheer climb up. A tricky ridge. Then an even trickier drop back down to the rugby club. It was a race Delilah had made her own. Even before she'd made the crazy descent Samson had heard so much about the last week. Which is why so many people had come down to the start to watch.

The fact Tyke was also lining up, the man who'd been the catalyst for her infamous run, was only adding to the drama.

'Wish me luck,' she murmured, placing a kiss on Samson's cheek.

'You'll be fine,' he said.

'What if I lose sight of Tyke?'

'You won't. And if anything happens, just be careful up there. No heroics, okay?'

She gave a small nod, one last kiss and then she moved over towards the start line.

'Give 'em hell, Delilah!' called out a voice.

'She'd better bloody had,' came Will Metcalfe's voice. 'I've got a tenner on with Troy!'

In the ensuing laughter, Delilah managed a smile. Raised a hand in acknowledgement. The crowd responding with applause.

'She's a bit special, that lass.' Samson's father had moved beside him, Eric Bradley with him, binoculars around his neck and Tolpuddle on a lead, Danny Bradley and Herriot there too. The Weimaraner immediately leaned into Samson's thigh.

'I'm not going to argue.' Samson was watching her. Seeing how she was working her way to the front. Alongside Tyke, who was no longer signing autographs, his customary smile having given way to something more focused. The look of someone who intended to win.

'Delilah's going to have to pull a rabbit out of the hat to beat that lad,' muttered Eric.

'Just as long as she doesn't do it in front of Sergeant Clayton,' responded Herriot with a dry smile, making them all laugh. The tale of the sergeant's post-mortem dizzy spell having already become Bruncliffe folklore.

Samson was too tense to laugh with them. An inexplicable knot of apprehension in his gut. It wasn't just about the race. It was about the case. He had the curious notion that somehow it was coming to a head. In a way they couldn't see.

A movement to the side of the field caught his eye. Ida Capstick, standing at Lucy's stall, deep in conversation with Nathan and Nina. Something serious about all of them which was at odds with the atmosphere of the day. As though they too shared his sense of foreboding.

Ida saw Samson looking and nodded. Saying something. All three now looking over, Nina nodding. Nathan's cheeks going crimson.

The lad was like his aunt in that respect. Never able to hide a thing.

Then Ida was striding across the field, coming Samson's way. Like a woman who had something on her mind.

'Morning, Ida,' he said as she joined them.

She opened her mouth to speak just as Danny leaned over, lowering his voice so only the group could hear.

'By the way,' said the constable, 'I had word from the sarge. That blonde woman at the surgery wasn't the mysterious Holly Campbell. He said to tell you him and Benson are sticking with it, trying to chase her down.'

'Is this connected to Vinny's murder?' asked Eric.

'Possibly that, and the death threats made against Tyke, too.'

Eric glanced at Samson's father. The pair of them looking at Ida.

'Happens there's something tha should know,' she said, regarding Samson with the same expression she'd had one of the many times when she'd broken the teapot. A mixture of contrition and defiance.

Samson's anxiety ratcheted up another notch.

DS Benson was the first to strike gold.

'Got her!' he exclaimed, shooting up out of his chair and nearly giving Sergeant Clayton a heart attack in the process. 'We've got her.'

The sergeant was round the desk in a second, looking at the screen.

'A listing in records for a certain Hayley Campbell,' said the detective. 'Turns out Hayley prefers to be known as—'

'Holly!' Sergeant Clayton let out a long whistle. 'Holly Campbell.'

'Indeed. According to this, she's named in an injunction from three years ago—'

'That's about the time she was kicked off Tyke's TV programme!'

They stared at each other for a heartbeat. Knowing this could be it. The clue which would shatter open the case.

'We need to find out what that injunction was for,' said the sergeant.

Benson nodded. Then pointed at Danny's desk.

'The lad's notes from his surveillance the day of the murder and from the CCTV. Go over them again. And again. If this lass was involved, she must be on there and we've missed it somehow. Meanwhile, I'll track down the finer details of this report and see what our Ms Campbell was up to which resulted in an injunction.'

Samson was processing the information before Ida had even stopped speaking.

'Where did Gareth see the trail bike?' he demanded. Heart pounding.

'On his way back from the dairy.'

The road which ran out towards the farm track Samson had used when on surveillance at Tyke's. The very same route he suspected the dead rabbit had been delivered by.

He glanced over to the fashion designer, poised for the start of the race. One hand on his GPS watch. Delilah right next to him.

What if DS Benson was right? What if Vinny King's murder had been a way of hurting Tyke? If that was the case, where would the killer strike next?

Samson could think of only one answer. An answer which chilled him to the bones. Because while he and the team, each in their own way, had done everything to ensure Tyke was as safe as possible, they hadn't done anything to prevent what Benson's theory predicted. And what better day to carry out such a heinous crime than a day like today when the town had all decamped to the rugby ground. Apart from the person who was next on the killer's list.

'Eloise!' he exclaimed. 'Where is she?'

'I heard Tyke saying she wasn't feeling too well,' said Ida.

'She's at the house?'

Ida nodded. Eyes widening. Sensing his panic. 'She's on her own!'

Samson was already moving, instructing Danny over his shoulder to stay and monitor Tyke and Delilah. Then he was running, through the crowds, past a startled Will Metcalfe, right in front of Nathan and Nina, Nathan's lurchers straining at their leads as he ran by.

Out into the car park, thanking the gods that he'd brought the Enfield.

As the starter's pistol fired into the cloudless sky, the scarlet motorbike tore out of the grounds of the rugby club and began haring across town.

There were no blondes matching the description of Holly Campbell. Not entering the station nor arriving by train. Either she hadn't been there or she'd worn a disguise of some sort.

Feeling weariness starting to get the better of him, Gareth stood up, stretched. Yawned. Perhaps a walk? Get some fresh air?

Or was it best to crack on? A man's life was possibly hanging in the balance, after all.

His mobile vibrated. Ida. The message short and sweet.

I've told Samson.

Thank goodness. The subterfuge had been gnawing at him. The fear that maybe they were adding to the jeopardy by keeping things quiet. Besides, it couldn't hurt to have another angle on things . . .

Another angle . . . That was it! That was how to narrow down the search.

He sat back down with a thump, Bounty jerking awake over in the corner.

'Just me, lass,' he murmured, but his focus was on the laptop.

Two cameras. Both situated on the gable wall above the lockers. One angled towards the car park entrance. The other facing the platform.

Realistically, most people would pass in front of both of them – coming through the entrance and then walking onto a train, or the other way around. A very small subset of people would appear on only one. Those who were going into the station building to book a ticket over the counter, which was a tiny percentage of travellers in this internet age. And those who were accessing the lockers.

What's more, it was less feasible that either of those in the subset would be arriving at the station by train. Which meant that Gareth could legitimately focus on the footage from the car park camera, searching for someone who appeared on it twice, coming and going, and was probably carrying a bag.

Reinvigorated by his deductions, Gareth started watching the video footage once more.

It started at a frantic pace. Like all races seemed to. The gun fired and then a blur of bodies was running up through the town to the bottom of the Crag, Delilah holding her place near the front, on Tyke's shoulder. Trying not to think about what was happening back at the rugby club. Why Samson had suddenly ridden off on his motorbike. Sensing somehow that protecting Tyke was more important than ever.

But then the climb began. Biting into the legs as the outcrop of limestone loomed over them. The ridiculous effort of scaling the incline tearing at the lungs. Delilah's only thoughts now about hanging on to the orange-clad figure ahead of her.

Self-doubt came next. The brain telling the body that what was being asked of it was ridiculous. That the sheer effort involved in getting up this steep hillside at this speed was impossible. Beyond her.

Delilah pushed the doubts aside.

One foot in front of the other. Seth's favourite mantra.

Ignoring the pain in her calves, the pressure in her chest, one foot in front of the other, she followed Tyke up the side of the Crag.

*

He reached the house in Low Mill in minutes, slinging the Enfield behind the Porsche in a scattering of gravel. She was in. Unless she'd gone for a walk?

Horribly aware of how isolated the place was, the surrounding walls and bushes now suggesting something sinister rather than seclusion, Samson ran across the drive, up to the front porch, ringing the bell, thumping on the door. Not caring if he scared her. Just needing to know she was safe.

One second. Two. Many more. Too many, even if Eloise had been in her studio at the back of the house. She should have answered the door by now. Another round of thumping and bell ringing. Still no answer.

Maybe she was in the bathroom?

Holding on to that one sliver of hope, he sprinted around the side of the house. Checking windows as he ran. Round to the rear patio, the kitchen, the bifold doors . . .

They were open.

He slipped his mobile out of his pocket, switched it to mute, and then eased inside. Wary about calling out. Afraid Eloise wasn't alone. Because there was an unnatural silence to the house. One he recognised. One which usually meant danger.

It took Gareth less time than he'd expected, his latest filter working a treat. Now he was faced with four possibilities. All four figures captured on a single camera.

Two of them he'd been able to discount straight away. Baggy, the mechanic, he'd recognised from his height and skinny frame and also because he was in his work overalls as he passed the camera. If Gareth had harboured any suspicions about the man, the fact he appeared onscreen carrying a parcel and departed empty-handed put paid to that, the lockers used to return online purchases as well as to collect deliveries.

The other person was Seth Thistlethwaite, those bushy eyebrows unmistakeable, even on the grainy CCTV footage. Judging by the length of time which passed between the first and second sighting of Seth, Gareth suspected the older man had been availing himself of the public conveniences inside the station building.

So only two remained. A woman, dark long hair, her head down looking at her mobile as she approached the camera the first time, large canvas bag over one arm. The second time, she had her back to the lens, the bag on the other arm, the shape of something weighing it down.

Holly Campbell in a wig? It was possible.

As for the other potential suspect – slender build, dark clothing, a baseball cap pulled low. No chance of seeing the face. But something about the way they walked made Gareth think it was a man. A rucksack was slung over his left shoulder. In the second shot, the camera managed to catch a brief profile. A bit of the right cheek, no more. And the rucksack. Still on the left shoulder but looking heavier.

Gareth started with the woman. Zooming in, trying his best to improve the image, wishing he had Delilah's prowess. Still not seeing enough to rule one way or the other in terms of a firm identification.

The man then. Hoping for more joy, he played the footage. Froze it on that brief peek of profile. The contours of the baseball hat, the lip of the brim, and below it, that tantalising glimpse of face.

He zoomed in, focusing on the cheek. The image so large now it was pixelated, a patch of darkness on the screen. What was that?

He zoomed back out. Seeing it in context. Peering at the screen, at the darker shade on the skin . . . He snapped backwards. The shock of recognising it for what it was. Then he was on his feet and scrambling for his mobile. This time too panicked to soothe the startled spaniel. If he was right, then the danger was a lot closer than they'd thought.

Picking up a knife from the kitchen, Samson moved quickly and silently around the ground floor, senses on high alert, ready for anything.

Eloise wasn't in any of the rooms.

He arrived at the bottom of the stairs. The most dangerous bit of any house search. Exposed the entire way up.

He stood for a few seconds, ears straining. Hoping to hear the sound of normality. But the heavy silence of the house pushed back at him. Pulse pounding, he began making his way up to the first floor, keeping his feet to the outside of each stair, wary of creaks. Of giving himself away and alerting anyone up there.

He reached the landing. A succession of doors in front of him. All open bar one. Moving rapidly now, he inspected the four main bedrooms. No one there. Likewise the two en suites and the bathroom. Which left the closed door. The rear bedroom Eloise had been using as an art studio.

He flung the door open and spun into the room. Knife ready.

Empty. Just a tumble of artwork on the floor, the drying rack turned on its side. He spotted the portrait of Tolpuddle lying there among the pile of paintings and drawings. And beneath them all, a sliver of turquoise. Something familiar about it.

He reached down. Picked it up. And felt the world go still.

Something wasn't right.

Sergeant Clayton had been going over Danny's notes from the day of Vinny King's murder and while he was no closer to spotting anything which could point to Holly Campbell's involvement, he'd worked through them multiple times and kept snagging on the same two things. Both were minor details, but something told him it was a minor detail which would crack this case.

For the life of him, though, he couldn't see how either could be relevant.

'There's something odd—' he began, as an exclamation burst from the desk opposite.

'Well I'll be damned!' DS Benson was staring at his computer in bemusement. 'You'll never guess what. That injunction which references Holly Campbell? It wasn't taken out *against her*. She took it out against someone else.' He looked up, shocked. 'Jake Ramsbottom!'

'Tyke,' murmured the sergeant.

'She claimed he repeatedly harassed her after she spoke out about her experience on *The Nines*. Not only that, but the address on the application to the court lists her as living in Italy.' Benson sighed. 'I don't know about you, but it doesn't make sense to me that she'd go to the trouble of getting an injunction and then stir things up by sending death threats. I'll see if I can track her down for a chat but my gut is telling me we're going to have to rule Ms Campbell out of our enquiries.'

The sergeant nodded. Staring at Danny's notes. At the oddities.

'In that case,' he said, 'perhaps this is worth a look.'

Samson stared at the picture in his hands, the swimming pool, the white diving board cutting across it. Feeling the rough texture of the paper beneath his fingers. A miniature version of the Hockney hanging in Vinny King's flat.

Nothing making sense, adrenalin clouding his thinking,

he let his mind drift. To Tyke and Eloise and Vinny. To a theft that wasn't a theft. To two investigations hitting dead ends. And a throwaway comment about rabbits being pulled from hats —

That was it! The dead rabbit!

The video doorbell on Rick Procter's old home had proved the threatening message hadn't been delivered via Tyke's front gates, so they'd presumed it had to have come from the rear. But there was another possibility. The most obvious one – one which Samson should have thought of.

It was like the last lever in a lock slotting into place. His mind open now. Thoughts tumbling. Reassessing. Coming to rest on the trail bike. Seeing the oil outside the derelict barn. The bike not parked there temporarily, but . . .

He snapped his head up, striding over to the window. There. A black figure. Running away from the house and across the fields. Towards the barn.

The dreadful truth dawned with Ida's voice in his ear.

Solve one and we might solve both . . .

He'd got it all wrong. And in doing so, had placed someone in the utmost peril. Left them in the company of a ruthless killer.

The painting dropped from his hands and he was spinning round, running down the stairs, fumbling with his mobile. Calling Ida as he raced out the front door, towards the Enfield.

'Ida!' he shouted. 'Delilah could be in danger! Tell her! Tell her now!'

36

'The timings are out,' stated Sergeant Clayton.

'In what way?' DS Benson had come around the desk and was looking at the constable's neat handwriting, the sergeant's own scrawls on a pad beside them. On the computer screen was the CCTV footage from Fellside Court.

'Take this one,' said the sergeant. He pointed at a line of writing. 'From when Danny was outside the house down in Low Mill.'

'"Target leaves lounge in haste."' Benson raised an eyebrow. 'That's a bit meticulous, isn't it?'

'I'd expect nothing less from the lad. But the point is, look at what happens next.'

The detective read the subsequent line of notes, clearly added after the fact and while the constable was sitting at a desk, the writing pristine and in the past tense.

'"Target appeared outside in changed clothes and drove off at speed in his Porsche."' He shrugged. 'And?'

'Look at the time that lapsed between those two events. Tyke leaps up from his sofa and exits the room, clearly having suddenly realised he'd brought his uncle's glasses home by mistake and in a hurry to return them. Yet it's several minutes before he appears outside, running for his Porsche. And when he does, he's wearing a different outfit.'

'I still don't see the problem.'

'Why did he go to the bother of changing before he left? Surely you'd just grab the car keys and go as you are?'

Benson looked unconvinced. 'Clutching at straws here, I think.'

'Okay, what about this.' Sergeant Clayton turned to the CCTV footage, playing a snippet of Tyke arriving at Fellside Court, baseball cap on, tracksuit bottoms and jacket covered in bright pink orchids. 'It's time-stamped. Twelve minutes past eight. Vinny is already dead upstairs but Tyke doesn't know that.' He paused the footage as Tyke entered the building, and held out a set of statements. 'Now look at these, Danny's notes from the witnesses that evening. Look at the time they say Tyke arrived in the hallway upstairs. And bear in mind, Geraldine was wailing like a siren up there, which Tyke must have been able to hear from the entrance hall.'

Benson flicked through the pages, a frown forming. 'None of them place him upstairs before quarter past eight.'

'At which point, according to both Clarissa and Geraldine, he came running along the corridor from the stairwell next to the lift. So it wasn't like he sauntered up there, but yet there are at least three minutes missing in the timeline.'

'Anything on the video to suggest what he was up to—?'

The sergeant's mobile interrupted them. He turned away from the desk, leaving the detective going through the CCTV footage.

'Hello?'

'Sergeant Clayton?' asked a woman, her accent suggesting it was the call from London he'd been waiting for. She introduced herself and then got straight to the point, a rustle of paper coming down the phone. 'You were enquiring about

Date with Destiny

Eloise Morgan? Let's see . . . so, she was arrested when a juvenile. Given a twelve-month rehabilitation order.'

'And the charges?'

'Theft. To be more precise, high-spec motorbikes. Seems she was stealing them to order for a gang. Wasn't a bike she couldn't ride. Judge went easy on her given her age and it being a first offence. Not sure it worked, seeing as she was up on vagrancy charges not long after.'

But Sergeant Clayton wasn't listening. In the back of his mind, a nugget of information dislodged itself and came to the fore. The Triumph trail bike. Bought, according to the previous owner, by a young lad who rode off like a pro . . .

For some reason he caught himself thinking about Eloise Morgan. That pixie haircut. More than proficient on a motorbike . . .

He was aware of the conversation being ended. Of putting his mobile on his desk. On the computer screen the CCTV footage was still rolling, Tyke's flamboyant clothing was disappearing inside Fellside Court, the door closing, making the shadows deeper and the man harder to see—

'There!' DS Benson hit pause and pointed, the frozen image dark, Tyke no more than a blur. But one of the pink orchids had caught the light, glinting slightly. 'He's turning left!'

The sergeant's attention snapped onto the screen.

'Now why,' he murmured, 'would he be doing that when the stairs by the lift are to the right? Someone is screaming blue murder upstairs and yet our lad decides to take a stroll?'

'Let it play,' Benson gestured towards the keyboard. 'See if he comes back across the foyer at any point.'

They watched in silence. The clock in the corner of the

screen ticking past the minutes. Not a soul passing the camera.

Sergeant Clayton stopped the video. Stared at Benson.

'That's gone past the time the witnesses say Tyke arrived at Vinny's flat. So he turns left in the foyer and then somehow, miraculously, appears upstairs a few minutes later from the stairs on the right without being caught on camera.'

'Christ.' Benson wheeled away from the screen. 'So what's to the left? The cafe? The kitchen—' He whipped back round. 'Dr Naylor. He said he used the kitchen to exit unseen.'

'You think Tyke nipped out that way? But why? And how come he doesn't show up on the CCTV coming back in?'

'Maybe,' said DS Benson, face grave, 'we had the right method when we suspected Dr Naylor. We just had the wrong person.'

And Sergeant Clayton saw it now. A deception in plain sight. It had been there all along – the curious change of attire before leaving the house; the inexplicable behaviour on the CCTV. Throw in a willing accomplice . . .

'Or even the wrong *people*!' he exclaimed. 'It's what that bugger always says. "Clothing gets you noticed." We were so busy looking at what was being worn, we forgot to check who was wearing it!'

He started telling DS Benson about the news from London. The detective was already reaching for the car keys.

They'd pulled out a good lead. Four of them. Two runners from Rossendale Harriers out front. Then Tyke. Then Delilah. She'd given it everything she had up the steep slope, trying to stay in touching distance with the leaders as the main field fell away behind her, knowing she was burning matches she wouldn't get back. But her plan was to stick with them and then make the most of the descent. She had local knowledge. Plus a natural agility on the steep scree, a fearlessness which enabled her to go faster. Or at least, that had been the case in the past.

Not allowing doubts to enter her mind, she concentrated on the last pull uphill, legs burning, lungs aflame.

One more massive effort, get alongside Tyke's shoulder on the ridge. Make him know she was there and force him out of his race plan. Then press him hard when they hit the drop and hope to God he made the first mistake.

Onto the ridge, the flat feeling like heaven, calves grateful for the temporary release. Flying now, feet nimble, dancing between the jagged edges of limestone, balance perfect. She was gaining on him.

He glanced back. Saw her. Slipped on a rock, staggered slightly. And she was there, right by his side. The path narrowing up ahead. A true ridge, deadly drop-offs on either side. Whoever reached it first would have the advantage.

She picked up her pace. And then her mobile sounded and her watch vibrated, and she was glancing down at the watch face. A message from Ida.

Gareth Towler was running. It wasn't a pastime he normally indulged in, his size not entirely suited to it. But no one had answered their phones. Either they'd rung out or been engaged. So running he was, as fast as his legs could carry him, thundering down Back Street before cutting through a ginnel and out onto High Street, the white marquees visible across the road.

Thankfully the roadblock was in place, traffic being diverted around the back of the rugby ground, allowing safe passage for the returning competitors when they came off the fellside. Gareth leaped the barriers, landing heavily the other side, almost falling. People turning now. Noticing him.

He didn't slow. Just kept on going, straight past a startled Harry Furness marshalling on the gate, and into the grounds. Looking for her. Ida.

She was with a group of people – Nathan and Nina, Eric Bradley, Joseph O'Brien, half of Bruncliffe, in fact. Danny was there too in his uniform, a pair of binoculars to his eyes. Everyone was staring up at the hillside. Something up there holding them in a state of what could only be described as terror.

'The dead rabbit!' Gareth exclaimed as he reached them. 'It was Tyke who collected it from the station! I recognised his bruised cheek on the CCTV!'

They began turning towards him. Something on the assembled faces telling him the news he had was already breaking.

Then Ida was nodding. Fear in her eyes. 'Samson just called. He reckons Tyke was behind the death of Vinny King. He reckons Delilah is in danger. I've sent a message to warn her but there's nowt else we can do until they're down . . .'

Joseph put a hand around Ida's shoulders, Tolpuddle beginning to whine deep in his chest. Sensing the agitation.

In the background came the sound of sirens.

The Royal Enfield wasn't cut out for this. But Samson had no choice.

Leaping onto the motorbike, he'd roared up the cul-de-sac and down a side road, bringing him to a gate which led onto the field behind Tyke's house. In the distance he could see her.

Eloise. Running. Almost at the far side and the derelict barn where he now knew the trail bike had been kept. Cursing himself for not checking inside it the day he found the oil, he entered the field and opened up the throttle, letting his bike have as much speed as he could manage. Bucking and bouncing, he raced across the rough ground. The Enfield sliding occasionally. Wheels struggling for traction.

She'd have the advantage of him. The trail bike built for such terrain. All the more reason to close as much distance as he could now, before she reached it.

But it was too late. She was there. Pulling aside the rotten door of the barn. The black Triumph kicking into life. It shot out of the barn and back across the field. Cutting away from him, heading east.

He skidded to a halt, wheeled around, following her. But she was already pulling away, distance growing between the two motorbikes, the Triumph covering the ground like a panther while the Enfield screamed in protest beneath him.

He knew where she was heading. Eloise Morgan was loyal to the last.

Running hard, Delilah only had a glimpse of the message. But it was enough.

Tyke's name. The word murderer.

Her feet faltered, a cry of alarm escaping her. Tyke, glancing her way. Seeing her looking up from her watch.

And that face, the part of Delilah which could hide no secrets, gave the game away.

He saw the shock. The fear. The revulsion.

Then he was twisting towards her, the path so narrow now, Delilah already at the very edge. Nowhere to go. In a blur of violence, his right arm landed on her left shoulder with force. Taking her balance.

And she was gone. Over the side. Arms out, nothing beneath her feet but air.

As the police car screeched to a halt at the barriers in the road, the rugby ground had fallen silent. An eerie quiet, the type that accompanies any unfolding tragedy, punctuated only by the whine of the Weimaraner Joseph O'Brien was struggling to restrain.

Sergeant Clayton and the out-of-town detective spilled from the car, racing through the entrance and into the mass of people, making straight for Danny Bradley. An urgent conversation, gestures up towards the Crag. The ongoing fell race.

Word spread. There was a killer on the fellside! And Delilah Metcalfe was up there right beside him.

The few pairs of binoculars to be had were trained on them. But even to the naked eye, the two runners could be seen, distant figures moving along the ridge. The bright orange one the easiest to see of all.

So when one of those figures suddenly started falling, a gasp of horror came from the watching crowd.

'He pushed her!' shouted Danny Bradley, knuckles white on the lenses of the binoculars. 'Tyke pushed Delilah over the edge!'

His shouts were drowned out by the roar of motorbikes. Cutting across the field at the back of the rugby club which had been used as an overflow car park. A black Triumph, made for the terrain. Some way behind it, the distinctive scarlet of the O'Brien lad's Royal Enfield, being ridden within an inch of its life.

Engine revving, the Triumph burst through the open gate, across the road and onto the track opposite. Heading for the bottom of the fell.

'It's Eloise Morgan!' exclaimed Sergeant Clayton. 'She's going for Tyke!'

Tolpuddle was stressed. A tidal wave of anxiety building within him. He could sense that something was wrong. The tension in the people around him palpable.

And he knew it was her. She was in trouble. Up there. On the hills where they ran together. Something terrible was happening.

He strained against his lead. A hand patting him. The soft voice telling him it was okay. But it wasn't.

Then the motorbikes went past in a roar of noise. He recognised the second one. Recognised the person on it.

More shouting, his lead going momentarily slack.

Tolpuddle took his chance. With a burst of strength, he ripped free from the restraint and started running. Through the crowd and towards the fells.

In a crowd frozen in shock, the Weimaraner was the spur they needed. As the grey shape streaked across the rugby ground and out the entrance, Danny Bradley spun round, thrust the binoculars at his grandfather and started running. Will Metcalfe took off after him, his brother Ash on his heels. Nathan and Nina too. Even Ida and Gareth. Tolpuddle acting like the Pied Piper until there was a horde of locals, all running towards the fellside.

The Weimaraner pulled away from all of them.

*

She landed heavily, rolled, hands grabbing desperately. A jutting rock, fingers clasping it, managing to stop the fall. Her face scraping down the scree. She lay there, panting. Fear. Exertion. Panic.

She was on the side of the Crag. The steepest bit. From her prone position, she could see Tyke, further along the path. Going fast. Uncatchable.

Below her, the sound of a motorbike. The black Triumph trail bike. Tyke's escape route. If he could reach it.

Anger coursed through her. He was worse than a cheat. A cold-blooded killer.

She pulled herself to her feet, the fellside falling away below her at a hideous angle.

Up was the sensible option. Back onto the path and hope that she could catch him. That he would tire. But she knew it was impossible. He had too much of a lead. Her only chance was to take the short cut, angling down across the fellside in order to cut him off.

She risked a glance down. The drop dizzying. Sickening.

With a deep breath and a prayer, she started running.

They could see it down below. The figure beginning to cut down the side of the Crag. That ridiculous gradient. A deadly route.

'She'll kill herself,' murmured Joseph, hand to his mouth.

'Delilah's Descent,' said Seth Thistlethwaite, shaking his head in horror.

No other sound from the crowd. Collective breaths being held as they watched Delilah Metcalfe try to defy death.

*

The scree slid and shifted under her feet. The ground at an absurd angle. Arms out, trying to stay balanced as her body pitched and swayed, she was half running, half falling, lurching down the fellside at a lethal pace. One wrong move and she would be dead.

All the time that perilous vista to her right.

Ahead she could see Tyke, on the official descent now. And at the bottom, the black Triumph parked and waiting.

Delilah went against every instinct and pushed herself to run faster.

The Triumph came to a halt ahead of him at the bottom of the path. Eloise's head twisted towards the fellside.

Samson gunned the throttle, forcing the Enfield to its limits. Expecting the Triumph to speed away and leave him for dust again.

But Eloise was taking her helmet off. Staring upwards.

He risked a glimpse. Saw the bright orange outline of Tyke coming down the path. Two runners well ahead of him. No sign of Delilah.

Still Eloise made no move to go. A look of dread on her face.

He pulled up in front of her, blocking her route, leaving the Enfield running while he leaped off and over towards her, his own helmet in his hands.

'You're under arrest—'

'No!' she said, shaking her head, hand going to her mouth, a tear slipping down her cheek. 'No more death!'

It was only then he looked. Up to where her focus was held. And he saw the small figure hurtling down the fellside, slipping, sliding, a head-first descent of the most reckless kind.

Samson's helmet fell from his numb hands and he started running.

Tolpuddle could see her now. Running diagonally across the fellside. He adjusted his trajectory, going up the steep slope, aiming for the main path on an angle that would meet with hers. Behind him, the footsteps of the people became fainter as he increased the gap between them.

Flat out. Panting. That huge heart of his thumping. Going as fast as his legs would carry him, the Weimaraner tore up the hill.

Tyke saw her coming. A sideways glance, barely able to believe his eyes. Delilah Metcalfe was running terrain that no sane person would deem runnable, rocks and debris rattling down the steep slope as she almost flew across it. And she was gaining on him. Coming at an angle that would have her on him in moments.

Waiting below was Eloise. He'd seen the bike approaching in the distance. Knew what it meant. Something had happened and the game was up. It was time to flee. To make the escape they'd planned in case of emergency.

He wasn't about to give up now.

Still moving, he reached behind him and unzipped his waist pack. One more casualty would make no difference. He was already in too deep. Then he turned and waited.

Delilah knew she had him. That falter as he turned to look at her. And now it seemed as though he was waiting for her. Arms behind his back.

She didn't pause in her headlong pace. Instead she used

it, propelling herself down the last bit of distance between them, and then lunging for him like a human missile.

From somewhere down below came a strangled shout that sounded like Samson. But Delilah was already committed.

'He's got a knife!'

Still some distance down the hill, Samson shouted at the top of his lungs, seeing the glint of the sun on the blade behind Tyke's back. But Delilah was already going for him in a full-on rugby tackle.

A tangle of bodies, a scream of pain and then Delilah was rolling away. Tyke getting to his feet. Knife in his hand as he advanced on her. And Samson was too far away to do anything about it.

Pain. Slicing across her thigh. Cutting through the shock of the impact as she brought them both to the ground.

She rolled away. Tried to get to her feet but her leg was bleeding, her entire body shaking. Instead, she started scrabbling up the path on her back, frantic. But he was already turning. Advancing towards her. That brutal blade shining.

'You always were a sore loser,' he grunted.

She felt everything go into slow motion. Her focus fixed on the knife. Fear, a metallic taste in her mouth. And death only seconds away.

Except for one little thing . . .

He came at them like a grey rocket. A full-grown Weimaraner with the bravest of hearts, and a loyalty which knew no bounds.

Judging his leap to perfection, Tolpuddle launched himself at Tyke, smashing into his side and sending him flying, the knife knocked from his grasp and clattering down the scree. And when Tyke went to get up and make a run for it, Delilah's sweet-natured dog, her hound who never gave anything but affection, bared his teeth and snarled and barked and terrorised the man back to the ground.

By the time Samson reached them, out of breath and sweating profusely, Tolpuddle had the situation entirely under control. And by the time the rest of the Bruncliffe posse arrived, Danny at the fore, Tyke was tied up with a dog lead, Samson was cradling Delilah in his arms and Tolpuddle was standing over them.

'Jesus, Delilah!' panted Will Metcalfe, doubled over, face puce and a hand clamped against his side. 'You could have bloody waited until he was on the flat!'

Delilah, face grazed and bleeding, grinned up at him. 'Where would be the fun in that?'

The burst of relieved laughter from those assembled on the fellside echoed around the dale.

37

By early evening, the Fleece was packed, as if by unspoken consensus the participants in the shocking events at the rugby ground had decided to congregate. To talk things through in the way Yorkshire folk do. When Samson and Delilah walked in with Tolpuddle, the place fell momentarily silent, and then raucous applause broke out.

'The hero of the hour!' said Will Metcalfe, raising his glass. 'To Tolpuddle!'

Glasses raised throughout the pub, the Weimaraner's name being chanted, pats raining down on him.

'Somebody buy that hound a pint!' called out Harry Furness.

'Don't you bloody dare!' retorted Troy Murgatroyd. 'I'll bar you for life.'

Laughter now. The mood a strange mixture of exhilaration from the fortunate outcome of what could have been a deadly morning, and a sombre realisation that a man they'd welcomed as one of their own had been responsible for the murder of his uncle and a near fatal attack on Edith Hird.

'We're proud of you as well, Dee,' said Ash Metcalfe, leaning down to hug his sister, Lucy Metcalfe and Herriot standing with him, Elaine Bullock just joining them, a large tray of drinks in her hands. Fresh back from a geology field trip to the Giant's Causeway with some of her undergraduates, the now full-time university lecturer had missed all the action.

'I hear you've been collecting rock samples with your face,' she said, head tilted to one side, glasses askew, as she assessed the damage to Delilah's cheeks and forehead. 'Next time take me with you and I'll show you how to collect them properly.'

Then she passed the tray to Ash and gathered her friend into a huge embrace.

'Seriously, Delilah,' she murmured, 'one day you're going to run out of lives.'

Delilah hugged her back. 'You'd have done the same.'

'Nah,' said Ash with a wink, 'Elaine would have just thrown rocks after him. But only the ones with no geological significance.'

Elaine aimed a kick in his direction before taking two pints from the tray, keeping one herself and handing the other to Delilah.

'Here,' she said. 'That's the least of what you've earned.'

'That's *my* pint!' protested Ash.

Elaine grinned at him, the others all laughing.

Ash was still complaining as Samson and Delilah made their way over to where a large group of their friends and family were seated around a crowded table – Joseph, Eric, Clarissa and Ana representing Fellside Court, Arty still at the hospital with Edith; Will Metcalfe and Nathan sitting either side of Ida, with Nina at the end; and Bounty, curled up under the table, Tolpuddle striding over to flop down next to her.

'Sit down, lass.' Ida was holding out a chair. 'Take the weight of tha leg.'

The St John Ambulance volunteers at the rugby ground

had done a good job of patching Delilah up, applying steri-strips to the knife wound and cleaning up the cuts and grazes she'd accumulated in her fall. The aching limbs and bruised body they couldn't do much about. Considering what could have been, she was counting herself lucky.

She wasn't the only one thanking those lucky stars. As she sat down, Ida squeezed her shoulder, Nina leaned over to kiss her cheek and Will ruffled her hair.

'That descent was mad!' said Nathan, full of awe. 'It's breaking the internet.'

'Completely insane,' muttered Will. 'Could have killed yourself, sis.'

'Here.' Another pint of beer placed in front of her, Seth Thistlethwaite staring at her from beneath his eyebrows. 'I told you to make me proud. You more than did that.'

Delilah shook her head. Fighting tears. 'I came last,' she said, smiling through the emotion. 'And only then because Samson carried me some of the way.'

It had been a strange sensation. Watching the race become a drama, police on the fellside, arrests being made, while the marshals were making sure all the runners got down safely. Determined not to have DNF next to her name in the Bruncliffe Hills records, Delilah had insisted on completing the final mile, leaning heavily on Samson, Tolpuddle not leaving her side. She'd crossed the line well after the rest of the runners and while, in her younger days, she'd scorned the concept of a participation medal, refusing to take one if she wasn't on the podium, today she'd taken it with gratitude. It was going to be hung up in her office.

'Last is good,' grunted her coach, eyes twinkling. 'Means there's room for improvement. I'll see you at training as soon as that leg's recovered.'

He walked off as Gareth returned from the bar with a coffee and a pint, placing them in front of the new arrivals. Seeing the beer already in Delilah's hand and a second on the table, he grinned.

'Going to be a heavy night!' he said. 'Mind you, it'll take a while to fill us in on everything.' He turned to Samson. 'Have you got any updates?'

'Like what the hell was going on out there today,' said Will.

'A scam gone wrong,' said Samson. 'Tragically wrong.'

Eloise had started talking almost straight away. Displaying a contrition that her partner in crime had yet to show as she outlined the scheme which had brought her and Tyke to Bruncliffe. And concluded in such horrific circumstances.

'Vinny was the target? That blasted Hockney of his?' asked Ida.

Samson nodded. 'Turns out Tyke was having major financial issues. The Porsche, the house rental, the supposed fashion show, it was all paid for on credit. Or not paid for at all. DS Benson finally managed to track down the elusive Holly Campbell out in Milan – or Hayley Campbell, as she now prefers to be known.'

The woman's name stirred guilt in Delilah. That they'd even considered her as a suspect when she was actually a victim. Someone who'd seen Tyke for what he was and had been subjected to such abuse after speaking out – to the extent that she'd had to take out an injunction against him – that she dropped off the internet, reverted to her real name and moved abroad. Hopefully she was feeling finally vindicated.

'Ms Campbell still works in the industry for one of the top Italian fashion houses,' Samson was continuing, 'and she gave Benson a lot of interesting insights about Tyke. She said this Retro Reversibles clothing line of his has met with a lacklustre reception and it could be the final nail in his coffin. There's even strong rumours that his TV show has been axed. So it looks like Tyke hit on a way of making a bit on the side. Commit an invisible theft.'

'Steal the Hockney, replace it with a copy and no one would be any the wiser,' murmured Gareth.

'It was a damn good copy,' said Joseph. 'If it hadn't been for the puzzle as to how the painting had been righted in the frame, none of us would have paid it a blind bit of notice.'

'Even the art gallery sticker on the back,' marvelled Ida. 'Identical.'

'Eloise takes the credit for all of that,' Samson said. 'She's an exceptional artist. Just a shame she didn't believe in her abilities as an artist in her own right. If she had, she might have been less inclined to go along with this.'

'But how the hell did they hope to sell a Hockney? Not exactly something you can stick on eBay,' said Eric.

Samson shrugged. 'DS Benson and Sergeant Clayton are still getting to the bottom of it all.'

'What I want to know is how Tyke managed to get in and out of Fellside Court without being seen,' said Ana, perturbed, Clarissa nodding in agreement. 'I want to be able to set my residents' minds at rest.'

'I can answer that,' said Danny Bradley, dragging a stool over to join them. 'One of the joys of being a subordinate – I get to go home earlier,' he grinned, and then looked pointedly from the pint of Black Sheep in Delilah's hand to the two untouched pints on the table. 'Is one of those going spare? It's been a full-on day and I'm parched.'

'Be my guest,' she smiled, passing one to him.

He took a long swig, sighed and went to take another.

'Get on with it, lad,' muttered his grandfather. 'We're on tenterhooks!'

'Oh, right. Sorry. So yeah, Tyke worked a switch with Eloise. CCTV and my own records show him entering the building in the afternoon when he went to visit his uncle. And then coming out just as you were all heading to the play. Only, it wasn't Tyke who came out. It was Eloise, dressed in the same crazy outfit.'

'"Clothing gets you noticed",' murmured Ida. 'The lad knew tha'd be looking out for what he was wearing.'

'So it was Eloise you followed back to the house?' asked Delilah.

Danny blushed. 'Yes, and I never suspected a thing.'

'None of us did,' said Samson, patting the constable on the back. 'But Sergeant Clayton said it was your detailed notes that cracked it.'

'Maybe. But still, I feel like an idiot. Thinking I was some hotshot undercover officer while the man I was supposed to be tailing was hiding out in a cleaning cupboard at Fellside Court.'

'I'm putting a lock on that blasted cupboard,' muttered Ida. 'Too many folk using it who shouldn't be.'

'If it's any consolation, Danny,' said Samson, gesturing at Delilah and the rest of the agency team, 'we were all chasing around looking for the mysterious person sending Tyke death threats, unaware that we were on a wild goose chase the entire time.'

Ida grunted. Perhaps the closest Delilah had ever seen her coming to losing her temper had been when Samson had explained to the team how the Dales Detective Agency had been used. A hit-and-run orchestrated by Eloise on the trail bike. The supposed messages, self-originated. Even the dead rabbit – part of a string of misdirections and sleights of hand, all done to make it look like Tyke's life was in danger.

As for the investigation itself, even there they'd been manipulated, Holly Campbell being offered up as a convenient smokescreen to throw them off the scent. And when Tyke suspected the team were getting too close to the truth, he sacked them, using the excuse that he wanted them to focus on finding his uncle's killer instead.

Ida had called down a heap of curses on the fashion designer's head, while Nathan had wanted to go straight round to the police-station holding cells with his lurchers. Nina had been the one to ask Delilah about the finances. About the hole in the agency coffers which would take some time to fill.

'Should have listened to thee,' Ida grumbled, casting a look at Samson. 'Tha wanted nothing to do with him.'

'I can't take the high ground on this,' said Samson, giving Delilah a sheepish smile that made her heart soar. 'My reservations didn't exactly stem from professional concerns.'

'Tha was jealous?!' Ida burst out. 'Tha needs tha head examined, lad. Eighteen months back and tha still doesn't know that – excepting that daft dog of hers beneath the table – this lass is the most steadfast person in town? If tha's about to be ditched, she'll tell thee first.'

There was laughter at the scant assurance Ida was offering, Delilah taking the chance to lean over and whisper to Samson.

'I'm sorry.'

'Me too. It's just you were acting so odd . . .' He gave her a shamefaced look. 'It didn't help that I saw a message from Tyke on your mobile, love heart and all. And when I tried to read it, I couldn't as you'd changed your pin. I jumped to conclusions.'

She laughed, surprised. 'Tyke put love hearts on all his messages! It didn't mean a thing. And as for the pin, I didn't want you to see I was talking to your father. It felt like such a betrayal somehow, to be turning to someone other than you for advice about our future.'

He smiled, wrapping his fingers around hers. 'I wouldn't care if you'd turned to Mrs Pettiford herself, so long as it meant you didn't leave me.'

She squeezed his hand. Pained at having caused him such torment. At having allowed her doubts about the wedding and the stress of the looming Rick Procter trial to almost tear them apart.

'Ida's right,' she murmured. 'You're stuck with me now.'

'I can't think of anything I'd like more.' His grin caused her cheeks to flame.

Samson watched the colour flare on Delilah's cheeks and wondered if anyone would notice if they slipped away.

'Samson? Do you know?' Nina was asking him something, a look of hurt on her face.

'Sorry? What?'

'Why go to all that trouble?' she said. 'Why didn't Tyke just steal the painting? Why did he have to involve the Dales Detective Agency?'

'I'm guessing it was to get the perfect alibi. Right from the start, he was insistent that I kept watch outside his house at night, even when I didn't see the point. The threats had all come in daylight, after all. But by making sure he was being "protected" – which necessitated someone monitoring his movements – Tyke was also making sure he would have a rock-solid defence for the time of the theft.'

'There was a bit more to it than that,' said Danny. 'When

DS Benson was interviewing Eloise, she said they'd heard of the Dales Detective Agency's reputation – in particular, your past undercover with the NCA, Samson – and they were worried. So Tyke devised a plan to keep you looking the other way, allowing him to conduct the perfect robbery right under your nose. Hence the fake death threats. And,' he glanced at Delilah, 'I'm sorry to say, Tyke's request for a website. All done to keep you both busy.'

'They certainly kept us busy,' grunted Samson, embarrassed. He'd been played for a fool, allowing his concerns for the fashion designer's welfare to override his instincts about what had happened to Vinny – instincts which had been trying to tell him that Vinny's death was the result of an interrupted theft. 'I suppose the fashion show was just a charade, too?'

'Yep. Once they had the painting, they were going to cancel the event, citing the risk to Tyke's life as the reason. They fully intended to be back in London by Wednesday evening.'

'But it all went wrong Tuesday night,' murmured Delilah.

'After which, they felt they had to stay around for a while longer, knowing it would look odd if Tyke hightailed it out of town when his uncle had just been murdered.'

Danny's blunt assessment triggered an upswell of sadness in Samson – while he might have been made to look daft by Tyke, poor Vinny King, who'd simply mixed up his glasses cases and thus returned home fatally early, had paid for his mistake with his life.

There were sober nods around the table.

'Crazy thing is,' mused Gareth, 'if the lad had just owned up, told his uncle what he was up to when he was caught red-handed, Vinny might even have helped him out. Loaned him a bit of money. Instead, Tyke panics, attacks him and sets off a spiral of destruction, ruining his own life along the way.'

'Huh, you sound like the sarge,' said Danny. 'He's always saying that each and every one of us is only one stupid act away from derailing our lives.'

Eric grunted. 'Difference is, Tyke compounded that mistake by attacking Edith! If Joseph and I hadn't been coming back from the dry cleaners, he'd have killed her for sure.'

'Has he admitted to any of that?' Samson asked Danny.

Danny shook his head. 'But we have Eloise's testimony. She witnessed Edith's reaction to the magazine in the doctor's surgery, saw the photo as it fell and guessed the game might be up. So she texted Tyke. According to her, she wanted them to leave town there and then. Use the money from the stolen painting to start a new life. But Tyke took matters into his own hands.'

'Huh!' said Eric. 'We're supposed to believe that lass wanted no part in what happened to Edith?'

'I think she's telling the truth, Grandad . . .' Danny paused. Then shrugged. 'It'll be common knowledge soon enough – Eloise Morgan is pregnant. She found out just after they got here and she says it changed everything for her. She tried to persuade Tyke to call off the theft of the Hockney, but he wouldn't. And then Vinny was killed, Tyke lost control and attacked Edith . . . By the time Samson arrived at the house this morning, hammering on the door, Eloise was a nervous wreck and, presuming the truth had been uncovered, she bolted. Part of me wonders if she didn't want it all to be over, one way or another.'

'Hard to have sympathy when she was complicit in such brutal crimes,' said Gareth.

Danny nodded. 'True. Although, I think Eloise was

manipulated as much as the rest of us. In fact, I think Tyke's been exploiting her ever since he found her begging on the street.' He turned to Samson. 'She didn't even know about the rabbit. Tyke ordered it and collected it from the station. Kept it in the freezer. He must have left it on the doorstep when he headed out and then later that day, Eloise got a text from him, telling her to open the door.'

'So her reaction was genuine, then?' said Samson. 'Because she had me convinced.'

'Totally. Tyke even timed it to coincide with Mrs Pettiford walking her dog down there. Maximum impact for minimum effort.'

'What a ruthless bastard,' muttered Will.

'Never trust a cheat,' said Ida. 'Happen Tyke showed his colours many moons ago. And I don't mean those blasted costumes of his.'

'Even they served a purpose,' said Samson.

Danny looked at him, impressed. 'You figured it out, then?'

'Yes. It took a while, but it was the only way they could have done it.' He noticed the expectant faces around the table and shrugged. 'Danny's explained how Tyke managed to stay inside Fellside Court while everyone thought he'd left. What he hasn't explained is how Tyke then managed to leave after the murder.'

'Through the door like everyone else, surely,' said Eric.

Clarissa shook her head. 'But he had to be seen entering the building again first. And how could he do that when he was *already* in there?'

'Exactly,' said Samson. 'I'd say their original plan was a simple switch back. They'd established a reason for Tyke – or Eloise dressed as Tyke – to go back to Fellside Court—'

'Vinny's glasses!' Clarissa nodded. 'Tyke took them deliberately!'

'Yes. The readers. The ones he thought his uncle wouldn't miss that evening while he was at the play. But Tyke didn't know Vinny had got the cases mixed up . . .'

'So Eloise comes back, dressed like Tyke, on the pretext of returning the glasses,' said Eric, frowning. 'Enters the building and then the real Tyke walks out, with the stolen painting tucked away in his clothing?'

'That was the plan.'

'But how was Eloise supposed to leave without being seen?'

Clarissa, addict of TV crime dramas, was already working it out. 'The kitchen,' she said, Danny nodding in agreement.

'Eloise told us the plan was for her to arrive as Tyke,' he said, 'and then, once she'd got that captured on the CCTV, to head straight for the kitchen, do a quick change into her normal clothes before leaving through the emergency exit and out into the car park. She would then lie down in the rear of the Porsche and wait for Tyke to make his formal exit and join her, before driving away with no one the wiser.'

'So she was in the Porsche when we arrived that night?' asked Samson, surprised.

Danny nodded. 'She slipped out of it after a reasonable amount of time had passed and entered Fellside Court as the concerned girlfriend, supposedly having walked from Low Mill.'

'Jesus,' muttered Will. 'They thought of everything. Even when it all went pear-shaped, they had it covered.'

'Literally,' said Samson. 'Even to the extent of Tyke's clothing.'

'Another thing I didn't spot at the time.' Danny grimaced. 'That quick change before the person I thought was Tyke left the house that evening. He was in such a damn hurry to return his uncle's glasses yet he'd taken the time to swap outfits? It seemed odd, but I thought no more of it, when I should have.'

Delilah gasped, comprehension dawning. 'Retro Reversibles! After Tyke killed Vinny he would have been covered in blood. He couldn't walk out of Fellside Court like they'd planned. He had to hide the blood somehow. So he simply flipped his clothing!'

'Which is why Eloise – pretending to be Tyke – had to rush upstairs at Low Mill and change too, before leaving in the Porsche. So that their outfits matched when they made the second switch.'

Eric groaned. 'Anyone else getting a headache with all this flipping and switching?'

'I lost track a while ago,' laughed Joseph. 'All I care about is that Arty messaged earlier – Edith will be coming home in a few days.'

'That's brilliant news!' said Delilah.

'Oh, and he asked if he was right. Was Vinny's Hockney a fake?'

Everyone looked at Danny, who shrugged. 'It's not our job to determine that—'

'Well put, lad! With that level of diplomacy we'll make a chief constable of you yet!' Sergeant Clayton was grinning down at them, DS Benson by his side, both men holding pints. 'Room for two more? I've persuaded my colleague here that it's time to leave the paperwork and do a bit of community networking.' He gave a broad wink, eliciting laughter.

There was a shuffling of seats, more stools being brought over, and the two policemen sat down.

'So,' asked Clarissa, barely giving them time to settle. 'Was it a fake?'

'Who knows?' said Sergeant Clayton. 'And, to be honest,

we've got bigger fish to fry. From what we've uncovered so far, it seems this isn't the first time Tyke and Eloise Morgan have pulled this stunt. We suspect they've been doing it for years – stealing from Tyke's wealthiest clients, the owners none the wiser that their precious artwork has been replaced with a replica.'

DS Benson was nodding, the rest of the group looking stunned.

'Have they admitted to it?' asked Samson.

'They're both staying schtum when it comes to this,' said Benson. 'But we found a series of photographs on Tyke's phone – clients posing in their homes wearing garments he created for them, all of them standing by a particular water-colour or oil painting. We reckon he used the fitting sessions with his clients to identify potential items for Eloise to copy because Eloise has a similar stash of photographs – her repro-ductions of those exact same paintings.' He shook his head. 'She's one talented young lady.'

'Too talented,' muttered Sergeant Clayton. 'As you can imagine, we're just beginning the awkward process of contacting a very long list of very famous people and having to suggest to them that they have an expert validate their works of art. We're not exactly getting a warm reception. Somehow think we should just let the buggers keep on believing they've got something valuable.' He turned to Clarissa. 'So, going back to your question, we don't have the time or the inclination at the moment to verify if Vinny's Hockney was a fake, but given that his final wish was to have it destroyed, I think we can surmise he didn't want it coming under any professional scru-tiny should his heirs have chosen to sell it. Draw whatever conclusions you want from that. Of course,' he continued, with a mournful shake of his head, 'if it was a fake, that's the biggest irony of all. Tyke went to all that effort and even committed murder, in order to steal something that was possibly worthless in the first place.'

The senselessness of it cast a gloom across the table.

'Christ, between Tyke and bloody Rick Procter, not to mention Bernard Taylor, we've had a lot to contend with in town of late,' muttered Will.

'Aye,' said Ida. 'But it's not all been bad. Happen we've had a black sheep come back that turned out not to be such a renegade after all.' She raised her glass at Samson. 'Here's to thee, lad.'

Samson grinned across the table at her. 'You've not broken another teapot have you, Ida? Is that what all this being nice is about?'

'Talking of being nice,' Ash leaned across, placing a pint, an orange juice and a bowl of chips on the table. 'For you two and Tolpuddle, from Troy, with strict instructions that the dog only has the chips.'

'On the house?' asked Delilah, raising an eyebrow. 'Not like Troy to be so generous.'

'All the money he's making on that blasted best man bet,' muttered Ida, 'he can afford to be.'

'On the subject of which,' continued Ash, grinning at his sister, 'thanks for finally sending out an invite! Thought I was being excluded.'

'But I didn't send—' Delilah began before Clarissa cut across her, eyes dancing with devilment.

'I got mine, too. Anyone else get one?'

'I got one,' said Eric. Grinning.

'Me as well,' confirmed Joseph with a big smile.

There were nods all around the table. Delilah looking strangely shocked. While Samson only felt relief. The wedding was actually happening. The minx had sorted it after all.

'By the way, Delilah,' Samson's father was saying, standing up to come round to her seat, a Spar bag in his hands. 'I forgot to give these back. Some of Tolpuddle's toys that were left at mine.'

He passed her the bag, Samson only half paying attention as Elaine, Lucy and Herriot joined them along with Harry Furness.

'Got my invite, too,' said Harry, slapping Samson on the back. 'So what about this best man, then? Made a decision yet?'

Samson's attention was divided. Something in Delilah's face as she peered into the Spar bag. A glimpse inside. What looked like the parcel his father had been carrying the day Edith was attacked. The Bruncliffe Bright Whites label catching his eye.

'Sorry?' Samson turned to Harry. Aware of Delilah hugging his father. Of tears in her eyes. 'Best man?'

'You know. The bloke—'

'Or lass!' said Elaine.

Harry tipped his head in acknowledgement. 'Or lass, who stands next to you at the altar and makes sure you have the ring!'

'Oh, right. I need to choose one.'

'No pressure or anything,' said Will, grinning.

Samson was conscious of everyone looking at him, expectant. Of Troy looking nervous behind the bar.

His gaze finally fell on Ida Capstick. And she smiled. A proper smile.

'Happen as tha knows who it should be, lad. Tha's known all along.'

And she was right. There had only ever been one contender.

Epilogue

It was a glorious June day. A day to make hearts turn to romance, the skies arching overhead in a brilliant blue, white puffs of cloud floating above the peaks, the lapwings in full-throated song as they soared up and down the dale.

Down below, in the town, things were unusually muted. Only a scattering of folk were in the marketplace. The three-storey DDA building on Back Street was completely empty. And there were more than a few empty chairs in the lounge of Fellside Court. An offcumden could be forgiven for thinking Bruncliffe was a sleepy place. Where not much happened.

For today, the townsfolk had decamped. All morning, the road to the north, which twisted out between stone walls along a steep valley, had been busy with a procession of cars and Land Rovers, and even some tractors towing trailers. All making the journey to the farm which lay at the far end of Thorpdale.

The people who emerged from these vehicles were dressed in their finery. Dresses and heels, suits and ties. Laughter filtering up as they joked with each other about how grand they looked. About how wonderful this all was.

They were met by the ushers, a gruff-looking man and a severe-faced woman, who showed them over to a large barn which was undergoing renovation, the roof yet to be replaced. On the grass on either side of the open doorway were two small pens containing several pink sheep, a silver letter spray-painted onto each one. Being sheep – and Texels to boot – they weren't the brightest and were making no effort to stay in formation, currently spelling out *MONSSA* and *LADHELI*, the randomness of their lettering making people laugh.

Taking as much pride in their roles as they did in their sheep, the ushers guided the guests inside.

There were no pews. Just rows of hay bales serving as seats. There was no altar. Just a platform made from pallets and covered with straw. But there were flowers. Tied to the blackened beams. Hanging from the new rafters which crossed the old walls. Decorating the spaces where windows had once been.

As they shuffled to their seats, a joyous expectation filled the crowd. Friends and neighbours. Colleagues who had become friends. They all had one thing in common. The reasons which had brought them to the barn. To Twistleton Farm.

One of those reasons was the man now standing at the front. Thick mane of dark hair gracing the collar of his suit, he was looking around, taking it all in with a smile.

'Are you ready, son?' Joseph O'Brien asked, straightening Samson's tie with one hand, Tolpuddle on a lead in the other.

'Seriously, Dad, I think you're more nervous than I am.'

Joseph smiled. 'Well, that could be the truth of it.'

For Samson wasn't nervous. How could he be? He was about to marry the most amazing woman in the world.

It had been a strange couple of weeks. Things going on around him which he didn't understand. A lot of whispering and halted conversation when he walked into rooms. And strict instructions from Ash, the man in charge of the renovations at Twistleton, that Samson was to stay out of the barn until after the wedding.

He gazed around, stunned by the transformation. It was a perfect setting for what was going to be a perfect day. Both sides of the aisle packed with people. Even on the groom's side, despite the fact that Samson's entire family was currently standing in front of him. He felt a pang of sadness that his mother couldn't be with them.

'She'd be proud of you, son,' Joseph murmured. Reading his son's mind.

'I know,' said Samson, smiling.

'And the rings?' asked Joseph.

'All sorted—'

The words faded into puzzlement, Samson watching Ida Capstick walking up the aisle in a smart dress and jacket, topped off with a fabulous hat, all in a shade of raspberry. But it wasn't her attire which was causing his wonderment. Or which was making the buzz of conversation circulating the barn turn to surprised whispers.

It was the young man walking by her side.

Thick mane of dark hair cut short, piercing blue eyes, and a confidence to him which came from birth, there was something about the lad as he approached and held out his hand. Something Samson recognised but couldn't place.

'Eli Longstaff,' said the newcomer, shaking hands, smiling now, Samson aware of a shocked gasp from his father. 'I'm your cousin.'

'Peas in a pod!' murmured Ida, nodding her head, gaze flicking between the pair of them, while the guests were all watching, taking in this exciting development.

Samson looked at his father. Who shook his head, shrugged. Stunned.

'I had a visit,' the lad continued, grinning, 'an invitation hand-delivered at the farm in Arkengarthdale. To be honest, I didn't even know you existed, Samson – all I knew was that Father had broken off contact with Aunt Kathleen and her husband.' He glanced at Joseph and gave an apologetic shrug. 'It all happened way before I was born, and with Father passing away last year . . . well, this seemed like a good opportunity to resume communication.' His grin turned into a hesitant smile. 'I hope you don't mind me coming today?'

Samson somehow found his voice. 'Not in the least!' he said. Amazement becoming joy. While his father was wiping his eyes, pulling the lad into an embrace, and then gesturing towards the front row of hay bales on the groom's side.

'Come on, Eli – let's take our seats.' Beaming with delight, Joseph led his nephew away.

'Well,' murmured Ida, patting Samson on the arm. 'Tha mother would have been so happy to know she had family here.'

Samson managed a nod, grateful to hear a familiar booming laugh provide a distraction as he fought to keep his emotions under control.

'Bloody hell, Samson!' Harry Furness laughed again as he approached, gesturing towards Eli sitting next to Joseph in pride of place. 'That's going to shake up the best-man odds. Reckon Troy's more nervous than the groom!'

The livestock auctioneer nodded towards Troy Murgatroyd, who'd taken a seat at the end of an aisle to give him an uninterrupted view of what was going on and did indeed have a distinctly apprehensive look to him. For, despite immense pressure over the past few weeks, Samson had refused to reveal his nomination for the role that was prompting such speculation. Not even to Delilah.

'Happen he's cause to be nervous,' muttered Ida. Then she glared at Harry. 'Hope tha's ready,' she said. 'Tha's got a lot of responsibility.'

Harry gave a jaunty salute. Grinned. And from outside came the rumble of an engine.

The bride had arrived.

Delilah was nervous. Not about the wedding. Or the commitment she was about to make. Or any of the many other worries and doubts she'd been harbouring.

She was nervous she was going to fall off the back of the transport which was taking her to the ceremony.

'TE20 three-point-linkage hold on tight,' urged Ida's brother, George, the excitement of the occasion reflected in the litany of tractor statistics punctuating his speech as, beaming with pride, he drove the Little Grey Ferguson out of the yard of the Capsticks' Croft Cottage, where Delilah had stayed the night.

The tractor trundled down the road, white streamers flying from its gleaming paintwork, a garland of flowers decorating the sides of the platform at the rear.

Standing on the platform were Delilah and her father.

'Well, lass,' said her father with a wide smile, 'you couldn't have chosen a better way to get there. I've not been on one of these since I was a lad.'

Delilah didn't have the heart to tell him she hadn't chosen it. That the wedding had all been planned without her knowing. That her only contribution had been a trip to Arkengarthdale to deliver an invitation in person. As for the rest, it was only thanks to some amazing people that she was getting married at all.

How Joseph and his army of helpers had done it, she didn't know. But done it they had. Rescued the day when she had almost ruined it.

And arriving on the Little Grey was simply the perfect way to start.

'Four-speed unsynchronized gearbox we're here,' said George, pulling up outside the barn of Twistleton Farm where Clive and Carol Knowles were waiting.

From inside came the hum of conversation. Laughter. And Delilah caught herself thinking about Samson's mother. About how much it would have meant if she could have been here to witness this occasion in what had been her home. She thought about Ryan, too. Of how happy he would have been to see his little sister marrying his best friend.

She ran her hand down her dress, letting her fingers drop to the discreet pocket and the small box within it. Nathan had called by Croft Cottage earlier and presented her with it. Inside was a fishing fly, immaculately tied.

One of Ryan's, Nathan had explained. An Iron Blue. In case she didn't have anything blue sorted.

Something old. Something new. Something borrowed. And a fishing fly.

Smiling at how her brother would have loved the gesture, Delilah tapped the box for luck, smoothed out her dress and, taking George's proffered hand, stepped down from the tractor.

'Made in Coventry 2088cc you look lovely!' he declared with a grin, nodding at her in approval. Then he gave a deep bow. Grinned again. And sat back up on the tractor, not a man for large social occasions. 'Continental engine tell Ida to bring me some cake,' he called out over his shoulder as he turned the Little Grey back towards Croft Cottage.

'Happen he's right, lass,' said Clive Knowles, craggy face wreathed in a big smile. 'You look a picture!'

'So do your sheep,' said Delilah, taking in the two pens of vivid pink Texels flanking the door. Silver letters on their sides glinting in the sunlight. The letters spelling out *MASONS* and *HELLIDA*.

'Supposed to be Samson and Delilah,' muttered Carol. 'But the silly buggers won't stand still.'

Delilah laughed. Touched at the effort the pair had gone to.

'You ready?' asked her father, placing her arm through his.

'Totally.'

And at some invisible signal – actually Ana Stoyanovic standing inside the door making a gesture to Grigore who gestured his brother Pavel – the haunting sound of a flute filled the air, silencing those gathered.

Delilah stepped into the barn. And her breath caught in her throat.

It was beautiful.

The simplicity of it. The joy of it. The view of the fells through the open roof and window spaces. The music so ethereal, like the first curlews after a long winter. And the people.

She took the time to look at each row. At every face. Knowing this was what made her town so special. Knowing this was what had made her who she was. And had brought her to this moment.

With tears in her eyes, she finally brought her gaze to the

front. Samson. Standing there. A future she couldn't have wanted more.

She took his breath away. That smile. The way she looked at everyone as she walked up the aisle. The warmth of her.

Then he noticed the dress. Simple. Stylish. Hem above her knees. He recognised it. He'd seen it so many times before in the one photograph which existed from the last time it had been worn.

'Hello,' she murmured as she came to his side. Tucking her hand into his.

'You look . . .' he stumbled, lost for words. 'That dress . . . How . . . ?'

She smiled. Turned to Joseph, sitting on the front row. 'Your father sorted it somehow. Is it okay?'

He nodded. Dumbstruck. His mother's wedding dress. Delilah wearing it. It was like a perfect circle. It was destiny.

'Shall we get started?' Harry Furness, auctioneer's voice booming, had stepped up onto the platform, hands raised. 'Who'll give me ten pounds?'

A riot of laughter around the room, Harry grinning, waving his arms in apology.

'Only kidding, folks! We're here today to bring these two together, not sell them . . .'

Samson leaned over to Delilah. 'Is any of this actually legitimate?' he murmured, grinning.

She grinned back at him. 'Not a bit of it. I left the legalities too late to sort, even for your father and his miracle-workers. We've got an appointment at the registry office in a fortnight.'

Biting back a laugh, he returned his focus to Harry.

'So let's get the rings blessed,' Harry was saying. 'And see who this mysterious best man is.'

There was a shuffle of hay bales as people craned to see. Which of the front runners would it be? How much would Troy have to pay out?

Samson turned slowly. Deliberately. Looked at the pew behind him. His father, Eli, Will Metcalfe, Ida Capstick. Everyone waiting to see which of them would step forward. And then Samson whistled.

Up the aisle, head held high, red bowtie looking resplendent on his grey attire, he came. The only best man it could ever have been.

Delilah let out a laugh. Will and many others let out groans. And Troy Murgatroyd grinned, looking over at Ida Capstick and nodding in respect. The only person in the whole town to have called it.

'Thanks,' said Samson, bending down to take the rings from the best man's collar and handing him a Dog-gestive in return.

Tolpuddle wagged his tail and sat down between them. The place where he was happiest.

It would go down in folklore as one of the best weddings Bruncliffe had ever known. Even though it wasn't a real wedding. Which, in a way, just made it more Bruncliffe. The roguish nature of it. The fact it didn't take itself seriously. The warmth with which it was celebrated and the joy it brought. Even the tears, Ida Capstick said to have been seen with a tissue at her eyes at one point, although she was adamant it was only a bout of hay fever.

They would party into the night. Pushing back the hay bales and bringing in trestle tables for a feast which lasted hours. Then clearing the floor for the band, the groom leading the bride out to the strains of 'Mr Brightside'. There was wild music and wild dancing and stories. So many stories. Of the past. Of the future. Many about sheep. And tractors.

Finally, when the moon was well up and the stars were dusting the heavens, they would make their way home through the darkened dale. To the town with the slate roofs, nestled in the fells, with the river running through it, and the railway. With the two tall chimneys at either end. And a wealth of history in between.

Acknowledgements

So there you have it. The curtain has closed, the stage is empty. All that remains is to share one last round of recognition for those who have helped bring this concluding chapter of the Dales Detective series to fruition. As always, I hope I have accurately reflected the expertise freely given. In return, I owe the following a ride on the back of George Capstick's Little Grey (conditional on his approval, of course!).

First up, a friend who knows his glacial overflow channels – yet again, David Dewhirst was on hand for flora, fauna and geology expertise when my own basic knowledge needed corroboration. He was also happy to get as excited as me about the history of medieval hunting practices, which was a bonus!

Another friend who has been a longstanding source of information over the series is Catherine Speakman. Not once has she baulked when I've fired random questions at her – from poison to pets and, this time, fell running, she has patiently answered my queries, usually just before cycling away from me up a steep climb. I also tapped into the extensive fell-running and coaching experience of Carol and Andy Evans, blindsiding them with an interrogation while they were out on a walk. Their enthusiasm for the topic was contagious – I've no excuses now for not attending their coaching sessions!

A final shout-out has to be sent across the fields to the Booth family. From the very first book, Liz, Dave, Rachael and Robin have not only answered my often ignorant farming questions, but also, right back at the beginning, before a word had been even put to paper, welcomed me to their farm during lambing time so I could get a real taste of the livelihoods I was about to portray. Huge thanks, all!

Given this is the tenth book, it's been a great oversight of mine that the following person has barely been acknowledged to date. Step forward into the spotlight, narrator extraordinaire Elizabeth Bower. The outstanding audio versions of the novels owe everything to her masterful interpretation of the written word. And, judging by the number of messages I get from audiobook users singing her praises, I'm not the only one who recognises Elizabeth's exceptional talent. Here's to working together again in the future!

Of course, books never get to the finished state without a lot of dedication from people other than the author. I'm lucky to have been surrounded by a fantastic team of folk who have all striven to make sure each novel has been the best it could be. My sister, Claire, has proven herself to be a brilliant first reader and sounding board. At Pan Mac, I've been in the luxurious position of having the support of two excellent publishers over the course of *Date with Destiny*, as Vicki passed on the mantle to Alex. Thanks, both! A special mention to Fraser Crichton, who has been a constant across all ten books, casting his sharp eye over every word and pushing me to be better. Thanks are also due to editorial manager Melissa Bond and the entire Pan Mac posse who have shown such great support for the series.

Across the channel, my usual *merci* to Camille and her colleagues – not least translators Dominique and Stéphanie – at